Taking a Chance on the Lucky One

Steve Trounday

PUBLISHED BY:
Duckingham Press

Taking a Chance on the Lucky One
Copyright © 2020 Steve Trounday

Print ISBN: 978-0-578-67463-6

Formatted for print by StevieDeInk. StevieDeInk.com
Edited by Marian Kelly. RavensGateEditing.com

Cover design by StevieDeInk.
Photos used to make the cover obtained from fotolia.com.

To Alex, enjoy the journey!

ONE

RANDY TRACED HIS fingers over the smooth skin of her breasts. "We shouldn't do this here."

Cynthia kissed his neck and ran her lips down his torso. "Mmm."

"Joe could show up at any time. It's too risky."

"I like the danger." She caressed his groin, and he moaned in pleasure. "You work in a casino. You should be accustomed to taking chances. Besides, Joseph's winning. He won't leave the blackjack tables while he has a lucky streak going."

"He did ask me to take good care of you. I don't expect this is what he had in mind, though, and he's not a man to anger."

Cynthia combed her fingers through his brown hair. "Let me worry about that. God, you're a stud." She stroked her fingernails down his inner thighs. "I'm glad I coaxed you into bed."

Randy offered her a wide smile. "Right now, I am too."

"We should do this more often. Why do I have to work so hard to get you in the sack?"

"I've been busy, and you're a married woman."

She winked at him. "It's all those girlfriends you have, isn't it?"

"I have to do something. You've been spending too much time at the Conquistador Resort with Conrad Hale. What's a lonesome boy like me supposed to do when you're not around?"

Cynthia's lips curled up. "Who are you trying to kid? You have beautiful women lined up waiting. And Conrad's an exciting diversion from my horrid marriage."

"I thought I was your distraction."

"That's what I like about you. We can have a good time without the messy relationship drama."

"We need to find a better place to rendezvous."

"I can't get enough of you." She rolled on top of him. Her chest heaved as she gasped in ecstasy.

A knock echoed through from the outer room of the suite.

Randy's heart started pounding. "I better get out of here."

Cynthia leaned back in the bed while he scurried out from under the sheets and put on his pants.

There was another thunderous knock.

She smirked at Randy, her white teeth glimmering. "I guess I should see who's calling."

He fumbled with the buttons on his shirt. "Wait until I'm dressed."

Cynthia shot him an annoyed look. "Whoever it is, I'm not inviting them in here." She slid out of the bed, put on a robe, and glided into the living room. She turned and pulled the double doors closed, then walked over to the mirror and primped her platinum blond hair as the pounding on the door grew louder. Irritated, Cynthia snapped, "I'm coming." She hurried to the door and opened it.

Harlan Samples stood there in a heavy black suit. An enormous man, he had to duck to enter the room. His dark hair was slicked back with some sort of shiny hair product, and his sideburns were long, cut just short of his jaw. "Mrs.

Nicosia, Mr. Nicosia's waiting for you in the casino." He peered with obvious suspicion at the bedroom doors.

She forced a smile, holding the collar of her robe together. "Let him know I'll be down in a while." Samples' size made her nervous, and she bit her lower lip. "I need to take a bath and make myself presentable."

He eyed her with clear skepticism. "I'll tell him you'll be there soon. You know he doesn't like to be kept waiting."

"Harlan, explain to him that it'll be worth it."

He stared at her for a moment. "Please make it quick."

"Relax; I'll be there as soon as I can." She batted her lashes at him.

Samples nodded, and Cynthia pushed him out of the suite and closed the door. She paused for a second, then ambled toward the bedroom doors. She opened one and moved into the room. There was no sign of Randy. "Where are you hiding?" she asked.

Randy crept up and embraced her from behind, kissing her neck. "I want you some more."

"He's expecting me."

"You'll get there...in time."

Cynthia spun around and held him close. He kissed her and led her to the bed.

RANDY KENNEDY STEPPED out of the elevator, adjusted his tie, and cruised confidently into the bustling casino. It was a busy Friday night. The sounds of the slot spin buttons being tapped and the bells ringing reverberated with a familiar rhythm. As a casino host for the Desert Palm Casino Resort, he was going to have a hectic night.

The Desert Palm wasn't a large resort by Las Vegas standards, but it was successful. It featured a compact casino, lavish hotel suites, and five award-winning restaurants. The resort made up for its small size by appealing to a sizable pool of high-rollers. The owner of the place, Walter Parker, was a stickler for quality and made sure every guest's visit was first class.

Randy strolled up an aisle of slot machines with the air of arrogance typical of an attractive man of twenty-eight. His expensive gray suit fit to perfection, and a tight shirt covered his muscular chest. He used his handsome face and charisma as a magnet, enabling him to make one sexual conquest after another.

Meandering through the casino, he stopped to talk with a voluptuous brunette cocktail waitress wearing a low-cut dress and juggling a tray full of drinks. "Hey, darling," he said, "let's meet after we get off work tonight. I have a bottle of champagne on ice that's just waiting for a celebration."

Her eyes chilled. "You told me you'd meet me last week, then stood me up."

"I had to work late." As usual in that type of situation, he was lying. "Frazier made me stay here 'til almost four in the morning."

Her expression showed that she doubted him but couldn't see past his seductive smile. "Midnight. My place."

"No, my condo. I'll pick you up at the end of your shift."

"Okay, Randy, but promise you won't stand me up again."

He raised his right hand. "I swear. I hope you're wearing those light-blue panties. They turn me on."

"They do?" She swept her hair back and gave him a coy grin.

He leaned over and whispered in an ear.

She giggled. "You'll find out later tonight. I better get over to the pit. The supervisor's giving me nasty looks."

"Sure. Hmm...I can't wait to see those blue panties...so I can take them off."

She arched an eyebrow, and with a devilish smile, walked away.

Randy chuckled to himself. He turned and suppressed a

groan at the sight of Carter Camp bearing down on him. Camp was everything Randy wasn't—skinny, with a pasty face and a rather bitter personality. Camp wasn't a good casino host by any measure, but his uncle owned the resort and he was immune from dismissal.

More than anything, it was apparent that Camp hated Randy. He was jealous, of course, but the revulsion festered within him. "Where've you been?" he asked. "Frazier's been searching everywhere for you."

Randy glared at him with contempt. "I've been taking care of a guest."

"I saw you in the Zanzibar Lounge an hour ago. You were flirting with Joseph Nicosia's wife. I doubt even gigolos come on that strong."

"How I host is none of your goddamn business."

"Joseph Nicosia's the most valuable guest at the Desert Palm Casino. He's down more than five million this year."

"I'm the reason Joe comes to Las Vegas in the first place. He thinks of me as a son, and you know it."

Camp put his hands on his hips. "Some son."

Randy blurted out an obscenity referencing Camp's mother and marched away. As he roamed through the casino, he muttered to himself. Camp had seen him flirting with Cynthia. In truth, she was always trying to seduce him. He shouldn't let her do it, but she was a beautiful woman and he was weak when it came to temptations of the flesh. He shook his head. He'd been pondering this for a while, though, and decided he wouldn't let it happen again.

JOSEPH NICOSIA SAT alone at a blackjack table, smoking a cigar and swilling expensive scotch on the rocks. His ever-present bodyguard, Harlan Samples, stood behind him with his arms crossed. Samples' eyes were menacing. Nicosia was a caricature of a man living through a midlife crisis. Gold medallions hung from his neck, and he was wearing a loud patterned shirt unbuttoned almost to the navel. What black hair he had was styled in an intricate swirl. If combed straight, it would probably drag on the floor.

Nicosia tried to combat his fear of aging with the only weapon he had: money. He was trying to use his wealth to buy back his youth. His riches were earned legitimately, as the owner of a string of successful payday loan shops, and in a less reputable way as one of the West Coast's most powerful crime bosses. He'd purchased a young and beautiful wife, had his chin lifted and stomach tucked, and was guzzling gallons of expensive herbal tonics that promised eternal life.

Despite the cash he'd spent, he didn't appear a day younger than his fifty-eight years. Awareness of this fact made him an angry and sometimes abusive man. "Where did you learn to deal?" he asked the blackjack dealer after she'd pitched two cards his way. Nicosia grabbed the cards and stared at them. "Jesus, lady, what did I ever do to you?"

The dealer smiled but didn't reply.

"Hit me. Be gentle." He scraped his cards across the green felt layout.

The woman drew out a ten.

"Damn it, I said go easy." He threw down the cards as the dealer scooped up his stack of orange chips and deposited them in the metal tray in front of her. She picked up the cards, shuffled the deck, and dealt out a hand.

"Where's Kennedy?" Nicosia asked. "I need to know the line on the Raiders game."

"I'll get the supervisor," she said, then turned toward the center of the blackjack tables and gestured to the pit boss.

The man walked over to the table and asked in a calm and even voice, "What can I do for you, Mr. Nicosia?"

Nicosia was studying the cards the dealer had dealt him. "Kennedy, find him."

"I'll see if I can locate Randy." The supervisor whistled on his way to the pit lectern and reached for the phone.

Nicosia split the two eights the dealer had given him and stacked another fifteen thousand dollars in chips on the betting circle. He tapped his finger on the first eight, and the woman dealt a two-card, placing it on the table. He bounced his finger again. The dealer drew a king. Beaming, he bobbed his finger in front of the other eight. The woman slid out a three-card. He swished his hand back vigorously, signaling for another card. The dealer spun out a nine.

Nicosia grinned and clasped his hands behind his head. "Beat that, baby."

The woman had a two-card face up; she flipped over the hole-card, revealing a five.

He raised his voice. "Wahoo."

The dealer pulled out another card. A two. She continued: a three, a four. She flicked over her last card. It was a five. The total was twenty-one. The woman glanced at Nicosia with an impish expression and seized his chips.

Nicosia was scowling profoundly. "No way. I can't believe it. This is ridiculous. I want another dealer."

The woman rocked from leg to leg with a stoic expression. "Please place your bet."

"Not with you."

She gave him a defiant stare. "Please make your wager."

"Didn't you hear me? I demand a different dealer."

The woman pointed across the pit. "You can always go to another table."

"I have no intention of moving. You go."

"Please place your bet, Mr. Nicosia."

"I told you, you stupid bitch; I demand a dealer other than you."

"You'll have to talk with the supervisor." The dealer pursed her lips, trying to remain professional. She looked desperately at the floor boss, who was still on the telephone.

After concluding his call, the supervisor headed to the table. "Is there a problem?"

"I insist on another dealer," Nicosia said. "This one's cheating."

"I am not," the woman said, indignation written all over her face.

Nicosia extended his finger toward the deck of cards she was holding. "A six-card twenty-one when I have thirty grand on the line and two hands of twenty? Not possible."

The supervisor said, "You know very well this casino doesn't play those games. We run an honest house."

"Bull. Get me a different dealer."

The boss shook his head. "I'm sorry, but we can't do that."

"Don't give me that crap. If you want my business, you'll switch to someone else."

"Please, Mr. Nicosia, there are twenty-five other blackjack tables open. You're more than welcome at any of them. I'll raise the limits if you want."

"I'm not going anywhere. Find me a different dealer, or I'll have your job."

"Joe!" a man said from behind him.

Nicosia glanced over his shoulder as Randy strode up to the table.

"What's the issue here?" Randy asked.

Nicosia shrugged. "Where've you been?" He pushed a stack of orange chips into a betting circle. The dealer cranked out two cards.

"I've been on a break. It seems like you've been causing problems."

Nicosia smiled. "A little."

"I thought you were winning."

"I was up a quarter of a million but lost it all in the last hour."

"Your luck will change again."

"I need to know the line on the Raiders game." Nicosia tipped over his cards, revealing an ace and a king. Blackjack. The dealer turned her own cards, exposing a seven and a ten. "And I would appreciate another dealer."

Randy waved his hand toward the woman as she paid out his winnings. "She dealt you a blackjack, for god's sake."

"Where's Cynthia? I've been waiting for her."

"She's up in your suite. She just returned from a shopping spree with Conrad Hale."

Nicosia frowned. "Hale thinks spending time with my wife will wheedle me into gambling at his casino. It's not happening."

Randy grinned. "That's what I like to hear. Do you still want to see the *Dance Las Vegas Dance* production?"

"Yeah, but I plan on eating first. I'm hungry."

"I've made you dinner reservations at the Copa Room for seven. I'll meet you in the showroom for the cocktail performance."

"Okay. I'm going up to the suite to see Cynthia." Nicosia hoisted himself up from the stool. "I have to get away from this bitch of a dealer."

Randy scowled. "Watch your mouth and give her a tip."

Nicosia dug in his pocket and pulled out a dollar token. He flung it across the felt layout. "Thanks for nothing, honey. Why don't you buy yourself some dealing lessons?"

RANDY SAILED INTO the host office, where he found casino manager Eric Frazier talking to a man in a dark suit that didn't quite fit. Frazier was an older guy with thinning white hair. Randy enjoyed working for him because he was fair, competent, and let him do his job with little to no interference.

The guy Frazier was speaking with looked about the same age as Randy. He was tall, over six feet, with a football player's muscular build, and he appeared a bit nervous, brushing his hand through his blond hair.

"Randy," Frazier said, "you're just the man I was looking for. This is Wayne Cork. Wayne, this is Randy Kennedy, one of our best casino hosts."

"The best," Randy said, his eyes showing amusement. He reached out and shook Wayne's hand. "It's nice to meet you."

"I've just hired Wayne," Frazier said. "I'd appreciate it if you'd spend some time with him tonight."

Randy nodded. "All right. Where've you worked before?"

Wayne scratched his cheek. "I've been employed at various sales positions in Los Angeles. I've never had a job in a casino. I do know my way around a craps table, though. I've wagered plenty." There was a prominent gap between his front teeth.

"Hosting experience shouldn't matter," Frazier said, his voice defensive. "I met Wayne at a golf tournament. He was in my foursome and persuaded me he has the right personality to make a great casino host."

"Sounds good," Randy said, peering at Wayne. "You'll like it here, but don't let Frazier push you around."

Frazier shook his head. "Don't let him fool you, son. I've been dealing with casino hosts for over thirty-five years. You don't manage them; you contain them."

Randy laughed. "You make us sound like zoo animals."

"Sometimes, I think you are. Now give Wayne a tour of the resort. Introduce him to some of our guests." Frazier turned to Wayne. "You'll learn a lot from this guy. All kidding aside, Randy knows his business. If you end up being half as good a casino host, you'll enjoy a long and rewarding career at the Desert Palm."

Randy smiled. "I can't take all this flattery. Come on, Wayne; let's get out of here before Frazier asks me to marry his daughter."

Frazier hooked a thumb to his chest. "I draw the line at that. I know your reputation with women. They don't call you the Lucky One for nothing." He looked back at Wayne. "Welcome aboard. I'm confident you'll do an outstanding job."

"Thanks, Mr. Frazier," Wayne said. "I promise you made a good hire."

Randy and Wayne walked out of the host office and onto the casino floor. The place was jammed with tourists seeking their fortunes on the games of chance, and they had to zigzag through the throng of people.

"Frazier's a cool dude," Randy said when they arrived at the blackjack pit.

Wayne put his hands in his pockets. "He's taking a risk employing my ass with no experience or customer list. I had to do some fast talking to convince him I could do the job."

"Well, he took you on. So, what do you know about being a casino host?"

"I don't know…We're supposed to take care of the VIP players. Make sure they're having a fun time, being taken care of, wined and dined. Right?"

"Yes, but a smart host can transform those guests into a meal ticket that'll keep him working and well-compensated for the rest of his life."

"That's why I wanted to be in the business. Well, that and betting on football."

"Most of the casinos in Vegas are pretty much the same: a few thousand slots, a hundred table games, and maybe a showroom or two. Every property has high limits. Even at the ones with volcanoes, pyramids, and Venetian canals, the casinos are close to identical. Sure, the big players expect a nice suite and fancy restaurants, but what keeps them coming back are the people. Us. Our relationship with these guests is what induces them to return. Our best players visit the Desert Palm because I get them here."

Wayne pointed to a blackjack table. "Don't they just like to gamble?"

"Of course they do. Many of them have the gambling bug, big time, but the odds at most of the casinos are the same. The paybacks on the slots are almost equal at every place, and a blackjack game's a blackjack game. As I said, the large joints all offer high-limit tables. It's the men and women employed here who draw the high-rollers to the Desert Palm. Let me show you." Randy pulled away from Wayne and walked up to an older woman playing a twenty-five-dollar slot machine. In her early eighties, she had permed gray hair and wore a rather unflattering blue dress. "How's my favorite girl?" Randy asked.

She smiled and continued to press the spin button on the slot. "Oh, Randy, I can't win a thing from this machine. I've invested almost five thousand. I have to go to the restroom, but I'm afraid to leave. I know when I walk away, someone will hit my jackpot."

"You want me to watch it for you?"

"Would you, honey? I do need to go."

"Anything for you."

"You're a peach." She leaned toward him, and he bent over and let her kiss him on the cheek. Her wrinkled skin took on even more creases. "Who's your friend?"

"Sylvia, this is Wayne Cork. It's his first night of work. He's going to be a casino host, the same as me. Wayne, this is Sylvia Gardner, the love of my life."

"Oh, you." She gave him a wide grin that showed her dentures. "It's good to meet you, Mr. Cork. Now Randy, protect my machine, and I'll be right back."

"Okay, Mrs. G."

Randy and Wayne watched the woman as she tottered away and disappeared in the sea of slot machines.

"She's a pretty nice old broad," Wayne said. "Except for the *ode to Bengay* perfume."

Randy chortled. "Nice, maybe. Filthy rich, with absolute certainty. She's a widow. Her husband was some kind of steel mill tycoon back east. She lost over a half-million dollars here last year."

Wayne's eyes narrowed. "No way. On slot machines?"

"Hard to comprehend, huh? And she's just one of hundreds of guests who lose that kind of money here. Your job's to find those people and keep them coming back to the Desert Palm."

Wayne gave a confident nod. "I believe Mrs. Gardner likes me. I saw a sparkle in her saggy eyes when you introduced her."

"No way, pal; she's mine. You go find your own rich senior citizen."

RANDY GAZED AROUND the casino with lustful eyes while leading Wayne toward the Desert Palm's showroom. "See all the women in this joint?" he asked. "So many females, so little time." He laughed.

Wayne leered at a passing cocktail waitress. "It's going to make it difficult for me to concentrate on my damn job."

"Don't approach it that way. Beautiful ladies are one of the best perks this place has to offer. And I see someone perky right now. Follow me."

Wayne said nothing, trailing behind Randy as he wound through a horde of Asian tourists and over to a carousel of slot machines. A striking dark-haired woman wearing a strapless white evening gown stood in the center of the carousel, wishing a guest good luck. She spotted Randy, smiled, and said, "Hello, baby. What time are you picking me up tomorrow morning?"

Randy pushed hair out of his eyes. "Eleven. I thought we'd go out to Red Rock for a picnic. Stephanie, I'd like you to meet Wayne. He's a new casino host."

She gave him a quick once-over. "Hi, Wayne."

"Hey," he said.

She looked back at Randy. "Do you need me to bring anything?"

Randy shook his head. "Nah. I'll pick up sandwich fixings at a deli on my way to your apartment."

"Why don't you spend the night at my place? We can grab something on our way to Red Rock. It'll save you some time."

Wayne turned away, obviously not certain if he was eavesdropping on a much-too-personal matter, his expression showing that he was a little annoyed that he had to listen to Randy's flirting.

"Can't tonight," Randy said, thinking about his rendezvous with the cocktail waitress. "I have to work late."

"So do I," she said. "I'm here 'til two."

Randy was unfazed, experienced at juggling his numerous sexual activities. "No, I've planned the perfect romantic date for tomorrow, and I don't want to do anything to spoil it. I need you drooling for me. A little wait will make it more fun."

"Randy. Please."

He kissed his finger and pressed it against her lips. "Tomorrow at eleven. I assure you, it'll be worth the wait."

She folded her arms across her chest. "Oh, all right."

"I'll see you in the morning. We're going to have a great time."

"I know." A wicked grin materialized on her face. "It was nice meeting you, Wayne."

Wayne appeared startled he was being brought back into the conversation. "Uh, sure, same here."

Navigating away from the slot carousel through a horde

of gamblers, Randy said, "She's a knock-out. You won't believe what she can do in bed."

Wayne nodded. "I bet."

"She has a friend who's almost as attractive. Want me to hook you up?"

Wayne seemed unsettled, his expression clouding over. "Thanks, but I got out of a bitch of a relationship a while ago, and I'm taking a break from women."

"That's crazy."

Wayne glanced back, gazing at the woman in the carousel of slots. "She is hot. Maybe a night with a woman like her would make me forget about Dee."

"Take my word for it, there are women in this town so stunning, you'll forget everything."

WAYNE WAS EXAMINING the large electronic board highlighting the betting lines of various football games. "The spread's six and a half. I'm going to make a wager on the Broncos."

"I wouldn't," Randy said. "I've heard their quarterback could be injured. I'd take the Ravens."

"No, believe me, Denver's a lock. I may not know a lot about being a casino host, but I know my football. I played in college, and it's my passion."

"Want to make a side bet?"

"How much?"

"A bill."

"A hundred-dollars? That's a little steep for me."

"I thought you said you knew your football. Put your money where your damn mouth is."

Smacking his fist into his palm, Wayne smiled with sudden machismo. "Okay, smart-ass. I can't resist a challenge like that. You're on. The Broncos at six and a half."

Randy grinned, a sliver of teeth showing. "Let's see now.

I've introduced you to two of the best benefits of being a casino host."

"What's that?"

"One, beautiful women. And two, sports betting."

"When do we work?"

Randy burst into laughter. "That's the best part. This is almost as tough as it gets."

TWO

CONRAD HALE LEANED back in his chair and asked with an edgy growl, "Goddamn it, why can't we persuade Joseph Nicosia to gamble at the Conquistador?"

"Randy Kennedy," Pete Sawyer said from across the desk. "He keeps Nicosia at the Desert Palm."

In Hale's tanned face, the wrinkles near his piercing black eyes were particularly evident. In his late forties, he had a slight build and capped, almost-too-white teeth. As the owner of the Conquistador Casino Resort and Tower, he was accustomed to getting what he wanted. "Damn it, Sawyer, why? The Conquistador's ten times the size of the Desert Palm. We have the best celebrity chef restaurants, the most lavish spa in Vegas, and the biggest stars in our showroom. I don't understand how this Kennedy can match what we have to offer."

Sawyer was the Conquistador's casino manager, a thin bald man in his sixties. He looked intently at his boss. "I've told you before, we must build up our hosting program. All the glitz in the world can't attract the best players. We need the personal contacts as well."

Hale's expression darkened. "I make those. It's my casino."

"Players like Joseph Nicosia are loyal to hosts, such as

Randy Kennedy. I can't emphasize that enough. We have to bolster our hosting program to be more competitive. We've lost three good executive hosts in the last six months. When Caesar's Palace stole Ted Sanford from us, he took five customers who'd each lost over a million-dollars last year."

Anger filled Hale's voice. "I hated Sanford...all the hosts, for that matter. They're free agents. They do what they damn well feel like."

"That's true, Mr. Hale, but they bring in the big players."

"I don't like it when I don't have control over my business affairs. I detest being at the mercy of these prima donnas."

"Unfortunately, it's a fact of life in the casino industry and you know it. Why don't you allow me to contact Kennedy? See if he's interested in moving over to the Conquistador."

Hale scrunched up his face. "I hear he's egotistical. I can't stomach the idea of him working here."

"Do you want Nicosia's business or not?"

Hale pounded his fist on the desk. "I'm getting it my way."

"All right, but with your permission, I'm going to speak with Kennedy. Nicosia isn't the only customer who's loyal to him. He has a dozen players who are almost as good. If we can lure him to the Conquistador, it would be a financial boon to the property."

Hale rubbed at the kink in his neck. "Talk with him, but don't put out an offer. If he shows some interest in leaving the Desert Palm, I want to speak with him first, before you discuss money."

"I'm sure he's well compensated at the Desert Palm. Walter Parker isn't a stupid man; I'm certain he pays Kennedy handsomely."

"I bet he overpays all his help. Parker runs that place as if it were a charity. Did I tell you I made another bid to buy the place? It's right next to us, and I want the land so I can expand the Conquistador. It frustrates me that he keeps turning me down. It's a competitive offer, mind you, and yet he says no each time."

"With employees the caliber of Randy Kennedy, he knows you'll keep upping the ante to buy his resort."

Hale grimaced and his nostrils flared. "I'll find a way to acquire that place."

"If we don't lock in Kennedy soon, you'll lose him to a competitor, whether you buy the Desert Palm or not. Word has it the MGM's trying to entice him over there."

Hale stared at Sawyer, his expression concerned. "I don't want that to happen. Yes, get in touch with Kennedy. I'd like to chat with him. I'm still working on Joseph Nicosia myself, however. It's a challenge I can't resist. I've found a new angle I believe might work. I'm directing my attention at his wife. She appreciates everything I have to offer."

CYNTHIA AND JOSEPH Nicosia sat in a booth at the Desert Palm's Oasis Showroom. Harlan Samples stood nearby, watching his boss and his wife with cold eyes. Cynthia was sipping a colorful tropical drink and playing with the paper umbrella perched on the rim of the glass. "Why are you in such a bad mood?" she asked with a sour look, pursing her lips.

Nicosia said with a snarl, "I'm not winning anything."

"Well, don't take it out on me. You're the one who loves gambling."

The corners of his mouth turned down. "It's my money, and I can spend it any goddamn way I want. I'm damn tired of your nagging."

"And I've had enough of your constant abuse."

"Someday I'll show you real abuse. Maybe you could use a good beating."

Fear swept through her, and she realized she needed to change the subject. "Joey, if a skilled gambler like you can't win at the Desert Palm, then something's wrong. Why don't you go over to the Conquistador and play there? Conrad Hale's wonderful."

Nicosia turned up his nose. "I don't like it there."

"He told me he'll give you anything you dream up. He said their pool-view VIP suites are magnificent."

"What wrong with the suite we have here?"

"Nothing, but if you aren't winning at the Desert Palm, I don't see why you won't try your luck somewhere else."

"Not at the Conquistador. I'm not a fan of Hale. He's arrogant."

Cynthia closed her eyes, smiling dreamily. "Well, I think he's fantastic. Did I tell you he's taking me out on Lake Mead in his yacht?"

"Fine by me, but I enjoy it here. My luck will change. It always does."

"Please, Joey. Why not? Do it for me, just once." Hale had promised her a sparkling bauble if she could convince her husband to vacation at the Conquistador Resort. She cuddled up to him, rubbing his groin through his slacks.

Aroused instantly, Nicosia let out a low moan. "I'll consider it." It was clear that the aching in his loins was now making it difficult for him to concentrate. "Let's go up to the suite."

Cynthia realized she'd gone a bit too far in her attempt to get Nicosia to visit the Conquistador. Now she was going to have to sleep with the unattractive man she'd only married for his money. "If you promise we can spend a night in a pool-view suite at the Conquistador."

"We can worry about that later."

She crossed her arms. "Give me your word we can stay there."

"Will it shut you up about this?"

Cynthia beamed, almost every tooth exposed. "I can't wait to see what a Conquistador suite looks like."

Just then, Randy and Wayne approached the Nicosias' table and Randy slid in next to Cynthia. Wayne propped himself against the booth and stood there uncertainly, looking nervous and licking his lips. He stared at Nicosia's scotch and looked like a man wanting a cocktail to calm his anxiety. Harlan Samples frowned at them with disapproval he didn't try to hide.

"Sorry I'm late," Randy said. "Joe, Cynthia, this is Wayne Cork. He's going to be one of our casino hosts. I've been showing him around."

Cynthia's eyebrows inched up. She shifted her attention to Wayne. "Is that so? Did Randy say your name's Wayne?"

Wayne wet his lips again. "Yes."

"Interesting. He's a host, the same as you, Randy?"

Randy smiled. "No one can be just like me, but I know he'll try."

Cynthia turned back to Wayne. "Wayne...Do I have that right; it's Wayne?"

"Ah, it is," he said.

"Well, Wayne, don't get me wrong, but are you sure you're the casino host type?"

His face reddened. "Why yes, Mrs. Nicosia."

"Being a casino host means having an attitude."

Wayne's tone of voice became defensive and a little harsh. "I can assure you, I have one."

Cynthia eyed him for a moment. "Time will tell if it's the right one."

"We're not going to watch the show," Nicosia said, plainly tired of the conversation his wife was pursuing.

"Why not?" Randy asked. "I hear *Dance Las Vegas Dance* is great. It's sold out every night this week."

"Cynthia and I want to go up to the suite." He had a lecherous gleam in his eyes. "I'll be down to the casino later on tonight."

Randy nodded as Nicosia grabbed Cynthia's arm and pulled her out of the booth.

"Use our table," Nicosia said. "I'm sure you two young men can find more suitable company than us."

"Thanks, Joe," Randy said. "We'll do that. I'll be here until midnight. If you need anything, tell the Hotel Operator to connect you to my smartphone."

"Okay, kid." Nicosia put his arm around Cynthia's waist. She smiled with coquettish fervor, and he escorted her out of the showroom, Harlan Samples following like their shadow.

"What a break," Randy said, sliding over to the center of the booth. "Have a seat, Wayne."

Wayne seemed a little tentative about slipping into the booth. "Is it all right for us to be watching the production without any VIP gamblers present?"

"Relax, the casino's biggest player instructed us to make ourselves comfortable. He also told us to get some company." Randy's eyes lit up. "I'll be right back." He sprang out of the booth and headed for the casino.

Wayne sat there with a furrowed forehead, wondering what he was up to. He scanned the showroom, hoping Eric Frazier wouldn't catch him slacking off on his first night of work.

Ten minutes later, Randy paraded up to the table with a brunette on one arm and a blonde on the other. "Wayne," he said with a huge grin on his face, "this is Mimi and Bridgette. They're staying in the hotel." Randy and the two women eased into the booth.

Mimi was the brunette. In her early twenties, she had brown eyes and a ski-slope nose and was wearing an expensive blue evening dress that clung to her body. Bridgette was the blond, about the same age as Mimi, with short-cropped hair. She, too, was dressed to impress.

"I found these beautiful women near the hotel lobby," Randy said. "They're looking for a good time."

"It seems we've found the right place," Mimi said, snuggling closer to Randy.

Wayne studied Bridgette with a lustful eye.

"What would you girls like to drink?" Randy asked, gesturing for a cocktail waitress.

"Something exotic," Mimi said. "I feel like celebrating."

"Exotic it is." When the waitress arrived at the table, Randy ordered a round of alcoholic beverages. He entertained everyone by telling tales Wayne wasn't sure were true. Wayne was impressed, however, with Randy's ability to enchant the ladies. Their conversation was interrupted by the dimming of the showroom lights and the center-stage entrance of a comedian. The man told jokes for about twenty minutes, and after his routine, the performers from *Dance Las Vegas Dance* entered the stage and put on a high-energy show. Mimi and Bridgette seemed enthralled by the nimble dancers, while Randy showed little interest and Wayne fidgeted, still uncomfortable, concerned his new boss might be lurking nearby.

As the dancers were finishing their final number, Randy leaned over to Wayne. "I need to go after the performance. I have a date."

Wayne gulped. "What do you want me to do with Bridgette and Mimi? I'm certain they expect us to keep them company."

"Then do that. Ever been with two gorgeous women?"

"Not at the same time."

"Welcome to Las Vegas."

Wayne gave him a sly smirk. "Maybe I *will* get over my ex."

"That's the spirit."

Wayne shook his head as the curtain lowered to the stage and the lights came up in the showroom. The audience continued to applaud and yell for more, but the dancers didn't return.

Randy asked, "Mimi, Bridgette, did you enjoy the performance?"

"It was wonderful," Bridgette said. "They're so talented. The men are hot."

Mimi said with a sexy wink, "Almost as attractive as you two."

Randy smiled, but it was wiped away when Carter Camp barged up to the table.

"I see you're hard at work," Camp said.

"What do you want, pissant?" Randy asked.

Camp glared at him. "I wonder what my uncle would say about the way you're throwing his money around. Are you deducting the cost of this from your paycheck?"

Obviously irritated, Randy snapped, "Get lost."

Wayne slumped down in his seat, wondering if he could lose his new job for screwing off. He'd spent most of his cash renting an apartment and was desperate for a paycheck.

"You'd like that, wouldn't you?" Camp snarled.

Randy said, "Go back on the gaming floor and at least try to pretend you're a casino host."

"If I followed your example, I'd find me a cocktail waitress and comp her dinner."

Randy sneered. "Yeah, right, like you could attract a cocktail waitress."

Bridgette and Mimi snickered.

Camp scowled at Randy, his eyes narrow slits. "If I were you, Kennedy, I'd be more concerned about the profits of this resort."

Randy shot out a puff of laughter. "If I were you, I'd kill myself. I'm off in half an hour, so don't you worry about it."

Camp seemed frustrated that Randy had a sarcastic rejoinder for every comment he made. "You're a disgrace." He spun around and stomped off.

"Well," Randy said, "it's fortunate I don't care what the unhappy camper thinks about anything. Let's forget about him."

"I want to go dancing," Mimi said.

"Oh, me too," Bridgette said, clapping her hands.

Randy said, "I'd love to, Mimi, Bridgette, but I can't tonight. There's someone waiting for me in the casino. Wayne here will take good care of you, though."

Wayne's mouth hung open a tad as he considered his chances of scoring with two beautiful women.

Randy climbed out of the booth and said his goodbyes.

Wayne pounded down the last of his beer and stroked his chin. His first night of work had been nothing like he'd expected. He could tell life as a casino host was going to be pretty damn interesting. He hoped the job would get him in a position to reap a serious financial reward.

THREE

RANDY WOKE UP with a beautiful woman in his arms. For a minute, he couldn't remember who she was. There'd been so many women, countless beds, and at times, he lost track of his lovers. He was the Lucky One. He remembered, when he noticed the mole on the nape of her neck, that this was Katie.

Sound asleep, she was breathing as if she didn't have a single care. Her contentment scared him, though. In her mind, he knew, he was the perfect man. She'd found what she was looking for in life and, for that reason, sought a more serious relationship. He wasn't ready for that. Not with Katie. He didn't want to spend the rest of his life with her. God, the rest of his life. Would he ever find someone he wanted to do that with? There was little likelihood, and he wondered how long he could string Katie along before he had to cut her loose.

DESERT PALM RESORT owner Walter Parker was seventy-nine years old, with a ruddy complexion framed by full white hair. A small man, he sat in his office reading the *Wall Street Journal* with his feet up on the desk, paying little attention to his nephew, who sat across from him.

"Uncle Walter," Camp said, "you have to do something about Randy Kennedy."

"What are you talking about?" the old man asked without looking up from his paper.

"Kennedy. He's out of control."

The casino operator sniggered. "How can you tell when a host's out of control?"

"Spend a day watching Kennedy, and you'll know."

Parker didn't care much for his sister's only son and had hired him because he was family. "The market went up three hundred points yesterday."

Camp lifted his voice. "You're not listening. You must address issues with Kennedy. He's a loose cannon. He could cost us a great deal of money."

Parker peered over the top of the paper. "Us?"

"Uh, uh, the Desert Palm. You."

Parker clicked his tongue. "You've never liked Randy. I don't want to get involved in your personal disagreements."

"You don't know what he's doing. Last night, I caught him in the showroom with two women. Neither one was a high-roller. He was drinking and having a wild time."

Parker turned a page of his paper. "I'll have a talk with him, but as long as he does his job, I don't care how he goes about it. He brings a lot of business to my casino."

"Boy, does he have you buffaloed."

Parker lowered the paper and glowered at his nephew. He didn't appreciate being lectured. "As I said, I'll speak with Randy at the appropriate time."

"That's it? You're not thinking about firing him, or at the very least writing him up?"

"Why would I dismiss Randy Kennedy? He's one of our best casino hosts. Legions of guests come to the Desert Palm because of him. I have no intention of terminating him. Do you believe we'd keep players like Joseph Nicosia if we fired him? I suggest you stop fretting about Randy and start working on your own career. Eric Frazier tells me you haven't made much progress attracting a guest following."

The look Camp gave his uncle was sharp. "I'm the one person in the Host Department obeying the rules. Kennedy's not the only host breaking company policy. Davidson spends his entire shift trying to line up free dinners in the gourmet restaurant, and I know Pauline Payson's swapping gifts for comps."

Parker's lips puckered. "Perhaps you'd be more comfortable employed in another department. There's an opening in the hotel. Assistant housekeeper. That job may better suit your skills and disposition."

Camp struck his fist on the desk. "No. I enjoy being a host, but I can't stand seeing the way the department's run."

Parker's face tinged pink. He picked up his silver-tipped walking cane and pointed it at his nephew. "Son, this operation's run the way I designed it. I didn't become the owner of one of the most successful casinos in Las Vegas by being an idiot. The hosts need latitude to attract the power players. The programs I've set up do just that. I don't want to hear another word about it. If I do, you're going to the Housekeeping Department whether you like it or not. Is that clear?"

Camp's lower lip popped out in a pout, and he bowed his head. "Yes, Uncle Walter."

"Fine. Now I have a lot to do, so why don't you get back to work?"

Camp stood, grumbling to himself as he slunk out of the office.

RANDY'S SMARTPHONE BLARED. He slid his finger across the screen and held it to his ear. The pulsating sounds of the casino made it difficult to hear. "You have a call holding," the Hotel Operator said. Randy was minutes into his shift. Wayne was with him, watching the tourists buzzing between the slot machines. Randy listened for the call to be connected.

"Mr. Kennedy?" a man asked.

"Speaking," Randy said, expecting yet another call from a casino guest.

"This is Pete Sawyer. I'm the casino manager at the Conquistador Casino Resort and Tower."

"Yes, Mr. Sawyer, what can I do for you?"

"Mr. Kennedy…Randy, may I call you Randy?"

"Yes, sir." Randy rolled his eyes at Wayne, who was waiting impatiently.

"Randy, do you know Conrad Hale?"

"I've heard of him. He owns the Conquistador."

"Mr. Hale was wondering if the three of us could get together for a little chat."

"About what?"

"Well, ah, we'd like to discuss the possibility of you coming to work for us."

Randy's heart quickened. Although he was happy at the Desert Palm, the thought of working at the Conquistador, one of the largest and most prestigious resorts in Las Vegas, was intriguing. "What do you have in mind?"

"I'd prefer we discuss this face to face. I'm having difficulty hearing you over the noise of the casino."

"Where would you like to meet?"

"Do you golf?"

"I'm a casino host. Of course I do."

Sawyer chuckled. "Yes, I guess it was a stupid question. Mr. Hale's a member of the Boulder Creek Golf Club. He has a tee time for Sunday morning at ten. We'd be honored to have you join us."

"I'd like to, but I must tell you I'm quite content at the Desert Palm. I'm not interested in a change of employer."

Wayne stared at Randy with his forehead furrowed, clearly curious about the conversation.

"I understand that," Sawyer said. "Mr. Hale and I just want to visit and see what direction you hope to take your career over the next few years. Our golf outing will have no strings attached. We'll play a nice round of golf and talk about your future."

"I'd enjoy meeting with you," Randy said. "I'll see you then."

"Very well, Randy. I look forward to it."

Randy tapped his mobile phone off and thought for a second. "Interesting," he said under his breath.

"What the hell was that about?" Wayne asked. "If you don't mind telling me."

"That was the casino manager at the Conquistador, Pete Sawyer. He asked me to meet with Conrad Hale, the resort's owner."

Wayne looked somewhat disturbed. "Are you considering leaving the Desert Palm? I need this job right now, and I'm counting on you to teach me the intricacies of being a host."

"Nah. This is a great place to work. Frazier's a good boss, and Walter Parker's the best. If the folks at the Conquistador want to laud my achievements and offer me a job, I'll listen, but it'd have to be one hell of a pay increase before I'd make a move."

"I'm being selfish, but teach me how to be a host before you think about leaving."

Randy laughed. "I've had other job offers. Some guy from the MGM called me last week, but the pay wasn't enough for me to consider leaving this place. I aspire to the big bucks."

"Me too. But I can't get respectable money if you don't show me the ropes first."

Randy smiled and pointed. "Right, so let's go over to the casino cashier—we call it the cage—and I'll walk you through the procedures the casino uses for issuing markers."

"Okay." Wayne nodded. "I was wondering when I'd be shown a function of the casino that could be considered actual work."

RANDY LED WAYNE across the casino, stopping just once to flirt with a cocktail waitress.

"Who's your cute friend?" the server asked him.

Wayne flashed the faintest of grins.

"Jennifer, this is Wayne," Randy said.

She reached out and squeezed Wayne's right biceps. "Whoa. I love boys with big muscles."

Wayne's smile grew. "Many hours at the gym."

Randy wasn't sure he liked the competition for Jennifer's attention. "Enough chit-chat, Wayne. We have work to do."

Not taking his eyes off Jennifer, Wayne said, "Oh, all right. Nice meeting you."

"This way," Randy said and turned away before Jennifer had a chance to respond. Wayne followed, giving her a lustful gaze and a quick wave goodbye.

The two men crossed the gaming establishment to the casino cashier, and Randy strolled up to a booth to its left. He made small talk with the security officer who sat in it while signing his name on a form attached to a clipboard, then handed it to Wayne. "Sign this."

Wayne inspected the paper. "What is it?"

"The cashier access log. We're going into the outer vault."

"Oh, okay." Wayne scribbled his name and gave the clipboard to the security guard.

A buzzer sounded. Randy pulled open the door and waited for Wayne to enter. After he moved through, Randy proceeded over to the counter to their right. A pretty woman with long auburn hair and brilliant blue eyes was on the other side of it, counting casino tokens.

"Well, who's this beauty?" Randy asked.

She peered at him, looking a bit wary. "Excuse me?"

"Randy Kennedy." He held out his hand. "Most pleased to meet you."

She waved her arm. "I'm Angela Grisham. I'm not allowed to shake hands across the vault counter. The Surveillance Department would disapprove."

He pulled his hand back. "Of course. I wasn't thinking. When did you start working here?"

"Last week."

"Well, welcome to the Desert Palm. I'm sure you'll like it here."

"So far, I've enjoyed it," she said, looking into his eyes.

"Where did you work before?"

"I've been at the Mirage for the last four years. A cashier here at the Desert Palm's an old friend and convinced me to make the change."

"I'll have to thank her."

She gave him a vague, noncommittal smile. "The cage at the Desert Palm has four ten-hour shifts, giving me three days off. You can't beat that."

"We hosts work all kinds of crazy shifts and hours."

Angela nodded. She ran her fingers through her hair and touched her sapphire necklace, which matched her eyes.

"Angela, this is Wayne Cork. He's new too—a budding casino host."

She studied Wayne for a moment. As with Randy, she appeared to be judging him. "Nice to meet you."

"Same here," Wayne said.

Randy focused on her with great interest. While attracted

to her beauty, he saw something in her eyes that disturbed him somewhat. He wasn't sure what it was that put him so on edge. "It's Wayne's second night of work, and I wanted to show him the marker and safe-keeping process."

Angela moved over to the credit area of the vault. "Come over here, Wayne."

Wayne walked to the counter and watched as Angela logged onto a computer.

"Do you know what a marker is?" she asked.

Wayne shook his head. "No, um, I haven't worked at a casino before."

"Okay, we'll take this slow. Stop me if I go too fast or you don't understand something."

Randy crossed his arms and listened as Angela took Wayne through the minutiae of the credit procedures of the Desert Palm. He chimed in occasionally, giving his thoughts on when he thought a gambler was a safe bet to receive increased credit.

"I guess I better start getting to know some of the customers," Wayne said.

"Guests," Randy corrected. "We don't have customers at the Desert Palm. We have guests. There's a big distinction. One that keeps this property one of the most successful resorts in Las Vegas."

Wayne flushed with a touch of anger, clearly not happy about being admonished. He glared at Randy. "Oh, okay. Guests."

Randy waved a finger. "Never let Walter Parker hear you refer to a guest as a customer. It's one of his pet peeves. That and the word employees. We're team members."

"You're kidding me, right?"

"Hey, be grateful you're not an associate. That's what they call them at Walmart."

Angela looked at Wayne and asked, "Are there any other questions I can help you with?"

Wayne glanced at Randy.

"Just one," Randy said with a crooked smile. "What time are you getting off work?"

Angela gave an almost silent gasp and gripped the edge of the counter. "Why do you want to know that?"

"I was wondering if you'd like to go out for a drink."

She shook her head. "I'm sorry, I'm not interested."

Randy gaped at her, surprised.

Amused, Wayne held his tongue, smirking.

Randy couldn't remember the last time a woman had said no to his advances. "Do you have a boyfriend?"

Angela blinked her blue eyes at him quite deliberately. "I'm not sure that's any of your business. Now, as I said, I'm not interested in having a drink with you. Thank you for asking, though."

Flustered, Randy said, "Um, ah, how about dinner at Mandalay Bay? Their gourmet room? Anytime you say."

Visibly trying to suppress a grin, she said, "No, thank you. I don't mean to be rude, but please leave it at that."

He drew his head back. "Okay, if that's the way you feel."

"It is." She smiled.

Randy tried to figure out why she was saying no to him. He realized her rebuff had made her irresistible, and he couldn't take his eyes off her.

"You better get back to work."

Randy's eyebrows twitched. "We're out of here, Wayne," he said and walked toward the door that led to the casino. Before leaving the room, Randy stopped and faced Angela. "I won't take no for an answer." His green eyes were ablaze.

She shrugged. "That's the one you'll always be getting."

He flexed his jaw and charged into the casino.

JOSEPH NICOSIA WAS sitting alone at a high-limit blackjack

table, puffing on an expensive Cuban cigar. A male dealer was pitching cards to him across the layout. Harlan Samples who stood nearby, grimaced at Randy when he came up to the table.

Nicosia peered over at Randy. "I'm winning."

Randy sat down on the stool next to him. "I told you your luck would change. How much are you up?"

"A couple hundred grand."

"Good for you. Do you feel like something to eat?"

"No, I'm on a winning streak, and I don't want to do anything to screw it up."

Randy glanced at the large stack of chips in front of Nicosia. "I don't blame you. Where's Cynthia?"

"She's with Conrad Hale."

Randy frowned. "Why the hell's she with him?"

"He's taking her out on Lake Mead in his yacht. He asked me to tag along, but I declined. Who wants to float around in a desert lake in this heat?"

"Why doesn't he leave you alone? He knows this is your home in Vegas."

Nicosia checked the cards in front of him and tucked them under a stack of orange chips. "It's kind of flattering the way he sucks up to us."

"Don't kid yourself, Joe. Hale has his eyes on one thing: your money."

"And the Desert Palm doesn't?" He was paid his winning hand, doubled the bet, and the dealer flicked two new cards his way.

Randy said, "You've been coming to Las Vegas long enough to know this place's different. If all you cared about was getting a larger suite, you'd have left us years ago."

Nicosia quietly mulled over what action to take with the cards. He gestured that he needed another one, and the dealer pulled out an eight. Nicosia gave a toothy smile. "Hale has Cynthia enchanted. The last three times we've come to Vegas, he's taken her all over town. This morning, he took her to the Forum Shops at Caesar's and lunch at the Bellagio. Now he has her working on me, trying to convince me to play at the Conquistador. To shut her up, I promised to stay there tonight."

Randy twisted his face in disapproval. "I wish you wouldn't."

Nicosia slid his cards under a pile of chips. "It's one night. To appease Cynthia. Hale's been treating her well, and she believes we're obligated to spend some time at his resort. She's the one you have to convince otherwise."

The dealer revealed his cards and again paid out Nicosia's winning hand.

"We love you, Joe," Randy said, "and we'll give you anything you ask. Just make any request, and it's yours. You know that."

Nicosia placed another ten-thousand-dollar bet on the table. "Sure, I appreciate it."

Randy rubbed his chin. He'd vowed to put some distance between himself and Cynthia Nicosia. Unfortunately, she'd once again filled the void with Conrad Hale. Somehow, he had to find a way to keep Cynthia occupied and away from that man. He was going to go about it in a different way this time. The last thing he wanted was to end up back in bed with Joe's wife.

THE THIRTY-FOOT YACHT, named the *Eldorado*, glided past one of the intake towers of Hoover Dam. The massive structure loomed above the boat, casting shadows across the bow.

Conrad Hale and Cynthia Nicosia sat in leather captain's chairs aboard the *Eldorado* and observed the dam as the boat progressed past its center.

"It's magnificent," Cynthia said.

Hale had his head back, eyeing the structure. "Quite an engineering feat."

Cynthia pointed. "Did you notice the art deco designs on the towers?"

"Have you ever taken a tour of the dam?"

Her nose wrinkled up. "You can go inside it?"

"Yes, there are elevators that take you down to the turbine generators. There's also a visitor's center. Built a while back, it cost more to construct than the whole damn dam." Hale grinned at his wordplay.

"I'll have to take the tour someday." Cynthia tossed her long blond hair over her tanned shoulders.

Hale picked up his glass and rattled the ice. "Can I get you another drink?"

"Yes, please. This is delicious. On a hot day like this, it's so refreshing."

He snapped his fingers, and a waiter in a white tuxedo stepped over to them, holding a tray. The man took their empty glasses and circled back into the cabin. Moments later, he returned with two fresh cocktails.

Cynthia took a sip and purred with satisfaction.

Hale said, "I'm pleased you were able to convince your husband to stay at the Conquistador tonight."

She squeezed her lips tight. "I don't want to talk about Joseph. I had to sleep with him to make the switch. You don't know how sickening that is."

He gave her a sympathetic nod, but his voice was cool when he said, "I appreciate the gesture."

Cynthia looked even more perturbed. "Why do you care about him? It's not as if you need his business. You have plenty of money."

Hale said charmingly, "I want you at the Conquistador. A

woman with your beauty should be staying at the best resort in Las Vegas. I have an idea. You're always talking about those home and garden shows you enjoy watching so much. I'm planning to remodel a suite at the Conquistador. Would you be interested in doing the interior decorating? I'll make it the suite you're staying in tonight."

Cynthia clapped her hands, and an excited smile spread over her face. "Oh, I'd love to. Is there a budget?"

Hale swayed his hand. "You can spend whatever you deem necessary."

Her eyes twinkled. "Oh, I have the perfect painting for the living room. I acquired it when I worked for an art gallery. It's an authentic Van Gogh. I'll loan it to you for a while. Right now, it's in storage. It's a great little canvas that needs to see the light of day and can be the centerpiece of my design. When can I start with the redecoration?"

He flashed his capped teeth. "Tomorrow morning. When it's done, we'll call it the Cynthia Nicosia Suite. It'll be yours whenever you stay at the Conquistador."

She fluttered her fake lashes at him. "I still don't see that happening often. Joseph told me he'd stay there just one night. Then he intends to go back to the Desert Palm. He's very attached to the place and very fond of one of their casino hosts."

Hale grimaced. "Yes, Randy Kennedy."

"Do you know him?"

"We haven't met. I've heard a lot about him, though."

"Joseph thinks he's the greatest. I like him too. As long as Randy works at the Desert Palm, you're wasting your time trying to get my husband's gambling business."

Hale turned to her and held her gaze. "I want you at the Conquistador."

"I have so many ideas on how I'll redecorate the suite.

Can I tear out walls? Dimmer switches, they should be everywhere. I'm going to use gold leaf. Yes, that'll make the bathroom elegant. This will be so much fun."

Hale sipped his cocktail and pretended to listen while she babbled on for the next two hours about her interior decoration ideas. He wondered if she had a tasteful bone in her body.

FOUR

WAYNE CORK APPROACHED Randy with a smug grin on his face. Randy laughed when he saw the rookie host. "What's up with you?"

"I just captured one hell of a player."

"Yeah? What kind of guest?"

"A thousand-dollar-a-hand blackjack player. Mildred Prichard. It's her first visit to the Desert Palm. She told me she owns a couple of apartment buildings in San Diego. She usually plays at the Charleston Resort. She's staying there."

"Is she married?"

"Yes, but her husband doesn't like to gamble. She left the Charleston because he was on her ass about her losses."

"That's not uncommon. You need to find something for him to do while she plays."

"He's a golfer, so I told her I'd keep him busy by taking him to the country club. She was grateful, and I can snare a free round."

Randy nodded in approval. "Good. Have you comped them dinner?"

"I will. I picked up a comp slip book from Frazier at the host office."

"Did you get her a player's card?"

"Yes, that's how I know she's a damn good one. She's already lost ten grand and has only been here a few hours."

"You should see if you can persuade her to switch hotels. Put her up in a suite. Play this right, and you'll have yourself a keeper."

"She loves betting on football almost as much as I do. I hope her husband and I get along."

"Don't worry about that. If the wife does, you're a lock."

"I've called the golf course and arranged a tee time for tomorrow morning. Would you like to join us?"

"No. I have a tee time myself. With Conrad Hale."

Wayne stared at him, visibly disquieted. "If he offers you a job, are you taking it?"

"I'm just golfing with him. I want to hear what he has to say. As I told you, I'm happy here at the Desert Palm."

Wayne looked at his watch. "I better get going. I'm supposed to attend to some kind of lame-ass orientation. Frazier tells me I'm meeting Walter Parker. He says Parker likes to introduce himself to all the new..." He made quotation signs with his fingers. "...team members."

Randy blew out a laugh. "What are you doing after work?"

"Nothing special. I recorded a college football game earlier. I was planning on drinking a twelve-pack and watching it."

"There's a party at a friend of mine's house. Care to join me?"

Wayne raised his shoulders. "I guess so. It's better than sitting home alone."

"A lot of beautiful ladies will be in attendance. It should be fun. I'll meet you at the sports book at midnight. We can take my car."

"All right."

"Nice job with the Prichards. You're catching on fast."

"I knew I would. I enjoy being employed at a place with a

sports book and sexy cocktail waitresses. By the way, when's payday?"

RANDY CRUISED THE casino, looking for VIP guests and any available female willing to converse. Walking past one of the busy blackjack pits, he ran into Nicosia's hulking bodyguard. "Sup, Harlan?" Randy asked and slapped him on the back. "Where's the boss playing?"

Samples frowned at Randy and grunted, gesturing toward a blackjack table across the pit. "Over there."

"How's he doing? Still winning?"

"Not my concern."

"Have you seen Cynthia? I was hoping to chat with her."

Samples said with a snarl in his voice, "You stay away from Mrs. Nicosia. She's a married lady, and you have no business with her."

Randy gripped Samples' left arm. "Harlan, I just want to keep her occupied while Joe gambles."

"I disapprove of the way you do that."

Randy's eyes narrowed. "There's nothing to be worried about. You're letting your imagination run away with you."

Samples obviously didn't like him and seemed dogged in his protection of Nicosia's interests. "I don't believe you. You better keep away from her. If Mr. Nicosia ever discovers you two in bed, he'll kill you with his bare hands. I'll help."

Randy swallowed hard. "H-Harlan, w-what kind of talk's this?"

Samples' eyes locked on Randy's. "You heard what I said." He turned, marched around the blackjack pit, and took a position behind Nicosia.

Randy wiped at the dew of sweat that had gathered at his temples.

RANDY STEERED HIS blue convertible under the Desert Palm's

porte-cochere and over to the curb. Wayne, holding a beer bottle, hopped in the vehicle, and they roared out of the parking lot and onto the Strip. The glare of the colorful neon lights was almost blinding. "Five ninety-nine ham and eggs," one marquee proclaimed. "Single-deck blackjack and girls, girls, girls," announced another.

"Could you stop by my apartment?" Wayne asked. "I spilled something on my tie, and I'd like to change. It's not far. Just off Tropicana."

Randy nodded. "No problem."

"Where's the party?"

Randy was driving toward the freeway on-ramp. "Green Valley. The house's awesome. My friend's father's a wealthy doctor. He's invited a lot of the big-wigs in town. I also expect some good babeage."

"You're sure you don't mind me coming along? I don't want to slow you down."

Randy smiled. "You couldn't if you tried. If I hook up with some female companionship, I won't abandon you. I'll make sure you get a ride home. Maybe you'll find someone of your own. How'd that play out with the women from the show? Mimi and Brigitte?"

Wayne shook his head. "I don't have enough money to keep those snooty women happy. We went dancing, but before I knew it, they were hitting on some rich guy with a fifty-thousand-dollar Rolex."

Randy chuckled.

"I'd have more luck with women if I could get past my obsession with my ex."

"What's her hold on you?"

Wayne fell back in the seat. "She's blond, great body, with the most beautiful green eyes I've ever seen."

"Sounds hot."

"She can be a raving bitch, though."

"Well, try to forget about her. There are thousands of gorgeous blondes in Vegas."

"It was an ugly-ass break-up, and we have some issues we still have to settle."

Randy pushed hard on the gas pedal, the car racing by the traffic. "Here's my advice: resolve them as soon as possible and press on."

"That's the plan, Randy. As fast and far as I can."

WAYNE LED RANDY into his apartment. "I'll just be a minute," he said.

"Okay," Randy said, surveying the living room.

"Sorry about the furnishings. I haven't had a chance to haul most of my crap up from L.A. I'll have to get back there soon to move it."

The place was empty except for a single folding chair and a television and DVR on the floor. "You don't have to be concerned about clutter."

Wayne nodded. "I never do. It'll just take me a second to get changed." He bounded down the hall.

Randy sat in the folding chair, but it was uncomfortable, so he stood and walked to a window, seeing the tall casino resorts, lit like candles, in the distance. He looked at the buildings for a while, then turned and inspected the bare, stark-white walls. *Color—this place needs color*, he thought.

Wayne burst back into the room sporting a fresh tie and jacket. "Let's go. I'm looking forward to this party. It's been a while since I've been out. I'm jonesin' for a good time."

Randy retrieved the keys from his pocket. "You'll have fun. I promise it's going to be one of the best parties you've ever attended."

"I could use a distraction."

The two new friends exited the apartment and climbed into Randy's car, both hoping for an entertaining night.

THE CROWDED ROOM buzzed with conversation. Groups of people in twos and threes huddled together, exchanging gossip. Everyone held a cocktail and had an opinion about politics and the general direction of the economy. One woman screeched out high-pitched laughter. "Oh, Randy," she said, "you're so funny."

He smirked at her. "And that was before her husband arrived."

She roared again, holding her stomach while her full breasts bounced. She was wearing a loud purple tank top and a miniskirt that was just short of indecent. Her long black hair was piled on top of her head in a nest of curls. It was more than obvious that she was thrilled to be standing alone with the Lucky One.

Randy asked, gesturing toward the bar, "Can I get you another drink, Roxanne?"

She caressed her empty wineglass. "That would be great."

"I'll be right back. Don't go away."

Her eyes were shimmering. "I won't."

Randy trekked through the bustling living room of the magnificent estate. The place had high ceilings, and the white adobe walls were covered with southwestern paintings. He elbowed his way to the bar through the throng of partygoers. A bartender in a black dinner jacket stood behind the counter, scooping ice into empty glasses. "What can I offer you, my friend?" he asked Randy.

"A chardonnay and a Heineken," Randy said, leaning against the bar and observing the people in the room. He noticed quick glances from several women and smiled. Gazing toward the foyer, he spotted Angela Grisham, and his palms moistened. She was wearing a white blouse, faded blue jeans, and high heels. On her, the casual outfit was elegant. Her long auburn hair was flowing over her shoulders. Errant strands of hair hung across her face, and she brushed them aside while conversing with a well-dressed woman in her late fifties.

"Your drinks, sir," the bartender said.

Randy was still eyeing Angela. "What?" He turned to the bartender.

The man held up the drinks and put them on the bar. "One chardonnay and a Heineken."

"Oh, yeah, thanks." Randy pulled out his wallet and extracted a five-dollar bill. "This is for you." He handed the tip to the bartender.

"Much appreciated, sir." The bartender tucked the money in his jacket pocket.

Randy picked up the drinks and set out across the room. Several acquaintances hoping to visit stopped him, but he had one thing on his mind: talking with Angela. She was now standing alone, and he wanted to get to her before another guy moved in.

He came up to her and asked, "Can I interest you in a drink?"

Startled, Angela peered at him, then at the Heineken and the white wine. "I only have two choices?"

Randy looked down at the drinks and back to her. He angled his chin to the right. "You seem like someone who would prefer a...." He glanced at the beverages. "...a chardonnay." He grinned, showing her his deep dimples.

She shook her head, smiling. "Neither. I'm sure that woman's waiting for her wine. It's not polite to give it away."

Randy peeked over his shoulder at Roxanne, who was staring into space, a vapid look in her eyes. "How do you know it's for her? Were you watching us?"

Angela blushed.

It was just a touch of pink, but Randy felt his heart jump at her reaction. He cocked an eyebrow. "Well?"

"I wasn't watching you," she said a little too defensively. "Why would I do that?"

He grinned again. "Then it must be Roxanne's outfit you were studying. Yes, she does have good taste in clothing."

Angela gave an easy laugh. "I suppose you'd think so."

He said in a mocking voice, "Oh yes, the tank top's sooo becoming."

Angela's smile was reserved. "I thought so."

He held up the wine. "I kind of feel stupid holding two drinks. People may assume I'm an alcoholic."

"You do look a bit thick. Give the chardonnay to your lady friend, and you won't appear so silly."

"I can't interest you in one?" His eyes searched hers.

She bowed her head, clearly not wanting to be drawn in by his magnetism. "No, thank you."

"Okay, let me deliver this drink to Roxanne, and I'll get you something else. What's your pleasure?"

"What do I have to say to make you leave me alone?"

"Nothing I can think of. How about a glass of champagne?"

She sighed. "Oh, okay. A soda with a lime would be fine."

"Great, I'll be right back." Randy walked to Roxanne, gave her the white wine, and told her he had some business to talk over with a friend and would see her later.

"You promise?" she asked with a whine.

"Yes." Randy pecked her on the cheek. He hurried to the bar, got a soda with lime, and returned to the foyer. Angela was nowhere in sight. He circled the area, weaving in and out of the hordes of guests, but couldn't find her anywhere.

"Kick-ass party," Wayne said from behind him.

Randy whirled around, juggling the Heineken and Angela's

soda. "Have you seen Angela Grisham? She's the cashier who took you through the marker procedures."

"No." Wayne chugged his beer.

"I went to get her a drink, and she disappeared." Randy's eyes roamed the room full of people, his forehead creasing.

"Maybe she's in the bathroom."

"Yeah, could be. So you're having a good time?"

"I am. You were right about the women. They're everywhere. I even snagged a couple of phone numbers. I'm taking your advice and pressing on." They both looked around the room, and when two blondes in matching evening gowns sauntered by, they stared in awe.

Randy let out a quiet whistle. "I told you. No one should go home alone tonight."

Wayne nodded. "Anyone in particular caught your attention?"

"One. Angela." Randy set his jaw.

"She doesn't seem to be too interested."

"Maybe that's why I want her so bad."

Wayne laughed. "Like me, you always crave what you can't have."

"You're right. But there's something about her I like. I can't put my finger on it." He took a swallow of his beer.

"She's a damn beautiful lady."

"No doubt about that. Not much of a personality, though. She has a chip on her shoulder."

"You're just unhappy she's blowing your ass off."

Randy shrugged. "I'll work past it, I assure you."

"You better hop to it." Wayne pointed at the front door with his chin. "She's getting out of here."

Randy turned and saw Angela, a sweater over her arm, heading out. "I'll see you in a while," he said. He bolted through the mass of people, dancing his way through the fashionable crowd, out the front doorway, and down the long winding drive. She was at the street, pulling open the door to a silver Prius. "Angela," he called out and ran toward the road, still juggling the beer and soda.

Angela's eyes met his, but she settled in the car and shut the door. Randy scurried around the vehicle to the driver's side and rapped on the closed window.

She rolled it down. "What do you want?"

Out of breath and panting hard, he said, "You forgot your drink. The soda with lime."

Her tone was low and harsh. "You're not understanding me, are you? I'm not interested."

"Ah, lighten up. You're not giving me a chance. You don't even know me."

"I have no reason to. You're not my type."

"And what's that?"

"Not you." She fired the engine and drove away from the curb. He stood in a cloud of dust, still holding the two drinks, and cursing under his breath.

FIVE

THE BOULDER CREEK Golf Course had a unique golfing concept, offering waterfalls and ponds, arroyos, oasis holes with swaying palms, and desert holes bordered by the playable sand.

"Nice swing," Conrad Hale said.

"Thank you," Randy said. His golf ball had rolled onto the green and stopped several inches from the cup of a lush oasis hole. The thick foliage made it difficult to believe they were in the desert.

"What's your handicap?"

"Right now it's about a ten. I haven't been playing as much as I'd like; I've been too busy."

"The Desert Palm does quite a lot of business," Pete Sawyer said.

Randy nodded. "It sure does." He put his club in his golf bag. "Walter Parker knows how to treat his guests well."

Hale said, "I've always admired what Parker's done with that place. Considering how small it is."

Randy looked at him. "It does a tremendous volume of high limit-play."

Hale said in a matter-of-fact voice, "In the last decade, the

Desert Palm hasn't been one of the growth properties in Las Vegas. It has, what, four hundred rooms and minimal amenities?"

Randy lowered himself onto the seat of a golf cart. "There's really no room for expansion, but as I said, Mr. Parker knows how to pamper his guests. The repeat business is phenomenal."

Hale sat in the driver's seat of the cart, and they drove along the path with Pete Sawyer not far behind in his own golf cart. They pulled up to a green, and Randy leapt out and retrieved his putter. He took Hale's putter out of his expensive golf bag and handed it to him.

Hale walked onto the green. "How does Parker treat his employees?"

Randy looked him in the eye. "Quite well. He has a loyal staff and treats us all like family. I've never worked in a better environment."

"It must be tough keeping the high-limit players without the proper tools."

Randy squinted. "And what might those be?"

"You have to admit, the Desert Palm doesn't offer all the amenities a resort as large as the Conquistador can provide. How many suites are there?"

Randy was lining up his shot. "Oh, I'd guess about forty."

Sawyer said, "The Conquistador has five hundred suites in a separate tower, all surrounding a private VIP pool area."

Randy did his best to not sound impressed. "Is that right?"

"Five hundred suites and the nicest spa and pools in Las Vegas. Our swimming pools make the ones at Caesar's Palace seem like children's wading pools. Have you ever seen them?"

Randy tapped his ball with the putter, and it dropped in the cup. "No, can't say I have. I've heard about them, though. Been told they're nice."

"I'd like you to come over to the Conquistador and see our operation." Hale hit his ball and watched it race past the hole and into a sand trap. "Damn it."

"Sure, I'd love a tour of the property. I've taken guests to your showroom many times, but as you'd expect, I usher them in and out as fast as possible. I haven't had much of a chance to poke around."

"It's spectacular," Sawyer said. "You must be aware the Conquistador's one of the top resorts in the world."

Hale said, "It's a great place for a host to work. Everything you'd ever need to indulge the high-limit players is available. We have the best restaurants, the grandest suites, and the most popular celebrities in our showroom. The Conquistador Tower's the tallest structure in Las Vegas, with unparalleled views."

Randy said, "Mr. Hale, I'm well aware of the amenities the Conquistador has to offer. I've been competing against you for the big players for many years."

"You've been quite effective," Sawyer said with an admiring smile. "You have some real whales in your pond."

"I prefer to think of them as my friends."

Hale said, "Consider what you could do with those friends of yours if you had the Conquistador at your disposal."

Randy nodded. "Some of them would be impressed. Others couldn't care less; they're just interested in hanging out with me."

"We know how good a host you are," Sawyer said. "We recognize that many of your players are loyal to you and not the Desert Palm."

Randy grinned mockingly. "Nor would they be to the Conquistador."

Hale gave Randy a brief nasty look. He shook his head, then both he and Sawyer took more putts, each bogeying the hole. The three of them scrambled into the golf carts and took the short ride to the next tee.

Hale jumped out of the cart and said to Randy, "We'd like to know whether you'd be interested in making a move. You'd enjoy working at the Conquistador."

"I'm always willing to discuss the possibility of a better job. I'm happy at the Desert Palm, but I'm not stupid. What kind of offer do you have in mind?"

Hale hesitated, glanced at Sawyer, then back at Randy. "We can increase the compensation you're receiving from Walter Parker by five percent, plus a five-thousand-dollar signing bonus."

Randy tipped his head to the side. "Five percent?" He grabbed the seven iron out of his golf bag.

"Yes. Keep in mind, your job will be much easier at the Conquistador. With our amenities, you won't have to work as hard to attract the power players."

Randy, with Hale and Sawyer behind him, took a few paces over to the tee. He turned to Hale and said, "I don't struggle all that much to get them to the Desert Palm. It may not be the Conquistador, but it's not a dump. It's a boutique resort."

Sawyer asked, "Then you're not interested in a change of employer?"

"Not for a five percent increase in compensation. I'm content at the Desert Palm. Without a substantial hike in pay, and I mean a significant boost, I'm not interested."

Hale scowled, his eyes black and severe. "I don't understand your loyalty to Parker."

"It has nothing to do with Walter Parker. My decision's purely financial."

"Working at the Conquistador's a much more prestigious job. Consider your career in the long term. Imagine what a hosting position at the Conquistador would do for your résumé."

Randy brushed blades of grass from his seven iron. "My résumé's made up of about twenty million in annual casino play from the guests I attract."

Hale pulled a tee from his pocket. "You're making a major mistake."

Randy waved his hand. "Please don't misunderstand. I appreciate the offer, but it doesn't meet my needs. Should you ever wish to present me a more attractive compensation package, I'd give it serious consideration."

"Let us talk it over," Sawyer said. He glanced at Hale, then at Randy. "We'd like to discuss this in private and perhaps get back to you."

Hale clenched his teeth, a muscle in his jaw pulsing. He didn't say a word.

"Very well," Randy said, pushing a tee in the ground and putting his ball in place. He stepped behind it, took a few practice swings, and then gave it a whack. The ball soared across the fairway, above a lake, rolled onto the green, and up to the cup of the short par three. "It's your turn, Mr. Hale."

WAYNE APPROACHED THE casino cashier's cage. He held a small gift-wrapped box Randy had given him and insisted he deliver to Angela. He didn't want to be Randy's mule but was trying to help the guy out. He figured it'd pay off in the long run. Wayne walked to her cashier window. "Can you spare a minute?"

Angela eyed him questioningly. "I suppose so."

"I have something for you."

"And what would that be?" Her tone was suspicious.

"It's from Randy."

Her expression darkened. "What is it?"

Wayne set the package on the counter and nudged it toward her. "He was adamant I give it to you."

"I wish he'd leave me alone." She scrutinized the wrapped gift. "I've told him I'm not interested."

Wayne gestured to the package. "Why don't you open the damn thing?"

Angela looked at the gift, then back at him. She tore the wrapping off the box, put the paper on the counter, and took the lid off. Inside were a tiny card and a heart-shaped locket. She read the note aloud: "*You've stolen my heart. Take a chance.*"

"What did he give you?" Wayne asked.

"Nothing. Just one of his mind games."

Annoyed, Wayne asked tersely, "What should I tell him?"

"To get lost."

"He's hot for you."

"Me and about twenty other women."

"He told me he can't stop thinking about you."

"Today. Next week, I'm sure he'll have his eyes on someone else."

"What could it hurt to go out with him once? Give him a goddamn break."

Angela threw her head back. "Break, yeah, my heart."

"You don't even know the dude."

"Neither do you. I know this: he considers himself god's gift to women."

Wayne pressed his lips together, plainly pissed he was even having this conversation. "Again, do you want me to relay a message?"

"His note says I've stolen his heart." She tossed the locket across the counter. "Here's a replacement."

ANGELA WATCHED WAYNE fade into a swarm of tourists, then tidied her work station, straightening a row of chip racks.

"What was that all about?" Dixie, the cashier next to her,

asked. She'd been counting a stack of hundred-dollar bills, which she placed in her cash drawer.

Angela smiled and stared out across the casino. "Randy Kennedy."

"You're not falling for him?"

"He doesn't think so." An older black woman piled chips on the counter in front of her. Angela stacked them up and exchanged them for currency. "Have a nice evening," she said.

Dixie shot Angela a disapproving look. "What do you mean he doesn't think so?"

Angela smiled. "I'm playing hard to get."

"I'd advise you to be impossible to get. He's no good. He's nothing but a womanizer."

"Oh Dixie, I'm not sure that's true."

"No, I know someone who dated him. She caught him with another girl. I'm told his exploits with woman are so well known he's called the Lucky One."

"There's something about him. It's in his eyes. A little boy, innocent but with a rebel streak."

"Innocent? You have to be kidding me."

"I'm serious. Something tells me that behind all that flash is a sweet person."

Dixie wagged an admonishing finger. "You're falling for his charms. He's just a peacock. He's a dirty nasty bird, but you're not seeing it because he has beautiful feathers."

"I know I'm right about him. Randy's not the jerk you believe he is. He's just confident."

"Then why are you being cagey?"

Angela smiled mischievously. "I want to be sure I have him pegged."

"Please be cautious, Angela. I know I'm right. He's bad news. A leopard doesn't change his spots. I don't want you to get hurt, like my friend."

"No, I'm pretty sure I'm right about him."

"Oh, lordy."

"I promise I'll be careful, but give me time to find out."

RANDY ENTERED THE Desert Palm still wearing a golf shirt and casual slacks. He bee-lined to the sports book, where he checked the spread on the Raiders-Chargers game. He didn't like it and decided he'd wait until later to make a bet.

Cruising through the casino, he was confronted by Carter Camp.

"Nice outfit, Kennedy," Camp said, giving him a resentful sneer. "I didn't realize hosts were no longer required to wear a suit and tie."

Randy was annoyed at Camp's incessant nitpicking and glowered at him. "I've been golfing. But that's none of your goddamn business."

"Do you ever put in a day of real work?"

Randy glared at him, turning toward the table games and walking away.

"My uncle wants to see you," Camp called after him in a superior tone.

Randy stopped and looked back at him. "What about?"

"Your job performance. He doesn't like your laid-back attitude and poor work ethic."

"You don't appreciate how I operate, but I can assure you Walter's quite pleased."

"Walter? Not Mr. Parker? God, you're arrogant. But you've gone too far. He's had it with your egotistical behavior, your total disregard for the rules."

"I interpret the policies as I see them. I've made this place a hell of a lot of money. You know it, and what's even more important is Walter does too."

Camp moved up to him and said in a forceful whisper, "I

bet he'd draw the line at your trying to coax our guests' wives into bed."

"You stupid son of a bitch."

"I'm watching out for my uncle's best interests."

"Trying to worm your way into the will."

Camp frowned at him.

"What's your problem? What've I ever done to you?"

"Oh, I don't know. Maybe I don't like being called a pissant or hate seeing you screw around all shift. You claim you're such a great casino host. If you spent half as much time taking care of our guests as you do trying to get laid, you might be worth something."

Randy aimed his finger at him. "You *are* a pissant." He marched away toward the pit.

"Uncle Walter wants to see you...I'm not kidding."

Randy kept going, shaking his head and growing angrier by the second. It took him three trips through the casino before he calmed. He chastised himself for letting Camp slither under his skin. *You're worked up for nothing,* he thought.

Spotting Nicosia at a blackjack table, Randy decided he'd better stop by and say hi. He went up to the man, pulled out a stool, and sat down. "What's up?" he asked.

Nicosia grunted a hello and turned his attention back to his cards. "I'm still winning. It's about time."

"You're due. Where's Cynthia? I haven't seen her in a while."

"I told you, we were given a suite at the Conquistador. It's pretty opulent."

Randy scowled. "I thought that was for one night."

"Hale's a smart man. He asked Cynthia to redecorate the suite. She loves design. Spends almost every waking minute watching those home and garden TV shows. Now it's all she's talking about—redoing a hotel suite."

Randy struck his hand on the layout. Camp had put him in a foul mood and this conversation was making matters worse. "He's an asshole who just wants your money."

Nicosia shrugged. "Tell that to my wife."

A BELLMAN CARRYING golf clubs followed Conrad Hale into his spacious office. The man propped the clubs against the back wall, and Hale tipped him twenty dollars. The bellman peered at the money, smiled wide, and left the room. Hale walked around his mammoth desk and took a seat. Pete Sawyer wandered to one of the big windows and looked out.

"That arrogant bastard," Hale said. "Who does he think he is?"

Sawyer turned to him. "Kennedy knows he's a good host. And he's right. You have to offer him much more money than the Desert Palm's paying or he'll never leave. It's the only way he'll consider making a move. He's made that quite clear."

"He's so egotistical, almost laughing in my face—taunting me to offer more money."

Sawyer crossed the room and sat in front of Hale's desk. "He's worth it, I tell you. I have a friend who's a pit boss at the Desert Palm. He says Kennedy's a high-roller magnet. He has one of those golden personalities. Everybody wants to be his friend."

Hale's left eye twitched. "I despise him."

"I understand you've been spending time with Joseph Nicosia's wife. I know you convinced them to stay in the hotel last night, but my games supervisors inform me he's been going over to the Desert Palm to gamble. He hasn't spent a dime here."

"I know. I was hoping the wife would be more of an influence. And boy, Cynthia Nicosia's a dicey broad. I need to be careful with that one. I believe she fancies me in a romantic sort of way."

Sawyer shook a finger at his boss. "That's the worst thing that could happen. Nicosia won't step foot in the Conquistador if he thinks you're stealing his wife."

Hale's expression was stern. "I recognize that."

"If you want my opinion, I'd cool it with Mrs. Nicosia and hire Randy Kennedy as a host. Mr. Hale...Conrad, don't let your personal feelings get in the way of a sound business decision. Invite Kennedy to the Conquistador and show him around. There's no doubt he'll be impressed. Then make him a reasonable proposal. It won't bankrupt you—the opposite, in fact. Nicosia alone is worth it. With the MGM's deep pockets, they're bound to make a strong offer sooner or later. We gotta get in first"

Hale stood and meandered to the window overlooking the casino floor. "What kind of salary do you think he'll accept?"

"Twenty-five percent more than he's making at the Desert Palm. That and the glitz of the Conquistador should convince him to change employers. I get the distinct impression he's intrigued by the idea of working at a top resort."

Hale was quiet for a while, a vein in his neck throbbing. "I'll offer him a ten percent increase. If he declines, I'll go to fifteen, but no more. At that point, I'll find another way."

"I'm not certain it'll be enough, but at least you're moving in the right direction. You won't regret it, I promise you."

Hale turned to Sawyer with hostile eyes. "You better be right."

RANDY TOOK THE elevator to the fifth floor of the pool-view VIP suites at the Conquistador Resort. He stepped out of the car and entered an elegant lobby. The penthouse floor at the Desert Palm was lavish, but it was no match for the grandeur of the Conquistador. A concierge desk, staffed by a neat and well-dressed young man, was straight ahead. The floors were marble and the high ceilings gold. The walls were dotted with expensive paintings.

Randy nodded to the concierge and strode down the hall, passing a series of suites. At room 507, he stopped and rapped on the door. He waited and knocked again, this time harder. A moment later, Cynthia Nicosia, holding a phone to her ear, opened the door and motioned for him to come into the suite. She placed her hand over the mouthpiece of the cellphone. "I'll just be a minute," she said. "Make yourself comfortable."

Randy entered the room, sat on a fluffy white sofa, and picked up a magazine.

Cynthia walked to the balcony doors and gazed toward the glistening swimming pools below. "It's not your painting, Kevin," she said. "It's mine." She listened while shaking her head. "Circumstances have changed since then. Get over it. Have you been drinking already?"

Randy watched her as she spoke. She was wearing a blue satin dress, and her blond hair was pulled back in a ponytail. She made an abrupt turn, and he glanced at the magazine, trying not to look like he was eavesdropping on her conversation.

Cynthia lowered her voice. "Don't you threaten me, you bastard. I'll tell Joseph you're hassling me." She held the telephone away from her ear as the person on the other end of the line shouted. After the yelling subsided, she put the phone back to her ear. "Are you through with your little temper tantrum?" She listened while taking the band out of her hair and releasing the ponytail, shaking her hair loose. "Leave me alone, damn it. I've said enough. This conversation's over." Cynthia hung up, paused, and then faced Randy. "What brings you here?"

"A social visit. I spend so much time working, I sometimes worry you're being ignored. That, and I wanted to see the suite you've been bragging to Joe about."

Cynthia smiled. "It'll be magnificent. Conrad's letting me

redecorate the space any way I see fit. Wait until you see what I'm going to do with it. It'll be the nicest suite in Las Vegas. I've been contemplating my design plans all morning."

"I wondered why I hadn't seen you. Hale's been keeping you busy."

She grinned and, in a sing-song voice, said, "Conrad's a wonderful man. I like him a lot. He gave me a tour all around Las Vegas, and yesterday, we spent a fabulous afternoon on his yacht at Lake Mead."

"You know he's only being nice to you because he wants Joe to gamble at the Conquistador."

Cynthia pressed her lips together firmly. "That's not true. We're becoming close."

"You can't believe that."

"Absolutely. I assure you, he's been far more than just nice."

Puzzled, Randy narrowed his eyes. "You're not hoping to get involved with Conrad Hale?"

Cynthia fluttered her lashes at him. "He's handsome. And sooo rich. I'm going to see if I can seduce him."

"Listen, Cynthia, fooling around with Hale will lead to trouble. Joe's bound to find out about it."

She flipped her hand at him. "I don't care if he does."

"Hey, Joe's the best thing that's ever happened to you. He's told me many times how much he cares for you."

"Ha," she said with a honking laugh. "He has a funny way of expressing it. Half the time, he ignores me, and the rest, he's yelling that I'm spending too much on clothes. He's always shouting. His verbal abuse is getting to be too much. I'm scared."

"You know Joe's just hot-blooded. He doesn't mean to be nasty."

"Well, Conrad doesn't treat me that way. He's kind, thoughtful, and attractive."

Randy raised an eyebrow. "And rich."

She bounced an eyebrow right back at him. "That too."

He didn't try to hide his expression.

"Randy, don't give me that look. I see nothing wrong with pursuing a man with money. Growing up, my family was poor. No, destitute. We lived out of the back of my father's station wagon, going to sleep hungry most nights. No friends, no toys. The one person I had to help me through that terrible time was my brother, Brett. If you'd lived our childhoods, you'd grasp for anything better too."

Randy swung his open hand in front of him. "See this suite? You've come a long way."

"Yes, little Cyndi Miller's moved up, and I'm pleased with myself, even if I've had to do some things I'm not proud of to get what I wanted. I gave up a lot to be where I am today."

Randy said with mocking sarcasm, "What, love?"

She lowered her eyes. "Yes, I suppose so."

"Are you falling in love with Conrad Hale?"

"I could be. He has all the attributes I'm seeking in a man. I feel a tingle when I'm around him. I'm sure he'll fall in love with me. Almost every man I've ever met does. Present company excluded." She winked at him.

"What about Joe?"

"He'll do just fine without me. He's rich and powerful. I know he cheats on me; he'll find someone."

Randy said vigorously, "He's powerful all right. Joe isn't your typical businessman. He's a man with mob connections and a pitbull of a bodyguard."

"If he loves me, he'll let me go."

"You're being naïve. It doesn't work that way."

"Conrad's been very attentive."

Randy shook a finger at her. "I'd go slow if I were you. I believe Hale wants you to get him Joe's gambling action and nothing more."

"You don't know Conrad like I do. It could become something exceptional."

"If you want out of your marriage because you no longer love Joe, fine, but don't expect Hale to rush into your arms. He cares about Joe's money. When you file for divorce, I'd bet my last dollar he forgets your name."

She gave Randy a stare with daggers in it. "You're being cruel."

"Jeez." Randy exhaled harshly. "I didn't come here to lecture you about your personal life. I thought maybe we could go shopping or something. I want to spend some time with you. Be a proper casino host."

Cynthia's eyes gleamed, her mood lightened. "I am kind of horny."

Randy put his fist to his chest. "I've been thinking a lot about that. You're a beautiful woman, but for us to sleep together is dangerous."

"It's just recreational sex."

"You're married to one of my biggest players, you plan to divorce him for Conrad Hale, and you're asking to make love with me. What's wrong with you?"

A wry smile crossed her face. "I can't help it; you're so cute."

"And you're spectacular, but I'm not stupid. We're not going down that road again. I've given this a lot of thought."

"You're sure?"

"Yes, but I want to keep you company...and away from Hale."

"Oh, Randy."

Curious, he shifted his head to the right. "Other than sex and interior design, what do you like to do?"

WAYNE SAT NEXT to Mildred and Ernest Prichard in a booth in

the Desert Palm's Mohave Steakhouse, working on building a relationship with the mature couple so he could show his boss it hadn't been a mistake to hire him. Doing so was a chore, but he kept reminding himself he needed the paycheck. When no one was watching, he poured a mini bottle of vodka in his water glass.

"Oh, I don't know what to order for dinner," Mildred said, reading the menu. She was wearing a purple paisley dress, and her gray hair was braided into a bun. Her face was wrinkled, the character lines of a woman who'd lived an interesting life.

"I'm having a steak," Ernest said.

"You always eat that. Why don't you try something different?"

Ernest didn't say anything but begrudgingly picked up his menu. He was dressed in a rumpled chocolate-brown suit and had slicked-back salt-and-pepper hair, thinning on the top. He was wearing thick-lensed glasses with unstylish black frames.

"Ernest's quite the golfer," Wayne said. "Mildred, you should've seen the putt he sank on the third green." *It was one of about ten he made on the hole*, Wayne thought.

Ernest's face brightened, and his teeth—it was obvious they were dentures—showed through the smile. "I was lucky. Thanks again for taking me golfing. I get bored while Millie gambles."

"Yes, Wayne," Mildred said, "we appreciate you taking the time. It's kept Ernest out of my hair. He drives me crazy when he doesn't have anything to do."

Ernest put his menu down. "What's that supposed to mean?"

Mildred leaned over and put her hand on his arm. "Oh, just hush."

Ernest seemed to almost wither away. He returned to the menu.

"I enjoyed golfing with Ernest," Wayne said. "I was able to escape from the casino for a while. We had an early enough tee time that it wasn't too hot. I've arranged for another one tomorrow morning. What do you say, Ernest, are you up for another round?"

"Okay," he said, his voice hoarse, "but I'm not sure I'm capable of doing all eighteen holes. Let's just play nine; my arthritis is acting up."

Wayne peeked at his watch. He could think of a couple hundred places he'd rather be. "Sounds great. How do you two like your suite?"

"It's quite nice," Mildred said. "You've been more than hospitable."

"My pleasure." More lies. That was what a host did for a living, Wayne had concluded. Lie.

"I did feel a little guilty about checking out of the Charleston Resort. After all, they've been giving me some nice comps. But I don't know anyone there, so I guess I shouldn't be concerned about it."

"You don't have a rapport with any of the casino hosts?"

"No, not in anything but a passing way. A lady came over while I was playing blackjack and asked how I was doing, but I didn't catch her name and she didn't seem interested in visiting. She was in such a hurry."

"Huh. That surprises me." He took a swallow of his vodka-infused water.

Mildred smiled at Wayne. "I enjoy the attention you're giving us. I appreciate your tips on which football teams to bet on."

Wayne thought for a bit. Maybe he could make some extra money off these old folks. "If you'd like, I'll wager for you when you're in San Diego. Call me, and I'll place bets on the teams of your choice." He didn't mention it was illegal.

"You can do that?"

"Sure. I will have to collect a ten percent fee for the service, though."

"That sounds like fun."

"Keep it to yourselves, however. I'm not doing this for every customer." Wayne picked up his menu and studied it. "I'm starving. I didn't eat lunch."

Mildred put down her menu. "I'm having the salmon."

"That sounds delicious. I'll order the same."

"I'm having a steak," Ernest said, recoiling in anticipation of a reprimand.

DURING THE FOOTBALL season, the sports book at the Desert Palm was almost always packed with fans looking to place a wager. Today was no exception, with long lines at the betting windows. "What do you think, Randy?" Anthony Chapman asked. "My gut tells me the Boys, but the Saints have been coming on strong." Chapman was a six-foot-six former UNLV basketball star, wealthy Las Vegas attorney, and frequent visitor to the Desert Palm. An African American man in his early forties, he was wearing jeans, with a tweed jacket over a white shirt.

"Go with New Orleans," Randy said.

Chapman scratched his close-cropped black hair. "I know Dallas was thrashed by Philadelphia last week, but I believe they're going to be the conference champions."

"I'd still take the Saints. They've been having a great year. I like that rookie running back. Have you seen his stats?"

The lawyer scrutinized the betting line intently. "What about the Seattle-San Francisco game?"

Randy studied the line. "The Forty-Niners are a definite."

Wayne neared the two men. "You're fricking crazy," he said.

Randy and the lawyer eyed him as he dropped into the seat next to them. "Don't listen to him," Randy said. "He owes me a hundred bucks from the Ravens-Bronco match-up."

"That was a goddamn fluke," Wayne said. "A Hail Mary with two seconds left. Who would've imagined it?"

The attorney smiled, nodding. "I thought so too." He held out his hand. "Anthony Chapman."

Wayne shook hands. "Wayne Cork."

"Wayne's one of our new casino hosts," Randy said. "He fancies himself a football authority. So far, he's been an expert at losing."

"Nice to meet you," Anthony said. "What's your pick in the Dallas-New Orleans game?"

Wayne checked the betting line. "I'd go with the Cowboys, no question."

"You're wrong," Randy said.

"Yesterday's game was a fluke. Want to go double or nothing on that bet?"

Randy jabbed his finger in the air. "You're on. I'll show you who knows his football. What do you think, Anthony?"

Anthony shrugged. "I'm afraid I have to go with Wayne. He seems like he knows what he's talking about. Did you play football?"

Wayne grinned and puffed up his chest. "I did. Two years at USC before I got hurt."

"So what?" Randy said. "That doesn't make you an expert. I've been following every NFL team since I was six."

Anthony said, "Sorry, Randy. This time I have to agree with Wayne."

Randy lifted up his hands. "You'll regret it. But hey, I can always use another hundred-dollars."

The lawyer stood up. "I'm placing my bets. I'll be back in a few minutes." Anthony walked away and queued in the line at a betting window.

Randy turned to Wayne. "What've you been up to?"

"Just finished having dinner with the Prichards—you know, the old couple I told you about. You didn't tell me that hosting can be such a boring job. Making conversation with these people sucks."

"It depends on the guests. Did you take the husband golfing?"

"Yes. Grumpy old bastard. He can't golf a lick, but I guess it's something I have to do. When I came back to the casino, I reviewed Mrs. Prichard's blackjack play. The computer shows she lost almost fifteen grand."

Randy gave him two thumbs up. "Congratulations. Get another fifty guests like Mrs. Prichard and you'll have it made for the rest of your life."

Wayne rubbed his cheek. "Jesus, that sounds like a lot of effort. I'm going to have to drink a lot to get through this job."

"What about Angela? Did you deliver my gift?"

Wayne screwed up his face and tugged at his collar. "Sort of. Don't have me do your dirty work again."

"What do you mean? Did you give her the package I gave you or not?"

"Yeah, she opened it." Wayne reached inside his jacket, pulled out Randy's locket, and handed it to him. "But she gave it back. Told me to tell you she wants nothing to do with your ass."

Randy's eyebrows drew together. "Goddamn it, why? I don't understand."

"How many chicks have you nailed at the Desert Palm?"

"Hell, I don't know. A few. What does that have to do with anything?"

"Randy, I've known you a short time, but I've never seen a guy move through women so fast. You attract them like no one I've ever been around before."

"So what?"

"Let's just say you've developed a name for yourself. One I'd give my right testicle to have. However, I don't believe Angela's impressed by your popularity."

"Oh, that's ridiculous. She doesn't know me."

"She's aware of your reputation. As Frazier said, they don't call you the Lucky One for nothing."

"Yeah? Well, she's crazy. I can name half a dozen women who are begging to slide into my bed. Does she think she's too good for me?"

Wayne shrugged. "I just know what she told me. She wants you to get lost."

"That's the last thing I'm going to do."

"What's your plan?"

"I'm not certain yet." Randy fell silent, deep in thought. "There's something about her. I can't give up."

SIX

IT WAS A busy night at the Desert Palm, and the casino felt alive with action. Jackpot bells rang across the floor, and dealer's calls announced the rolls of the dice. Nicosia took a puff on his cigar and said to Randy, "My luck changed, so I decided to give it a rest." They were in a casino lounge at the bar, and Nicosia was sipping a scotch on the rocks. Harlan Samples, ever protective, was parked about ten feet away with his arms crossed.

"Are you still up?" Randy asked, pulling out a stool and sitting down.

"Yeah, about fifty thousand. I was up almost three hundred grand but ran into a hot dealer. I'd sure appreciate it if this casino would give me a new one when I ask."

"We don't do that, Joe. Let's not go into that again. Switch tables if you don't like the dealer."

A smile crept over Nicosia's face. "You can't blame me for asking. I love keeping the dealers and bosses off guard. When I intimidate a dealer, I believe I'm luckier."

"You go too far. How would you feel dealing to someone like you?"

Nicosia wiggled his eyebrows. "They know I'm a sweetheart."

"That's what you keep telling me." Randy grinned.

Nicosia laughed, loud and strong, and took another swig of his drink. "I wonder what that wife of mine's up to."

"I spoke with her a little while ago. She's all enthusiastic about redecorating the suite at the Conquistador. I wish I could keep her from Hale. It's in my best interest to shield both of you from that man."

"You're right. If I were in your shoes, I'd do the same. But don't worry; I won't gamble there."

"How about another drink?"

"Sure. Tonight, I feel like getting drunk."

Randy drummed his fingers on the bar. "I want a shot too."

Nicosia gestured for the bartender, who walked over and took their order, poured the drinks, and pushed them across the counter. Nicosia picked up his glass. "A toast."

Randy held up his shot. "To what?"

"To good luck."

"Hear, hear."

In one swift movement, both men downed the whiskeys.

ON THE OTHER side of the casino, Carter Camp pointed, saying in an excited voice, "See that, Uncle Walter? Kennedy's drinking on shift."

Parker watched Randy conversing with Nicosia and nodded.

Camp waved his arm. "What did I tell you? He has zero respect for the rules. This is nothing; at least he's with a casino guest this time. You can't believe some of the stunts I've seen him pull."

Parker looked at his nephew. "I've told you I'll have a word with Randy. His behavior's none of your concern, though."

"Now you know I wasn't exaggerating. You've seen it for yourself."

"I said it's not your business." He grabbed his cane and trotted away from his ill-tempered nephew. Parker wound through the busy casino and moved up the steps into the Arabian Lounge. He strolled up behind Nicosia and put his hand on the gambler's shoulder. "Mr. Nicosia, I trust you're having an enjoyable stay at my establishment?"

Nicosia smiled, while Randy elbowed his empty shot glass out of the way.

"Yes, Mr. Parker," Nicosia said. "I'd like to be winning more money, but as usual, everything's first class."

Parker said, "I've told you before—please call me Walter."

Nicosia jiggled his finger. "That's right, and you're to call me Joe."

"How many times have we had this conversation?"

Nicosia chuckled. "A few."

"We haven't had a chance to chat since our Labor Day party. I apologize. How've you been?"

Nicosia inhaled smoke from his cigar. "I've been doing well. Business is up."

"Is Randy taking good care of you?"

Nicosia leaned over and patted Randy on the back. "You bet. You have a gem in this guy. Best damn casino host in town."

"That's what I like to hear."

Randy smirked, quite self-satisfied.

Parker said, "As always, should you need anything and young Mr. Kennedy's unavailable, please ask for me in person. I'm at your service at all times."

"I appreciate that," Nicosia said.

"Thank you for the business." Parker gazed at Randy. "Son, would it be possible for you to stop by my office sometime late tomorrow afternoon?"

Randy's grin faded. "Sure. Any particular reason?"

"I'd prefer to discuss it in private." There was an edge to his voice.

Randy's forehead furrowed. "Oh, okay."

"I'll see you tomorrow. Joe, it was nice visiting with you. I hope you find the best of luck at my casino."

"Thanks, Wally," he said.

An annoyed frown passed over Parker's face, and his lips thinned. He suddenly veered away from the bar and into the casino.

"Uh, oh," Randy said. "Busted."

Nicosia's eyes narrowed. "What'd you do?"

"Walter saw me drinking. I'm not supposed to be consuming alcohol while on shift."

"Ah, that's crap. If you need me to talk to Wally, I will."

"No. I can take care of myself." Randy noticed a smug and beaming Carter Camp across the lounge. "I know where my troubles are coming from and how to handle it."

Nicosia shrugged, trying to shake the last drops of whiskey out of his glass and onto his tongue. "If you say so. But just say the word, and I'll call the old man."

"Don't worry about it." Randy caught the attention of the bartender, who came up to them. "Two more, please."

The bartender poured fresh shots and set them in front of Randy and Nicosia.

"This is good hootch," Nicosia said.

"It's my turn to make a toast."

Nicosia held up his whiskey. "Shoot."

"To getting even." Randy clicked his drink against Nicosia's, raised his glass in defiance, and smiled at a stunned Camp. He slugged back the liquor.

Visibly enraged, Camp stomped away.

RANDY STOOD IN the Desert Palm's parking lot next to Angela

Grisham's silver Prius. He'd spent the entire evening with Nicosia, drinking copious amounts of liquor, and was very intoxicated. He glanced at his watch, trying to focus on the blurry hands. It was twelve-fifteen. A sliver of a moon was creeping toward the center of the sky. The stars were all but washed away by the glow of the neon lights along the Strip.

Randy heard voices and saw two women walking toward him, talking and laughing. They slowed as they approached him, tentative in the darkness. When they were close enough, Randy recognized Angela and a woman he knew also worked in the cashier's cage.

"Evening, ladies," he slurred.

"What are you doing out here?" Angela asked.

"Nothing." Randy staggered a few feet back. "I wanted some one-on-one time with you."

"I'm not interested in speaking to you."

The other woman put her hand on Angela's arm. "Would you like me to hang around?" she asked. "I don't mind."

"No, Dixie. I'll be fine. I know your husband's waiting for you to get home. I'll see you tomorrow."

Dixie was looking at Randy with a disapproving frown. "If you're sure."

"I'll be okay. Say hi to Jimmy for me."

Dixie pursed her lips. "All right. I'll see you later." She scowled at Randy and, high heels clicking, crossed the parking lot to her vehicle.

"Please, Angela," Randy said after Dixie had started her car and driven away. "I hoped we could talk."

"You're drunk," she said.

"Nooo. I've just had a couple. Why wouldn't you take my locket?"

She swept her auburn hair over her shoulder. "I don't need

a gift from you. I want nothing to do with you. Why can't you understand that?"

"I'm dense." Randy flashed a boyish smile. "I think I looove you."

Angela's blue eyes widened in surprise. "Love? Ha! You *are* drunk. How much have you had?"

He concentrated on trying to stand still and not fall over. "I told you, a few shots. I had to have them to soothe my aching... aching heart."

Angela bit her lower lip, trying not to smile. "Go home and sleep it off."

"I'm not leaving until you tell me you looove me too."

"Well then, you're never going home." She unlocked her Prius with the key fob and pulled open the door. She settled in the car, shut the door, and rolled down the window.

"Please, Angela, give me a chance." Randy lost his balance and lurched forward, grabbing the hood of the car to keep himself from falling to the pavement.

"I'm not taking chances with you. You're a mess."

"I'm... I'm lovable." Randy staggered over to the driver's side of Angela's car.

Gazing into his eyes, she again bit her lip. "Go home."

"Can't. Toooo drunk to drive."

"Call a cab."

"I don't have any... any money. I left my wallet at home."

Angela scowled with growing irritation. "God, you're pathetic."

"Will yooou give me a ride home?" He was hanging on the door and leaning through the window. The pungent smell of whiskey wafted through the vehicle.

She waved her hand and coughed. "Your breath's intoxicating."

"So's my looove for you."

Angela let out a sarcastic laugh. "Oh brother."

"Pretty please."

She studied him for a moment, undoubtedly trying to decide what to do. "I'll take you home because you might hurt yourself or someone else if you drive. But I don't want you bothering me ever again."

Randy smiled, pleased, and stumbled to the passenger side of the Prius. He struggled to open the door and get inside. "I live in Green Valley. I looove you, Angela."

Angela pushed the ignition button and started the car. She glanced over at him. His eyes were closed, and he was snoring. She watched him breathe, her heartbeat still rapid. He was egotistical, an arrogant womanizer, and a drunk. Just what she didn't need.

SEVEN

RANDY WOKE TO the sound of a jackhammer outside his bedroom—the city crews working on the street. He forced himself out of bed and shut the open window, but the pounding in his head continued. He had vague memories of the previous evening, remembering that Angela had driven him home but little more.

He did dream about her. He smiled at the thought, but the movement hurt, and he massaged his aching temples. He pulled on a pair of shorts and walked down the stairs.

Randy's home was a condominium in the fashionable Green Valley area of the Las Vegas suburb of Henderson. The place had a classic design, with high ceilings and over-stuffed furniture. The walls were white, and the floor was covered with copper-colored tile. A large potted palm tree leaned over the sofa. As Randy plodded toward the back of the house, the cool tile felt good on his bare feet.

Entering the kitchen, he squinted, trying to block out the bright sunshine pouring in through the windows. Randy headed straight for the refrigerator. A picture of him with his mom and dad when he was a child and one with a former girlfriend adorned the door. He yanked it open and grabbed a carton of orange juice. He gulped at least a quart of the golden liquid and returned the almost empty carton to the refrigerator, then trudged to the living room, where he flopped down on a puffy leather sofa and covered his eyes with his hands. Randy thought again about Angela, feeling a strange sensation he couldn't quite understand. He remembered telling her he loved her—he hadn't said that to a woman before. Well, not and meant it.

What was he doing wrong? Why wouldn't she go out with him? He knew his drunken performance hadn't done much to bolster his chances.

His mobile phone rang, interrupting his thoughts, and he lurched at the device, trying to silence the blare. He lifted it to an ear and said hello in a gravelly voice.

"Randy?" a man asked.

He rubbed his hand over his face. "Yeah?"

"Randy, it's Pete. Pete Sawyer from the Conquistador Resort."

"Hey, Pete, what can I do for you?"

"Mr. Hale and I had a long discussion about you, and we'd like to make another offer."

Randy kneaded his temple. "How much?"

"We want to show you around the Conquistador before we discuss money. Are you free this morning?"

Randy closed his eyes and winced. "I suppose so."

"Fine, then. I'll have a limousine pick you up at ten."

Randy groaned. "Ten?" He checked the clock on the far wall. "Could we make it eleven?"

"Certainly. Give me your address, and I'll have a limo there at eleven."

Randy rattled off his address and tapped the phone off. He rolled back on the cushions, his stomach doing flip-flops. Eventually, he pried himself off the couch and lumbered over to the mirror above the fireplace. His skin was sallow and eyes bloodshot. He had a lot of work to do if he was going to look even halfway presentable for a job interview.

CONRAD HALE SAT in his office, reviewing the previous day's financial statement. Business had been good, and he wondered how much better it would've been if Joseph Nicosia had gambled at the Conquistador. He picked up the phone and dialed. When Cynthia Nicosia answered, he asked, "How's your redecoration project coming along?"

Her voice was matter-of-fact. "I need another worker to help with the wallpaper, and people who can do tile work. And a limousine to take me to a high-end furniture store and a fabric place. The ones I know that stock the items I want are in the World Market Center and the Fashion Show Mall."

Hale nodded. "Anything you need is at your disposal."

"That painting I told you about? A friend of mine's been storing it for me, and she's having it shipped to Vegas today. It's called *Sunflowers in a Vase* and will be the perfect centerpiece for the living room wall."

"I can't wait to see it. I want you and Joseph to stay in the suite every time you visit Las Vegas."

"I'd rather stay in it with you."

There was an abrupt silence as Hale registered her words. "Ah, Cynthia...I believe...you should focus on your interior decoration."

"Oh, why not? It'll be fun." Her tone was flirtatious.

Another few seconds of awkward silence ensued, and Hale tipped back in his chair. "You have shopping to do. I'll talk with you later." He hung up and shook his head.

RANDY SAT IN the black stretch limousine, clasping his hands behind his head and reclining in the soft leather seat. As the limo cruised down the Strip, he saw the tourists peering at it, trying to see through the tinted windows. He wondered if they thought he was a Hollywood celebrity.

When the limousine passed the Desert Palm, Randy felt a twinge of guilt but forgot about that when the car drove into the entrance of the Conquistador. The limo sped up the road, and he admired the tall fountains on both sides of the driveway. Manicured hedges and lawns surrounded each one. Splashes of colorful flowers were accented by swaying palm trees. The one-hundred-ten-story Conquistador Tower loomed over the resort.

The limousine glided under the ornate porte-cochere and stopped at the curb. A doorman in an elegant red conquistador outfit opened the door to the limo and held it, waiting for Randy to exit. Randy smiled at the royal treatment and slipped out of the car. As he stood there, adjusting his tie and buttoning his jacket, he heard his name being called and turned to see a waving Pete Sawyer.

"Randy," Sawyer said, "welcome to the Conquistador."

"Thanks." He shook Sawyer's hand firmly. "I'm excited about the tour."

"Mr. Hale's waiting for us in his office." Sawyer grasped Randy's elbow and escorted him toward the gleaming entrance. "He's pleased to be meeting with you again."

"Somehow I doubt that."

"Please don't misunderstand Mr. Hale. He's accustomed to getting his way and was taken aback by your negotiation technique. I've talked with him, and he wants very much for you to work here at the Conquistador. I believe you'll be much more receptive to the offer he has in mind."

Randy nodded. "I'm willing to listen."

"This way." Sawyer ushered Randy through the dramatic entry of the Conquistador. The interior of the resort was immense. To their left was a four-story waterfall that cascaded into a lagoon. To the right was the lobby, where lines of people were queuing up to check in and out of the four thousand hotel rooms. The enormous fish tank behind the registration desk stretched from one end of it to the other, hundreds of tropical fish swimming past the waiting tourists.

Opposite the lobby was a bridge leading over a flowing stream to a lounge, where a pasty-faced trio of musicians was trying to enliven a half-dozen stoic barflies. The lead singer was attempting to make conversation with the customers, but they were either too hung over or two disinterested to care. The trio soon gave up their attempt at banter and played a stale version of the lounge favorite, *New York, New York*.

Directly ahead of Randy and Sawyer was the casino, its centerpiece a full-sized replica of an Aztec temple. The giant stone structure terraced its way to a ceiling covered with skylights. Intricate stone ornaments of Aztec gods were prominently displayed along the top of the edifice. Green flower-covered vines crept down the stone steps of the temple.

Randy's gaze was focused on the monument.

"It's something, isn't it?" Sawyer asked.

Randy looked at him. "Sure is."

"Have you seen the light show?"

"No, but I've heard about it."

"From seven in the evening to midnight, there's a laser light show every hour on the hour, with colored lasers shooting out of the top of the ruin and bouncing around the casino. It's incredibly fun to watch."

Randy noted the elaborate carvings in the stone. "I'm amazed at the architecture."

"Mr. Hale traveled to Mexico many times before he built this portion of the resort. He made certain every inch of the temple was authentic. He even hired Aztec Indians to supervise the construction."

Randy craned his head back. "I've always wondered why

a resort named the Conquistador had an Aztec temple as the focal point of the casino."

"The Spanish conquistadors conquered the Aztecs. Mr. Hale wanted to celebrate the bravery of the Spanish warriors."

"I wonder what the Aztec Indians think about that."

Sawyer lifted his shoulders. "I don't know, but it makes for a dramatic resort."

Randy followed Sawyer down a couple of steps and into the main casino of the Conquistador. The area was crowded with gamblers, frumpy snow-birds alongside men and women in expensive dresses and suits. Rows of blackjack tables stretched out the length of a basketball court. Sawyer gestured to the gamblers. "As you can see, we cater to a wide range of customers. When you have a resort as large as the Conquistador, you're able to appeal to a vast array of visitors. We accommodate both the high and low end of the economic strata."

Randy watched a man in bib overalls tapping the spin button on a dollar slot machine while a woman in what appeared to be an expensive French original sat behind him, staring intently at the spinning reels on her penny machine. "Yes, quite a mixture of guests."

"We're going to show you the entire resort and give you an idea of what makes this place special. The tower's a landmark in Las Vegas. Mr. Hale will be the tour guide; his office is this way." Sawyer led Randy to the foot of the simulated Aztec ruin and into a dimly lit passageway.

"This is how you get to Hale's office?" Randy asked.

Sawyer bobbed his head. "Yes."

"It seems more like the entrance to a ride at Disneyland."

He smiled. "Mr. Hale has a flair for the theatrical." At the end of the corridor was a single elevator. Sawyer hit the call button to the right of it, and the doors clanged opened. He held them, and Randy entered the car.

After a short ride, the elevator doors parted, and both men strode out into an elegant lobby. A waterfall to their left tumbled into a lily-covered pond filled with colorful koi. A petite blond woman sat behind a desk in the far corner of the room, staring at a computer screen. She looked up when Randy and Sawyer approached and said, "Mr. Hale's expecting you."

Randy flashed an easy smile at the woman. "Hi, beautiful, what's your name?"

"Ava."

"Ava's a sexy name. I'm Randy."

She offered him a broad grin. "It's nice meeting you."

"Enough with the flirting," Sawyer said, opening one of the double doors to their left.

Randy winked at Ava. "I'll talk with you later."

She stared at him, obviously captivated. "Okay."

"Randy," Sawyer said impatiently, "Mr. Hale's waiting."

Randy winked at the secretary again, turned, and drifted into the office of Conrad Hale. The space was flooded with light, and he raised his hand to block the over-powering rays of the sun. Surveying the room, he figured the office was somewhere near the top of the Aztec temple.

"Good morning, Mr. Kennedy," Hale said, sitting behind a massive plank of a desk. "It's good to see you again."

"Great office," Randy said. He crossed the room to a wall of windows. Through the glass, he saw the entire Conquistador casino laid out below him—acres of slot machines and rows of blackjack, roulette, and craps tables.

Hale stood and moved over to Randy. "It does have an unbelievable view. You should be here during the laser light show. You'll find no better vantage point."

"I bet." Randy stepped away from the window and inspected the office. Slanted glass surrounded three sides of the room, each window with its own distinctive view of the casino below. The furnishings were sparse, but elegant. The floor was an alternating pattern of stone and bamboo.

"I'd like to show you around my resort before we discuss a compensation package."

"That would be fine," Randy said with a faint smile.

"I want you to see all the advantages you'd have as an executive host at the Conquistador." Hale put his hand on Randy's shoulder and escorted him through the doorway and into the office lobby. "You'll find that every tool you could ever desire is at your disposal."

They drew near the elevator, and the doors swooshed apart. Hale boarded the car, Randy and Sawyer trailing after him.

"You'll be impressed," Sawyer said.

"I already am," Randy said.

Once in the casino, Hale directed them through the labyrinth of betting options and over to the hotel lobby. He said, "Our customers' pampering begins right here at check-in. Of course, we don't make our best players stand in line with the masses. We have a special check-in room like no other in Las Vegas."

Hale walked to the right of the registration desk, to an ornate gold door marked *VIP Services*. He pulled it open, and Randy and Sawyer followed him into a large room with Cherrywood paneling, expensive Persian rugs, and crystal chandeliers. Half a dozen tables, each surrounded by plush brown velvet chairs, were sprinkled around the area. A grand piano sat in one corner, a musician playing a soft classical tune.

At two of the tables, well-dressed women in navy blue uniforms were attending to customers. At one, three Asian men in business suits sat captivated by a lanky blonde, who was explaining the amenities of the resort. A man wearing a turban occupied another table; his eyes dark and brooding, he appeared somewhat anxious.

A busty brunette in a red silk evening gown came up to Randy carrying a tray of hors d' oeuvres. "Would you care for a snack?" she asked. "The caviar's delicious."

"Yes, thank you," he said, taking a toast point topped with caviar. He bounced his eyebrows at her in a seductive manner and took a bite.

She smiled. "Would you care for some champagne?"

"No, thank you, I'm fine."

"As you can see, Randy," Hale said, "we make our customers' check-in experience as enjoyable as possible."

Randy brushed a crumb from his lips. "It's quite impressive."

"This way." Hale went to the back of the room, opened a door, and the three of them passed into an elevator lobby. "These private elevators are for our VIPs. As you can see, there's easy access to the casino." He gestured to the double glass doors in front of them, which faced the gaming floor. A woman security guard manned the entrance. "Our VIPs don't have to mingle with the unwashed when going up into the hotel. These six elevators go straight to the five VIP floors, which surround our private pools."

Randy looked at the security guard, remembering how he'd had to do some fast talking to gain admittance to the elevators when he visited Cynthia earlier. He'd been lucky; the guard had been enamored with his green eyes. He had no intention of letting Hale know he'd already seen a Conquistador hotel suite.

"All of our VIP suites are in this five-story wing of the hotel," Sawyer said, his pride once more apparent.

Randy nodded.

"I want to show you a typical suite," Hale said. "Pete, do you have a key?"

"Yes, sir," Sawyer said, showing a keycard to his boss,

and they entered an open elevator. Sawyer pushed a button on the panel, and the car climbed with speed. At the fourth floor of the hotel, the elevator doors rumbled apart, and the three men padded out of the car.

Randy recalled his visit to the Nicosias' suite and how awestruck he'd been at the surroundings.

Hale said, "We have a commercial kitchen for the VIP wing, which insures prompt room service and quality meals."

"Room four-twenty," Sawyer said, gesturing to their right. His voice echoed through the long hallway, and their heels clicked on the marble floor as they proceeded past the concierge. Sawyer stopped in front of a set of double doors and tapped the keycard over the lock. A green light blinked on, and he turned the knob and swung open the door. He held it, waiting for Randy and Hale to enter the suite.

The living room of the suite was huge. "Spacious," Randy said. "The furnishings are nice." The space was done in warm colors, with vibrant paintings on the walls. A built-in bar dominated one side of the suite. Crystal snifters were suspended from a rack above, and the bar was well-stocked. A grand piano, complete with candelabra, was to their left.

Hale said, "I supervised the interior decoration of each suite in this hotel." His expression was self-satisfied. "I spare no expense in making sure our VIP customers feel special."

"I can see that," Randy said, walking to a sliding glass door. Through it was a balcony that overlooked lush pools and gardens.

Hale motioned to his right. "Take a peek at the master bedroom."

Randy sauntered into the bedroom and noted the large sunken hot tub in the corner of the room. A round bed sat in the center of the area on a step-up platform, a shear veil hanging around it from the mirrored ceiling.

Sawyer reached for a switch on the wall and flipped on the hot tub; jets of water foamed and gurgled. He said, "The view of the pools from the hot tub's unparalleled. Perfect for a romantic interlude."

"If you'd like," Hale said, "I can make arrangements for you to spend the night in one of my suites."

"I might take you up on that offer," Randy said. "Do you provide female companionship?"

Sawyer cleared his throat. "I suppose, if that's necessary."

Randy chuckled and held up his hands. "I was kidding. I'm impressed with this suite."

"We have larger ones," Hale said, "on the top floor."

"All of them are occupied," Sawyer said, "or we'd show you one. You should see the Coronado Suite."

"That's all right," Randy said. "If this one's any indication, I bet it's out of this world."

"It is," Hale said. "Let's go back to the casino. There's much more of my resort I want to show you. The best is yet to come. You must see the tower."

RANDY, HALE, AND Sawyer returned to Hale's plush office at the top of the Aztec temple after a thorough tour of the resort. Randy and Sawyer sat in small chairs in front of Hale's desk. Hale's chair was throne-like, and Randy wondered if he thought he was some sort of Aztec god.

"What's your opinion of the place?" Hale asked.

"Extraordinary," Randy said. "It's clear the Conquistador's a successful hotel and casino."

"That it is. We've grown from a little motel like the Desert Palm into the third-biggest resort in Las Vegas."

Randy chose not to react to Hale's blatant putdown of the Desert Palm. "Do you have more expansion plans?"

Hale smiled. "I sure do. I intend to devote a billion dollars to development. Another thousand rooms, additional casino, and a second showroom. I won't stop until the Conquistador is, without question, the largest and most lavish resort in the world."

"That's a mighty ambitious goal."

"It is, but who'd have thought, when I inherited a flea bag motel from my father, that I'd transform it into the Conquistador Casino Resort and Tower."

Randy nodded. "You have a point."

Hale said in a determined tone, "Let's talk business. You've seen what we have to offer our customers. An executive host position at the Conquistador would be a real boost to your career."

"I'm wowed by your operation, but as I told you, I'm content at the Desert Palm. I'd only make a change of employer if the right financial deal came my way."

"I'm prepared to offer you ten percent more than you're making at the Desert Palm. That includes the bonus package."

Randy crossed his legs. "No, thank you, sir. I'm getting a performance review next month, and I expect my annual raise will be at least that much."

"Consider the advantages you'd have at the Conquistador."

"We've gone over that before, and I don't see the benefits outweighing the flexibility and autonomy I enjoy at the Desert Palm."

Hale glared at Randy and glanced over at Sawyer.

Sawyer squirmed, his eyes pleading for Hale to cough up more money.

"You're a tough negotiator, Mr. Kennedy," Hale said. "Tell me, what would it take for you to leave the Desert Palm?"

Randy put his finger to his lower lip. "Well, let's see, I can envision making a move for twenty-five percent above my existing compensation level."

There was a flash of fury in Hale's eyes. "Fifteen percent."

Randy tightened his jaw. "Not enough."

"Twenty percent, and that's my final offer."

Randy stroked his chin, deliberating.

Hale frowned. "Did you hear me? Twenty percent above what you're making now. It's a hell of a deal. Sawyer insists you'll be worth the investment."

"And you don't agree?"

"I trust Pete on matters like this, and I don't want you going to a competitor. Now, what do you say?"

"It's an interesting proposal; I'll need a little time to think about it."

Hale's features were firm, his lips pursed. "Fine. Forty-eight hours. After that, my offer's null and void."

"All right." Randy stood up and straightened his tie. "I'll get back to you in two days. Thank you for the tour of the Conquistador. I know you're a busy man, and I appreciate the time you've taken."

"Say yes to my deal, and it'll have been well-spent."

Randy smiled at him. "Yes, Mr. Hale, if I do that, it'll be the most productive time you've expended in quite a while."

RANDY PAUSED AT the entrance of Angela's townhouse, trying to put on his best contrite expression. He knocked on the door and waited a moment, hearing footsteps on the other side. Angela opened the door, and he could tell she was surprised to see him standing there. Unspeaking, she put her hand on a hip.

"May I come in?" Randy asked.

Angela shook her head. "I'd rather you not. How'd you get my address?"

"A woman I know in the personnel office gave it to me. I came to apologize."

"Okay. Do that." She stared down, clearly trying to avoid his gaze.

"I know I made an ass of myself last night."

Angela looked up. "That's a confession, not an apology."

"I made a fool of myself in the parking lot of the Desert Palm, and I want to apologize for my behavior."

"Apology accepted. Is that all?" She didn't look him in the eye.

He squirmed a little and yanked at his shirt collar. "Um, well, I was wondering if we could start over with a clean slate. Forget last night and try a new beginning."

Her expression wasn't encouraging. "I'll accept your apology, but let's leave it at that."

His voice rose. "I'm a nice person. You'd realize that if you'd give me a break."

"I'm sure you're a fine human being. I haven't thought any different."

"Then why not give me a chance?"

Angela seemed to consider his request. "My better judgment tells me it'd be a mistake."

"Wayne says you think I'm a womanizer."

She skewed her chin to the side. "Aren't you?"

He glanced toward his shoes, then back up. "No...Okay, I've dated quite a bit, but I'm not a womanizer."

"Randy, we're not the same kind of person. We're not right for each other. When I first saw you, I'll admit I was intrigued, but that's since diminished."

He wondered if she was lying. "Angela, go out with me one time."

"I'm sorry, but the answer's no."

He stared at her. "I don't understand."

"I'm sure you will in time. I appreciate the apology. I've got to get ready for work."

"I was once known as the Lucky One. Not anymore." He was still staring at her as she shut the door. Deep in thought as he walked toward his car, he felt glum, something he hadn't often endured. He wondered if he was reacting this way because he had real feelings for her or if it was just the first time he'd run into a woman who'd been so adamant about turning him down.

EIGHT

WAYNE STOOD IN front of the sports book betting board, shaking his head. He couldn't believe his eyes. The Saints had beaten the Cowboys by fourteen.

"That's two hundred bucks you owe me," Randy said. "Wait until I see Chapman. That'll teach him not to listen to me."

"Two hundred-dollars," Wayne moaned. "Damn it. I wouldn't have made the bet if I knew the goddamn quarterback was going to get himself hurt."

"I told you—I know my football."

Red tinged Wayne's cheeks. "Oh, I suppose you knew before the game that the starting quarterback wouldn't finish."

Randy shrugged. "Sort of."

Wayne frowned. "What do you mean?"

"One of Joe Nicosia's associates told him the quarterback had a sore shoulder. I knew the Dallas coaches wouldn't risk aggravating it any more than they had to, so I was certain they'd pull him out of the game. Dallas needs him to be whole for the conference game next week, so why risk it?"

"You son of a bitch. That's cheating."

"No, that's smart betting."

"I don't agree."

Randy grinned. "Okay, since I did have a little inside information, I'll give you a break. I'll go triple or nothing on the Eagles-Dolphins game."

Wayne looked at the betting board. Miami was favored by seven. "Who do you take?"

"Miami."

"I better not. I won't be able to pay you back until I get my first paycheck. I spent my last dollar on cocktails last night. I don't want to go deeper in debt, and the Dolphins make me nervous."

"Suit yourself. Enough about football. You getting this hosting business down?"

"Well, I suppose so. A floor boss introduced me to another senior couple who love to play roulette. The Wilsons from Seattle. There's one problem, though. When I took them to lunch in the coffee shop, I ran into the Prichards. You know — Mildred and Ernest, my first big capture. When Mrs. Prichard saw me with the Wilsons, the old bag was jealous. I believe she wants me to spend all my time with them."

Randy nodded vigorously. "That happens. Wait until you have a stable of high-limit players, and they're all here at the same time. They'll try to jerk you in ten different directions. You'll just need to learn to parcel out your time. When you're with a guest, you have to make them feel like they're the most important person in the building. That'll satisfy them most of the time."

"I hope all my guests aren't as stiff as these two couples. All they talk about are their aches and pains."

Randy laughed. "Now you know the real truth about hosting."

"At least I can golf on the company's dime."

Randy rubbed his chin between his finger and thumb. "I met with Conrad Hale this morning."

Wayne narrowed his eyes. "Hale, from the Conquistador?"

"The very same."

"Did he up his offer?"

"Yes, to an 'I can't say no' level."

Wayne's expression was quizzical, one eyebrow lifted. "Are you taking it?"

"I don't know. It's a lot of money. Working at the Conquistador could be a host's dream."

"I've heard Hale's an asshole."

"The biggest."

"The money's that good?"

"Could be. The opportunity to work in a facility like the Conquistador's hard to pass up."

"Well, for what it's worth, I'd appreciate it if you turned the job down. You're my one friend at the Desert Palm. If you go to the Conquistador, I'll have to learn how to be a host from Carter Camp."

Randy snorted. "In that case, you're screwed."

DIXIE AND ANGELA were in the Desert Palm's vault, sorting casino chips. It was the job of the cashiers to separate the Desert Palm's chips from the other Las Vegas casinos' chips so they could be exchanged. "You've been awfully quite," Dixie said. "Is everything okay?"

Angela shrugged. "Yes. I've just been preoccupied."

Sarcastically, Dixie asked, "Anyone in particular?"

"You know me all too well."

"I can't believe you're still interested in Randy Kennedy. Especially after last night. He was wasted."

"I know, but for some reason, I can't help myself."

"What do you intend to do?"

Angela suppressed a sigh and nibbled on her lower lip. "I don't know. I've been giving him the cold shoulder. He came to my townhouse this afternoon and apologized for his behavior."

Dixie turned a serious expression on her. "I see a pattern here. He's a stalker."

"Listen to this: last night, he said he loved me."

"An old line that guys use when they're trying to lure a woman into bed."

"What if it's true?"

"He was blasted, drunk out of his mind. He doesn't know you well enough to be your friend, let alone in love."

"Dixie, I have real feelings for him. Ones I'm not able to describe. I drove him home last night. Of course, he was too drunk to drive; I had to. He fell asleep before we even left the parking lot. I couldn't stop looking at him; he's so handsome."

"Angela, how many times must I tell you to look further than skin deep? Like I told you before, a leopard doesn't change his spots. He's nothing but heartache. Do you want a boyfriend who chases other women and is drunk every night? Are you going to be his designated driver every time you go out?"

Angela raised her hands in surrender. "Enough, okay? You're right. My heart tells me one thing, and my brain another. But I guess I should listen to you." Her lips twisted. "I'll do my best to forget about him."

"That's better." Dixie smiled, and the tiny wrinkles around her eyes edged up. "You're an attractive woman. We both know there are dozens of men who'd love to go out with you. Good ones, who'll care for you the way you deserve."

"You think so?"

"I know it. God, what I wouldn't give to have your beauty and be young again."

Angela shook her finger. "You're not that old."

"I feel like it. That's what three kids and a mortgage will do to you."

The sigh she'd been trying to hold off came out. "I'm tired of being single. I want to share my life with someone."

"Sometimes, I wish I were still a carefree bachelorette, but it's really nice to come home to a loving family after a bad day at work. Despite the aggravation."

"Yeah, I envy you."

"Cheer up, kid. You'll find your Prince Charming."

"I hope so. If not, can I move in with you?"

Dixie rolled her eyes, and the two cackled with laughter.

RANDY WALKED INTO Walter Parker's outer office and sat on the edge of the secretary's desk. "Is the top guy in?" he asked her.

"Yes, Randy," she said and tucked a wisp of her long dark hair behind an ear. She was a slim young woman in a tan dress with a white blouse. She peered at Randy, and the desire in her eyes was unmistakable. "What've you been up to?" she asked in a seductive voice.

He waved his hand back and forth. "This and that."

"When are we going out again?" She smiled at him, her pink lips turned up.

He blinked a few times, Angela popping into his mind. He stared at the woman, wondering why he didn't feel like flirting. "I've been very busy."

"Well, you should take me out for drinks."

"As soon as I can find the time. I better meet with Parker. Would you tell him I'm here?"

"Sure." She picked up the telephone and waited for an answer. "Mr. Parker, Randy Kennedy's here. Very well, I'll send him in." She hung up and tilted her head toward the office. "Go on in."

"Thanks, Gina." He stood, crossed the room to the open double doors, and passed into the office of Walter Parker.

The place was large and comfortable, decorated with dark, heavy furniture and lots of pictures on the walls, showing Parker with almost every celebrity who'd performed in the

Desert Palm's showroom. The casino owner sat in a large chair, the cushions enveloping his slight frame. Despite his feeble appearance, his eyes showed an inner strength. "Take a seat," Parker said. "Can I get you anything to drink? A soda, coffee, water?"

Randy sank into a chair and crossed his legs. "No, thank you, sir."

"I appreciate you stopping by."

"Anytime, Walter; you know that. After all, you're the boss."

"Randy, how long have you worked at the Desert Palm?"

Randy tapped a finger on his knee. "I don't know; let's see, about five years. Yeah, five years in November."

"Five years. Yes, you've come a long way in such a short period of time."

"I'd like to think so."

"You've done a good job of cultivating our top guests. Despite your youth, you've managed to attract some of the biggest players in Las Vegas. I commend you."

Randy stared piercingly at Parker. "When's the shoe dropping?"

"I beg your pardon?"

"You didn't ask me to your office to discuss my hosting successes. Make your point, Walter. What's on your mind?"

Parker seemed taken aback, and his eyebrows moved together. "You're not one to go along with the expected decorum, are you?"

"What's that?"

"When someone's asked up to my office, they sit there, twitching nervously and nodding like robots at my every word. You're not doing that."

Randy shrugged. "Why should I? We're not strangers. Sure, you're a multi-millionaire casino mogul, but I don't see why we can't have an enjoyable conversation. Now, what have I done to warrant this summons?"

Parker smiled, the creases around his mouth fanning out. "Son, you remind me a lot of myself. Neither of us has much regard for rules or conventions. We both know what's right, what's going to make the Desert Palm money. Our methods may be unorthodox, but the results are dramatic."

"I couldn't have said it better myself. Is that what this is about? My disregard for rules?"

"Not everyone understands your actions. Some see them as very wrong."

"You know how much money I bring into this casino. Yes, some of my tactics are unconventional, but I get the job done."

"Yes, you do, but that's not the point. I have other casino hosts and team members to worry about. Your behavior, while productive for you, would create disruption and havoc on the casino floor if everybody followed your example."

"This sounds like a lecture from that weasel, Carter Camp."

"You do know he's my nephew?"

"You think he's a weasel too. It's written all over your face when you're near him. We both know he's the worst casino host in the history of the industry."

It was obvious Parker was attempting to repress a smile. "My opinion of my nephew, good or bad, has nothing to do with our conversation. I know you and Carter have a personality conflict, but I can assure you, his dislike of you has nothing to do with what I'm trying to articulate."

"Why did you wait so long to say something?"

"As I told you, I understand how you operate. I want you to enjoy your job. Eric Frazier's a fan of yours and has kept me at bay. I've let as much slide as I can, but I have to tighten up before I start having problems with the rest of the team."

"What do you want me to do?"

"Don't change everything. Just be more conscious of your activities and how the rest of the hosts may perceive them. And no drinking while on duty."

Randy grinned, thinking about Conrad Hale's job offer. "If you insist, Walter."

"That's my boy." Parker rested his head on the back of the chair and pressed his hands together. "Now, before you leave, I need to know. The brunette carousel girl who works swing shift, what's her name?"

"Stephanie?"

"Yes, Stephanie." Parker's eyes twinkled. "God, if I were forty years younger...Tell me, Randy, I know you've been out with her. Was it as good as I'm guessing?"

RANDY WANDERED THROUGH the casino and over to the keno lounge, where Anthony Chapman sat contemplating his next bet. Randy plopped down next to him and picked up a blank keno ticket from the holder attached to the chair. He picked up a keno crayon and doodled.

Anthony said, "I should've listened to your advice on the New Orleans-Dallas game."

Randy circled several of the numbers on the ticket. "Yeah, Anthony. Never bet against me."

Anthony squinted. "You seem kind of down. What's wrong?"

"Nothing. I just have a lot on my mind."

"Anything I can do to help?"

Randy turned and focused on the lawyer's face. Anthony was a successful man, and Randy admired his drive and confidence. Of all the guests Randy dealt with, he was closest to Anthony, who wasn't that much older than him. They had a real friendship—one that went beyond the Desert Palm. "Maybe. I've been offered an interesting proposition. I want to hear what you have to say about it."

Anthony stood and gestured to the right. "Let's go to a lounge and visit."

"Uh, if you don't mind, I'd rather go to the Waldorf. I'm getting a little heat from above about drinking at the Desert Palm. I'm off work in fifteen minutes."

"Sure. I have a pocket full of chips I need to cash out. I'll meet you at valet parking in twenty minutes. We can take my car."

"Thanks. I have a difficult decision to make, and I'd like to know your opinion."

THE OLD WALDORF Bar was a popular hangout for many of the casino workers in Las Vegas. The tavern wasn't quite dingy, but it still had a well-worn atmosphere. Randy and Anthony walked past the long bar and took a seat in the rear of the establishment. Televisions tuned to various sports channels lined the walls of the room. In the center of the bar, two off-duty blackjack dealers were playing pool. Their rumpled white shirts hung out over their black pants. Just hours earlier, the dealers had been pitching cards to high-limit gamblers. Now they looked like poorly dressed penguins.

A waitress in too-tight jeans cruised up to Anthony and Randy. "What can I get you gentlemen?" she asked.

Randy winked at her. "You know what I've always wanted, but besides that, I'll take a Heineken."

The waitress said indignantly, "I'm not going there again. A Heineken and a…" She gave Anthony an expectant gaze.

"Make that two."

The waitress nodded and went back to the bar.

Anthony asked, "Are there any women in this town you don't know?"

Randy shrugged. "A few. There's a new one I have my eye on, but she keeps turning me down."

Anthony chuckled. "That's a first. So tell me, what's this decision you need to make?"

"Conrad Hale offered me an executive host job."

Anthony reached for a bowl of peanuts and grabbed some. "Hale, huh?"

"What do you know about him?"

"My firm's done work for the Conquistador. He's a successful man, to say the least. Driven. Some say a visionary."

"I admire that."

"He also has a reputation for being ruthless. He always gets what he's after."

"He's made the Conquistador hyper-successful."

"Yes, and killed his father in the process."

Randy propped an elbow on the table and rested his chin on his hand. "How so?"

"I don't know whether you remember this, but there used to be a motel where the Conquistador stands. A motel owned by Hale's father."

"I know. He told me he inherited a run-down place."

"Did he tell you he tried to have his father committed to a mental institution?"

Randy shook his head. "No, that didn't come up."

"Hale's always had grand ideas. He worked for his father at the motel. It wasn't much of a business, but it had a great deal of land and, as you know, the location's superb. Anyway, it was young Conrad's intention to open a casino next to the motel. His father was vehemently opposed to the idea. A devout Mormon, he didn't want anything to do with running a gambling operation. Conrad filed papers with the authorities, trying to get his father declared insane and committed to a sanitarium in Reno."

"Wow. I take it he didn't succeed?"

"No. In the middle of a major argument, the elder Hale suffered a fatal heart attack."

Randy's eyebrows went up. "You're kidding, right?"

"Conrad Hale put unbelievable pressure on his father."

"Regardless of how he got there, the Conquistador's one hell of a resort."

"So is the MGM. You declined their host job."

"They weren't offering the kind of money Hale is. If they had, I would've given them serious consideration. Having a large casino like that on my resume would be nice."

"You believe you need to bolster it?"

"I can't see being employed at the Desert Palm forever."

"I thought you enjoyed working at the DP."

Randy nodded. "I do, but Parker's tightening the rules and I'm losing some of my autonomy."

Anthony smiled. "We both know how much you like regulations."

"Another thing—I can't move into management at the Desert Palm. I suppose if I planned to spend the rest of my life as a casino host, I could stay there as long as I wanted. I like working for Walter—he's a fair man—but it's a family operation. The level of advancement in a joint like the Desert Palm's limited when relatives are employed there too. I'd imagine that, in ten years, that slime-bag Carter Camp will be in charge."

"I doubt it. I don't consider Camp management material."

"He's family and has a business degree from UNLV. Sooner or later, he's taking over the resort."

"Oh, I hope Parker's smarter than that."

The waitress delivered the beers, and they both took a drink. Randy said, "At the Conquistador, I'd have a real chance at advancement. An executive casino host position there would open up a lot of opportunities. At some point, I could work at Aria or the Bellagio for the really big money."

Anthony gestured at him. "It sounds like you've made up your mind."

"No, not yet. I know Hale's a jerk. The story about his father makes me dislike him even more. I don't know what I should do."

Anthony slugged back more beer, wiping the foam from his lips. "Not positive what I'd do if I were in your situation either."

"If I go to the Conquistador, can I expect you to follow me there and get your casino play?"

"I'm not sure, Randy. I don't like wagering in the mega-resorts. They're too impersonal."

"I'll be there."

"Not twenty-four hours a day."

Randy looked at the lawyer, somewhat bothered. "But we're friends."

"Always will be if I have anything to say about it. That doesn't mean I'm gambling at the Conquistador. If you leave the Desert Palm and it changes, I might make a switch."

Randy grinned.

"Then again, maybe I'll go to Sam's Town."

Randy eyed him warily. "You bastard."

NINE

ONCE AGAIN, RANDY was at the Conquistador Resort, heading for the hotel suite Cynthia Nicosia was redecorating. He checked his watch; it was noon. Approaching the double doors of the suite, he knocked hard. Cynthia opened one door and motioned for him to come in. She was wearing designer jeans and a light-pink blouse. Her hair was up off her shoulders, and around her neck was an expensive gold necklace encrusted in diamonds.

"You look nice," Randy said, stepping into the living room. "Very sexy."

She gave him an appreciative smile. "Thanks. What brings you by?"

"Joe asked me to take you to lunch."

"Randy, I can't. I don't have the time. I'm still working on decorating. For the last two days, I've had men in here pulling twelve-hour shifts. It's turning out nice, don't you agree? The Van Gogh painting I had shipped up from L.A. just arrived, and I can't wait to see it on the wall."

Randy laughed. "I haven't seen you this excited about something in a long time." He inspected the room. Workers were everywhere, wallpaper was going up, and the finishing touches in tile were being installed around the wet bar. He heard more construction in the master bath.

Cynthia seemed pleased, a slight smirk on her lips. "It's nice having something to keep me busy. At home, I sit around all day doing almost nothing."

"If you're bored, why don't you go back to your art gallery job?"

"Joseph won't allow me to work. You know how old fashioned he is about women."

"He's letting you work for Conrad Hale."

"Conrad's not paying me. Joseph considers it a hobby."

"Hale's getting a good deal."

Her voice became sultry. "There's a whole lot more I expect to do for Conrad."

Randy shook his finger at her. "I'm telling you, be careful."

"I can't wait to finish this suite so I can show it to Conrad. I know he'll love what I've done. Better yet, if I work this right, I'll be able to lure him into bed."

"If Joe catches wind of this, it's going to get nasty."

"If I can seduce Conrad, I won't need him anymore."

"It doesn't work that way."

She beamed at him, but her mouth was pouty.

"Okay, have your fun with Hale. Don't say I didn't warn you, though." Randy took a deep breath. "I told Joe I'd take you to lunch. Give me a rain check."

"Let's get together later tonight." Cynthia looked at him with excitement in her eyes. "I'd like to go to the top of the Conquistador Tower. Did you know there's a rollercoaster up there?"

"Yeah, there are all kinds of amusement rides."

"I do have a passion for rollercoasters. I've ridden them all over the country. They're so much fun."

"I saw it when Hale gave me a tour of the property. This one's pretty lame."

"No, I watched a hotel video. Riding it will be a breath-taking. And scary. It travels off the side of the tower."

Randy shrugged. "I guess. I'll pick you up at seven, and we can go to the top of the tower for a drink."

EVERY BLACKJACK TABLE at the Desert Palm was full, except for one. That table had a betting minimum of ten thousand dollars, and just one person was willing to wager that much on a hand. Joseph Nicosia slammed his cards down on the layout. "Goddamn it, lady, why are you doing this to me?"

"Gee, I'm sorry," the young dealer said. "I want to lose, but this seems to be my lucky day."

He shot her an irritable glower. "Honey, you're kicking my ass. When's it going to be my turn?"

She smiled and flicked new cards in his direction. "Maybe this hand."

"I hope so. I'm not leaving Vegas until later in the week, and at the rate I'm losing, I'll have to declare bankruptcy."

"If you're in financial trouble, you shouldn't gamble so much."

He rolled his eyes. "I was being sarcastic. I'm loaded. I was up a quarter-million until I ran into you. You haven't been a dealer for long, have you?"

She shook her red hair off her shoulders. "Can you tell?"

"You don't look old enough to be working here. Shouldn't you be at cheerleader practice or something?"

"I'm over twenty-one." She paid out on his winning hand.

"What's your name?"

"Can't you read my nametag?" She pointed to the one on her blouse.

Nicosia sneered. "Violet? What kind of name's that?"

"My eyes, they're violet." She dealt him two cards.

"Mine are brown. They don't call me Brownie." He peeked at the king and two of clubs.

"What is your name?"

"You *are* new. My name's Joe. I was christened Joseph, Joseph Nicosia, but most people call me Joe." He scraped the cards on the layout.

"Joe, huh. Well, if you don't mind, I'm calling you Brownie." She dealt a ten.

Nicosia roared with laughter and beat his fist on the table. "I don't look like a frigging brownie." He threw down the cards.

"Sure you do." She raked in his losing hand and a stack of ten one-thousand-dollar chips. "You put on a tough guy image on the outside, but inside, you're sweet as can be. Just like a brownie." She whirled two cards toward him after he pushed more chips into the betting circle.

Nicosia laughed again. "I like you a lot, Violet." He picked up the cards and glanced at them.

"Same here, Brownie." She fluttered her lashes at him a few times.

"Care for a drink when you get off work?"

Violet leaned forward and asked in an admonishing tone, "Is that a wedding band I see on your left hand?"

He rubbed the ring. "I'm not asking you to go to bed with me. Yet." He ogled her. "Besides, we have an open relationship. At least I do. Hey, hey, hey. Come on, enjoy a drink or two with me."

"I don't know. I wouldn't want a jealous wife after me."

"Ah, don't worry about that. She believes I'm on a winning streak. I haven't been to bed in days. She knows I don't allow her near the casino unless she's summoned."

"Isn't that convenient for you?"

"How about that drink? What time are you off work?"

"In half an hour."

He chucked his cards on the layout in disgust. "I'm taking

a little break. I'll meet you at the Zanzibar Lounge in thirty minutes." He scooped up his mound of chips.

Violet smiled. "Okay, I'd like that."

He flung a thousand-dollar chip to her. "Buy yourself something nice."

She gazed at it with obvious delight, an even bigger smile on her face. "Thanks, Brownie. Considering how lucky I've been, you don't have to be so generous."

"My pleasure. After we down a few drinks, maybe my luck will change."

CYNTHIA LED CONRAD Hale through the double doors and into the redecorated hotel suite. "What do you think so far?" she asked, twirling around with her arms stretched out wide. "Isn't it divine?"

Hale surveyed the living room and nodded his approval. "You've done a spectacular job. I don't know how you pulled this off so fast."

"When I set my mind to something, it happens. That, and your workmen were a little afraid of me. I was a slave driver."

Hale laughed. "You had an army of them in here. The Van Gogh's nice. The lighting's just right."

Cynthia gestured to the painting. "I hung it myself. Do you like the frame? It matches the furniture. I was lucky to find it at a great little import store off Tropicana Avenue."

"We need to get it alarmed. Until it is, we're not renting this suite to the general public."

"That's wise, Conrad. It's quite a valuable work of art."

He pointed to the chandelier hanging over the dining table. "That's stunning."

"I still have some finishing touches here and there. I'm unhappy with the wallpaper behind the bar and will be changing it out. There's still more tile work to do."

"Does Joseph like the suite?"

Cynthia's tone became sullen. "He hasn't seen it yet. He's on a winning streak and hasn't been around. I wouldn't care if he never comes back."

"You know I want his business."

"I expect you to want me even more." She grinned lasciviously. "Follow me. You must see the bedroom."

Hale gave her an uneven smile, his expression tense. "Okay, let's see what you've created." He walked into the bedroom. It was done in dark colors, and he gazed around the room. "Earthy."

"No. It's chocolate, tan, and timeless, and it makes me amorous." She ambled over to Hale, put her arms around his neck, and kissed him.

"Cynthi—" She put her finger on his lips.

She pushed her breasts against his chest, gave him a deep penetrating kiss, and looked him in the eyes. "I'll wager I can get you feeling passionate too." She locked her plump lips back on his.

Hale said through a mouthful of kisses, "Cynthia, we shouldn't."

"Shhh. Just enjoy." She nibbled her way up to an ear.

"But, your husband..."

She rubbed his groin through his trousers. He was erect in no time, and a grin stretched over her face. "That's it, baby," she said and continued to caress between his legs.

Hale's face contorted with pleasure. "Ah, jeez, Cynthia. Oh yeah." He panted hoarsely.

Cynthia undid his belt, unzipped his slacks, and let them fall to the floor. She yanked down his shorts. "Hi there, big boy." She stroked his genitals.

Hale moaned. "Oh man, that feels good."

"I'm taking you to a level of ecstasy you haven't experienced before."

ANGELA SAT IN the team members' cafeteria of the Desert Palm, nibbling on a chef's salad, alone and feeling somewhat blue. She stirred her fork though the lettuce, then put it to the side of the dish. She wasn't hungry.

A man behind her asked, "Mind if I join you?"

Angela turned to see Carter Camp. In the past week, she'd noticed him lurking around the cashier's cage quite often. Every chance he had, he was at her window, wanting to converse. She hesitated, wondering if she could find a polite way to say no, then decided she couldn't. "Um, sure, have a seat."

"Thanks." Camp eyed her with unmistakable interest. "You look as if you could use some company." He flopped down in the chair next to her.

She peered back at him, not enthralled by his staring. "Just having a bite to eat."

"Are you getting comfortable with your new surroundings?"

"Everyone's been nice."

"The casino sure is busy today. The slots are packed."

Angela nodded. "Yes, they are. This is the first break I've had all shift. I haven't been able to get away."

"My uncle will be pleased."

"Who's your uncle?"

"Walter Parker. The owner of the Desert Palm."

"I didn't know that."

"Yes. A little later on, I'll go up to the executive offices and take a gander at the financial statements."

"I understand Joseph Nicosia's lost over two hundred thousand this morning."

Camp's eyes narrowed. "That's news to me. I was told he was up almost half a million."

"No, he started losing big time. You're a host; I thought you'd know those kinds of details."

"W-well, yes, but Nicosia isn't one of my guests. I can't

keep track of all of them when the action in the casino is so strong."

She took a sip of her iced tea. "Oh."

Camp clearly felt he needed to offer more explanation. "Nicosia's Randy Kennedy's guest. Kennedy and I don't like each other, so I'm often left in the dark about his players."

"What's up between you two?"

Camp's features crumpled. "Are you kidding? I can't stand the man. He's a bum, but unfortunately, my uncle thinks he's great, so I have to tolerate his behavior."

"You're not his boss?"

"No, not yet. But in time, I will be. When I'm the boss, there will be some major changes in the way the Host Department is run. I'll clamp down on Kennedy's ass so fast his head will spin."

"Is that right? I've been told he's a good executive host."

"He believes he's better than he is."

Angela pushed her salad plate away. "He can be rather arrogant."

Camp hunched forward. "Angela, I was wondering if you'd be interested in attending a party with me. It'll be a huge celebration, with great food and entertainment."

Angela was caught off guard by his invitation. A date with Carter Camp was the last thing she'd ever considered. "What kind of party?"

"A birthday party. It's my uncle's eightieth. His secretary and my Aunt Marian are putting the whole thing together. They want as many team members as possible to be present. It's a surprise. Many important people will be there, and I even expect a few celebrities."

"Uh, I don't know, Carter. I heard about it from my supervisor, but I'm so new here, I wasn't planning on participating. When is it again?"

"Tomorrow night. Please, I'd love for you to go with me."

Angela thought for a moment. Camp wasn't the man of her dreams, to say the least. He seemed so dull and awkward, the direct opposite of Randy Kennedy. Maybe that was what she needed—a date with someone who wasn't so enthralled with himself. She figured she could probably ignore his apparent lack of a personality. Why not, she decided. She didn't have anything better to do. "Okay. That sounds like fun. What time's the party?"

Camp's eyes glimmered as if it was the first time any woman had ever said yes to him. "Sixish. It's in the main ballroom here at the Desert Palm. My uncle's supposed to arrive at six-thirty."

Angela took a slow breath. "I don't work tomorrow. Do you want to meet here or pick me up?"

He said, excited, "I'll come get you."

"All right, let me give you my address." She took a notepad and pen from her purse and jotted it down. "I live off Flamingo in the Sagewood Townhouses."

Camp took the note and glanced at it. "I know the place."

"Go to the middle of the complex. My townhome's by the swimming pool."

"I haven't been on a date in a long time. I'm minutes the counting...counting the minutes."

Angela gave him a questioning look. "Who's going to be at the party? What celebrities?"

"Comedian Wayne Bell's a close friend of my uncle's, so I bet he'll be there. I hear the judges from *America's Most Talented* are in town, and they've been invited. As you know, my aunt has also invited the Desert Palm management and most of the team members."

"Will Randy be there?"

Camp grimaced, his eyes just slits. "All the hosts will be in attendance. Eric Frazier's made it mandatory."

Excellent, Angela thought. Maybe it'd do Randy good to see her on a date with Carter Camp. It would knock his ego down a peg or two. In truth, though, what she wanted to do was make him jealous.

THE DRAMATIC CONQUISTADOR Tower loomed over the resort. Ten stories taller than the Stratosphere Tower on the other side of town, it was built when the current owner of the Stratosphere outbid Conrad Hale on the purchase of the property. In retaliation, he constructed the larger tower.

The top of the Conquistador Tower featured a large pod with four levels. The upper observation deck included several of the most exciting amusement park rides ever created. The rollercoaster was the most popular attraction, taking passengers around the pod at a terrifying speed. A massive white art deco spire climbed from the upper level observation deck up another 125 feet, and a floodlight graced the top. The lower level observation deck offered unparalleled views of Las Vegas and had a large cabana area. The next floor down had a rotating cocktail lounge and several restaurants. The bottom of the pod featured numerous wedding chapels and a popular nightclub.

Cynthia and Randy rode the glass elevator to the top of the tower in silent anticipation. Randy had a death grip on the back rail, and his skin was a sickly white. He was afraid of heights and had avoided the tower since its construction. Now, in just days, he'd unfortunately ridden to the top on two occasions.

Randy didn't want Cynthia to know he was uncomfortable and tried to keep his feelings hidden. Fortunately for him, she was too engrossed by the view to see the fright in his eyes. The ride up the tower took less than a minute, and when the elevator doors parted, Randy led Cynthia to the lower level observation deck. Hundreds of people were milling about the deck and enjoying the view. Randy crossed over to the outer railing with trepidation.

"Oh, what a sight," Cynthia said.

Randy's hands were trembling, and he was getting more uncomfortable with each step. "We sure are up high."

She dismissed his words with a wave of her hand. "I've been in scarier high places. The sky deck at one of the skyscrapers in Chicago has these balconies with glass floors. When you go out on them, the sensation's unbelievable."

Randy grabbed the railing. "This is high enough and scary enough for me."

She chuckled. "Afraid of heights?"

He didn't answer, clenching his jaw and staring out over the city. A swarm of tiny cars were working their way up and down the Strip. Pedestrians looked more like ants than people.

"The Strip's fabulous in the dark," Cynthia said. "The lights of the resorts are so pretty." She turned and observed the rollercoaster above them with delight. "Look at that." She pointed to the excited people riding the contraption.

Randy peered up at the rollercoaster, hearing the shrieks of the passengers as he watched the cars barrel forward, then slide over the edge. The cars swooped down and around the tower, then up near the large white spire in the center of the structure. "Let's go to the cocktail lounge and have some drinks." He knew there was no way he could board the rollercoaster sober.

Cynthia smiled and flipped back her hair. "Okay. A margarita sounds tasty."

Randy licked his lips, and they made their way to the tower doors. Once in the lobby, he felt his heart rate begin to slow and relaxed a little. They took the stairs down one flight to the cocktail lounge and were seated in the middle of the room. A rather flamboyantly dressed waitress came up to their table and asked them what they'd like to drink.

"A margarita on the rocks," Cynthia said.

"Vodka straight up," Randy said. "A large one."

The waitress nodded and walked over to the bar.

"Why so thirsty?" Cynthia asked.

He lowered his head. "I feel like getting buzzed."

"Isn't this place fun? I love the view. Oh, the lounge's revolving. See, Randy, it's making a slow circle."

He glanced at the large windows and back to her. His face was ashen, but he tried to put on a brave facade. "You're right; it's cool."

The cocktail waitress soon returned to their table and placed the drinks in front of them. "Do you need anything more?" she asked.

"I'll take another of these," Randy said, holding up his vodka.

"Yes, sir." The waitress raised an eyebrow as she watched Randy pound back his cocktail in a single motion. "And you, miss?"

Cynthia sipped her margarita. "No, thank you. One drink will satisfy me."

The woman smiled and left them alone.

"Jeez, Randy," Cynthia said. "Do you want a buzz or are you hoping to get drunk?"

There was a nervous twitch below his right eye. "I haven't decided yet. Regardless, I'll be a gracious host and make sure you're having a good time."

"Speaking of hosting, Conrad tells me he's offered you a job here at the Conquistador."

Randy's smile was a bit restrained. "He did."

"Are you taking it?"

"I'm not certain. I'm still mulling it over."

"Why? It seems like a fantastic opportunity."

"There are a lot of pros and cons. I enjoy working at the

Desert Palm, and if you'll excuse me, I don't think much of Conrad Hale."

"Don't be ridiculous. He's a pussycat."

"I'm not sure I want him as a boss. He's definitely no Walter Parker."

"You're worrying for nothing. Take his offer and come work at the Conquistador. It's a fabulous resort. The pools, the shops, they're marvelous."

"I won't get Joe to move to the Conquistador if he finds out you want to leave him for Hale."

She touched a finger to her chin. "Oh, I didn't consider that."

"If you're serious about pursuing the crazy idea of seducing Hale, you need to keep Joe as far away as possible."

"It's not a crazy idea. I'll make a wonderful Mrs. Conrad Hale. I did woo him into bed. I told you I would. He's a wonderful lover. I'm a tad smitten."

"No good can come from you two getting together. You're going to get hurt."

"I couldn't be hurt by Conrad. He's so sweet. He can free me from the tyranny that's Joseph Nicosia."

"Joe's my friend; you are too, for that matter. I'm keeping out of it. I'm not getting involved in your personal problems."

Cynthia sighed, a quick burst of air. "I don't feel like talking about this anymore. I want to ride on the rollercoaster."

Randy flinched. "I can't change your mind?"

"No. I bet it's a thrill."

"I need another drink."

"One more?"

"Okay, two."

"Randy, you'll puke when the rollercoaster starts to move."

"No, I'll hold it in." He hoped if he knocked back enough alcohol, he wouldn't remember any of it.

WAYNE ESCORTED THE Wilsons to a roulette table and made sure they were comfortable. The older couple stacked casino chips on the red and black numbers with a vengeance.

"If you need anything," Wayne said, "tell the dealer. I have some paperwork to do in the host office, but I'll be back in a little while."

"Thank you, Wayne," Mrs. Wilson said as she watched the spinning ball. "We'll be fine. Wish us luck."

"Sure. Good luck." Wayne smiled, pleased he was getting a break from the crusty old folks. He strolled across the casino, weaving between the slot machines, and entered the host office. Inside, he found Carter Camp at his cubicle, his feet propped on the desk. Camp was humming to himself.

"What are you so happy about?" Wayne asked.

Camp smirked. "Found myself a date."

"Does she have all her shots?"

Camp glared at Wayne. "I see you're picking up Kennedy's bad habits. Don't ever speak to me like that again or I'll have you fired. Kennedy may be able to get away with that kind of talk, for now, but not you."

Wayne lifted his hands in a surrendering motion. "Hey, asshole, I was kidding. Don't be so goddamn grouchy. No harm was meant. Who's your date with?"

Leering, Camp grinned. "Angela Grisham, from the cashier's cage."

"Angela?" Wayne tried to picture the two of them as a couple, and his eyebrows drew close. "The hot chick with the beautiful blue eyes? Works swing?"

"I'm taking her to my uncle's surprise party tomorrow night."

"Angela Grisham?"

"Why do you sound so astounded?"

Wayne was thinking about Randy. "Oh, I'm not. I just never considered you her type."

"What sort did you expect?"

"I don't know. Maybe someone a little more...athletic... gregarious. I can't envision you and Angela together. She's a knockout."

"You'll see tomorrow night at the party. You're coming, aren't you?"

"I have to. Frazier said he'd write my ass up if I didn't show."

Camp rubbed his hands together. "I can't wait."

"Did you know Randy's asked Angela out?"

Camp scowled. "No, but I don't care who she's dated in the past."

"They didn't hook up."

Camp's mouth fell open, and his voice was an octave higher when he said, "Why not?"

Wayne shook his head. "You'd have to ask Angela."

"She turned him down?"

"It's none of my goddamn business. He gets enough tail anyway."

Camp crossed his arms. "Well, I've been successful in one-upping the mighty Romeo. Angela Grisham's chosen me over that blowhard. I can't wait until the party. I want him to see her with me."

"I wouldn't press my luck if I were you."

Camp snickered. "Revenge is sweet."

Wayne gave him a hard look. "I'd be mindful of Randy's retribution. He can kick your butt."

RANDY ESCORTED CYNTHIA back to her hotel suite, then walked over to the Desert Palm. He hadn't ridden the rollercoaster. He couldn't do it. His fear of heights was too overwhelming, and he'd decided he didn't want to get drunk enough to give it a try. He'd begged off, saying he had to go the restroom, and put Cynthia in a rollercoaster car with a teenage boy who'd volunteered to be her companion. The kid couldn't keep his eyes off her ample breasts. Randy tried to watch as the rollercoaster sped to the edge of the tower, but he had to turn away. His hands were moist just contemplating how it must feel. It sobered him up fast.

Nearing the Desert Palm host office, he ran into Walter Parker.

"Randy, my boy," Parker said, "may I have a word with you?"

"Sure, Walter. What's up?"

"We need to talk." His inflection was rather severe.

Randy bristled. "Oh, all right."

He followed Parker through the casino, and they settled at a private table near the back of a lounge. Randy saw Nicosia across the bar and was surprised to see him fawning all over a buxom young blackjack dealer.

"What would you like to drink?" Parker asked, raising his hand and flagging down a cocktail waitress. The woman scurried over to the table, eager to wait on the owner.

"I'll have a soda with lime," Randy said.

"Dewar's neat," Parker said. The waitress jotted down their orders and headed toward the bar. Parker turned to Randy. "Son, I've heard some disturbing news, and I want to discuss it with you."

Randy frowned. "What is it?"

"I've been told by a reliable source that management at the Conquistador Resort's trying to steal you away."

Randy's heart rate ticked up. "Well, yes, sir. Conrad Hale asked me to move over there as an executive host. I guess I should've mentioned it when we were in your office yesterday afternoon."

"I wish you had." There was a not-so-subtle hint of irritation in his voice. "Are you taking it as a serious offer?"

"It's generous, and I have to consider it."

"I see." Parker's expression was troubled.

"I haven't made up my mind yet, though. It's a difficult decision and not one I'm making without thorough deliberation. I told Hale I enjoy working at the Desert Palm, for you, and I needed some time to think about it."

"How long?"

"He gave me forty-eight hours. He made his offer yesterday morning."

The cocktail waitress returned to the table and placed their drinks in front of them. She must've sensed they were involved in an intense discussion because she didn't speak and hurried away.

Parker took a sip of his scotch. "If you don't mind telling me, what kind of money are we talking about?"

Randy folded his arms. "I don't see why not. Hale offered me twenty percent more than I'm making now, plus a signing bonus. I'm sure you'll agree it's a substantial increase."

"I'm willing to match it."

"I appreciate that, but my decision isn't based solely on pay."

Parker cocked his head. "I thought you liked working here."

"I do, but I don't see much of a chance for advancement. It's no secret that at some point your nephew will be in charge of the Host Department. In time, the whole damn place. I have to be realistic. I understand blood's thicker than water, and sooner or later, he's going to be my boss. I couldn't work for Carter Camp. Not in a million years."

"Carter's future with this company has yet to be determined. Don't be concerned about that now."

"In a year or two, I may have to be. That's why I need to evaluate all the opportunities coming my way. I may not get a proposal like Hale's again."

"Clearly you've made up your mind; you're taking Hale's job."

"I haven't come to a final decision, but I'm leaning that way. I want you to know I appreciate all you've done for me and no matter what I choose to do, I'll be forever grateful."

"I'd hate to see you go. It won't be the same around here. That and I stand to lose a great deal of money to the Conquistador. I expect a substantial portion of your guest base will follow you there."

Randy shook his head. "Not all of them. I know several guests who prefer the intimacy of the Desert Palm. They may visit me at the Conquistador from time to time, but their home will always be here. You've built up a great business."

Parker took a full breath. "Maybe I'm too damn old for this. I'm almost eighty, you know. I'm tired of the hassles of running an operation as complex as the Desert Palm. The competition from the mega-resorts is getting brutal."

Randy pointed at Parker. "No one competes better than you."

"It's becoming more difficult every year. The large joints like the Conquistador and the Venetian make it nearly impossible. The days when you could put forward good odds in the casino, value-priced food, and a comfortable room and expect people to flock to your place are over. You need gimmicks like volcanoes, rollercoasters, and singing gondoliers. The casino industry has changed, and I'm too damn old to be chasing after young bucks like Conrad Hale."

"Walter, you've developed one of the most successful resorts in Las Vegas. Don't minimize what you've accomplished."

"I'm not. I'm proud of the Desert Palm, but sometimes, I believe it's about time I retired."

Randy was having trouble keeping the skepticism from his expression. "You're not ready for that."

"The truth is maybe I am, and I've had some intriguing offers for the resort. Pretty lucrative ones."

"Your retirement would make my decision to leave much easier."

"Well, isn't that ironic."

"Regardless, I've very much enjoyed hosting at the Desert Palm. I have friends here, and if I do take Hale's job, I'll miss this resort something fierce. That's what's making this decision so difficult."

Parker nodded, stood with the help of his cane, and buttoned his jacket. He lowered his eyes to Randy. "Thank you for taking the time to speak with me. I appreciate you being so candid. It's going to be an interesting few days. I know you'll make the right decision, and I hope I make the correct one as well. Good night, Randy."

"Have a nice one." Randy finished off the last drops of his soda and watched Parker walk to the elevators. He felt a hand on his shoulder and turned to see Wayne.

"What are you doing here?" Wayne asked. "I thought you worked day shift today."

"I did. I came back to take Cynthia Nicosia to the top of the Conquistador Tower. She wanted to ride on the rollercoaster."

"Why didn't you call me? I'd have been happy to do that for you. I love the Bloody Marys at the Cabana Bar. They have bacon and avocado in them."

"It was no big deal. She's an attractive woman, and I enjoy being with her."

Wayne frowned. "You're not crazy enough to be hitting on her?"

"I don't need to; she comes on to me."

Wayne's face suddenly darkened. "You're not...you haven't been trying to sleep with her?"

"We've done it a couple of times, but no more."

"You slimy bastard; she's a married woman."

"What's with the judgment? You don't strike me as being so pious yourself. I understand she's married, and I'm making sure we don't end up in bed ever again."

Wayne bent toward him and said in a whisper, "You told me Nicosia's a mobster."

"It's a rumor."

"You have balls. Someday, they'll find you at the bottom of a lake."

Randy held up his right hand. "I swear to you, I'm keeping my pants zipped. Besides, Cynthia has her sights set on Conrad Hale. She wants to leave Joe for him. She's not interested in me; I don't have enough money."

Wayne's eyes narrowed. "Hale? The casino owner?"

"I don't want to talk about this anymore. How about a beer? It's almost time for you to get off shift." Wayne didn't answer, and Randy could see he was trying to register the thought of Cynthia Nicosia with not just him but Conrad Hale. "What do you say? Let's go to the Waldorf and down a couple."

Wayne shook his head. "Nah. I'm going to get drunk and play some poker at the Bellagio."

"Whatever floats your boat."

"You're one crazy prick." Wayne walked away, zigzagging through the slot machines.

Randy watched him get lost in a crowd of gamblers. He then set out for the Old Waldorf Bar. For a whole lot of unrelated reasons, he was feeling rather depressed.

TEN

CONRAD HALE LOOKED over his desk at Pete Sawyer and said, "I've had a productive day. I just got off the phone with Walter Parker. He's a stubborn man. He keeps changing his mind about selling the Desert Palm. One minute I have a deal and the next it's off. Right now, it's on, so I must move fast."

Sawyer crossed his legs. "You scared him last year when you told him you wanted to buy the Desert Palm so you could tear it down and expand the Conquistador."

"I know. That was a tactical mistake."

"An understatement if I ever heard one."

"This time, I told him I was interested in buying the Desert Palm as an operating business. I promised him I had no intention of demolishing it. He seems ready to finalize a deal."

"What do you need with a small resort? The Desert Palm's too tiny, and there isn't enough land to enlarge and make the whole project viable in the long run."

"Well, I am going to knock it down, but Parker doesn't need to know that now. I have some great expansion ideas for the Conquistador. I plan on doubling the size of the shopping gallery. Ours isn't big enough. Besides, it's one of the most valuable pieces of land on the Strip. I know Parker's had overtures from Sal

Wyman at the Charleston, and I don't want him to get control of the property."

"It seems like you've finally upped the ante enough."

"At last. I'm not sure why he was being so obstinate."

"Parker's not dumb. He knows the longer he bargains, the more money he'll receive."

"Maybe so." Hale tipped his chair back and clasped his hands together. "I'm a tough negotiator, though. Each time we talked, I knew I was making progress. It's about time he retired and enjoyed his money."

Sawyer brushed a piece of lint off his sleeve. "He's earned it."

"That he has. Cantankerous old geezer, though. I dug into his past, and he has a vicious streak." Hale rubbed his hands together. "Pete, I can't wait to get my mitts on the Desert Palm. There's another bonus—when Parker sells me his resort, I'll acquire his guest list and all his loyal customers."

"Mr. Hale, if I didn't know you better, I'd think you weren't so much interested in the land under the Desert Palm as obtaining its players, and Joseph Nicosia in particular."

A wide smile covered Hale's face. "I've been after that man's action for a long time. I knew I'd get it one way or the other."

"The deal hasn't been signed yet. Aren't you getting a little ahead of yourself?"

"No, Parker's capitulated."

"Just to keep you from hounding him."

Hale's grin broadened. "I'm positive there's no way he'll back out this time. I'm meeting with him again later this afternoon. Like I said, I'm sure I can expedite the matter. My purchase price is fair, and I'm certain he's ready to sign the papers."

"He's an admirable man who's worked hard to develop a solid business."

"I told you, I'm offering him a hell of a price. All things considered, he's getting more than he should."

"We still have to honor our commitment to Randy Kennedy and get him to sign an employment contract."

"I'll secure him by default with the purchase of the Desert Palm."

"You'll regret it if you don't give him that pay increase. If he's angry, he'll be swept up by the Mirage or Mandalay. Don't take that risk. Get a signed employment agreement."

Hale's expression was unhappy but understanding. His phone console buzzed, indicating his secretary was on the line. He pressed a button. "Yes, Connie?"

"Cynthia Nicosia's here to see you."

Sawyer scowled at Hale.

"Give me a minute, then send her in."

"Yes, sir."

Hale eyed Sawyer, embarrassed, pink coloring his cheeks.

Sawyer peered disapprovingly at him over the top of his reading glasses. "Mr. Hale, you—"

Hale interrupted, raising his left hand. "Stop. I know. I don't need a lecture from you. I'll put an end to it."

HALE GLANCED UP when Cynthia entered his office wearing a tight red satin dress with a pair of matching crimson pumps. Wanting to avoid an uncomfortable situation, Pete Sawyer excused himself, and Cynthia took a seat in front of Hale's desk.

"So, how does Joseph like your redecorations?" Hale asked.

She frowned. "He hasn't seen it yet. He must still be winning. He won't leave a blackjack table if he's up." Cynthia was fishing for something in her purse. She pulled out a lipstick, put some on her lips, and checked the results in a compact mirror, pursing her lips. Satisfied with the look, she closed the compact and placed it in her purse, which she set on the edge of the desk.

Hale rapped his knuckles on the desk. "Damn it."

"Let's go up to the suite. I put some extra touches on the decorations, and I want you to see them. Besides, I'm feeling unbelievably affectionate." She wiggled her eyebrows in a sexy fashion. "I'd love a repeat of yesterday afternoon. You're a fantastic lover."

Saying nothing, Hale rose from his chair. He turned his back to her and walked to one of the big windows in the front of the office, where he gazed down on the busy casino below. He cleared his throat. "Cynthia, I'm not in the mood."

Cynthia stood, floated up behind him, and massaged his shoulders, nuzzling his neck. He continued to stare out into the casino with a frown on his face. She nibbled at an ear. "Come on, baby. I know some tricks that'll send you over the top."

She stretched her hand toward his groin, but he pulled away before she could touch him and glared at her scornfully. He couldn't believe she'd coaxed him into bed. She was good and had had him aroused so fast his judgment was clouded. It was a regrettable tryst, though. Now that he was certain he was well on his way to purchasing the Desert Palm and would be employing Randy Kennedy as a casino host, spending time with Cynthia Nicosia was unnecessary. "I've been contemplating this all day," he said. "Yesterday afternoon was a mistake. You're a married woman, and it's best if we not see each other in any way but as friends."

"What?" she screeched, tossing her blond hair back. "What the hell are you talking about?" She reached for him, grabbing his shoulders.

Hale shook her off, moved back behind his heavy plank of a desk, and sat in the leather chair. Struggling to keep his tone light, he said, "I've been thinking this over since our rendezvous yesterday. No good can come from an affair."

Cynthia stormed to the front of Hale's desk. "I can't believe you're saying this." Disappointment was written all over her face and moisture brimmed in her eyes. "I thought we could be falling in love."

He felt the blood drain from his face. "You're joshing me!"

Tears cascaded down her cheeks. "I wouldn't have slept with you if I didn't feel you cared for me."

"You seduced me, and you know it. I enjoyed our time together—it was fun—but it was a one-time fling."

Her voice became almost inaudible. "I was thinking about leaving Joseph for you."

Hale choked out a laugh. "You're a little delusional. I wouldn't recommend parting with your husband unless you want to be alone."

"You bastard." Her lips were pressed tight, her eyes angry. "How can you do this in such a blithe manner?" She grabbed the shoe off her foot and threw it at his head.

Hale dodged it, and it bounced off the window and clattered to the floor. "There's no need for violence."

"The hell there isn't. No man treats me like this. I'm not some whore you can spend the afternoon with, then dump the next day. No way. What, is there another woman? I bet it's that cocktail waitress I saw you talking to the other day."

"There's no other woman, but it's none of your goddamn business if there were. Cynthia, yesterday was pleasurable, but it was also ill-advised. There's no need for you to get this hysterical."

"You haven't seen hysterics yet, buddy. No one treats me like this. I mean it. I'm not letting you do this."

Hale turned his hands up. "I'm sorry, but you have no choice."

"I'm telling Joseph you've been trying to entice me into bed."

"Don't be ridiculous. Why would you do that?"

Cynthia crossed her arms. "Revenge is going to be mine, baby face. I'm telling my husband how you've been trying to seduce me for months. He won't gamble a dime in your stupid casino. He'll stay at the Desert Palm forever." Her lips turned up in a defiant curl.

He glared at her. "By the end of the day, I'll have purchased the Desert Palm. By the end of the year, the place will be leveled and the land ready for another expansion of the Conquistador Resort."

She put a hand on her hip. "That's what this is all about, huh? Randy Kennedy was right; you never wanted me, just Joseph. You're willing to spend millions to get Joseph Nicosia to gamble at your resort. What an ego. Well, I have news for you—it won't happen. When I tell him how you lured me into bed, he'll have every bone in your body broken."

"You're not being rational. I don't want to continue a physical relationship, but I still want to be friends. It's not necessary to resort to brutality."

"Are you begging me for mercy?"

"Cynthia."

Fresh tears streamed down her cheeks. "Say our affair's not ending and we have a future with each other."

Hale stared at her with a stony face, shaking his head slowly.

There was loathing in her eyes. "I hope your insurance is paid up."

He exploded out of his chair and marched around the desk and over to her. He grabbed her by the arms. "I don't take threats from anyone. Not you, not anybody." He shook her.

Cynthia shrugged. "Take that up with Joseph."

Hale backhanded her across the face.

She bleated in pain. "How dare you!" It came out on a hiss.

"I mean it, Cynthia; let this pass. Keep your mouth shut and move on."

"You fool." She wiped her mouth where he'd stuck her, looking to see if she was bleeding. "You don't know me very well."

"I'm telling you to keep quiet."

"Or what?" She picked up her purse.

"Or it may be the last thing you ever do," he snarled.

With fear in her eyes, without her missing shoe, she limped out of the room.

RANDY HUNG UP the phone and paused a minute before walking through the crowded casino, disturbed by the fear in Cynthia's voice. Going into the host office, he spotted Wayne. "You're just the man I wanted. I was hoping I could track you down."

Wayne smiled. "Why's that?"

"There's a problem I need to take care of, and I was wondering if you could help me out. I have a dinner date with a guest, Sylvia Gardner, and I'm not able to keep it. Would you mind taking my place?"

Wayne hoisted his shoulders up. "If she doesn't care, it's fine by me."

"You remember Sylvia—the woman you met on your first night of work? *Ode to Bengay*. She's asked about you a few times. I'm sure she'll enjoy your company."

"Dining with blue-haired old ladies seems to be my goddamned fate this week. What time?"

"Five. She likes to eat early. I've made reservations in the gourmet room. It shouldn't take more than an hour. She doesn't eat much. I'll meet up with you later tonight at Walter Parker's birthday party."

Wayne said sarcastically, "Doesn't that sound like a hell of a way to spend an evening? A birthday party for an eighty-year-old man. What are the party favors going to be—wrinkle cream?"

Randy laughed. "Oh, you should walk by the Arabian Lounge on your way to meet Sylvia. Jennifer Crichton's working today and looking hot."

Wayne didn't say anything, just smirked with a touch of lust in his eyes and walked out of the office.

WHEN CYNTHIA OPENED the door to the suite, Randy was taken aback by her appearance. She looked haggard, tears seeping from the corners of her eyes. Her hair was in disarray, and she was wearing an unflattering white terrycloth bathrobe.

"Cynthia," Randy said. "What's wrong?" He loped into the room, shut the door, and put his arms around her waist. "Are you all right?"

Cynthia blinked through the tears, her mascara streaming. "Oh, Randy, I don't know what I should do."

"Sit down and tell me what's going on." He led her to the sofa, and they both took a seat. He pulled a handkerchief from his jacket pocket and brushed the tears from her cheeks. In a calm and reassuring tone, he said, "Everything will be fine. What's got you so upset?"

Cynthia fought for composure, her eyes bloodshot. "My life's falling apart. Conrad..." Her lips quivered. "He's broken off our affair."

Randy grinned widely. "Is that all? That's no loss. The man's an ass. You don't need him."

"You don't understand what he meant to me. He was my ticket away from Joseph. I can't take the abuse anymore. Now I don't know what to do."

Randy took her hand and patted it. "If you want to leave Joe that bad, then just do it."

"I'm afraid of being alone."

"You can make it on your own. I know you're a strong woman. Get a job in a gallery, like you had before."

Cynthia sniffed away more tears. "I won't need to work. There's no issue with money. I have *Sunflowers in a Vase*. It's worth way more than a million dollars."

"What's *Sunflowers in a Vase*?"

"That's it right there." She pointed to the painting above the fireplace mantel. "*Sunflowers in a Vase* by Vincent van Gogh."

"Is it Joe's?"

"No. I'm not getting into the details, but let's just say I acquired it in a rather unconventional way."

"Is it stolen?"

Cynthia shook her head. "Not stolen, but switched out with an excellent replica. The real owner doesn't know I have it. It's my little insurance policy in case something goes wrong."

"That sounds stolen to me." Randy eased up from the couch, took a couple paces to the fireplace, and scrutinized the painting above it. "Joe doesn't know you have this?"

"No. No one does but my ex-boyfriend, Kevin, and of course Conrad."

Randy stroked the frame. "Why did you hang it here?"

"I thought it would be fun to have it as part of my redecoration of this suite. I also thought this would be a good place to hide it from my ex."

Randy turned to her. "What's his claim on it?"

"He helped me get hold of it in the first place. At the time, Joseph was pursing me, and I could see that my relationship with Kevin was coming to an end. I decided to keep the Van Gogh for myself. I took it one night when Kevin was passed out after a drinking binge. He's furious. He keeps threatening me. Anyway, having the painting sent here is one of several mistakes I've made in the last few days. I have to pack it up and take it back to L.A."

"What's your plan?"

Cynthia's taut face was filled with anxiety, and she clicked her tongue. "Maybe I should just run away and go live with my brother, Brett."

"Where's he?"

"In West Hollywood. I need to call him. Our relationship's been pretty cool for the last few years, and I have to mend some fences. Brett hasn't liked the men in my life. He hated Kevin, detested him. He didn't think much of Joseph either. Since I married him, we haven't spoken much." She was silent for a second and wiped away a tear that had run down her cheek.

Randy returned to the sofa and sat next to her. "I'm sure he'll be glad to hear from his sister."

Cynthia rubbed her eyes. "I hope so."

"That's the right attitude." Randy dabbed more tears from her cheeks with his handkerchief.

Cynthia stood and walked to the mirror on the wall. "Oh, my god. I'm a mess."

"You're showing your sexy vulnerable side."

She gave a short hoot of laughter. "You consider me beautiful?"

"Yes, I do. Even more so on the inside. Within that stunning exterior of yours is a person who's sweet, if not somewhat naïve." He smiled at her in the reflection.

She stepped away from the mirror and sat back down on the couch. She grasped his hand and gripped it tight, caressing his fingers and kissing his knuckles. "I need to be with you."

"We're not going there, Cynthia."

"Please, just this once. I can't bear to be alone. I want to be with a man who believes I'm beautiful on both the outside and the inside. I yearn for someone who cares for the real me." She leaned over, trying to kiss him.

Randy pushed her away. "Stop it. I'm not sleeping with you. It's too dangerous. Joe could show up."

"He's at the Desert Palm. He doesn't like playing here. Besides, he's probably on a lucky streak. He'll be there for hours."

"It's not happening. I told you, I've thought a lot about this."

"Will you at least cuddle with me?"

Exasperated, he stared at her. "For a little bit. Keep your hands above my waist."

"We'll see."

His voice was stern. "I mean it."

Cynthia stood, reached out, and clasped his hands. "Okay. Just hold me for a while." She pulled Randy up off the sofa, and he followed her into the bedroom.

ELEVEN

FOR A SECOND night, Joseph Nicosia was in the Zanzibar Lounge, snuggling up to Violet, the blackjack dealer. He nuzzled her ear and said, "You're so alluring."

"Brownie, not now. This is a public place. I work here and could be fired if I'm not careful."

"Don't you worry about that, my darling Violet. Me and the owner of this resort are close."

She caressed the back of his hand. "You know Mr. Parker?"

"Sure, me and Wally go way back. Can I get you another drink?"

Violet said in a squeaky voice, "I don't know, I'm a little tipsy."

"Bull, you're just relaxed. I haven't slept in days and I'm feeling wired." He snapped his fingers at a passing cocktail waitress. "We need another round."

The woman shot him a cross look but, knowing he was a high-roller, took his order of a couple whiskeys with beer chasers.

Nicosia dug inside his jacket and lifted out a book of matches. He patted down his pockets. "Damn. I'm out of cigars."

Violet tilted her head toward the bar. "The waitress can get some for you at the gift shop."

"Not Cubans. That's all I smoke. It's okay, though, I have

some in my suite. Harlan, come here." Nicosia motioned to his bodyguard, who was propped on a nearby bar stool.

Samples walked up to his employer. "Yes, sir."

"I'm out of Cubans. There's a box of them on a table in the suite. Here's the keycard. Bring me two or three. Hurry. While you're over there, see what that wife of mine's up to. Make sure she stays put. Violet and I don't want to be disturbed."

"Okay. I'll be right back." Samples set off for the exit.

"Now, where were we?" Nicosia asked, gazing into Violet's eyes. "Oh, I remember." He held her hand and nibbled his way up her arm.

"Brownie," she squealed.

"Violet, let's blow this popsicle stand."

"Where do you want to go?"

He massaged her shoulder. "Somewhere we can be alone. I'll have one of the hosts arrange for a room."

"Oh, all right." She hiccupped. "Excuse me. I'm a little inebriated. Inneebbreeateed." She giggled.

"I love the way you say that, honey-bunch. Inneebbreeateed. Baby, I have a hankering for somebody named Violet."

"Not someone called honey-bunch?" She tried to focus on his face.

"Her too."

"Well, I'm in the mood for a tasty brownie."

"Grrr." He buried his face in her cleavage. "Let's get out of here now."

"What about Harlan?"

"Who?" He showered her neck with kisses.

"The giant man you sent to get the cigars."

Nicosia waved a dismissive arm. "Ah, forget about that. He can catch up with us later."

Violet's cheeks were flushed. "Brownie, you're making me hot."

He pawed the inside of her thighs. "Not as turned on as me, gorgeous."

ANGELA STARED IN the mirror and winced. The stylish party dress she was wearing reflected in her blue eyes but didn't hide her gloom. She combed her auburn hair and swept it over her shoulder.

She took in her image one last time and was making a goofy face in the mirror when her doorbell rang. She left the bathroom and descended the stairs to the front entrance, sighed, and opened the door to a grinning Carter Camp.

Camp was dressed in a black tuxedo with an aqua bowtie and cummerbund. The cut of the outfit made him appear weak and bony. "Hi, Angela."

"Hello," she said and backed up, signaling for him to enter. "Come in. I'll just be a minute."

"Sure." He walked into the townhouse and closed the door. "This is for you." He brought his hand from behind his back and handed her a clear plastic box containing the largest and most hideous corsage Angela had ever seen.

"Oh my." She tried to conceal the revulsion. "It's...it's enormous."

"Do you like it? I picked out the flowers myself."

She held up the box with the blue-and-orange arrangement. "I, I haven't seen carnations in that color combination on a corsage before."

"Let me put it on."

Her heart sank into her stomach, her mouth hanging agape. "Um, oh, okay."

Camp opened the plastic container and took out the mass of flowers. He placed the corsage on her shoulder and attempted to attach it to her dress with a long stickpin, pricking his finger. "Ouch."

Angela seized the corsage and his wrist before she too was jabbed. "Tell you what, let me go to the bathroom and put this on. It'll be safer for both of us."

"I guess you're right." He stuck his pin-pricked finger in his mouth and licked off the blood.

Angela recoiled. "Make yourself comfortable." She pointed to the sofa in the living room. "I'll be back in a bit."

"Take your time." Camp ambled over to the sofa and took a seat.

Angela trekked up the stairs to the bathroom. She gazed in the mirror, then at the flowers. She pinned the corsage to her dress and appraised herself in the reflection, almost crying at the sight of the gross pile of carnations jutting from her shoulder.

What will Randy think of this? For some silly reason, she'd been hoping to make him jealous. One look at her now, and he'd have the uncontrollable urge to laugh.

She stood there for the longest time before hearing Camp shout from below. "Angela, we better get going. We don't want to be late for my uncle's surprise party. Is everything okay?"

"Yes, Carter." She shook her head, knowing she couldn't avoid the inevitable. "I'll be right down."

FULLY DRESSED, RANDY lay on top of the bed with his hands behind his head, thinking about Angela.

Cynthia was next to him, naked and under the sheets. "You're not being very comforting," she said. "Please, baby. I need to be with a man."

He continued staring at the ceiling. "It'll have to be someone besides me."

Cynthia was quiet for a bit, her arms crossed over her chest. "I'm going to get even with him."

Randy pushed his head back against the pillow, stretching his neck. "Who?"

"Conrad."

"Cynthia, you're better off without him. Let it drop."

She reached over and put her arms around him. "Make love to me."

There was a loud thumping sound in the adjoining room, and both Cynthia and Randy glanced at the doors with alarm. "Who's there?" Cynthia asked, sliding out from between the sheets. Randy flew off the bed and up against a wall. She put her finger to her lips, directing him to stay quiet.

She grabbed a robe and put it on. "Who is it?" she asked, louder. Cynthia opened the door, crept into the living room, and skulked over to the entry foyer. An empty box of Joseph's cigars was on the floor next to the doors. She picked it up, placed it on a table, and looked around the room. It was apparent that whoever had been in the suite was gone. She put her hand to her chin, trying to figure out what had just happened. "You can come out, Randy. There's no one here."

Randy peered around the bedroom door. "Who was it?"

"I don't know. It must've been the maid."

"You're sure?"

"No, but whoever it was is gone."

"I'm a little spooked."

"Yeah, me too." Cynthia clutched her robe together and walked back into the bedroom.

Randy picked up his jacket. "How'd you like to go to a party?"

"No, I'm not up for that."

"It'll be good for you to forget about your problems. It's a surprise eightieth birthday celebration for Walter Parker. It should be fun."

Cynthia closed her eyes for a second. "Oh all right, I'll go to your party. It better not be dull."

"It's just what you need to get your mind off Conrad Hale."

HARLAN SAMPLES POKED at the Conquistador elevator call button and rocked from heel to heel as he waited for the car to arrive. "Hurry up," he said, tapping some more on the down button. When the doors rumbled open, he entered the car and pushed 'casino' on the elevator panel.

Samples' face was rigid, and he muttered to himself as the car descended. "I knew he was doing her."

The elevator arrived at the casino floor, and Samples bolted out of the car. He ran out of the Conquistador Resort, down the long driveway, and over to the entrance of the Desert Palm. He crossed the casino to the Zanzibar Lounge, where he'd last seen his boss. Not finding him or his lady friend, he went over to the bar and got the attention of the bartender. "Where's Mr. Nicosia?" he asked.

The bartender grinned. "He left with the dealer he's been groping."

"Where to?"

"Not certain. I suppose he's up in a hotel room. The way they were pawing each other, I'm certain they're having a good time."

"Damn." Samples stomped toward the registration desk.

CONRAD HALE SMILED and looked across the desk at Walter Parker. "Now that we've come to an agreement on my purchase of the Desert Palm, why don't we invite the lawyers back in the room so we can finalize the details?"

Parker hit a button on the phone console and asked his secretary to send in the waiting lawyers. When the men and women were seated, Parker said, "I insist on assurances that my team members' jobs will be protected."

Hale nodded. "Without question."

"I mean it," Parker said emphatically. "The people who work here mean the world to me, and I don't want anything to disrupt their lives."

"You employ a good workforce here, and after a thorough examination of the financial statements, it's clear you have a well-run and profitable operation. I won't do anything to change that. Your employees and customers will see nothing but business as usual."

"I prefer to call them team members and guests."

Hale gave a flippant wave of his hand. "Whatever. Well now, Walter, you have to agree that the price I'm paying is more than generous."

Parker considered Hale's words with an ill-tempered glare. "It could've been better."

Hale dismissed that comment with another flick of his hand. "Boy, I envy you. With the amount of money you're making on this deal, your golden years are going to be fantastic. And without all the headaches associated with running a casino and hotel."

"Perhaps you should consider retirement too, if you find operating a large resort such a burden."

Hale's lips bowed in a seemingly involuntary smile. "Don't be absurd. I have too much I want to conquer."

"I bet you do. You're an aggressive man."

"That's true. I thrive on growth and change. You have to keep building or you die."

"There's little room for expansion at the Desert Palm. Except for our rather small parking lot, there isn't any vacant land available."

"True. This deal would be better if there was more space for development, but I understand that's not possible. However, the Desert Palm will be a great addition to my portfolio, and I'm happy with its profitability. It makes more money than half the resorts on the Strip."

"Due in most part to my loyal team members. I must emphasize that I don't want the Desert Palm to be demolished so you can expand the Conquistador. I need assurances my team members won't lose their jobs."

"That's not in my plans right now."

"I want it in writing, Conrad. I insist it be part of the sales agreement."

Hale wagged his finger. "That's not necessary."

"I believe it is."

Hale squirmed and fidgeted with the ring on his pinky finger. "Walter, I'm trying to make this as simple as possible. You know deals like this can get complicated. Trust that I have your best interest at heart."

Parker narrowed his eyes. "Let's get this over with."

Hale smiled. "Marvelous." He turned to his team of lawyers. "You know what to do. Write up the final contracts and get them back to us as soon as feasible. Davis, deliver my gaming application to the Control Board pronto."

A well-coiffed heavy-set lawyer with a deep voice said, "Yes, Mr. Hale."

Hale looked at Parker. "I feel like celebrating. What do you say, how about we go out and enjoy a few drinks?"

Parker pressed his palms together and tapped his fingertips. "I'm going to a party tonight. I'm not supposed to know this, but my wife's throwing me a surprise eightieth birthday celebration. It's hard to keep a secret in this place, but I'll do my best to act astonished."

"It's your birthday? Why didn't you tell me? With the money I'm paying you for the Desert Palm, you can buy yourself one hell of a gift."

Parker half-shrugged. "Most of the money from the sale will be bestowed on my charitable foundation."

"Charity? It's being donated to charity? You're giving it away?" Hale stared at Parker. "You and I are very different people."

Parker rolled his eyes. "That's an understatement. Anyway, why don't you join me at the party? All my top management and many line team members will be in attendance. It's as good a time as any to break the news of your acquisition."

"I'd be honored to participate in the festivities. It'll give me the opportunity to meet your staff—correction, mine—in a celebratory environment."

Parker stood and straightened his tie. "Well then, let's go to the casino and find my wife. I'm to meet her near the escalators. I'm sure she's concocted a reason to lure me to the ballroom." He picked up his silver-tipped walking cane, and Hale followed him out of the office and toward the elevators.

"I always enjoy a good party," Hale said.

Parker's cane clicked as they strolled down the marble hallway. "Please go along with the charade. I know my wife's gone to a great deal of trouble setting up this gala, and I don't want to do anything to hurt her feelings."

"You have my word, Walter. I promise you this will be one fantastic surprise party."

Parker tipped his head to one side. "It'll be even more so when everyone hears I'm selling the Desert Palm Casino Resort...to you."

TWELVE

THE BALLROOM OF the Desert Palm was large, with a high ceiling decorated with multi-colored balloons. Paper streamers arched from each of the four walls to the center of the space. A crowd of almost a thousand people were milling around, and the air was electric with the sound of laughter and the hum of voices. A twelve-piece orchestra was playing big band tunes to the delight of the small number of brave souls on the dance floor. Tuxedo-clad waiters were scurrying around, making certain everybody had refreshments. "Have you seen any celebrities?" a well-dressed woman asked her friend.

The woman looked at the people around her. "No, not yet, but I've heard the winner of last year's *America's Most Talented* is here somewhere."

"You're kidding! Oh, what I wouldn't give to meet him."

Her friend nodded, her eyes roving around the ballroom.

The well-dressed woman petted the mink shawl on her shoulders. "Marian Parker sure knows how to put on a party."

"I know. It's going to be one of *the* social events of the year. Do you know what time Mr. Parker's scheduled to arrive?"

"No, but the bandleader will get everyone's attention right before he comes into the ballroom."

"In the meantime, let's track down the winner of *America's Most Talented*."

The other woman nodded, and the two took off across the room like schoolgirls searching for the captain of the football team.

Randy and Cynthia entered the ballroom and worked their way through the throng of people to one of the many bars. He ordered a champagne cocktail for her and a Coke for himself. Drinks in hand, they wandered to a standing table in one corner of the room.

Cynthia was wearing a blue evening gown with an expensive gold-and-diamond necklace. Randy was having little success convincing her to make conversation. "Do you plan on pouting all night?" he asked.

She frowned. "I told you earlier, I'm not in the partying mood."

"Well then, start drinking." He raised his soda.

"That's not a bad idea. It might deaden the pain."

Randy let out an annoyed breath. "Will you forget about Hale?"

"I'm trying, but whether I do or not, I still have to decide if I'm going to leave Joseph. If I don't, I'll end up in bed with him. The very thought repulses me."

Randy scratched his cheek. "I wonder where he is. I looked around the casino, but I couldn't find him. I asked one of the pit supervisors, and she said she hasn't seen him for quite a while."

"He'll show up at some point. You can't keep Joseph away from the blackjack tables for long."

Randy took a sip of his Coke.

Cynthia held up her empty glass. "I need a refill."

Randy lifted an eyebrow. "That was fast. Jeez."

"I'm thirsty. Be a sweetheart and bring me another one."

He took her glass. "Okay, I'll be right back. Watch my

soda." Randy turned and threaded his way through the ever-growing crowd of people. Approaching a bar, he spotted Wayne and navigated in his direction. Pushing over to him, he said, "Hey, what's happening?"

Wayne shrugged. "Not much. I had dinner with Mrs. Gardner. For that, you owe me big time. What a bitch. She's been losing on the slots and is grumpy. Anyway, I thought I'd better get here before Mr. Parker arrives. I wouldn't want the old guy to believe I skipped his birthday party."

"So many people are here, I doubt he'd miss any of us."

Wayne cast his gaze around the room. "You're right. How long have you been here?"

"We just arrived. I brought Cynthia Nicosia. She's had a rough day, and I figured the party would be good medicine."

"I thought you wanted to put some distance between yourself and her."

"Somehow that isn't working out."

Wayne stared at him, shaking his head. "Oh, before I forget, I got a paycheck advance. I have your money." He reached in his wallet and extracted two hundred-dollar bills, handing them to Randy.

Randy took the currency and shot him a satisfied smile. "Anytime you'd like to bet again, let me know."

Wayne gave him the middle finger. "You can go to hell."

Randy laughed. "Listen, I have an idea. It's almost six, and Jennifer Crichton should be off work any minute. I see the way you look at her—you do her with your eyes every time she walks by. I'll go to the casino and see if she's interested in coming to the party. She can be your date."

Wayne leered, the gap between his front teeth prominent. "You're sure she doesn't have a boyfriend?"

"She doesn't and thinks you're cute, muscle boy. She told me that."

Wayne's grin was growing. "She is hot."

"A habanera. Let me deliver another drink to Cynthia, and I'll go find Jennifer. It won't take me long." Randy gestured for the bartender.

THE PARTY GOT louder as the big band played old Glenn Miller tunes. Randy was helping to ignite a conversation between Wayne and Jennifer while Cynthia continued to chug champagne cocktails as if her life depended on it. From the corner of his eye, Randy watched Angela enter the ballroom with one of Carter Camp's hands on her back, guiding her through the crowd. Randy gasped.

Camp saw Randy and, with a plainly satisfied smirk on his face, veered his way, slowly working through the growing crowd. Randy felt like fleeing but locked his knees, clenched his jaw, and didn't budge.

Wayne had spotted Camp too and said to Randy, "Jennifer and I are going to find some alcohol with a kick. I'm thinking shots. Try not to get in a fight with that asshole."

Randy was focused on Angela. "We'll see."

After winding through the swarm of people, Camp sidled up to Randy. "Good evening, Kennedy. You know my date, don't you? Angela Grisham." He gave him a smug, toothy grin.

Randy put on an obligatory smile. "Sure, I know Angela." He pointed to the flowers on her shoulder. "What a *beautiful* corsage." He paused, and his voice sounded completely different when he added, "You're astonishing this evening." His eyes burned into hers, and she held the gaze.

"She sure is," Camp said, pulling Angela closer to him. "She's one of the most attractive women in the room."

Angela tipped her head down then back up. "Stop it, you two. You're embarrassing me."

Randy winked at her ever so subtly. "Angela, I'd like you to meet Cynthia Nicosia. Cynthia's Joe's wife. Cynthia, this is Angela Grisham. She works here in the cashier's cage."

Angela shook Cynthia's hand. "It's a pleasure to meet you."

"Good evening, Mrs. Nicosia," Camp said.

Cynthia finished off her cocktail and wiped her mouth with the sleeve of her dress.

Camp looked at the two women. "Well, ladies. What can I get you to drink?"

"White wine," Angela said. "A chardonnay."

"I'll have another one of these," Cynthia said with a slight slur. She lifted her empty glass. "It's a chchchampagne cocktail."

Camp nodded. "Fine, I'll be back soon."

Cynthia staggered toward him. "I'll go with you."

Camp eyed Randy with apprehension, a weak smile on his lips, clearly not certain he wanted to leave him alone with Angela. "Okay. Let's go to that bar." He pointed, then leaned down and pecked Angela on the cheek.

Looking surprised, she touched her face where he'd kissed her.

Camp sneered at Randy; then he and Cynthia dove into the crowd and waded to the bar.

There was an awkward silence. To break the tension, Randy said, "You *are* striking this evening." Again, he stared into her eyes.

"Despite the *beautiful* corsage?" She seemed to be trying to hold back a grin but couldn't.

Randy chuckled. "I assume Camp picked it up at a local mortuary."

"He means well."

"If you say so."

"He's been quite sweet...maybe a little boorish."

Randy raised both hands in the air. "If Camp's the kind of man you want, it's fine by me."

Angela studied him. She seemed transfixed by his eyes.

For the next five minutes or so, they stood in uncomfortable silence and watched the horde of people. Randy wanted to say something more but couldn't find the right words. Finally, frustrated and tired of the anxiety he knew they both felt, he said, "Angela?"

She peered into his eyes.

He felt a tingling all through his body.

Angela blushed a faint scarlet.

Randy was about to continue speaking when Camp stepped between them.

He passed Angela a glass of wine. "Here you are. I arranged for the wine steward to bring this up from my uncle's wine cellar. It's a 2002 Cullen's chardonnay from Australia. I know you'll enjoy it."

Angela took a sip. "Yes, Carter, it's delicious."

Camp beamed at her. "I knew you'd like it."

"Where's Cynthia?" Randy asked.

Camp gestured to a bar with his beer. "She's getting another drink. You better keep tabs on her. She's plowed. I don't want her spoiling my uncle's party."

Randy nodded. "I'll go find her. Angela, it was nice seeing you." He put his hand on her arm and again felt the tingling sensation. "I hope you have a good time this evening."

She smiled, a warm and earnest one. "You too."

Randy saw a flicker in her eyes. He was dizzy and his heart felt like it was going to burst. He'd never felt this way before.

Camp visibly cringed when he saw the spark between them. "You better go find Mrs. Nicosia."

Randy forced himself to turn away from Angela. He slapped Camp on the back and vanished into the mass of people.

THE BANDLEADER STOOD on the ballroom stage and tapped on the microphone. "Ladies and gentlemen, may I please have your attention?" Hearing no drop in the volume level of the room, he tried again. "Please, folks, I need you to quiet down." The microphone squawked, and that caught the attention of the crowd. "Thank you." The room quieted, and everyone looked his way. "I've just been informed that Walter Parker's on his way to the ballroom. In a few moments, we'll turn off the lights and wait for his arrival. When he enters, the lights will go back on and everybody will yell 'surprise'. After that, we'll all sing *Happy Birthday*."

The room buzzed with excitement.

"All right, hit it."

The lights in the ballroom dimed, and there was a murmur of voices from around the room. "This is rrrrdiculous," Cynthia said with a more prominent slur. "What do they think we are, children?"

Randy put his finger to his mouth. "Shhh."

"Here he comes," a man in the corner of the room said in a hoarse whisper. Snickers and muffled laughter floated across the ballroom.

Marian Parker, a sturdy woman in her late seventies, led her husband through the entrance of the darkened ballroom, Conrad Hale trailing close behind. "I want you to see something," Mrs. Parker said, eyeing her spouse lovingly.

"It's pitch black in here," Mr. Parker said. "What on earth do you want to show me in the ballroom?"

The lights flashed on, and the mob roared, "Surprise!"

Mr. Parker looked somewhat sheepish as the band played and everyone sang *Happy Birthday*. He wagged his finger at his wife and kissed her.

He's a good actor, Hale thought with surprise. *If he hadn't told me about it, I'd buy it myself.* You could tell from her glowing smile that Mrs. Parker believed he was surprised.

When the singing concluded, there was a large round of applause. Parker raised his hand. "My goodness, I don't know what to say. Thank you, all of you. This is such a shock, and I'm moved and a little embarrassed. Thank you so much."

Everybody in the room applauded again, and the band played *Memories*. Marian Parker held out her hand. "May I have a dance with the birthday boy?"

He grinned, his wrinkles more pronounced. "I'm far from a boy, my dear, but I'd love nothing better." He took her hand and led her to the dance floor, his cane tapping against the wooden floor. More applause ensued.

Left alone, Hale took a glass of champagne from the tray of a passing waiter and scanned the room with an overwhelming sense of satisfaction. By this time tomorrow, he'd own the Desert Palm, and his ever-growing casino empire would prosper even more.

He watched the Parkers' slow glide around the dance floor. An adoring group of employees watched as their patriarch and his wife gazed into each other's eyes. Hale was almost jealous of the reverence Parker's employees felt toward him. *That will all change,* he thought. *As soon as Parker makes the announcement that he's selling the Desert Palm, life for these people will never be the same.*

CYNTHIA HANDED RANDY her empty champagne glass. "Fetch me another drink? M still thirsty."

He set the glass on a table. "You've had enough. I'll get you a soda."

"You're th' one who... who told me to looooosen up."

"Well, you're plenty loose enough. Let's dance."

She grimaced. "Don't like dancin'."

"I do and want to shake some booty."

"Then dance with her." Cynthia pointed at Angela who

was sitting at a cocktail table with Carter Camp. "You been starin' at her all... all night."

"Have I?" Randy looked across the room at Angela. He could tell she was struggling to pay attention to Camp.

"Yes. What's goin' on tabeen you two?"

"Nothing." Randy's tone was dejected. "Believe me, not a goddamn thing."

"Has anyone toooold her?"

"What do you mean by that?" he asked, his voice shaded with disbelief.

"She's in looove with you."

"I wish."

Cynthia frowned. "You do?"

He didn't respond, still eyeing Angela and Camp.

Cynthia staggered a little to the left. "Well, she's in looove with you."

"What gives you that idea?"

"She's sneakin' peeks at yous. She's beauuutiful, I'll give yoooou that. I'm kinda envious."

"You're drunk."

"And I wanna get drunker."

Randy took a deep breath. "Oh, all right, I'll get you one more drink. But remember, sooner or later, you have to sober up and tackle your life straight on."

"Nooo, gonna stay wasted f'rever."

THE DANCE FLOOR filled up as more people joined the Parkers. The lines at the bars were now ten deep, and as the alcohol flowed, the volume in the room increased.

Camp raised his voice to be heard over the din of the gathering. "Someday, Angela, I'll run this whole place."

She adjusted the corsage on her shoulder. "You have pretty grand aspirations."

"Yes, I do. This resort needs new blood, and I'm just the person to make the right changes. I have some great ideas on how to improve this property."

"What does your uncle have to say about your plans?"

Camp traced the rim of his beer with his finger. "He's from a different era and doesn't give my thoughts much credence."

"Do you believe he'll give you control of the Desert Palm?"

"I'm the single viable heir. Uncle Walter and Aunt Marian didn't have any children. I earned a degree in hospitality management at UNLV, and I'm the only one capable of taking the reins of this resort. My mother's close to Uncle Walter, and I'm sure she can convince him I'm the right person to follow in his footsteps."

"Well, I hope you're successful."

"I will be. I'd be even more so if you were by my side."

Angela almost choked on her chardonnay, patting her chest. "Carter, this is our first date, and you're moving a little too fast."

"I realize that, but I'd like you to know I think you're special."

"I appreciate that. Let's take our time."

"Fair enough."

Angela felt her insides sink with dread. She didn't know what else to say.

THE BALLROOM FELL silent as Eric Frazier began to speak. "Walter Parker's one of the great Las Vegas pioneers." He stood at a lectern on the stage in front of the orchestra, wearing glasses and reading from index cards. "While Steve Wynn was creating the Mirage, Bellagio, and Wynn Las Vegas and Conrad Hale was developing the Conquistador Resort, our Mr. Parker was steadily building his own empire. He did it in a unique way, however. He's always been concerned about his much-loved team members and known that by taking care of them, he'd ensure that the money would follow. With his vision, he's created one of the most successful resorts in Las Vegas.

"I remember the first time I ever met Mr. Parker. I was a dealer at the Golden Nugget downtown. He'd just lost a thousand dollars at my blackjack table, and I told him not to worry—his day would come. He said with that expression we all know so well, '*My day won't come with the turn of the cards. My day will come from hard work.*' I decided that minute that I wanted to work for him.

"That was almost forty years ago, and oh, what an adventure it's been. Back then, the Desert Palm was little more than a bar with a small restaurant that had a reputation for good food. The casino was a couple of slot machines and a single blackjack table in the lobby. Look around you, ladies and gentlemen." Frazier stretched out his arms. "See what Walter Parker's built with hard work. Then, of course, there's the Walter Parker Foundation. Millions have been given to charity through the generosity of that organization. I'm proud to have been on his team all these years." Frazier turned to Parker, who was standing near the lectern, and held up a glass of champagne. With a tear in his eye and a shaky voice, he said, "I salute you, Mr. Parker. Happy birthday, and may you have many more years of success and joy."

The people in the room applauded and many chanted his name.

Parker approached the lectern, hooked his cane on its side, and stood there, feeling the love and adoration wash over him. He raised his hands and lowered them in a half-hearted attempt to quiet the exuberant crowd. The chanting grew louder.

Parker smiled. "Please, my friends. Please." He gestured

for quiet again, this time more emphatically. "Thank you. Thank you very much." The applause continued unabated.

"Enough," Parker barked. "I have a few thoughts I'd like to express." The tone of his voice quieted the room immediately.

Parker said with a quaking voice, "Thank you, my dear friends. You'll never know what this means to me. Listening to Eric Frazier a minute ago brought back so many memories. Good ones, although there were some tough times as well. This place wasn't an instant success. As many of you know, there was a long period when my beloved Marian and I slept on cots in the back room behind the bar. Not an ideal situation for a young couple." Laughter sprinkled throughout the ballroom.

"Eric was right—we worked hard, very hard. But Marian and I didn't do it alone. I see many people out there tonight who've toiled side by side with us all these years." He paused, taking in a deep lungful of air. "Wilma Jenkins, over by the hors de oeuvres table, was one of the first people I hired to work in my restaurant. In my opinion, she's right up there with the best damn waitresses who ever lived. You remember the early years, don't you, Wilma?"

Wilma beamed at Parker and nodded.

Parker smiled at her. "Boy, I had big dreams back then. Surveying this room full of people I consider family, I guess you can say I've fulfilled them. The Desert Palm and all the team members who work here are my pride and joy. For what you've done for me and Marian, I can't thank you enough. I guess that makes what I have to say a little bittersweet."

A profound hush fell over the ballroom. It became so quiet, you could almost feel the silence. The crowd waited, breathless, for Parker to continue.

"For as long as I've owned the Desert Palm, I've had a passion. For growing, getting better, offering our guests the best in service. Alas, my friends, I'm afraid my zeal isn't what it used to be. I'm getting up there now, as you all know. This isn't my thirty-fifth birthday; it's my eightieth. An eighty-year-old man deserves to slow up a little and enjoy life. I've earned that right."

Parker took a sip of water from a glass on the lectern. His voice trembling, he said, "So now, after much soul searching, I've made up my mind. Tonight, I'm announcing that I'll be retiring and selling the Desert Palm Resort to Conrad Hale and the Conquistador organization."

Gasps of shock echoed throughout the ballroom. Wilma Jenkins swooned, and the gentleman next to her had to keep her from falling to the floor. Sniffles and muffled cries danced across the room.

Parker raised his hands in a calming gesture. "Now, please. I promise you, this is the right thing for all of us. You deserve a dynamic leader with vision. A man who'll take the Desert Palm into the future. I believe Conrad Hale's the best person to move this resort forward. In my negotiations with him, I've made it clear your welfare's my utmost priority. He's assured me he intends to operate the Desert Palm just as I have. None of you needs to worry about your jobs."

Voices filled the room. "Please, no, Mr. Parker," a distraught woman shouted.

Parker shook his finger. "Don't make this any harder for me than it already is. I haven't lied to you before, and I'm not tonight. This will be good for everyone. I've worked all my life, and I deserve a little enjoyment in my twilight years. Does anyone disagree?"

The room became silent again. Randy started clapping, a loud and deliberate beat. More people in the room joined him, and soon there was a thunder of applause from around the ballroom. "We love you, Mr. Parker," a man called out as the ovation continued. "You ought to have the best."

Parker smiled, and his wife joined him at the lectern. He hugged her with palpable affection. Then they turned and waved to the room full of admirers.

CARTER CAMP'S FACE was gray. "I can't believe it," he said, looking at Angela. "I won't accept that my uncle would do this."

Angela took a sip of wine. "I'm surprised he didn't tell you that he intended to sell. Didn't he give you any indication he wanted to retire?"

Camp didn't answer, gnashing his teeth as he watched his aunt and uncle chatting with well-wishers.

Angela stroked her fingers through her hair. "Carter, did you hear me? Did your uncle ever mention he might sell the Desert Palm?"

Camp shook his head without looking at her. "No, never. I can't understand why he'd make this announcement without informing me first. What am I supposed to do now?"

"Your uncle said Mr. Hale wasn't making any drastic changes in management. If we all work hard, I'm sure our jobs are secure."

"Right," Camp said sarcastically, "you believe that?"

"I always try to see the positive side of everything."

"Naïve, if you ask me." Camp's tone was cold, and he was still staring at his uncle with a dark expression.

Angela glared at him. "I'm not naïve. I'm pragmatic. If we apply ourselves, we have a good chance of keeping our jobs. The Conquistador's one of the premier resorts in Las Vegas. If we play our cards right, who knows—there may be a lot of room for advancement."

"Not the kind I was hoping for. I wanted to run the Desert Palm at some point. That's not going to happen now. Not under Conrad Hale. No, I won't work for that man. He has to be stopped."

"It doesn't appear you have much choice."

"I've got to talk my uncle out of this insane idea."

"It's a little late for that. He's not going to change his mind now."

"If you'll excuse me, Angela, I need to make my opinion known to Uncle Walter. Somehow, I have to force him to reconsider." He stood and, with a determined air, made his way through the throng of people.

CAMP RUSHED BY Randy, almost knocking the drunken Cynthia to the ground. "Hey, waaatch it," she said, steadying her champagne glass and licking the spilled alcohol from her fingers.

Randy called after him, "I guess your plans to become a casino mogul have been dashed. Who'll take care of you now?"

"You son of a bitch," Camp snarled over his shoulder as he marched off through the ballroom.

Randy sighed. "I don't know why I'm being so glib. I doubt I'll be around much longer either."

"What are you talking about?" Wayne asked. "You'd be working for Hale one way or another." He downed a shot of whiskey.

"No, with Hale purchasing the Desert Palm, I'm irrelevant."

Wayne coughed. "You're crazy. He offered you a great job at the Conquistador because he knows you're one damn good casino host."

"He doesn't care about me as a host. He had his eyes on my guest list and has now bought it for, oh, I'd guess several hundred million dollars."

"That sleeeaze-bag," Cynthia said, trying to bring the room into focus. "Someone has to put him in... in his place. Somebody should tell...ooold man Parker that Hale's a... a jerk."

"It won't do any good, Cynthia," Randy said, propping her up when she listed to the left. "Money talks and Hale has a lot of it. Walter wants to enjoy his retirement. I don't blame him for taking the cash and having an enjoyable time in his golden years. Why endure unnecessary stress at his age?"

Cynthia pointed to Hale. "Looook at tha' bastard. He's sooo arrogaant. Th' truth about Conrad Hale musht be told."

Randy was now attempting to keep her from falling to her right. "Maybe so. Why don't you mind your own business and let others do that?"

CONRAD HALE STRODE up to the lectern and tapped three times on the microphone. "May I please have a minute of your evening?" he said, tapping twice more. Heads throughout the ballroom turned in his direction. It didn't take long for the people in the room to realize who he was, and the place quieted.

"Thank you," Hale said, gripping the top of the lectern. "For those of you who don't know me, I'd like to introduce myself. I am Conrad Hale, and it's a great honor for me to be here tonight."

A hum of excited murmurings reverberated through the ballroom.

"Let me begin by making my own toast to my good friend Walter Parker. Please join me." Pete Sawyer moved up next to him, holding two glasses of champagne. Hale took one, his eyes quickly scanning the room. "You know, I've had great success with the Conquistador Resort. Back when it was a little motel run by my father, I worked at the front desk, checking in the weekend tourists. During that time, I had great dreams for the future. Do you know who my inspiration was? Of course, it was Walter Parker.

"I'd heard the stories about how he'd taken a patch of land in this remote section of the highway to Los Angeles and developed it into one of the most successful resorts in Las Vegas. I wondered if we could do the same with our motel. After all, if

Walter could make the desert bloom, why couldn't I? I mirrored his path in many ways, and today, the Conquistador Casino Resort and Tower has few rivals in the world. Despite my success, I've always had a soft spot in my heart for the house that Walter Parker built: the Desert Palm. I must tell you, Walter agreeing to sell it to me was one of the proudest moments in my life. The Desert Palm Resort's a thriving monument to Walter, and I guarantee you, I'll do everything in my power to keep his dream alive. Now, please join me in toasting a great man." He raised his glass of champagne. "To Walter Parker, Mr. Philanthropy. Relish your retirement, my friend. You've earned it."

Hale smiled at Parker, lifted the glass of champagne to his mouth, and emptied it. "I want to say a couple more words before I get off the stage and let the party continue. I realize that many of you were startled by tonight's announcement. Let me pledge to you that you have nothing to fear—"

"Liar," Cynthia shouted, staggering onto the stage and stumbling up to Hale. "This man's nothin' but an igamo... egomaniacal liar. He doesn't caaare about the Desert Palmss or its... its employees. He can't wait to start up the bulldozers." She grabbed the lectern for balance and wailed loudly, "Conrad's one of the most eeevil men on the pplllanet."

"Cynthia," Hale snapped with a mixture of embarrassment and astonishment. He looked to Pete Sawyer in desperation, saying into the microphone, "Will someone get this woman out of here?"

Hushed voices rolled throughout the ballroom. Something scandalous was clearly happening and the gathering was witness to the excitement.

Cynthia slurred, "Oh, you... you'd love to have me thrown away, wouldn't you? Just like these nice people. Yooou don't care about aaanyone by yooourself."

165

Hale attempted to pull her from the lectern. "Get off the stage."

Cynthia broke free of him and latched onto the microphone. It screeched once, then she said, "I know Conrad's gonna tear down th' Desert Palm tree hotel. He told mmme so yestaday after we made love—sweeeet whoopsie. Ev'ry time we're together, he tells me his ambish...anbishions to take over th' Strip. Wait until my husbing-husband finds out. You aaall know him, right? Jooseph Nickkkosia." She hiccupped loudly. "Can you believe I... I was thinkin' about leavin' him for Conrad? Whatt-a mistake."

"Get her off the stage," Hale said to the three security guards rushing to the lectern. "She's crazy."

The security guards surrounded Cynthia and attempted to dislodge her grip on the microphone. Cynthia wouldn't let go. "You gotta stop Conrad. I know how wickeding he is. He's gonna demolish the Desert, the Deserts Palm and destroy all you guyses."

More guards ran to the lectern and attempted to remove Cynthia. She scratched one of the men on the chin when he yanked her hair. The audience in the ballroom took in the spectacle with mouths open. "You're hurtin' me," Cynthia screamed.

Randy tore across the stage, calling out Cynthia's name. "Let her go," he shouted, pushing one of the security guards off her. "I'll take care of her. Back off."

Mascara tinted tears ran down Cynthia's cheeks. "Heeelp me, Randy."

"Goddamn it, let go of her," Randy said with more emphasis. "I'll get her out of here. Leave her alone." Cynthia reached out for him, and Randy pulled her into his arms. "It's all right, Cynthia. It's okay." He peered at the guards. "I'll take her to her hotel." The men backed away and let Randy maneuver Cynthia away from the lectern. As he led her off the stage, they passed Conrad Hale.

"You little bitch," Hale said through clenched teeth. "How dare you humiliate me like this? You'll regret it, I can assure you that."

Before she could respond, Randy tugged on her arm, hurrying her away from Hale and out of the ballroom.

Hale was left alone on the stage in front of a room full of people staring at him with disdain. He paused for a second to compose his thoughts, then walked up to the microphone. "Ladies and gentleman, I apologize for that scene. It's obvious the woman's drunk out of her mind and doesn't know what she's saying. I want you to know I have the best of intentions for the Desert Palm Resort."

Silence filled the room, and the skepticism on the faces of the people didn't dissipate as Hale continued to speak.

THIRTEEN

RANDY ASSISTED THE sobbing Cynthia to the sofa in her suite and handed her a handkerchief.

Cynthia sniffled. "Oh, Randy, what am I going to do?" The realization of what she'd done seemed to be sobering her up rather quickly.

He was irritated. "Did you have to mention in front of a thousand people that you slept with Hale? Joe's sure to find out by the end of the evening."

"I had to have revenge on Conrad. No man can treat me like that and expect to get away with it. The champagne cocktails gave me the courage. M still a little woozy."

"Well, it wasn't a smart thing to do. If Joe divorces you, which is likely, you won't see a penny in alimony. You admitted in front of a room full of people that you committed adultery. Joe's lawyers will make you pay for your infidelity. Let's not even mention the beating he'll inflict."

Cynthia's chest heaved, and she cried, tears pouring down her cheeks. "My... my life's ruined."

"You talked about divorcing Joe. There's no doubt it'll happen now; he'll help you pack."

"Oh, god. I gotta call my brother—see if I can stay at his

place. There's so much I have… I have to do." She gestured to the Van Gogh on the wall. "I have to take that down and get it out of the Conquistador." Cynthia stood and wiped her eyes. "I'm leaving Las Vegas tonight. M not waiting around for Joseph to return."

Randy nodded. "Yeah, I suppose that's wise."

"Would you call me a limo to the airport? I need to pack and get the painting ready, but if I stay focused, it won't take me long."

Randy checked his watch. "I'll meet you here at nine and go with you to the airport."

"Thanks, Randy. In return, I'll tell you something interesting about my ex-boyfriend."

"What's that?"

"Not now. On the way to the airport."

"Okay. I'll be back in a bit. Everything will work out fine."

"At some point, maybe, but first I have to get out of town with that painting before Joseph and my… my ex find out I'm gone."

WALTER PARKER GLARED across his desk at Conrad Hale. "Mr. Hale, you've embarrassed me in front of my wife and team members. I demand an explanation and an answer to Mrs. Nicosia's charges."

Hale waved his hand. "No one's more mortified about what's just happened than me. I apologize, but you surely realize the woman's crazy. She was so drunk, she couldn't stand up without staggering."

"Then you have no intention of tearing down the Desert Palm?"

"That's not currently in my plans."

"It's clear you told Mrs. Nicosia something different."

Hale's voice climbed higher than normal. "You're not

listening to that woman, are you? The whackjob should be committed to an asylum. She's clearly insane."

"She said you slept with her."

"Another lie." Hale dropped his eyes.

"You deny it?"

Hale stared at his lap. "Absolutely. The woman was drunk and delusional." He looked up at Parker. "Walter, I'll admit I've been trying to woo the Nicosias to the Conquistador and have wined and dined Cynthia, Mrs. Nicosia, in the process. But it was a business relationship. You can't begrudge me the right to lure new customers to my casino. I'm confident you too have attempted to attract a big player to the Desert Palm by schmoozing his wife."

"I draw the line at sleeping with them."

"So do I."

"Then explain Mrs. Nicosia's actions this evening."

"I can't. It was the alcohol. She must've misconstrued my kindness."

"Regardless of where the truth lies, Mr. Hale, her words have done considerable damage. In front of my staff, she said you were demolishing the Desert Palm. The fear in my team members' eyes was unmistakable."

"I'll be able to reassure them."

"I'm not sure I believe it. I stood in front of that room and promised them I was making a decision that wouldn't affect their income. I gave my word my retirement and the sale of the Desert Palm would be a benefit for everybody. Now I'm not certain I was right."

"Don't be ridiculous. Of course it's the correct decision. You deserve to enjoy your golden years. Work more with your foundation. The sale of the casino will be the best thing for everyone."

"This incident's disturbed me deeply, and I must think about my plans to sell with more care."

Hale tugged his earlobe. "You can't be serious. We have a deal."

"The papers have yet to be signed."

"You're going back on your word?"

"Circumstances have changed."

"That's ridiculous. Nothing's different. I'm willing to spend hundreds of millions—a substantial price, all things considered—to purchase the Desert Palm. What's changed?"

"The shock and sadness on my team members' faces moved me. I'm not positive selling to you is the right thing to do."

"You want more money? That's it, isn't it? You're using this incident as a way to squeeze additional cash out of me."

"No, Conrad, money has nothing to do with this." Parker leaned back and frowned at Hale with cold contemptuous eyes. "I need to reflect on this some more. I'm waiting until tomorrow before I make my decision. I'm going to speak with Mrs. Nicosia when she's sober and coherent."

"Why talk with her?"

"I have to hear what she has to say about tonight's outburst. I want her to explain when she's clear-headed that you didn't tell her you were razing the Desert Palm."

"You'll get no facts from Cynthia Nicosia. She's a liar. Plain and simple."

"Perhaps. I'd still like to speak with her. After that, I'll make up my mind. Until then, consider the negotiations for the sale of the Desert Palm on hold."

"Walter, let me remind you we have a deal."

"How could I forget? After I've spoken to Mrs. Nicosia, I'll give you a definite answer."

"You have no choice. Do I need to get Frank Titan involved again?"

Parker glared at him. "If you'll excuse me, there's a casino full of team members who need to be reassured their livelihoods aren't being destroyed." Parker pushed up from his chair and walked out of the room, his cane clattering with each step.

Hale sat there scowling darkly, a vein in his neck throbbing. "Damn it," he said between gritted teeth. "Damn you, Cynthia. Damn."

RANDY SHOVED A spoonful of ice cream in his mouth. He sat with Wayne and Jennifer in the twenty-four-hour coffee shop at the Desert Palm. "What a night."

"You'd think there was a goddamn full moon," Wayne said, sipping a beer.

Jennifer asked Randy, "Were you able to calm Mrs. Nicosia? She sure was upset."

He nodded. "She still is. She's leaving town before Joe can catch up to her. I'm taking her to the airport in about half an hour."

"Where's she going?" Wayne asked.

"Her brother's place. I believe it's in West Hollywood."

Jennifer said, "I wouldn't like a pissed off husband after me. One of the blackjack dealers told me he's connected with the mafia."

Randy swept his hair out of his eyes. "I'm kind of concerned about that. But she has a painting in her hotel suite that's worth a lot of money. If she can sell it, I'm hoping she'll have enough to disappear for a while."

"A painting?" Wayne said. "Who's the artist?"

"It's a Van Gogh."

"Damn. And she has it in her suite at the Conquistador?"

"Not for long."

Wayne glanced at his watch. "Jennifer, can I interest you in a couple more drinks? Maybe a little dancing? I'd like to see you swivel your ass."

"That sounds like fun," Jennifer said with a gleam in her eye.

"Cool. I promised a customer... guest that I'd stop by and visit. She's lost almost twenty grand, so I owe her the courtesy. It won't take long. I'll meet up with you at the Zanzibar Lounge."

She beamed. "Okay, hot stuff."

Randy said, "I have a bet to place—football—and I need to check my messages in the host office; then I'll head over to the Conquistador to usher Cynthia out of Dodge. One of the pit supervisors told me Joe's upstairs with some woman he picked up. I hope he's having fun and stays with her for a long time. I don't want him going to the Conquistador until Cynthia's long gone."

CAMP WALKED ANGELA to the door of her townhouse and stood there with a grim expression. She was sure that they both felt disconcerted.

"I regret that our first date was ruined," he said.

Angela smiled weakly. "Oh, it was fine. I'm sorry Mr. Parker gave you such a shock."

"It'll turn out fine. I'm certain my uncle will call off the sale of the Desert Palm. He'll want to investigate Mrs. Nicosia's allegations before proceeding. That'll give me time to talk him out of it."

"It seems like he's ready to retire. Even if the transaction with Hale doesn't go through, he'll sell to someone sooner or later."

Camp shook his fist. "I can't let that happen. Somehow, I have to convince him to keep the property. I'll soon be ready to step into his position, and then he can retire."

"After tonight, I hope he doesn't sell to Conrad Hale. I believed Mrs. Nicosia when she said he was planning to bulldoze the Desert Palm."

Camp nodded. "I did too. I'm sure my uncle does as well. I'm going over to the Conquistador tonight to have a conversation with Mrs. Nicosia. I must speak with her when she's not hysterical. If she's telling the truth, then the sale of the Desert Palm's absolutely off."

"Could be. Thank you for inviting me to your uncle's party."

"I wish it'd been less eventful. I was looking forward to spending some time with you."

Angela smiled again but didn't reply.

"Angela, would you like to have coffee with me the day after tomorrow? The lattes at Frenchman's Bistro are excellent."

Feeling a little sorry for him, she figured she could be polite and one afternoon of coffee and conversation couldn't hurt. "That would be nice."

Camp was almost glowing. Obviously, her acceptance of another date had changed his mood. "Great. I'll pick you up at three-thirty."

"Very well." Angela unlocked her door. "I have to be up early tomorrow, so I better get to bed. Thank you again." She swung open the door and stepped into her townhouse.

Camp's eyes showed a hint of disappointment that he wasn't receiving a goodnight kiss. "Take care."

"Have a nice night." Angela closed the door.

Camp stood there for a minute, contemplating the night. It'd been one of emotional highs and lows. He now had two tasks he needed to accomplish. One was meeting with Cynthia Nicosia and stopping the sale of the Desert Palm. The second was convincing Angela to be his girlfriend.

HARLAN SAMPLES KNOCKED on the door of a Desert Palm hotel suite. The door to room 734 opened a crack, and Violet eyed him warily. "Yes?" she said, holding a blanket around her body.

"Is Mr. Nicosia here?" Samples asked in his typical brusque manner. "I need to talk with him."

Violet turned into the suite. "It's your friend, Harlan. He wants to speak with you."

Samples heard his boss's voice, and a moment later, Nicosia stood in the doorway, wearing a pair of boxer shorts and nothing more. His hair was standing straight out in a style reminiscent of Bozo the Clown. "What do you want, Samples? Can't you see I'm busy?"

"I must have a word with you, sir. It's serious. I didn't mean to interrupt, but there's something you have to know."

Nicosia set his jaw and held open the door, motioning for Samples to enter. Samples trudged into the hotel suite, and it was clear from the look on his face that he was uncomfortable. Beads of sweat were forming along his upper lip.

Violet was sitting on the sofa, adjusting the blanket above her chest.

"What's the problem?" Nicosia asked.

Samples gestured to Violet. "I don't believe she should hear this. It's a private matter."

Nicosia glanced over at Violet. "Hey, babe, we need a few minutes. Why don't you go in the other room and powder your nose or something? I promise it won't take long."

"Okay, Brownie. Maybe I'll use the Jacuzzi. When you're finished with him, you can join me." She gave him a wicked smile.

Nicosia leered at her. "I'll be there in a jiffy."

Violet rose from the couch and moved into the bedroom.

After the door closed, Nicosia turned to Samples. "This better be damn good. Do you see what you're interrupting?"

Samples nodded. "Yes sir, and I apologize. I just... it's just...this is important, and I knew you needed to know."

"About what?"

"It's Mrs. Nicosia."

"Yeah?"

"Well, um, she's with someone."

"So? Stop being so evasive and get to the goddamn point."

"I went to your suite to pick up your Cubans. When I entered the outer room, I heard voices in the bedroom. I heard Mrs. Nicosia and Randy Kennedy."

Nicosia's nostrils widened. "You're sure?"

"Yes, sir. There's no mistake."

"You're positive it was Kennedy?"

"Mr. Nicosia, I heard them both as clear as can be. I know what was happening. I've had suspicions for a while."

"Damn it. I trusted them."

"What are you going to do?"

Nicosia's eyes blazed. "What do you think?" He picked up his clothes from the floor, quickly pulled them on, and blew towards the door.

THE ELEVATOR AT the Conquistador Resort clanged to a halt on the fifth floor, and Randy entered the corridor. He looked at his watch; he was running late. The concierge desk was unmanned. He walked down the empty hall to the Nicosias' suite. One of the double doors was ajar. He slipped through the opening. "Cynthia? I have a limo waiting."

He crossed the foyer and went into the suite. The living room was dark, but he saw a light coming from under the doors to the bedroom. He fumbled his way across the room, tripping on something while edging through the space, opened one of the bedroom doors, and peered in. He looked at the bed and scanned the empty room. "Cynthia," he said, louder than before. "Where are you?"

Randy walked past the bed and into the bathroom. Not finding her there, he returned to the living room of the suite. In the light emanating from the bedroom, he saw that something was wrong. He felt his way to the coffee table and inched to the lamp near the wall, groped for the switch, and flipped on the light. Chairs were tipped over, a broken vase on the floor. The Van Gogh was no longer hanging on the wall above the fireplace, an empty frame propped against the wall. Panicked, he gazed around the room. He gasped when he saw her, realizing what he'd tripped on when he first came into the suite was the body of Cynthia Nicosia. He glanced down and saw there were streaks of blood on the tip of his shoe.

Creeping up to the woman lying on the white carpet, Randy felt as if he were moving in slow motion. Cynthia was on her back. Randy saw that blood had oozed from the top of her head. Her cheeks were battered and bruised. The gold necklace he'd admired earlier was missing. He leaned over and picked up her right hand, feeling her lifeless palm. He let go, and it fell in a pool of blood, tiny droplets spraying onto his white shirt. He crouched farther, trying to find a pulse in her bloody neck. Nothing. "My god," he said, trying to make sense of the scene before him, his mouth open.

With a loud bang, the double doors to the suite crashed open, and Joseph Nicosia and Harlan Samples burst into the room. It was a tossup as to who was more surprised. Still crouched over Cynthia's body, Randy eyed the two men in disbelief. He said in a shaky voice, "She's dead, Joe."

Nicosia charged up to Cynthia and stared at the body. "What did you do to her?"

"I didn't do anything. I just got here myself and found her this way. Somebody killed her."

Nicosia's face was crimson. "You murdered my wife."

Randy stood. "Don't be ridiculous. Why would I want to kill Cynthia?"

"You were squatting next to her. You've got blood on your hand and shirt."

Randy looked down and saw the blood on his hand,

splattered over his shirt, and on the cuff of his shirtsleeve. His heart sank at the realization of how it must appear. He wiped his bloody fingers on his shirt. "Don't be crazy. I was checking to see if Cynthia was alive. I was feeling for a pulse when you and Samples came in. I wouldn't kill your wife. I liked Cynthia; you know that."

Nicosia said in slow vengeful voice, "You liked her, slept with her, and killed her."

The hair on the back of Randy's neck stood upright, and he felt a chill. "Joe, that's not true. You know me better than that."

"I thought I did, but that was before I found out you were banging my wife."

Randy tried not to let his expression give him away, not sure if he was succeeding. "I'm not sleeping with Cynthia."

"I heard you with her earlier this evening," Samples said accusingly. "I listened to you in there, on the bed with Mrs. Nicosia."

Randy licked his dry lips. "You're making the wrong assumption, Harlan. I was with her, but it was nothing sexual."

Samples' expression was as black as his tone. "I know what I heard, and it was you and Mrs. Nicosia. I'm not wrong, and there's no good explanation for you being in bed with her."

Randy's eyes darted over to Nicosia, who was glaring at him with fire in his eyes. He clasped his hands pleadingly. "Please, I didn't murder Cynthia."

Nicosia pointed at him. "You also said you never slept with my wife. You lied about that, and you're lying about killing her."

"Oh god, she was upset. Nothing happened tonight. You're letting your imagination run away with you. I didn't kill her. Please listen to me."

"You're a fool."

Randy was paralyzed with fear, his mind blank, grasping for the right words.

"You murdered my wife, and I'm going to make you pay."

"Damn, Joe, don't say that. We've always been good friends. You know I wouldn't take her life."

"Samples." Nicosia tilted his head at Randy. Samples surged over and clenched beefy fingers on Randy's shoulder.

Randy struggled to shake off Samples' hand. "Let go of me, you oaf. I didn't kill Cynthia, and I'm not going to let you take me out for something I didn't do."

Samples grabbed Randy by the collar. "We'll see about that."

Randy doubled up his fist and swung at the bodyguard. Samples was quick and ducked, Randy's fist swishing past his face. The power of the missed punch flung Randy to the floor. Samples roared, barreling at him with fury in his eyes. Randy saw a heavy bookend on the floor next to Cynthia's body and grabbed it as Samples came toward him. He scrambled to his feet and swung the bookend at Samples' head. The bookend hit Samples' jaw, and the man grunted with the force of the impact and fell to his knees.

Randy tossed the bookend when Nicosia rushed at him and bolted for the open doors, running down the hallway, Nicosia's shouts ringing in his ears. He pushed the fire door open and bounded down the stairs, skipping steps and hopping over railings as fast as he could. Popping out of the fire exit five floors later, panting heavily, he sprinted away from the Conquistador to his car at the Desert Palm. Once in the vehicle, he sped out of the parking lot, wheels screeching. In the thick Las Vegas traffic, it took him almost thirty minutes to reach his condo.

As he thought about his circumstances, sweat trickled down his temples. What was he going to do? He had to call the police. *Wait*, he thought, trying to assess his situation. He suddenly had a vivid memory of the bookend he'd used to hold off Harlan Samples. There was blood on it before he hit the man. Blood and blond hair. Had he touched the murder weapon? He shook his head. If there was ever a solid murder suspect, he was it.

Randy drove his BMW around the corner of the condo complex and saw a cop car idling in front of his unit. He slowed but didn't pull into his parking space. There were two policemen walking up to his door.

Adrenaline pumped through Randy's body. He shifted his car into gear and raced out of the complex. He cruised to an intersection, first looking left, then right, chewing on his lower lip. He didn't know what to do, where he should go. Crazy as he knew it was, he decided it would be best if he sought refuge at Angela Grisham's townhouse.

LIEUTENANT ANDRE SCHULTZ walked into the hotel suite and up to the body of Cynthia Nicosia. The flash of a forensic photographer's camera lit the room. Schultz studied the woman, then approached a uniformed policeman. "Hi, Alex," he said. "Who do we have here?"

Sergeant Avery took a notepad from his jacket pocket and flipped it open. "The lady's name's Cynthia Nicosia. Her husband's Joseph Nicosia, a high-roller."

Schultz's droopy eyes looked questioningly at him. "From Beverly Hills?"

Avery glanced at his notepad and nodded. "Yes, do you know the guy?"

"I've heard of him. Rumor has it he has some sort of mob connections in Southern California."

"No kidding?" The sergeant's voice was clipped.

"What's the story with Mrs. Nicosia?"

"The husband claims she was killed by a Desert Palm casino host. A man named Randy Kennedy. Nicosia says he entered the suite and found Kennedy crouching over the body. Says he confronted him, and the guy took off."

"What's the cause of death?"

"A bash to the head. She's got a lot of abrasions on her wrists and face. There was quite a struggle. As you can see, there's a great deal of blood." He gestured to an object on the floor. "That bookend there's the probable murder weapon. Forensics will be processing the fingerprints soon."

"And the blood trail going to the bedroom?"

"Kennedy must've stepped in her blood sometime after the struggle."

"Any sign of this suspect?"

"A black and white's on its way to his home, and we've sent out an APB."

"Where's Mr. Nicosia?"

Avery pointed his chin to the right. "In the bedroom. He's an asshole."

"Okay. Make sure your people are careful around the footprints."

"I will, Lieutenant."

Schultz marched into the bedroom, where he found Nicosia shoving a handful of shirts in a suitcase. "Excuse me, Mr. Nicosia," Schultz said. "I'm Lieutenant Schultz with Las Vegas Metro. I'm sorry about your loss."

"I bet you are," Nicosia said derisively.

Schultz's frown dug deep ruts in his forehead. "That's uncalled for. I'm sorry your wife has passed."

"She didn't pass. She was murdered." Nicosia stuffed more clothing in the suitcase.

"This is a crime scene, sir. You can't take anything from this suite."

"I'm checking out and going to the Desert Palm."

"That's fine, but nothing's leaving this hotel room. Is that clear?"

Nicosia slammed the suitcase shut.

The lieutenant reached in his jacket and retrieved a notepad. "I'd like to ask some questions, if you don't mind."

"I've already answered more than enough. I know who killed my wife, and I'd appreciate it if you'd catch the bastard and leave me alone."

"Why do you believe this Randy Kennedy murdered your wife?"

"I saw him squatting over her, blood on his hands and clothing."

"But you didn't see him actually kill your wife."

"I didn't have to. He had blood all over him. My wife's dead. It doesn't take a brain surgeon to know what happened."

Schultz jotted down a few notes with a pen. "What relationship did this Desert Palm casino host have with you?"

"We usually stay there. Kennedy's been my personal host for years."

"And your wife knew him well?"

Loathing bloomed on Nicosia's face. "I found out tonight that he slept with her. I should've known better. He considers himself quite a ladies' man and has poked half the women in Vegas."

"Did your wife ever complain about him?"

"No, Lieutenant, but none of that matters. He killed Cynthia. Now stop wasting my time and go after him."

"I'm sure we'll have him in custody soon."

Nicosia looked at the lieutenant with hard dark eyes. "Better be, for his sake."

"What do you mean by that?"

"I have my own associates out searching for the murderous Mr. Kennedy."

"This is a police matter, and you're implicating yourself in a potential murder."

Nicosia gave him a quick irreverent smile. "It's not just a police matter when it involves me."

ANGELA DESCENDED THE stairs of her townhouse and walked over to Randy, handing him a long-sleeved gray Polo shirt. "This is my brother's. You're about the same size, so it should fit. Take it and go. I don't want you here."

"Please, Angela. I didn't kill Cynthia. I've got nowhere to go." Randy rapidly unbuttoned the bloody dress shirt and tossed it in the corner of the room—the very thought of Cynthia's blood on it made his skin crawl. He pulled on the Polo shirt.

Angela walked over to the blood-splattered shirt and leaned over to pick it up—but stopped herself. She looked at it with fright and disgust. "Randy, you have to call the police."

He shivered, rubbing his arms. "And take the fall for a murder I didn't commit? I can't do that."

"Well, you can't hide out forever. Sooner or later, you have to talk with the authorities."

"Right now, I'm sure I'm the number one suspect in Cynthia's murder. I'm almost positive I handled the murder weapon. At least, what I guess killed her. It was a bookend, and it had blood all around the base." Randy put his hands over his face. "With my fingerprints on the murder weapon and Nicosia's accusations, I'm as good as on death row." He stared at her through his fingers and slid his hands down his chest with a harsh sigh.

"If you're innocent, they won't convict you."

Randy took a shallow breath. "The jails are full of people who aren't guilty."

"Do you have a lawyer?"

"No...I don't know." Randy hesitated for a second, his mind racing. "I suppose Anthony Chapman might agree to be my attorney."

Angela gestured to the telephone on the wall. "Call him."

"I will. I just need to think through what's going on."

"What do you believed happened?"

"I'm not certain. I suppose it could've been a robbery gone wrong. A priceless Van Gogh was missing, leaving only the frame, as was the necklace she was wearing earlier. Then again, it could've been Conrad Hale. I heard Walter Parker was calling off the sale of the Desert Palm after Cynthia's blow-up. You saw how she embarrassed Hale. He threatened her as I was escorting her off the stage."

Angela shook her head. "Hale wouldn't murder a woman after she'd just made a fool of him in front of a thousand people. No way. He's smarter than that. He'd never kill her immediately after she made such a spectacle."

"Yeah. I suppose you're right, but his threat was serious."

"What about Nicosia? Maybe he killed his wife. After all, she cheated on him with Hale."

"If he did it, he's an excellent actor. You should've seen his face when he came into the suite and saw she was dead. Pure shock."

"Both Hale and Nicosia have motives, that's for sure."

Randy raised a finger. "There's another possibility. I know Cynthia was having some problems with an ex-boyfriend. She said she was hiding the Van Gogh from him; he may have killed her for it."

"Great. Three people with strong motives and no way to prove anything. Randy, it's impossible for you to investigate

Mrs. Nicosia's death while you're a suspect. Turn yourself in and let the police find out who killed her."

He raised his voice. "Until they do, I'll be behind bars."

"I've been told Anthony Chapman's a good lawyer."

"He'll have to be." Randy gazed at her intently. "You do think I'm innocent, don't you?"

She stared at him, then nodded. "Yes, I do, but you're in a lot of trouble. I don't want you here."

There was desperation in his eyes. "I didn't kill Cynthia. You said you believed me. You're going to have to have faith I'm doing the right thing. I need your help getting to the bottom of this."

Angela was unsettled, unsure what to do. "I shouldn't." She shook her head. "Against my better judgment, I'll let you stay here for a little while. But tomorrow morning, I insist you call your lawyer. Agreed?"

Relieved, Randy shot her a grateful look. "Thank you. My god, thank you."

FOURTEEN

THE FOLLOWING MORNING, Randy was surfing the news on Angela's iPad. A headline screamed at him: *Casino Host Wanted in Connection with Murder.* He tapped on it and saw his picture plastered below the masthead. He couldn't bear to read the copy. "Did you see this?" He turned the tablet toward Angela.

She walked across her kitchen and poured coffee in her cup. "Yes, I did. You have to turn yourself in. It's the best thing to do."

"You know I can't do that. With Nicosia's testimony and my fingerprints on the murder weapon, the police have no incentive to search for the real killer. I'm sure that as far as they're concerned, this is an open-and-shut case."

Angela stared at him, plainly agreeing but disturbed. "Then what are you going to do?"

"I have to think. Right now, it's all so confusing. Getting around Las Vegas will be almost impossible. I'm going to call Wayne Cork and ask him to give me a hand."

Angela shot him a sideways glance. "The new casino host?"

"Yeah. He seems like a decent enough guy, and I know he'll help me out."

"Can you trust him? You haven't known him long. He's kind of sarcastic, drinks like a fish, and well, I guess I'd say he's a bit strange."

"Maybe a little."

"You must have other friends you can trust."

"Not really. I've never had many male friends who weren't customers. A few ex-girlfriends."

She frowned at him.

"I have to take a risk and call Wayne. There's no other way I can find out what's going on. I need people like you and Wayne to help me determine what happened."

"Before I do anything, I want you to call your attorney."

"I will."

Angela picked up the phone and held it out to him. "Now."

NICOSIA AND SAMPLES were in a cocktail lounge at the Desert Palm Resort. Nicosia was nursing a whiskey and staring out across the casino.

"We can't find Kennedy," Samples said. "We've been looking all night."

Nicosia puffed on a cigar. "He's staying with one of his girlfriends, I'm sure."

Samples massaged his bruised and aching jaw. "You're right, but that could be any one of a hundred women."

"Get some help. Call Los Angeles and have them send up some of the boys."

"How many?"

"Phone Straub. He'll know what to do. He can help me with my other problem; Conrad Hale."

Angry, Samples thrust a thumb to his chest. "I don't need that crazy bastard's help."

"This is his specialty."

Samples glared at his boss.

"We have to hurry, though. I don't want the cops getting to Kennedy before we do." Nicosia narrowed his eyes. "That man killed my wife, and I want some revenge."

"You'll get it, sir."

Nicosia gave Samples a look that made him swallow nervously. "Retribution is mine. Find Kennedy."

RANDY HELD THE phone away from his ear as Anthony Chapman shouted, "Goddamn it, Randy, get your ass to the police station."

Randy brought the receiver back to his ear. "I'm not doing that, Anthony. You can refuse to help me, but that won't change my mind. You know I'm a man of my word, and I'm telling you I didn't kill Cynthia Nicosia."

More calmly, Chapman said, "I believe you. But you're just making matters worse by not turning yourself in. It seems like the police have a strong case against you. The longer you're on the run, the more they'll believe you're guilty."

Randy wiped his brow with his shirtsleeve. "I'll tell you what, head over to the police station and talk with them. Find out what's going on and see what they think happened."

Chapman raised his voice once more. "The newspapers printed what they believe went down. Every TV station's covered it as well."

"If you think the cops have an open mind about my situation, I might, and I mean might, consider surrendering myself."

There was silence for a moment as Chapman thought. He then said, "Where can I reach you?"

"I better keep that a secret for now. It could put you in a compromising position with the police. I wouldn't want you to have to lie to protect me. I'll keep in touch."

"This is wrong, Randy. As your attorney, I'm telling you to turn yourself in."

"I just can't. Will you help me or not?"

"You're not giving me much of a choice. I'll do what I can."

"Thank you. You won't regret it, I assure you."

"I already do. Okay, I'll drive down to Metro and see what they say. I'll have my mobile phone with me. Call me later today."

"I'm going to owe you my life."

"Right now, my friend, I'm not sure it's worth owning."

WALTER PARKER GLOWERED suspiciously at Hale. "Conrad, what do you know about Cynthia Nicosia's death?"

Hale was sitting in front of Parker's desk, his legs crossed, an expensive Stefano Ricci shoe waving in the air. "Same as you, I suppose—what I've read in the morning paper. I have to tell you, though, I'm not surprised Kennedy killed her. He was a firecracker waiting to explode."

"I have a difficult time believing he could murder anyone. There must be another explanation."

"The news says the case against him is strong."

"And the motive?"

"A horn dog like Kennedy? A love triangle or something like that."

"Perhaps, and excuse me for being so direct, but some might say you had a motive for killing her."

"Because of her unfortunate outburst at your birthday party?"

Parker nodded.

"My dear Walter, I have an unshakable alibi."

"What might that be?"

Hale pointed. "You."

Parker was surprised, his eyebrows pulling together. "Me?"

"While Cynthia Nicosia was meeting her premature demise, I was with you. She was killed at eight-thirty, when we were right here, discussing the sale of the Desert Palm."

Parker steepled his fingers. "I apologize for being doubtful, but I needed to know for certain. You knew I intended to speak with Mrs. Nicosia about her accusations against you. Her death's made that impossible. I had to know you didn't take the ultimate step to keep her quiet."

Hale's cheeks had just a touch of red in them. "I'm offended. Have you that little trust in me?"

"If what she said last night at my birthday party's true, I have no reason to accept your word."

"As I told you yesterday, she was lying."

"I'll never know now, will I?"

"That's water under the bridge. I came here this morning to complete my purchase of the Desert Palm. It's a fair price."

"It should be higher, and you know it."

"We've covered this. Thanks to Frank Titan, the price is settled. As a businessman, I'll do what I have to do to increase the value for my stockholders. I'm purchasing the Desert Palm Resort on the terms we agreed to earlier. Now, why don't you start thinking about that cabin you have in Montana?"

Parker rubbed his arms. "It's too cold up there."

"With the millions I'm paying you for the Desert Palm, you'll be able to buy a nice island in the balmy Bahamas."

"It's clear I have no choice in the matter."

"Stop resisting it and enjoy."

ANTHONY CHAPMAN SHIFTED his weight in the uncomfortable metal chair in Lieutenant Schultz's office. "Lieutenant, my client's not guilty of Cynthia Nicosia's murder."

The detective leaned back in his chair and put his hands behind his head. "The evidence says otherwise. His prints are all over the murder weapon."

"There's a good explanation for that."

"I bet there is," Schultz said, his voice dripping with sarcasm. "What, he was rearranging the furniture?"

"Very funny. Randy told me the bookend was on the floor next to Mrs. Nicosia's body. When rushed by Nicosia's bodyguard, he grabbed it to protect himself."

"Get real, Chapman. What do you take me for, a fool? There's no question Kennedy's the killer. His fingerprints are on the murder weapon, and more smudged prints were found on the decease's body."

"Of course they were on the woman—he was checking for a pulse. Did you find any other prints on the murder weapon?"

"None."

"The murderer must've wiped them clean or was wearing gloves."

"Nicosia says Kennedy killed his wife."

"You believe that mobster?"

"I see no reason why he'd lie."

"Now it's you who should get real. A known gangster's wife is found dead in mysterious circumstances—immediately after telling an entire room full of people that she slept around on him, no less—and you're taking his word that he's innocent."

"Joseph Nicosia's never been convicted of a crime."

Chapman peered at the lieutenant in disbelief.

"If your client's not guilty, why's he on the run?"

"He knows how bad it looks. He's scared. I've been trying to talk him into giving himself up, but he knows the evidence points to him."

"He's right; it does. Where's your client now?"

"I don't know; he won't tell me. I've only spoken with him on the phone."

"Oh, come on, you're hiding him. How would you like it if I hauled your butt to the State Bar and we discussed your part in aiding a fugitive with them?"

Chapman pounded his fist on the desk. "Goddamn it, I'm not hiding him. I don't know where Randy is."

"If you know what's good for both you and your client, you better convince him to give himself up."

"I'm trying, but he's stubborn."

"That obstinacy's going to result in him getting the death penalty."

Chapman studied Schultz's face. "He didn't kill Cynthia Nicosia. You have my guarantee that I'll do all I can to persuade him to turn himself in to the police."

"Here's my promise." The lieutenant stood, pulling up his baggy pants. "If Kennedy doesn't surrender himself by tomorrow morning, any thoughts I may have had about listening to his side of the story will be gone."

"I know." Chapman shook his head. "Damn."

ANGELA KNOCKED ON the door of Joseph Nicosia's suite at the Desert Palm and waited nervously. She glanced down and saw that her hands were shaking. She'd spoken with Nicosia before, at the cashier's cage, but that was different. Now, she was planning to question the man about his wife's killing, interrogating a rumored member of organized crime. She shuddered at the notion. *I must be out of my mind,* she thought. Why had she let Randy seek refuge in her townhouse? Unfortunately, she knew the answer; she had real feelings for him. For that reason, she had to know the truth about Cynthia Nicosia's murder and would do whatever it took to find out.

The door opened, but Harlan Samples' girth blocked her view of the inside of the suite. He eyed her suspiciously. "Yes?"

Angela cleared her throat. "May I speak with Mr. Nicosia?"

"Who are you?"

Her breathing was heavy. "A-Angela Grisham. I, I, I work in the main cashier's cage."

"What do you want?"

During the drive to the hotel, she'd rehearsed what she was

planning to say. "I've come to give my condolences to Mr. Nicosia and discuss the status of his markers. With the grief I'm sure he must be enduring, I'm assuming he doesn't have the time or inclination to worry about these details. The management of the casino asked me to inform him he can take as long as necessary to pay on his account."

"Fine, I'll let him know." Samples started to close the door.

Angela slid a shoe in front of it and stopped him. "I'd like to tell him in person."

"I'll relay the message."

She knew she had to expand her lie. "Mr. Parker requested that I deliver the message in person and ensure this hotel's taking care of all Mr. Nicosia's needs. Please ask him if I may have a minute of his time." She compressed her lips, hoping her expression made it clear she wasn't taking no for an answer.

Samples fiddled with his ring and stared at her. After a second or two, he said, "Okay. Wait here. I'll see if he's available."

Angela smiled weakly as he turned into the suite and closed the door. She rubbed her hands together, her palms feeling cold. She dreaded speaking with Nicosia, unsure what she was going to say, and the urge to forget all this and flee was over-whelming. Remembering the bleakness in Randy's eyes was the single thing forcing her to continue.

A short wait later, Samples returned and motioned for her to enter the suite. She followed the hulk of a man through the living room and into the bedroom. Nicosia was wallowing in a large hot tub in one corner of the room, one meaty hand holding a cigar and the other a Bloody Mary. Angela was thankful he was wearing a swimsuit. When their eyes met, she felt an unexpected chill.

"Don't just stand there," Nicosia said, switching off the

gurgling jets. "Take a load off." He gestured with his cigar to the chair next to the hot tub.

"Yes, sir." She walked across the room and sat down.

He took a pull on his cigar. "What's this about my markers?"

Angela again cleared her throat. "First, I'd like to offer my condolences for the loss of your wife. It was a terrible tragedy. I've met her, and she was a sweet woman."

"I appreciate that. Now what about my markers?"

"This trip, you've run up a total of one-hundred and fifty thousand dollars. Considering the situation, I'd imagine worrying about this debt's a low priority. We understand that and want you to know you're welcome to take as long as you need to repay."

He sipped his drink and puffed some more on the cigar. "That won't be necessary. I'll be settling my account when I check out in a couple of hours. The Desert Palm employed my cherished wife's murderer. For that reason, I doubt I'll ever be returning. I intend to close my account and forget this place. My business manager in Beverly Hills is wiring me the necessary funds."

"Mr. Nicosia, please don't fault the Desert Palm for your misfortune. I know this was a tragic event, but we value your patronage and hope you'll visit us in the future as a satisfied guest."

"What? Satisfied one of your employees murdered my wife? No way."

"I'm sure Randy Kennedy had no involvement in your wife's death."

"Young lady, there's no question at all. The man's a liar and a killer."

She shook her head. "I don't believe it."

"Think what you want, but I saw him crouched over my dead wife with blood all over his hand and shirt."

Angela considered this for a moment but decided to plow forward, no matter how uncertain she was. "Forgiving me for being so bold, but there are those in the casino who say you murdered your wife."

Nicosia gaped at her, flabbergasted. "You're being more than bold. Accusing me of killing my wife? Don't be absurd."

"I'm not accusing you of anything, but your wife made quite a spectacle of herself last night. I was there. She admitted to an affair with Conrad Hale, a motive if I ever heard one. Do you have an alibi?"

Nicosia barked out a short laugh and waved his hand. "I don't require one, honey. I didn't murder Cynthia."

"So you have an alibi?"

"If I need one, which I don't. Kennedy, that son of a bitch, was sleeping with my wife and murdered her to keep her quiet about their affair."

Angela gave him a hard stare. "He denies any involvement in her death." She regretted the words the minute they left her mouth.

"You've spoken with him?"

Her heart raced. "Oh, oh no, I heard through friends who've talked with him. He insists he didn't do it."

"What friends?"

She pressed her hand to her chest. "Um. Casino folks. You know, hotel gossip. It may not even be true."

Nicosia focused on her with sudden mistrust. "Who sent you here? Why would the management of the Desert Palm send a casino cashier to my suite to discuss my outstanding markers?"

Angela brushed wayward strands of hair from her forehead. "I'm employed in the Credit Department. I wanted to ease your mind about your debt."

"Why dispatch you?"

"I've told you, I'm a cashier who works in credit."

"Where's the credit manager, Simone Fletcher? Forget that, why isn't Wally Parker here?"

"It's apparent you think I'm not the appropriate person to act as an ambassador for the casino on this matter." She stood on feeble legs. "I'm sorry for intruding. I'll tell the upper management you wish to speak with them. I apologize if I've upset you."

"I have every right to be unhappy. This casino values my welfare and business so little that they send a clerk rather than an executive to do their bidding. One who accuses me of killing my wife."

Trembling, Angela brushed back her hair again. "I didn't mean that. I told you about idle speculation on the casino floor, which clearly shouldn't be a concern to you if you have an alibi."

"A good one too. Not like your friend Kennedy. Let me tell you something, sweetheart. If you do know how to contact Mr. Kennedy, give him this message…"

His tone was menacing, and she was petrified, feeling cold.

Nicosia pantomimed a cut throat with his finger. "…he's dead."

Her hands shook even more.

"Now, get the hell out of here. I'm tired of this conversation, and I'm sick of you."

Speechless, Angela turned, her knees wobbly, and exited the room.

RANDY PACED THE floor of Angela's townhouse, the helpless feeling becoming unbearable. He was trapped with nothing to do but worry. Hoping for something to take his mind off the situation, he snatched the TV remote from the coffee table and flicked on the television. He realized that was a mistake the second the images appeared on the screen.

The six o'clock news on Channel Three was just beginning, and his picture flashed across the small flatscreen. The anchorwoman said, "Authorities are still searching for Desert Palm casino host Randy Kennedy in connection with the murder of Cynthia Nicosia, a guest at the Conquistador Casino Resort. Joseph Nicosia, the deceased's husband, confronted Kennedy soon after the homicide. Mr. Nicosia claims Kennedy fled the hotel suite after assaulting his bodyguard."

"Assault," Randy said. "The man was going to kill me." He shook his head. "I can't stay here doing nothing while my goddamn life goes down the drain." He switched off the TV. "I'm finding some answers."

RANDY CREPT UP the stairwell of the Aztec temple inside the Conquistador Resort, fueled by adrenaline, making it to the eighth-floor landing. He stopped to catch his breath before pulling open the stairwell door and entering the executive office lobby. It was a little after seven at night, and the area was deserted. A ray of light was streaming from beneath the doors to Conrad Hale's office. Randy crossed the room and placed an ear against one door. He heard Hale's booming voice. It sounded like he was on the telephone.

Randy grasped the doorknob, pushed the door open a crack, and peeked into the room. He could see the back of Hale's chair across the desk. Through the windows, Randy saw the flashing colored lights of the evening laser show. He slunk into the office and to a far corner and waited with heightened anxiety as Hale continued to talk. Randy held his breath, his heart thundering.

Hale concluded his call and swiveled the chair around to hang up. He put the receiver in place and sorted through papers on his desk.

"We need to talk," Randy said.

Startled, Hale glanced at him, then the phone.

Randy focused intently on him. "Don't call anyone. I only have a few questions."

Hale pointed at him. "You're a wanted man."

"Tell me something I don't already know. And for a crime I didn't commit."

Hale started to stand up.

"Sit down." Randy charged toward the desk, his gaze fierce. His muscular physique and dominating presence were an advantage over the much smaller Hale.

Hale put his hands up. "All right." He sat back down.

"What happened to Cynthia Nicosia?"

One corner of Hale's mouth twisted up. "I assume you killed her."

"Funny, Hale. Try this scenario on for size. Cynthia embarrassed you and caused the sale of the Desert Palm to be canceled. In a mad rage, you went to her suite and beat her to death."

"That's ludicrous."

"Is it? She ruined your business deal and also made public your affair. I'd say that's a sound enough reason to commit murder."

"Again, that's preposterous."

"What about the Van Gogh? It's missing. Do you have it?"

Hale picked up a pen and tapped it on the desk. "I didn't know it was gone."

"You didn't report its disappearance to the police?"

"I told you, I had no knowledge it wasn't there. I didn't go to the Nicosias' suite. I heard the crime scene was a bloody mess, and that's the last thing I wanted to see."

Randy scratched his head, unsure whether to believe him.

Hale examined his manicured fingernails. "Not that I care to spend ten seconds with you discussing my innocence, but I have a solid alibi. During the time of her murder, I was in Walter

Parker's office, discussing a man named Frank Titan—forget that—I was pleading with him to reconsider his decision not to sell the Desert Palm." Hale sneered. "I have an unassailable alibi—your wonderful Wally Parker."

Randy considered Hale with a steady eye. "That's everything I needed to know."

"What did you expect to prove by coming here?"

A clattering sound came from the lobby. It spooked Randy, who quickly glanced at the doors. He turned back to Hale. "I had questions I needed answered. You've done that. Good evening, Mr. Hale."

Randy spun toward the door and ran out of the office. Rounding the corner in the lobby, he tripped on something, and tumbled to the floor. He was glancing back to see what tripped him when another noise sent him scrambling to his feet and sprinting to the door to the stairs. Like he had the day before, he descended the stairwell as fast as possible, skipping steps and bounding over the railings.

Back at the top of the temple, Hale seized the phone and dialed. "Pennington, this is Conrad Hale. Call the police. Randy Kennedy's in the executive offices. Yes, that Randy Kennedy. Hurry." He hung up, then rotated his chair to face the wall of glass and watched as the blazing lights from the laser show bounced around the casino below.

A gloved man moved into the office, pulled a putter from the golf bag that was leaning against the rear wall, and tiptoed up behind Hale. He swung the putter back and brought it down across Hale's skull three times. The man returned the putter to the golf bag and shuffled out of the office as the dead body of Conrad Hale slumped forward.

FIFTEEN

BACK AT HER townhouse, Angela folded her arms, an angry scowl on her face. "Tell me why you slept with Cynthia Nicosia. As if I don't already know."

Randy lowered his head. "Does it matter?"

"Yes, damn it. You've asked me to trust you, but you haven't given me the whole story."

"I told you the truth—I didn't kill Cynthia."

Her already intense voice notched up. Seething she snapped, "I've gone out on a long limb for you. After my visit to Nicosia, I'll probably lose my job. I'm running around like some amateur detective, yet all I find are half-truths. You ask me to believe you, to take you into my home and hide you from the police, yet you don't trust me enough to tell me the truth. I want you to leave this instant." Her cheeks were scarlet as she pointed to the front door.

"I'm sorry." Randy laced his fingers together. "I didn't sleep with Cynthia last night, like Nicosia thinks. It's all a misunderstanding. She was upset after her outburst at Walter Parker's party. I tried to console her, but that's the extent of it. Not a bit of that matters, though. I didn't kill her."

"Based on the circumstances, I'll be the one who decides what's important. I'm taking a huge risk having you here."

"Why *are* you taking the risk? Why didn't you call the cops?"

"I, I, I don't know." She averted her eyes and turned from him. "I believe you're innocent. I don't like the thought of you going to jail for a crime you didn't commit."

He walked up to her and placed his hand on her shoulder. "Look at me."

Angela shook her head.

Randy stepped around and lifted her chin with his finger, gazing deep into her eyes.

She pushed him away. "Don't. Please. I'm confused enough as it is."

"Thank you. You'll never know what it means to have you on my side."

"I shouldn't be doing this." She assessed his grateful expression. "Damn. Damn." She shook her head again. "For now, I'll do what I can, but you have to promise to tell me everything."

Randy gave her a grateful look, well aware how lucky he was she was helping him. "Thank you."

She stared at him. "Changing the subject, I wonder if Carter Camp spoke with Mrs. Nicosia last night. He told me he was going to confront her about her outburst at Mr. Parker's party."

"Maybe their conversation turned violent. Perhaps he should be another murder suspect."

"That seems unlikely."

"Camp was pretty upset about the Desert Palm being sold. What if he lost it?"

Angela narrowed her eyes. "There's no motive for him killing her no matter how angry he was."

"Yeah, I suppose you're right. Tell me about your meeting with Joe. What did he have to say?"

Angela wrapped her arms around herself and shuddered. "What a creepy man. He says he has an alibi if he needs one but that he doesn't."

Randy's eyes probed hers. "He looked so shocked when he saw that Cynthia was dead. He must be telling the truth."

"I'm not sure. He seemed confident enough, but we shouldn't rule him out as a suspect. Randy, he's dangerous. He wants you dead."

"I know he does."

"This is serious. Your life's in real danger. You'd be much safer if you surrendered to the police."

"I can't do that. Going to the cops will only save my life until the lethal injection. I have to find out who killed Cynthia. It's my only hope."

"I don't see how you can find out what happened."

"We're making progress. Joe has an alibi, dubious as it might be, and so does Conrad Hale."

Angela's lashes fluttered. "Hale? How do you know that?"

"I confronted him earlier this evening. I took the bus to the Conquistador. Hale claims he was meeting with Walter Parker when Cynthia was murdered."

"So where does that leave us?"

"If Nicosia and Hale are in the clear, it must be her ex-boyfriend. He's connected to the missing Van Gogh, and I'm sure it has something to do with her murder. I'll wager whoever has it killed her."

"Maybe." There was a knock at the door, and Angela flinched. Having Randy there put her on edge. She looked with trepidation at the front door. Another knock followed, this one louder. Angela approached the door hesitantly and peeked through the peephole. "It's Wayne."

"It's okay. I called him. He's trying to help."

WAYNE SWEPT INTO the townhouse holding a bottle of Coors and took a seat on the sofa. Randy and Angela sat next to him and enlightened him on their visits with Nicosia and Hale.

"Wayne," Randy said, slouching forward, "like I told you on the phone, Cynthia had an ex-boyfriend who was giving her a hard time. He threatened her on more than one occasion. He should be a suspect in her murder, right along with Nicosia and Hale. I have to track him down."

Wayne's eyes narrowed. "How the hell will you do that?" He took a deep slug of beer. "Do you know the ex's name or what he looks like?"

"No. I need to contact Cynthia's brother and see if he knows where to find the ex. The brother's name's Brett Miller. I tried finding him online but the name's too common—there are a hundred Brett Millers in Southern California. So my only other option is to hope her brother's at her funeral."

Wayne scratched his nose. "Like you asked, I called the mortuary. Mrs. Nicosia's funeral is tomorrow at two at the Forest Lawn Cemetery in the Hollywood hills."

"I have to go. It's my best chance to talk to her brother."

"You need to contact Anthony Chapman," Angela said. "See what he found out from the police."

Randy heaved himself off the couch and moved over to the phone, picking up the receiver and dialing. After the third ring, Chapman answered. "Anthony, it's Randy."

"Jesus, what've you done?"

"I told you, I didn't kill Cynthia."

"I'm not referring to her."

Randy frowned. "What are you talking about?"

"Why did you go to Conrad Hale's office?"

"To find out if he had an alibi for Cynthia's murder."

"Did you kill him?"

"What?" Randy demanded, his voice climbing. "Are you crazy?"

Angela walked over to his side, concern on her face.

Anthony said, loud enough for Angela to hear, "Conrad Hale's dead, and you're the number one suspect in his murder."

Reeling, Randy grabbed Angela's shoulder to brace himself. "My god, Anthony, that can't be true."

"Hale was found dead minutes after he called hotel security and told them you were in the executive offices."

"I was there. I spoke with him, but I didn't kill him."

"Well, someone did."

Angry, Randy raised his voice again. "Hale told me he was with Walter Parker at the time of Cynthia's murder, and then I left his office. I wasn't there five minutes."

"Was anyone else with you?"

"No, we were alone."

"What about outside?"

"No." Randy paused, his mind numb. "I, I don't know. I wasn't looking for anyone but Hale. After I spoke with him, I ran out of there as fast as I could. I knew he'd be calling security."

"Hale was bludgeoned in his chair; his back was to the assailant."

Randy shook his fist. "Nicosia. It had to be one of Nicosia's boys. Joe wanted him dead for his tryst with Cynthia."

"That's not what the police believe happened."

"There must be surveillance video of the area. It'll show who was in Hale's office."

"As I understand it, Hale was a privacy fanatic. There are surveillance cameras all around the Conquistador but not in his Aztec temple lair."

"Dammit."

"With Hale found dead minutes after he called security about your visit, what else are the authorities going to think?"

"But I didn't kill him or Cynthia. You have to believe me."

"My opinion doesn't matter. You couldn't be in bigger trouble, my friend."

Randy clenched his jaw, frustrated. "I know that. God, what should I do?"

"For starters, turn yourself in before anyone else ends up dead and you're the suspect."

"Cute. I'm not doing that. With Hale dead, my situation's worse than ever."

"You have that correct, pal. If you don't go to the police this minute, you can find yourself another attorney."

"Fine, if that's the way you feel."

"I do."

"All right then, it's been nice knowing you." Randy slammed down the phone. He closed his eyes, trying to clear his mind.

Angela put her hand on his shoulder. "Are you okay?"

He didn't answer.

She patted him on the back. "What's going on?"

Randy opened his eyes and turned to her. "It's not good. As you probably heard, Conrad Hale was murdered. They believe I killed him."

Angela's mouth hung open.

"Jesus," Wayne said, taking a long pull of the Coors.

Randy bent over and put his hands on his knees. "Joe had him offed. I'm sure of it. I knew he'd seek revenge for Hale sleeping with his wife."

Angela said, "I'm positive you're next on his hit list."

Randy stood up and ran his finger over his lower lip. "I understand that."

"Turn yourself in."

"I don't trust them to see I'm innocent. As long as I'm wanted by both the police and Nicosia, I'm safer here."

Wayne said, "I take it Chapman isn't too happy with that decision."

"Yeah, it's unfortunate, but he's now my ex-lawyer. He gave me no other choice."

"So, what's next?" Angela asked.

"It's a waste of time to search for Hale's killer. I suspect it was a mob hit, Nicosia's revenge. We need to find out who killed Cynthia. If it's not Nicosia or Hale, then it must be the ex-boyfriend."

"You know, Randy," Wayne said, "I've been thinking about that. You're being too generous, letting Nicosia off the hook; he had ample reason to murder his wife. She cheated on him, and I bet he's humiliated."

"He claims to have an alibi," Angela said.

"What about other scenarios? Cyndi could have been killed by one of Nicosia's enemies. I'd guess he'd have plenty of those."

"Yes, that's possible, I suppose," Randy said.

"It sounds like we're going to be running around in goddamn circles."

"Keeping me from death row should be worth it."

Wayne's and Angela's eyes drifted to each other, and they didn't speak.

ANGELA AND RANDY were dozing on the sofa after hours of dead-end speculation. Wayne had left earlier, excited about another date with Jennifer Crichton.

A car door slamming woke Randy, and he sat up, straining to hear. He sprang off the couch, careful to stay away from the living room window, ran into the kitchen, and peeked through the blinds. In the parking area, he saw two men in black suits standing next to a dark-blue Mercedes Benz.

Randy's heart quickened. He dropped to his knees and crawled back over to the sofa. "Angela," he whispered and nudged her, holding a finger to his lips. "Someone's outside. I'm pretty sure it's Nicosia's guys."

The color drained from her face. "What do we do?"

"I'm not certain. Is there another way out of your townhouse? A side exit?"

"Just into the garage. And there's a balcony upstairs."

The muscles in the pit of Randy's stomach tightened. "Okay, stay here. Don't answer the door if they ring. I want to take a look around." He headed for the stairs and hiked up, then dashed into Angela's bedroom and to the sliding glass door. He opened it and eased onto the balcony.

It was a moonless night, and he peered over the railing to the pool area below, which glistened turquoise in the bright underwater lights. He saw Harlan Samples conversing with a man who could've been his clone—big, tall, and dressed in black. The two men strolled away from the pool and along the side of the townhouse. Randy slipped back into the bedroom and almost jumped out of his skin when he bumped into Angela. "I thought I told you to stay downstairs," he said.

She glared at him. "I have a mind of my own. I do what I believe is right, not what you tell me to."

Irritated, he pursed his lips. "Nicosia's goons are everywhere."

"How'd they know you were here?"

"I don't know. When you visited with Joe this afternoon, he must've thought we might be together."

"Short of calling the police, any ideas how we get out of this situation?"

"Let's lie low. They don't know for sure I'm here." He hesitated. "I hope. Maybe they'll go away."

There was a pounding on the front door, loud and so vehement it shook the townhouse.

Sarcastically, Angela asked, "Any other bright ideas?"

The hammering on the front door switched to a sound like something very large and very angry colliding with it. The sound of breaking wood echoed up the stairwell. "One. I assume you can swim."

Randy and Angela heard the thunder of footsteps crashing through the first floor of the townhouse. They ran to the balcony, climbed the railing, and jumped as far out as they could into the pool below. They surfaced with ragged gasps, then swam to the side closest to the townhouse and held onto the edge, staying in the shadow of the pool wall and hoping not to be seen.

Randy popped up and gazed at the balcony. He saw Harlan Samples walk through the sliding glass door and ducked back down. Samples glanced over the railing, but he didn't appear to spot them. Randy inched up again and watched Samples re-enter Angela's home. "Follow me," he said, and they pulled themselves out of the pool as quietly as possible, their clothes clinging to their bodies. Their shoes made a squishing sound while they jogged through the maze of buildings in the townhouse complex and to a street.

WAYNE DROVE HIS Ford truck along Interstate 15 toward Los Angeles. "How wanted do you think you are?" he asked. Angela and Randy, still wet from their quick dip in the pool, were sitting next to him. They'd called him from a payphone, asking for a ride.

"What do you mean?" Randy asked.

Wayne pointed to the highway in front of them. "Do you suppose the police have set up a roadblock?"

Randy thought about that. "They have no reason to believe I'd leave Las Vegas."

Wayne and Angela stared straight ahead in silence, looking unconvinced. An awkward minute later, Wayne said, "You're a suspected murderer on the loose."

Randy didn't respond, not sure what to say.

"Where are we going?" Angela asked.

Randy turned to her, the stress visible on his face. "If you both don't mind, Cynthia Nicosia's funeral."

Wayne said, "Fortunately, I'm off work for the next two days."

NICOSIA WALKED PAST the bar in the den of his opulent Beverly Hills mansion. "I saw on the late news that Conrad Hale was taken out."

Robert Straub's eyes were a chilling black. Behind his back, never to his face, he was referred to as Crazy Eyes. There was insanity in them. He was a small, dark-haired man in his mid-fifties. Despite his size, he was as dangerous as an agitated cobra—a professional assassin. "This Kennedy's a vicious man. Two murders in as many days."

Nicosia handed Straub a glass of whiskey. "He did me a favor by killing Hale, but I still have a job for you. I want you to eliminate Kennedy."

Straub sipped his drink. "I thought your boys were on his trail."

"They were. Against my better judgment, I let Samples convince me he could handle it. I was informed where we could find Kennedy; he was staying with a woman named Angela Grisham. However, I was just told a half-hour ago that Samples botched the whole goddamned thing and he got away."

Straub swirled the liquor around in his glass and took another sip.

"I need you to give a little leadership to my guys."

Straub finished off the whiskey in one swift movement. "I'd prefer to work with my own people."

"The more men we have looking for Kennedy, the better. Your boys alone can't cover a city the size of Las Vegas. Plus, for all I know, he's left town and could be half-way to New York by now."

Straub smiled as the warmth of the alcohol spread through his stomach. "I'll talk with your guys, but let me decide the best way to approach this."

"You've earned that right."

"I'll meet with your men and locate Kennedy, but I won't

be able to make the hit for a couple of days. I'll be in Mexico; I have a previous commitment with the Quinones family."

"I understand. I can wait a short while. Give my best to Jose."

"I'll do that. Now let's talk money."

SIXTEEN

A LONG LINE of limousines cruised the narrow streets of the cemetery. It was an overcast day, and the weather fit the occasion. The hearse leading the motorcade turned on-to a side road and parked next to an open grave. Two tall men dressed in black hopped out of the hearse, walked around the vehicle, and opened the back door. They pulled the coffin out, placed it on a metal cart, and pushed it to the side of the hole in the ground. They lifted the coffin over the grave and positioned it on vinyl straps. One man arranged flowers around the site; then they both proceeded back to the hearse and waited for the mourners to congregate.

A crowd of Joseph Nicosia's associates and business partners soon surrounded the coffin. The group consisted primarily of husky men who hoped to one day take Nicosia's place as the head of the West Coast crime syndicate. There was also a scattering of relatives and friends.

Randy, Angela, and Wayne watched the mourners from a nearby knoll, far enough away to feel safe from observation. As a further precaution, Randy had dyed his hair platinum blond.

Frustrated, Randy said, "I wish we could get closer."

"Are you crazy?" Wayne asked. "Coming here wasn't a good idea."

Randy frowned. "Jesus, will you lighten up? You've been uptight all goddamn day. What's wrong with you?"

"I don't like cemeteries or funerals with lots of gangsters."

Randy pushed his lips together, annoyed. "We can't do anything from here. We have to see if Cynthia's brother's down there."

"Let me find out," Angela said. "I can ask a few of the mourners if they know him." Now that she'd committed to assisting Randy, she shoved away any thoughts of the police and the certainty that what she was doing was wrong. She was going to do what it took to prove his innocence.

Randy's eyes met hers. "I don't know, Angela. Joe may see you, and it could be dangerous."

Angela lifted her hands. "Like you said, we can't do anything from here. One of us has to go to Mrs. Nicosia's service, and it can't be you. The pissed-off look on Wayne's face makes me think he's not up for it either."

"She's right," Wayne said, staring at his shoes. "I don't want to go there."

"I'll stay in the back and be as inconspicuous as I can."

Randy put his hand on her shoulder. "Please be careful."

Angela gave him a jerky nod, circled around a large headstone, and picked her way down the hillside toward Cynthia's funeral. She approached the mourners with care, made her way to the back, and stood there with her head bowed, trying not to draw any attention to herself. That would be difficult, as she wasn't dressed for a funeral. She was also wearing oversized sunglasses that covered her face, which she'd purchased when they stopped at a drugstore to get Randy's hair dye. Hopefully, if Nicosia spotted her, he wouldn't recognize her.

The ceremony was just beginning, and Angela fixed her attention on the priest.

"She was a vibrant woman, full of life," the cleric said with a nasal twang. "The Lord took her home much too soon, but it consoles our hearts to know she's now at peace."

Muffled sniffles emanated from several of the people in attendance as the preacher droned on. Nicosia stood stone-faced as his wife was eulogized. His knuckles were white as he clenched his fists ever tighter. When the priest was done, at his urging, Nicosia strode over to the burial site and placed a single pink rose on the coffin. For a fleeting instant, his eyes showed grief, and just as rapidly, they became hard and cold again. He moved away from the grave and set out for his limousine, his closest associates, led by Harlan Samples, trailing behind.

Angela leaned forward when Nicosia passed, then scrutinized the remaining mourners. She glanced at the middle-aged woman next to her and offered her a feeble smile. "Such a shame," she said.

"Yes. She was much too young to die."

"Did you know her well?"

"I'm her husband's first cousin."

"I'm sorry for your loss."

The woman folded the handkerchief she was holding. "She was his third wife, and I'd hoped he was in a relationship that would last. This is a tragedy."

"Did she have a large family?"

"Other than Joe, just a brother, as far as I know."

"Is he here? I'd like to give him my condolences."

The woman surveyed the remaining people gathered around the gravesite. "Yes, that's him against the tree." She pointed. "You can see how much pain he's in. I can't stand seeing someone that distraught."

Angela saw the man wipe his tear-filled eyes. The grief was contagious, and she looked away. "I feel sorry for him."

"We all do. If you'll excuse me." The woman dabbed a tear from her cheek and rambled toward the road.

Angela watched her for a minute, then turned toward the gravesite. She said a quick prayer as the mortuary attendants lowered the coffin into the hole in the ground.

ANGELA CLIMBED BACK up the knoll and skirted her way around a large marble crypt. "Over here," Randy said. Wayne waved to her from behind a tall granite headstone.

Angela zigzagged past a cluster of grave markers and joined them.

"What did you find out?" Randy asked anxiously.

Angela gestured to the solitary man still leaning against a maple tree and staring at Cynthia's grave. "That's her brother."

Randy rubbed his hands together. "Let's go talk with him."

Wayne said, "You two go and speak with Mrs. Nicosia's brother. I'll go get the truck."

"All right," Randy said, and he and Angela marched down the hillside while Wayne trudged back to his Ford.

Cynthia's brother took a final drag on his cigarette and threw it to the ground as Randy and Angela walked up to him. Thin, in his late twenties with thick light-brown hair that hung to his shoulders, he had a skimpy goatee in its first days of development. He was attractive in a skinny, Calvin Klein model sort of way.

"Hello," Angela said with a compassionate smile.

The man pushed hair out of his bloodshot eyes but said nothing.

"Are you Cynthia Nicosia's brother?" Randy asked. "Brett Miller?"

An irritated glower fell over the man's face. "Yeah, and I'm not good company right now."

"It's tragic," Angela said. "You have our sympathies."

Again, Miller didn't say anything, his eyes reflecting anger.

"We were friends of hers," Randy said. "I can't believe she's gone."

"She didn't have to die," Miller said. "It wouldn't have happened if she hadn't married that asshole Nicosia."

"We should introduce ourselves," Angela said. "I'm Angela Grisham, and this is Randy...Randy King." She figured the L.A. media were covering Mrs. Nicosia's murder and Randy's last name could be well-known. She'd decided against his earlier suggestion of Herman Dorchester.

"Are you going to the reception?" Randy asked.

Miller took a pack of Marlboro Silvers from his pocket. He pulled a cigarette out, stuck it in his mouth, and lit it up. "I don't want to be anywhere near Nicosia. That event's for him, not my sister."

"We understand," Angela said.

Miller wiped away a tear that was forming in the corner of his eye.

Randy and Angela could clearly see he was embarrassed by his show of emotion.

Miller fought for composure, biting his lower lip. "Do you know how much it rips me up that she's dead? I didn't have the chance to say goodbye and tell her that I loved her."

"It must be terrible for you," Angela said.

Randy said, "Brett, I knew Cynthia pretty well, and she told me she loved you very much. She explained what a rotten childhood you two had and how she wouldn't have made it if it weren't for you."

Miller appeared comforted by those words, and his voice turned hopeful when he asked, "She said that?"

"Yes, and I know she intended to get in contact with you to reconcile."

"I hadn't heard from her in a while."

"She said you disapproved of the men in her life."

Miller nodded. "That's an understatement."

"What do you know about her murder?"

"Just what I've been told by the police. Some casino guy in Las Vegas. I'm certain that one way or the other, Nicosia was involved."

"We're not so sure of that," Angela said.

Miller took a drag from the cigarette. "Why do you say that?"

Randy said, "We think it's possible her death may have had something to do with an ex-boyfriend—the guy she lived with before she married Nicosia."

Miller's eyes narrowed. "Kevin Delfino? I thought she was rid of him."

"He was still lurking in the background. She complained to me that he was stalking her. He wanted a painting she had—a Van Gogh. We believe it may have had something to do with her death. What can you tell us about him?"

Miller inhaled a final puff from his cigarette and tossed it to the ground. "I'm surprised he wasn't at the funeral. He was obsessive about my sister. None too pleased when she married Nicosia."

"Do you know anything about this painting?"

"Delfino could have something to do with Cyndi's murder?"

"It's a distinct possibility."

"Listen, I need a drink. Why don't you meet me at the Blue Lamp Pub on Sunset Boulevard in half an hour? I'll tell you all about Kevin Delfino and how he screwed up my sister's life."

"WHAT DID HE have to say?" Wayne asked when Angela and Randy climbed into the truck.

"He doesn't like Nicosia," Randy said. "Says Cynthia's ex-boyfriend was obsessed with her."

Angela said, "Brett's meeting us at a pub and telling us what he knows about him."

"Which one?" Wayne asked.

"It's called the Blue Lamp. It's on Sunset. Do you know where it is?"

Wayne raised his shoulders. "I suppose I can find it. Do you guys mind if I just drop you off? I'm taking advantage of being in L.A. to get my furniture out of storage. It may take me a while. My crap's spread out in three separate storage units from Marina Del Rey to Irvine. I also want to visit my uncle's place in Santa Monica. He's giving me a leather sofa."

"Not a problem," Randy said. "How do we hook back up?"

"I'll let you off at the Blue Lamp, rent a U-Tote trailer, and pick up as much of my furniture as I can. I'll meet you back at the bar in a couple hours."

Randy stared at him, the weight of his plight heavier by the minute. "All right. Thanks again, both of you. I appreciate what you're doing; you'll never know how much."

Wayne crossed his arms. "I hate to say this, and I'm sorry, but I don't like being in this position. This whole goddamn thing makes me nervous."

Angela nodded, wondering how she'd ever let herself get into this situation.

RANDY, ANGELA, AND Brett Miller were tucked into a dark booth in the back of the Blue Lamp Pub. The establishment was decorated in a Bohemian style, with an eccentric arrangement of art and sculpture. Famished after a day on the run, Angela and Randy gobbled hamburgers and french fries. Brett said he was content with an imported beer.

"I like this place," Angela said. "The painting over there would look great in my living room." She pointed to a Jackson Pollock-style contemporary canvas.

"It's one of my favorites," Brett said.

"Brett's the artist, am I correct?" Randy asked.

A sheepish smile flitted over Brett's face. "How'd you know?"

"Cynthia told me you were a painter. She mentioned you showcased your art in a bar."

"My god, you're gifted," Angela said. "What I wouldn't give to be able to paint. What a wonderful way to make a living."

"I wish it paid a little better," Brett said.

"But still, wow."

Brett pulled out a pack of cigarettes. "Don't get me wrong. I suppose I make a decent living. I'm not the quintessential starving artist, but I'm not rolling in dough. I supplement my income by doing odd jobs. Do you mind if I smoke?"

Randy asked, "Isn't it illegal to do that in a restaurant in California?"

"The owner of this place doesn't think much of the law. Neither do most of his customers." Brett lit up a cigarette and breathed in, enjoying the nicotine rush. "Ah, I need this to calm my nerves. The last few days have been pretty rough."

"I know what you mean."

Brett exhaled a stream of smoke. "How's that?"

"Cynthia's death. It's been a shock for all of us."

"You said at the cemetery you suspect Kevin Delfino."

Randy scratched his arm. "It comes down to Cynthia's missing Van Gogh. I know Delfino wanted the painting bad. He may have murdered her for it. I'm sure it was taken by the killer."

Angela said, "Brett, tell us what you can about Delfino. What do you know about this painting?"

Brett aimed his finger across the room. "That work over there—the one hanging above the cash register—I painted it three years ago. That's about the time Cyndi started going out with Delfino. What a loser. Alcoholic. Lazy. Sarcastic. I didn't like the dude and knew that five minutes after we met. I could tell he was a schemer, always searching for a way to get rich quick." Brett put the cigarette to his mouth and inhaled. He held the smoke in, then continued to speak as puffs shot out of his mouth. "When Kevin first met Cyndi, he was putting together some sort of internet scam. You know, the kind where unsuspecting people are convinced to send money or give out their credit card numbers."

Angela said, "A friend of mine was taken in by one of those cons."

"He didn't get it off the ground. He was having software problems and was afraid what he was doing could be traced by the cops. Anyway, when Cyndi told me what he was trying to do, I blew my stack. I was mean. I have a temper and a wicked tongue."

"Did she defend him?" Randy asked.

"She didn't, but you must understand how poor we were growing up and why money was like a drug she had to have."

"She told me that you were homeless as children."

"We were, and that made Cyndi want, more than anything, to have a life of wealth and comfort, and she did what it took to achieve that. It's why she was always attracted to men she felt would give her that lifestyle. Delfino promised her the moon, but I kept nagging at her, trying to make her feel guilty about the potential victims. That was when Delfino switched directions and came up with the art fraud."

Randy leaned forward. "Forged paintings?"

"When Cyndi met Delfino, she was employed at an art gallery in Beverly Hills. She loved being in a place that dealt with high-income clientele. Believe it or not, she became pretty knowledgeable about art."

Angela asked, "What kind of scam did they have going?"

Brett sipped his beer. "Randy's right—forgeries. They had a good artist, who'd paint replicas of various pieces of art. Cyndi would then switch the paintings at the gallery.

"What was Delfino's role in all this?"

Brett took another drag on his cigarette. "He peddled the originals. He collaborated with a guy who'd hawk the paintings on the black market. Cyndi would sell the forgeries at the gallery, and if needed, Kevin would act as a so-called art expert and appraise the works. They had it all figured out.

"The gallery had a wealthy customer who had terminal cancer. She owned a Van Gogh that she wanted sold after her death, with the money going to a charity. Delfino saw an opportunity to make the big bucks he'd always wanted. Of all the really valuable art out there, Van Gogh's paintings are the easiest to copy. The old woman didn't die for almost a year, so there was plenty of time to make a credible forgery. After her death, they made the switch at the gallery and sold the forgery to a local businessman."

"You mentioned they had a good artist," Randy said.

"Yeah, a guy named Gus Hadley. He's damn talented, and if he ever tried, he'd make a real name for himself."

"Where does Nicosia fit into this?" Angela asked.

"Nicosia came into the gallery all the time. Almost all the forged paintings Cyndi sold were to him. As you know, my sister was quite a beauty, and he was smitten. She took a fancy to him right away, always seeking a sugar daddy. I don't believe she loved him, but I know she loved his money."

"And that left Delfino in the cold?"

"Yep. She married Nicosia and quit working at the gallery. Kevin lost not only his girlfriend but what he'd hoped was an easy source of income."

Randy nodded. "Cynthia told me she took the original Van Gogh one night when Delfino was passed out."

Brett's face darkened, and he sucked more smoke from his cigarette. "I regret I didn't spend more time with her. No matter how much I disapproved of the men in her life, I loved her. For the rest of my life, I'll lament not being more understanding."

"Don't be too rough on yourself," Angela said. "No one can blame you for not wanting her to be involved in criminal activities."

"She told me she loved you very much," Randy said.

"That means a lot," Brett said. "It drives me crazy, though, when I consider how bad her life ended up as a result of getting involved with those two men. If one of them is her killer, I want nothing more than to avenge her murder. Maybe by doing so, I can make amends for my emotional abandonment."

Randy sipped his orange soda. "Do you have any idea where we can find Kevin Delfino?"

Brett stubbed out his cigarette in an ashtray. "No. I haven't seen him since Cyndi married Nicosia."

"What about Gus Hadley?" Angela asked. "Would he know?"

"Not positive, but he might be aware if someone's trying to fence the Van Gogh. He pays attention to that type of gossip. He has a studio in Long Beach, by the port."

"Will you take us there?" Randy asked, almost begging. "We need someone to introduce us. I'm certain he'd be much more forthcoming if we were with someone he knows."

Brett rubbed his temples, appearing exhausted. "I suppose I can do that. Even though Gus and I have had heated arguments about him painting fakes, we've always gotten along. I'll take you out there tomorrow morning."

"Thank you, Brett," Angela said. "With your help, we might be able to find your sister's killer."

Brett reached for another cigarette. "I'll do what I can."

CARTER CAMP ADJUSTED his tie and slipped out of the car. He smiled at the single red rose he was carrying. He ambled up the pathway to Angela's townhouse and stopped when he saw the damaged front door. He moved to the threshold and pushed open the battered door, creeping around the splintered doorjamb. "Angela, are you home?" he called out.

Camp wandered through the living room and kitchen, then ascended the staircase to the second floor. He entered Angela's bedroom and called her name one more time. There was silence. Long white curtains blew out of the open sliding glass door. He stepped out onto the balcony and glanced down to the pool below. Several sun worshipers were lounging around it, oblivious to the world around them.

Heading back into the townhouse, Camp rushed down the stairs to the living room. On the floor in the corner was a man's white dress shirt. He walked over and picked it up. Dried blood stained the cuff and breast pocket and tiny splatters dotted the fabric. He dropped it and fumbled for his iPhone. Frantic, he punched 9-1-1 and told the operator he needed the police.

LIEUTENANT SCHULTZ INSPECTED the shattered front entrance of Angela Grisham's townhouse. "What time did you arrive?" he asked Camp.

Camp tapped his finger on his wristwatch. "A few minutes before three-thirty. Angela and I had a coffee date."

"I wonder why no one reported this before you arrived. You say this has something to do with the Nicosia murder?"

"Come see this." Camp led the lieutenant across the living room and grabbed the dress shirt, holding it up. "Note the monogram—R.J.K. This is Randy Kennedy's shirt. There's blood splattered all over it."

Schultz gingerly took the garment from Camp and inspected it. "You're sure it's Kennedy's?"

"Yes, sir. He was wearing it at my uncle's birthday party. My uncle's Walter Parker, the owner of the Desert Palm Resort. I remember the monogram. Kennedy was wearing that shirt the night Cynthia Nicosia was murdered."

"What was his relationship with Ms. Grisham?"

"She's a cashier at the Desert Palm. Her connection with Randy was mostly work related. I know he'd had his eye on Angela and she'd spurned his advances. That's why I'm so concerned. He broke down the door to get inside her townhouse. She's missing. I shudder to think what he's done to her."

Schultz's eyes narrowed. "You believe Kennedy's abducted Ms. Grisham?"

Camp waved his arm. "She's not here."

The lieutenant tipped his head. "She may have gone of her own volition."

"Look at the front door, Lieutenant Schultz," Camp said, his voice raised. "We had a date at three-thirty. She wouldn't miss that without calling me. She's very conscientious."

"This doesn't make sense."

"The man's deranged."

"Excuse me, Lieutenant," a burley uniformed police officer said, lumbering into the living room.

Schultz turned to face the man. "Yes, Jameson, what is it?"

"A late model BMW registered to Randy Kennedy is parked in the garage."

Schultz looked to Camp. "What kind of car does Angela Grisham drive?"

"A Prius. It's parked in a space outside. I passed it when I arrived."

The lieutenant ran his finger over the bridge of his nose. "Both of their vehicles are here. Why do you suppose they left them?"

The police officer said, "I'm sure Kennedy knew we'd be searching for his car."

"Yes, but we weren't interested in the Grisham woman. Hers would go unnoticed."

The officer shrugged. "There must be a reasonable explanation."

"I'm certain there is. We need to find out what it is."

AFTER BRETT EXCUSED himself and left the Blue Lamp Pub, Angela sat back in the booth and sipped her soda. She yawned. Dark circles were forming under her obviously tired eyes.

"It's been a long day," Randy said. His eyes were also weary, and he rubbed them.

Angela looked at him with a worried expression. "Are you confident we're doing the right thing?"

"God, I hope so. I don't know what else to do."

"I feel like a criminal."

Randy touched her hand. "You don't have to do this. Say the word, and I'll get you back to Las Vegas." Angela was quiet, and he tried to decipher her expression.

She peered into his eyes. "I must be crazy, but no. I'm not going back there without you. You should surrender yourself to the police, but if you insist on tracking down Mrs. Nicosia's killer, I'm resigned to giving you a hand."

"I appreciate that; it means a great deal." His voice was soft and his eyes burned into hers.

She took a deep breath and turned away. "I'm out of my mind, but you're welcome. I truly believe you're innocent."

"Why? No one else does."

Angela continued to stare across the room, openly afraid of her emotions. "I just do. Can we leave it at that?"

"Why won't you let me inside that shell of yours?"

She turned to him. "I don't know what you're talking about."

"You try to pretend you don't have feelings for me."

Angela was silent.

Randy gripped her hand tighter. "Angela, I've told you I have feelings for you. I know I was drunk when I said it, but it's true." He paused, still uneasy about saying the words. "I'm falling in love with you."

She waved her hand. "Oh, don't be ridiculous. You know too little about me to be in love. That line may have worked on your vast number of girlfriends, but it won't on me. I'm not succumbing to the so-called Lucky One's spiel."

Randy bowed his head. "I'll admit I've had a few girlfriends. Okay, maybe more than my share, I suppose, but I swear to you, I haven't told a woman I loved her and...."

"And what?"

"And meant it."

Angela shook her hand loose from his grasp. "But you've said it. How, may I ask, is a woman supposed to know when you're telling her you love her to get her into bed and when you're saying it because you do?"

"I don't know how to respond. The same way you know whatever it is that makes you believe I didn't murder Cynthia Nicosia or Conrad Hale."

Seemingly stumped for an immediate reply, she said after a minute, "Randy, it may be true I feel an attraction to you, but the part of my brain that recognizes that fleeing from the authorities is wrong also tells me I cannot commit my heart."

"Give me time. I'm certain you'll realize I can be trusted."

"I hope so," she said softly.

"That's all I ask. Give me a chance. With time, you'll realize my feelings for you are sincere."

She gave him a weak smile, her hands trembling. "Let's take this one day at a time." She peeked at her watch. "Wayne won't be here for a while, and I need some fresh air. Do you mind if we take a walk? There's a park just up the street." She put her sunglasses on.

"That sounds perfect." He slid out of the booth and held his hand out to her. "I'd like nothing better than take a walk with you."

AFTER THEIR WALK in the park, Wayne picked Randy and Angela up at the pub and they checked into the Sleepy Hollow Motel, a block off Sunset Boulevard.

Angela assessed the motel room with a disgusted expression. "This sure isn't the Ritz."

Randy agreed, his eyes sweeping over the linoleum floor and cheap, weathered paneling. The two beds had stained and wrinkled covers. "It couldn't be a more complete opposite, but I can't use my credit cards and I want to conserve cash. I'm sorry we have to share a room."

Wayne said, "At lease, no one will have to share a bed. I didn't get to my uncle's place to pick up the sofa. I'm staying there tonight."

"Lucky you," Angela said. "No cockroaches to contend with."

"I'm not so sure about that. My uncle's a bachelor and not much of a housekeeper."

Randy looked at Angela and said, "I promise to be a perfect gentleman."

She eyed him carefully. "I expect so."

He smiled.

"I wish this room had a telephone. I left my cellphone in my townhouse. I have to call my parents; they're going to be worried."

Randy flopped down on a bed. "My phone was ruined when we jumped in the pool. I'd be afraid to use it anyway. I'm pretty sure the cops can locate you if it's turned on."

"I'm no help there," Wayne said. "I have a prepaid plan, and I used up all my minutes this afternoon. I saw a phone booth by the manager's office, though." He glanced around. "So, will this do? I gotta get to my uncle's."

"Yeah, it'll have to suffice," Angela said.

With a shrug, Wayne left them there, promising to be by first thing in the morning.

Angela pulled back the sheets on one of the beds to see if there were any unwanted creatures. "I'm so tired I could sleep on the floor." She brushed a foreign object off the rumpled bed sheets. "Ick."

"We could sure use a little shuteye," Randy said. "We have a lot to do tomorrow."

Angela nodded. "If you'll excuse me, I'm going to take a shower and hit the sack."

Randy got off the bed. "Have you been in the bathroom?" He stuck his head through the doorway and checked out the room, catching his reflection in the mirror and startled by how different he looked with blond hair.

She angled her head. "No, why?"

"From the looks of this place, I'd be careful about stepping into a warm, moist environment."

Angela screwed up her face even more. "Maybe you're right."

"Hopefully, this will be over soon and we won't have to stay here long."

Angela shook her finger at him. "If something crawls across my face in the middle of the night, it'll be over quicker than you think."

SEVENTEEN

ANTHONY CHAPMAN WAS back at Metro Police headquarters in Lieutenant Schultz's office. The air-conditioning didn't seem to be working, and a fan on the corner of the desk was doing its best to cool the room. It was failing, and both Chapman and Schultz were sweating.

"I get the impression, Lieutenant," Chapman said, "that you don't believe Angela Grisham was abducted by Randy."

Schultz frowned, and his expression hardened. "I didn't say that."

"Then what do you believe happened?" He pulled his handkerchief out of his jacket and wiped his face.

"It's clear something happened at her townhouse. The front door was smashed in, and she appears to be missing."

Chapman kept the handkerchief out, knowing he'd be using it again. "Yet you don't suspect Randy of being behind her disappearance?"

"I'm not saying that at all. It's just that some of the pieces of this puzzle don't quite fit."

"Such as?"

"Why was your client—"

Chapman interrupted. "Ex-client."

Schultz's brow furrowed. "You're not his lawyer?"

"No, he relieved me of that dubious honor when I insisted he turn himself in to the police."

"Then why are you here?"

"You may find this difficult to understand, but I don't think Randy killed Cynthia Nicosia."

"And Hale?"

"That was Nicosia retaliating after Hale's affair with his wife became public. It was a mob hit, and you know it."

"I know no such thing. Your client—excuse me, ex-client— was in Hale's office five minutes before the man was found dead."

"Why would Randy kill him?"

"He was probably in a jealous rage. He'd just found out that Hale slept with Mrs. Nicosia. He killed her first, then went after Hale."

"That's just guessing."

"So you say."

"What about Angela Grisham? How does she come into the picture?"

Schultz scratched his head. "That I don't understand. I can't explain her disappearance. All I know is that a shirt we presume to be covered with Cynthia Nicosia's blood was found in the living room of her townhouse. We're pretty sure the shirt's Kennedy's. It has his monogram on it. And his BMW was there, parked in the garage."

"Yeah, so he was hiding at Angela's townhouse. Think about it, Lieutenant; he was there, and someone found him."

"Who?"

"Nicosia."

"You have no proof of that."

"You can't believe that he's not after Randy."

Schultz whisked his hand through his thinning hair. "Nicosia did tell me he was looking for Kennedy."

"He intends to kill him."

"No, I made it clear he was to leave this matter up to the police."

"He's a criminal, for god's sake. He's not going to listen to you. He's sure Randy murdered his wife, and I bet he'll do just about anything to find him."

The lieutenant wiped sweat from his brow with his shirtsleeve and stared at Chapman.

"That means Randy's in grave danger," Chapman prompted.

"You haven't heard from him?"

"No, not since the other night."

"So you don't know where he is?"

Chapman dabbed his temples with the handkerchief. "No. I suspect he was hiding at Angela Grisham's home and is now on the run. What are you doing to find him?"

The lieutenant scowled at Chapman. "I have the entire Metro force searching for him. We'll catch him soon, I'm sure."

"You better locate him fast, because if Nicosia tracks him down first, you're going to have another homicide on your hands."

WAYNE DROPPED ANGELA and Randy off at the Blue Lamp Pub and headed for another storage unit. He appeared very hung over and was bitching about having to drive out to Irvine.

As arranged, Brett Miller showed up at the bar and joined them in a few cups of coffee. Well-caffeinated, they jumped into Brett's car and drove down Highway 405 toward Long Beach. Angela sat in the front with Brett, and Randy was in the back. The morning commute was heavy, with bumper-to-bumper stop-and-go traffic, making progress slow.

Brett drove in silence, concentrating on the freeway, and his mind seemed far away.

"Tell me about Cynthia," Angela asked him. "What was she like growing up?"

The question pulled Brett out of his daze. He glanced at her. "Rambunctious," he said with a faint smirk. "To say the least."

"I bet she was," Randy said with a knowing smile.

"She was always in trouble, often finding herself in some kind of sticky situation that involved the cops."

"Like what?" Angela asked.

Brett thought for an instant. "Hmm. Let's see. From the time she was five years old, she'd wander off. Once, she sneaked on a bus and ended up in Anaheim. My old man and lady were too drunk to worry that something was wrong, so I was the one who called the police when I couldn't locate her. They didn't find her for two days."

Angela wrinkled her nose. "Was she all right?"

Brett chuckled. "Yeah."

"Where did she go?"

"To Disneyland. She wanted to visit Mickey Mouse."

"Amazing," Randy said.

"That was just the beginning of Cyndi's adventures. She was caught shoplifting at least three times. Nothing a normal little girl would take, like candy or dolls, but expensive clothing and jewelry."

"Your parents did nothing to stop her?" Angela asked.

"Always too wasted." Brett braked hard to avoid a tractor-trailer that had cut him off. He shouted an obscenity and flipped-off the driver of the truck, blaring the horn.

Angela said, "It sounds like it was pretty rough growing up."

"I got used to living that way, out of the back of a station wagon."

"What about Cynthia?" Randy asked.

Brett looked at him in the rearview mirror. "If you knew Cyndi, then you know she'd never be able to adapt to that life."

"Where are your parents now?" Angela asked.

Brett coughed out a harsh laugh. "Who knows. They went out one night and didn't come back."

"They abandoned you?"

"It didn't matter; they'd dumped us in spirit years before."

"How old were you?" Randy asked.

"Cyndi was thirteen, and I'd just celebrated my seventeenth birthday."

"What did you do?" Angela asked. "Where did you go?"

Brett closed his eyes for a moment and inhaled deeply. "I got a job working in a restaurant. First as a busboy, then as a short-order cook."

"And Cynthia?"

Brett went silent, his gaze roaming across the traffic in front of them. He licked his lips. "She worked as a prostitute." He stared straight ahead, his lips pressed tight. "I put a stop to it as soon as I found out." He gripped the steering wheel hard, his knuckles white, and said in a broken voice, "I didn't want her working the streets and took on two jobs so we'd have enough money to live. But it was too late. Cyndi did get out of the business, but whatever innocence she had was gone.

"She came out of the experience a changed person. She vowed if she was going to sell her body, it would be for more than forty bucks in some seedy motel. She skipped from relationship to relationship, each man a little wealthier than the last. She was a woman on a mission. Money. She'd drop one guy for another if the next man had more cash.

"I'm not sure where Kevin met Cyndi, but he had the same insatiable desire for the dollar. Once he'd talked her into the forgery con, he thought he had it made for life."

Randy said, "It sounds like they could've had a sweet deal."

"No. Delfino was a drunken loser, and Cyndi had started to recognize that."

"And she saw Joseph Nicosia as a tempting option."

Bret nodded. "His money and power were irresistible to her. She got him to walk her down the aisle a year after they met." He slowed the car and took the Long Beach exit on Highway 710, merged into the flowing traffic, and sped back up.

"What about you?" Angela asked. "How'd you end up as an artist?"

For the first time since they'd gotten in the car, Brett's face brightened. "I've always loved to draw."

Randy said, "Living out of a dilapidated station wagon doesn't expose you to much in the way of fine arts."

Brett chuckled. "No, but when you don't have a TV, video games, or a computer, you turn inward. I have a vivid imagination, and I drew on any scrap of paper I could find. As I got older, I spent more time honing my skills. I enrolled in art classes and was lucky—an instructor recognized some talent and took me under his wing. He was a real mentor, and like I told you yesterday, I've made a decent living off my paintings. I've developed a following for my work and supplement my income by painting for a local building contractor."

Angela said, "From the works I saw at the Blue Lamp, your talent's amazing. I'd love to see more of your paintings."

Brett gave her an appreciative smile. "I'd be happy to show them to you. I have a little studio at my house, not far from the Blue Lamp. I do abstract paintings most of the time, landscapes on rare occasions, and even less often, a portrait or two."

Angela beamed at him. "It's a date."

Randy eyed her suspiciously, wondering if she was coming on-to Brett Miller. "Believe it or not, I also have an appreciation for good art."

"You do?" Angela asked, turning to shoot him a doubtful look.

"Sure, I love paintings."

"Who's your favorite artist?" Brett asked.

Randy struggled for an answer. "Uh, I don't know...no, no, Norman Rockwell."

Angela asked skeptically, "Norman Rockwell?"

"Yes, he's an American classic."

"That he is," Brett said. "As you know, my works are about as far from his as you can get. I'm a little more colorful and outside the box. Some people find my art difficult to understand."

"I prefer eclectic work," Angela said.

Randy said, "I'm certain contemporary art can become a favorite of mine as well."

"Somehow I find that hard to believe."

KEVIN DELFINO SAT down on a bench in the back room of the Kwik Money Pawnshop. "I'm ready to peddle *Sunflowers in a Vase*. The Van Gogh."

Yazzie, a Native American man in his early forties, raised an eyebrow. He handed Delfino a beer and whistled. "Now's not a good time to fence a Van Gogh."

Delfino twisted off the bottle cap. "Why not? A year ago, you told me it was worth almost a million and a half."

"The Feds have been cracking down. They're doing a lot of undercover work."

"Goddamn it."

"There's also a chance Eugene Serrano could find out. I'm sure he'd be surprised to discover the one in his living room's a fake."

"You think Serrano would hear about it?"

"Van Gogh owners are a tight-knit group. He'd find out within days if it was on the market. I'm not risking that. Serrano's not a nice man."

Delfino took a long pull of his beer. "Damn it. I have to unload that painting."

"Why did you take so long to decide to sell?" Yazzie opened his own beer.

Delfino blinked at him. "Dee and I had a little disagreement on how to best split the money. Her marriage to Nicosia complicated the matter."

Yazzie rubbed his stubbled chin and gave Delfino a dark look. "I hear Cyndi was murdered. You must be broken up."

With a chilling lack of emotion, Delfino said, "Yeah, I can't stop crying. At least I have the Van Gogh to console me." He took a long slug of his beer.

Yazzie shook his head. "You're a ruthless mother. The news says she was killed by a Vegas guy."

Delfino's lips twisted. "I've heard that too. That reminds me, I have a gold-and-diamond necklace to pawn."

Yazzie stared at Delfino, then threw his beer cap toward a trash can. It hit the wall and bounced in. "Anyway, dude, Van Goghs are hot right now and there's no way I can sell it. Things have to cool off first."

Delfino drained the beer and threw the empty bottle at the trash can. "Goddamn it. I'm desperate. I need the money."

"You must have some cash tucked away."

"My passion for the ponies and football ate it up. All I have left is the necklace and the Van Gogh."

"A necklace I can do, but I won't touch the painting. Too damn hot. The last thing I want is Serrano on my ass. Sit on it a couple of years, and we can try to unload it in Europe."

"There has to be someone out there who'd be willing to purchase the Van Gogh."

Yazzie chugged his beer until the bottle was empty. "Good luck finding them. Well, Big K, I have to get back to work. It was nice seeing you again. If you ever tire of freelancing, let me know. I can always use a vicious bastard of your caliber."

Delfino pursed his lips. "If I can't figure a way to sell the Van Gogh, I may just give you a call."

BRETT STEERED THE car off the freeway and onto a street that led to the port warehouses in Long Beach, passing shabby buildings that had long ago seen better days. "Gus Hadley's studio isn't far from here."

Randy said, "Brett, I've been thinking—if Hadley and Delfino are good friends, it would be a mistake to tell him Delfino's a suspect in Cynthia's murder."

Brett glanced over his shoulder at him. "Maybe. So what do you propose we do?"

"Let's not question him about Delfino. This may sound crazy, but let's tell him we're gallery owners and have a client who wants to buy *Sunflowers in a Vase*."

Brett looked back at Randy again. "Gus would question my helping someone buy a painting on the black market."

"Explain you're tired of being a starving artist and are doing it for the money."

"Would he believe that?" Angela asked.

"I'm sure you could be convincing."

"It's an idea," Brett said. "I'm also concerned Gus won't be too cooperative if he believes we're searching for Delfino as a murder suspect. I don't know how good of friends they are. I suppose I could pull off the ruse."

"Okay, how do we do it?"

"Follow my lead. I think I know what to say."

"Tell us about this guy."

"He's a character. You'll find him easy to like in a strange sort of way. I don't appreciate the fact that he paints forgeries, but besides that, he's a kick in the pants. We need to be cautious, though. Gus is smart, and if we're not careful, he'll see right through what we're doing."

"We'll take our cues from you."

"That's wise." Brett drove down a long narrow alley.

DIXIE HOLIDAY SAT in the Desert Palm team members' cafeteria, sipping a cup of coffee and reading the front page of the newspaper. She shook her head, unwilling to accept the news that Angela had disappeared with fugitive Randy Kennedy. She gasped when she read about the shattered front door of Angela's townhouse.

Carter Camp pulled out a chair and sat next to her, gesturing to the newspaper. "Pretty unbelievable."

"Carter, I'm sick with concern. You know how close we are. Angela's like a daughter."

"You haven't heard from her?"

Tears filled her eyes, and she fumbled through her purse, searching for a tissue. "The police asked me the same question." Her voice shook. "No, I haven't heard a word."

"Kennedy must be unhinged. First two murders and then a kidnapping."

Dixie said in a whisper, "This might sound absurd, but I'm not sure she was abducted?"

"Of course she was."

She dabbed at her eyes with the tissue. "I have my doubts."

He frowned. "Why?"

"Angela's romantically interested in Randy."

"I don't believe that."

"I wish it weren't true. I thought I'd convinced her he was no good, but in my heart of hearts, I'm not certain I got through."

"I know for a fact she spurned his advances."

"I hate to say this, but she did that to see if his feelings for her were real."

"No way. She's been on a date with me. We were supposed to go on our second one the day she was kidnapped."

"I'd like nothing more than to see Angela end up with a fine man like you."

"She will." He glared at her. "If we can rescue her from that murderous jerk."

"I know you won't understand this, but if Angela's with him by choice, at least I know she's not in imminent danger. If she's with him against her will, then she's in real trouble. For that reason, like it or not, I hope she chose to leave with Randy."

"Dixie, that's crazy logic. I've seen Angela's townhouse. The front door was bashed in. Kennedy's dress shirt was in the living room with Cynthia Nicosia's blood all over it."

"Stop it." Dixie put her hands over her ears. "I can't hear this. I may be naïve, but for my own sanity, I won't accept that she was taken hostage."

"Put on blinders if you like, but I know the truth. Angela's in jeopardy, and I'm going to find her." Camp stood and buttoned his jacket. "She's not with Kennedy because she wants to be, and I know it."

Dixie closed her eyes and sighed, a mournful sound.

"I'm going to rescue her." Camp thrust his nose in the air and stomped away from the table.

EIGHTEEN

BRETT STEERED HIS car through the alley and drove along the wharf. The docks were bustling, with cargo ships being unloaded by tall cranes, and a mass of workers driving forklifts were zipping between the containers. Brett pulled the car over in a wide spot in the road and turned off the engine. "This is as close to Hadley's studio as I can get."

"He lives around here?" Angela asked.

A forklift buzzed by, and Brett said with amused sarcasm, "Charming, don't you agree? He lives in the top floor of an old warehouse. You'll be surprised; it's quite nice."

"Lead the way," Randy said, yanking open the car door and hopping out.

Brett led them through a cramped passageway between two brick buildings. The tall structures blocked the sun, and he bound purposefully down the corridor, Randy and Angela struggling to keep up. Brett stopped in front of a heavy metal door, waiting for them to join him. He flung it open and held it as they entered. Inside, an ancient elevator was illuminated by a single naked light bulb that hung from a chain.

"Is it safe?" Angela asked.

"I guess so," Brett said, shrugging. "I've never had a problem."

"Do you come here often?" Randy asked.

"I've been a few times."

Angela inspected the elevator. Incredulous, she said, "Is this a rope hoist?"

Brett laughed. "No, it's an industrial elevator. It once lifted engine parts, so it must be strong."

Randy boarded the car. "Seems secure to me."

Brett and Angela followed. Brett pressed a green button, the iron doors clanged shut, and the elevator rose. At the top floor, eleven stories up, the elevator banged to a stop. Angela frowned and peered at Brett. He smiled, and the doors rumbled apart. "This way," he said.

Randy and Angela trailed after him. At the end of a grayish hallway was an unmarked steel door. Brett knocked forcefully. He waited a second and knocked again.

The clicking sound of locks being turned could be heard, and the door swung open. Gus Hadley stood there with wide eyes, obviously surprised to see them. He was in his mid-forties, his red hair shaved close to his head. His skin was pale, thin wrinkles forming near his temples. "Brett, my friend," Hadley said. "What the hell are you doing here?" He didn't wait for a response. "Damn, I've missed you." He flung himself at Brett and gave him a hearty bear hug.

"Hey, Gus," Brett said and patted him on the back.

"God, it's been ages." Hadley released Brett. "Come in. Come in. And who are these gorgeous people?"

"Gus, this is Randy and Angela. They're friends of mine."

Randy reached out and shook Hadley's hand. Angela did the same and gave him an engaging smile.

Hadley pointed to the center of the large room. "Please make yourselves comfortable."

Despite the odd location of the studio, it was a fantastic space for an artist to work. The furnishings were expensive, and the red brick walls led up to high windows that circled the entire place. Light flooded through them at interesting angles, creating unique patterns of shadows on the walls. Three brass ceiling fans spun around and around.

"You have a beautiful home," Angela said. She walked over to admire a sculpture perched on a pedestal against the wall. "Did you do this?"

Hadley sauntered over to the figure. It was a freeform creation of a man holding the moon. "That depends. Do you like it? If so, I did. If not, I found it at the dump." He roared with laughter at himself.

Randy gave Brett a look that said, *is this guy crazy?*

"I like it very much," Angela said.

Hadley grinned, his cheeks bulging. "It's yours."

"Oh, I couldn't."

"Poppycock. I want you to take it."

"Thank you, but I can't accept. The offer's appreciated, though."

Appearing somewhat hurt, Hadley flicked his hand. "As you wish."

"I do appreciate the gesture."

Hadley turned from her. "Well now, what can I get you to drink? Champagne? I'll make Mimosas."

"I'll have a Diet Coke," Brett said. "If you have any."

"That sounds good," Randy said.

Angela nodded, making it unanimous.

"Party poopers," Hadley said. "Okay, colas it is." He walked into the kitchen area, opened the stainless steel refrigerator, and pulled out three bottles of soda and popped off the tops. He returned to the living room portion of the studio. "Sit down. Sit down." He handed each of them a soda, and Randy and Angela took a seat on a tan leather sofa.

Brett propped himself on a red wooden stool. "How's everything?"

"Marvelous. You have to see my latest work." Hadley scurried across the room and snatched a painting from an easel. "I finished this last night." He glided back to the living area and passed it to Brett. The canvas was flecked with colors in abstract shapes.

Brett moaned in appreciation. "Oh, this is nice. I've always said you're a unique talent."

Hadley beamed with a mouthful of somewhat crooked teeth. "Quite a compliment coming from you. Angela, Randy, as you must know, this man's one of the finest artists on the West Coast. Someday, his creations will be hanging in museums with the Masters."

Brett waved his open hand dismissively. "Enough of that." He looked back at Hadley's painting. "You should be proud of this."

Hadley crossed his arms. "Unlike my other works? Are you still angry at me for making copies of overpriced pieces of art?"

"No Gus, I've come to terms with that. It's your life. Do with it whatever you want. What else are you working on?" Brett gestured to another easel, which supported a canvas covered with a white cloth.

Hadley glanced at it and frowned. "Something that's not ready for viewing." He took the abstract painting out of Brett's hands and returned it to the easel. Then he ambled over and flopped down in an overstuffed paisley chair. "Brett, I hear you're doing pretty well. I read about your showing at the Miriam Gallery."

Brett rolled his eyes. "Oh yeah, lots of accolades, but not many sales. It's tough in this economy. I'm working for Benny Cartwright to keep my landlord at bay."

"Is he still building apartment houses?"

Brett drank a swallow of his Coke. "Yep, a real palette for a renowned artist like me."

"Ho, ho. Stick with it, kid. With your talent, I know you'll make it big soon."

"Wouldn't that be nice?" Brett sounded a little defeated, bowing his head. "All joking aside, my financial condition's why we stopped by."

"You're not here to visit an old friend?"

Brett gave him a puckish smile. "Sure, but I have an ulterior motive. I've got some money problems."

Hadley's eyes narrowed. "Oh?"

"When I found out they were giving me a show at the Miriam, I became a little overconfident. I racked up almost twenty-five thousand on my credit cards."

"I thought you were smarter than that."

"I know. I was giddy before the show. Unfortunately, my expectations were much too high, and my paintings didn't sell as well as I'd hoped. My bills are mounting, and I have to get some relief. Anyway, Randy and Angela own a gallery in West Hollywood. They've been exhibiting some of my work."

"We too recognize his talent," Randy said.

Angela said, "We know assisting Brett now will pay off in the future."

Brett said, "To help me, they've agreed to pay a commission if I can aid them in acquiring a certain painting. A Van Gogh—*Sunflowers in a Vase*. We're pretty sure it's coming on the market. That's why we're here. More than anyone, I know you have your ear to the ground when it comes to that type of thing."

Hadley's lips compressed, and his pale skin seemed to turn even whiter. He stared across the room, puzzlement in his eyes. "You should ask your sister. As I recall, she sold that painting, or a mighty fine facsimile, to Eugene Serrano, the real estate developer."

"Haven't you heard?" Brett said grimly. "Cyndi was murdered."

The confused look on Hadley's face dropped away, replaced by disbelief. "Oh my god, what happened?"

"It occurred in Las Vegas. The police suspect a guy who works at a resort up there."

Hadley's cheeks and ears reddened with anger. "Why would he do such a thing?"

"You know Cyndi and men. Sooner or later, she was bound to cross one who didn't like it."

"Damn. I can't believe it. I'm stunned. She was always so nice. Why would something like this fall upon such a beautiful woman?"

Brett stroked his budding goatee. "Did you paint a copy of *Sunflowers in a Vase* for my sister and Kevin Delfino?"

Hadley nodded. "Sure. A few years ago."

"Cyndi ended up keeping the original, but it's been missing since her death."

"If the real painting's on the market, Serrano will discover he has a fake. Oh boy. I hear he has a temper. I bet he explodes."

Randy asked, "Do you know how we can reach Delfino?"

Hadley paused, then shook his head. "Um, no, we had no reason to stay in touch once he got out of the art scam."

"How about Serrano? How can we get in contact with him?"

"I've heard he spends most of his time at a restaurant on Santa Monica Boulevard called Tapas. He owns the place and has an office in the back."

"I wonder if he'd talk with us."

Hadley shrugged. "Couldn't say."

Angela said, "We have a client who's interested in purchasing the Van Gogh and willing to make a strong offer."

"I sure need the commission," Brett said.

Hadley scratched his cheek. "I'll nose around and see what I can find out. Again, I'm sorry about Cyndi. I'm heartsick."

"So am I."

For the next half-hour, Brett and Hadley reminisced about Cynthia, telling funny stories. Hadley then babbled on about the latest gossip in the sometimes chaotic and almost always incestuous world of art. "Did you hear that Chuck Shay's sleeping with the director of the Chassen Museum of Art?"

"Missed that one," Brett said with a smirk. "Well, we better be going. It's been great visiting with you." He stood, and Angela and Randy followed his lead. They walked toward the front door.

"I'd enjoy seeing your latest works," Hadley said.

"I'd like you to. Let's get together in a couple of weeks."

"It was nice meeting you," Angela said. "Thanks for the Coke."

"Yes, Gus," Randy said, "listening to you has been fascinating. I hope we can locate *Sunflowers in a Vase* and make a sale."

"I'll ask around," Hadley said.

"That would be appreciated. We'll be in touch."

"Thanks," Brett said. He waved goodbye, and they left the studio.

BRETT TOOK THE freeway leading back to Los Angeles. He opened the window a crack and let go of the steering wheel to light a cigarette. "Gus is quite a character."

"He's a pleasant man in an odd way," Angela said.

"It seems like we're in the gallery business," Randy said.

Brett gazed at him in the rearview mirror. "I guess you are."

"I don't mean to pry, Brett," Angela said, "but you aren't in financial trouble, are you?"

He took a drag of his cigarette. "Was I convincing?"

She nodded. "Very."

"No, I don't have money problems. I'm doing quite well. My showing at the Miriam Gallery was so successful, I'm about ready to give up house painting for good."

"I'm happy for you."

He smiled. "Thanks."

Again, Randy didn't like the look between them and glared. "How far is this restaurant?"

Brett said, "About forty-five minutes north if the traffic's not too bad."

"Put the pedal to the metal."

"In a hurry, are you?"

"I want to find that painting and your sister's killer."

Brett exhaled a stream of smoke out the window. "I know you were friends, but why are you playing detective and spending all this time on something that's better handled by the police? I don't understand your motivation."

Rubbing his chin, Randy wasn't sure how to answer.

Angela jumped in, saying, "The man the authorities suspect of killing your sister's a good friend of ours. We don't believe he did it, and we're trying to save his life by finding the real murderer."

"You're some friends."

"You wouldn't want your sister's killer to go free?"

Brett brushed hair out of his eyes and tucked the strands behind an ear. "I don't know enough about what happened to draw any reasonable conclusions. All I know is what the police told me. They said the evidence against this guy is indisputable."

"He didn't do it," Randy said with a little too much emotion.

Brett glanced back at him, obviously startled. "If you say so."

"I know the guy really well, and he's innocent."

"I don't suppose the two of you would go to all this trouble if you thought he was guilty."

Randy's eyelids drooped. "It all comes back to the painting."

"It's a valuable work. It was one of Van Gogh's last creations."

"It's a good motive for murder," Angela said.

CARTER CAMP WAS sitting in his uncle's office, staring out the window. "Uncle Walter, I'd like to take a leave of absence."

Parker was reading the newspaper and, as usual, paying scant attention to his nephew. Without looking up, he asked, "What for?"

"You're aware Angela Grisham's missing?"

"Yes, it's here in the paper."

"Kennedy abducted her."

Parker peeled down a page. "So the *Review/Journal* says."

"I want to find her."

Parker put down the paper and took a sip of coffee from his mug. "How do you propose to do that?"

Camp rubbed his temples. "I can't sit here doing nothing."

"It's a police matter."

"I know that, but it's hard to concentrate on my job when I know Angela's in trouble."

"There's little you can do."

Camp stopped massaging his temples and started twiddling his fingers. His head was lowered. "Ah, I need to ask a favor."

"If you want a leave of absence, go ahead. I'll clear it with Frazier."

"No, it's more than that."

Parker blew out an aggravated breath. "What might that be?"

"I'd like you to offer a reward for any information leading to the whereabouts of Angela Grisham and the capture of Randy Kennedy. If he kidnapped her, and I'm sure he did, then a reward's the best way to find out where he's hiding. A million and a half dollars ought to get us some tips. For that amount of money, someone's bound to turn him in."

Parker said indignantly, "I'm not putting up that kind of cash."

"Please. It's the only sure way we can find Kennedy."

Parker took another swallow of his coffee. "I still can't believe Randy's responsible for those murders."

"I know he abducted Angela. I'm the one who called the cops when I found her front door destroyed."

"I can see you have real feelings for this girl."

"More than you know. That's why I'd do anything to locate her. I don't have the means, but you do. If you put up the million and a half bucks, I'll spend day and night making sure everyone knows about the reward. Someone will turn Kennedy in."

Parker tapped his fingers on the desk. "Carter, let me think about this. A million five is a lot of money."

"I'll pay you back. Even if it takes years, I promise I'll pay you."

This was the first time Parker had ever seen his nephew so passionate about the welfare of another person. Of course, it was still self-serving, but he was surprised. "Okay. If it'll help us determine what's going on, I'll put up the reward."

Camp clapped his hands. "Yes. Thank you, Uncle Walter, thank you. It'll be a worth-while investment, I promise you."

Parker picked up the paper. "For your sake, it better be."

LIEUTENANT SCHULTZ LEANED back in his chair and propped his feet on the desk. It hadn't been a good morning, and he was looking forward to quitting time, planning to see his grandson play t-ball. The kid was talented, and Schultz was already imagining him as a starting pitcher for a big league team.

A rap on the door brought Schultz back to reality. He saw Officer Avery through the worn plastic Venetian blinds and motioned for the policeman to enter. Avery opened the door and came in to sit in the chair in front of Schultz's desk.

"How goes the wars, Alex?" Schultz asked, pulling his feet from the desk.

"Trying to keep up, Lieutenant."

"Any sign of our boy?"

"No, but Vegas is a large city," Avery said in a tone that said they couldn't search everywhere. "We'll keep at it."

"I'm getting a lot of heat from Commissioner O'Leary. He wants a quick arrest."

"We all do, sir. I have the lab results on the bloody shirt found in the Grisham woman's townhouse." He handed the report to Schultz. "The blood's Cynthia Nicosia's."

Schultz thumbed through the folder. "There wasn't much doubt about that. When will forensics have the results on the Hale murder?"

"In a couple of days. They're backed up due to the gang shootings in North Las Vegas. While we wait, we've been interrogating Kennedy's friends and co-workers."

"Yeah, and what do they have to say?"

"He's a popular man. None of them believe he's a killer."

Schultz gave the folder back to Avery. "I'm still baffled by the disappearance of Angela Grisham. A murderer on the run doesn't stop to kidnap someone. It's more probable she's with him by choice."

"No one I interviewed knows of any connection between the two other than at work."

"That doesn't make sense." Schultz took a gulp of his coffee. It was cold and bitter, and he made a face.

"There was one woman, a cashier at the Desert Palm—hold on, let me get her name." Avery opened a notepad and flipped through the pages. "Yes, here it is, Dixie Holiday. She works with Grisham in the casino cashier. When I asked her about Kennedy, she hesitated a bit before saying she knew of no relationship."

Schultz pushed his coffee cup to the side of the desk. "Do you think she wasn't telling you everything she knows?"

"That wasn't my impression at the time, but now that you mention it, I'm not positive. She was rather evasive."

"I want to talk with her. What was her name again?"

"Holiday. Dixie Holiday. A real nice lady."

Schultz wrote that out on a piece of paper. "What shift does she work?"

Avery checked his notepad. "Swing. Two to midnight, the same as Grisham."

"I'll put a little pressure on her. Let's see if we can get this goddamn investigation moving."

As BRETT DROVE his Honda into the parking lot of Tapas Bar and Grille, Angela noticed the spelling of *Grille* and frowned. "I know it's trendy to spell grill that way," she said, "but to me, a grille is on the front of a car and doesn't do much to tempt my palate."

There were only a few vehicles in front of the restaurant. Brett pulled his car up next to a silver Lexus, and they hopped out of the car and walked under a green canopy to the entrance. Randy heaved open the thick wooden door and waited for Angela and Brett to enter.

The lectern in the tiled corridor was deserted, as was the bar to their left. They stepped down into the restaurant and maneuvered between oak tables that were set and ready for the dinner crowd. Spotting a busboy in the back of the restaurant, they weaved over to him. "Excuse me," Randy said, "do you know where we can find Eugene Serrano?"

The teenage Latino didn't look up from his task of placing silverware on a large oval table.

"Did you hear me?" Randy asked, louder. "We'd like to speak with Eugene Serrano."

"No hablo Ingles," the kid said.

"The owner," Angela said.

He shook his head.

"Senor Serrano," Randy said. "Donde puedo encontrarlo?"

The busboy's face reflected surprise, and he pointed to the door in one corner of the restaurant, near the bar.

Randy nodded. "Gracias."

The teen picked up a handful of spoons from a tray. "De nada."

Angela's expression said she was impressed with Randy's language skills.

He grinned. "One of my many hidden talents. My grandmother taught high school Spanish. She made me learn."

"Nowadays, it must come in handy."

They walked across the restaurant and stopped at the closed door. A metal plate on it said *Office*. Brett knocked, and they heard shuffling on the other side. A tall young blond woman wearing a tight gray sweater opened the door. Her sizable breasts filled out every inch of the cloth. She appeared somewhat startled by their presence. "Sorry, we're not open until five."

"How's the food here?" Randy asked.

She beamed, seeming enamored by him. "I like it. The best small plates in Southern California."

"I'll have to give it a try sometime."

"As I said, we open at five."

"That's not why we're here," Brett said.

She primped her hair, unable to keep her eyes off Randy. "If you need the chef, he's not here. He's at the market and won't be back for about half an hour."

"We're looking for Eugene Serrano," Angela said.

The woman squinted at her. "Eugene?"

"Yes," Randy said. "We'd like to speak with him."

She folded her arms over her chest. "And who are you?"

"I'm Randy and this is Angela and Brett." He held out his right hand.

She uncrossed her arms and shook his hand but looked suspiciously at him. "I'm Mitzie. What do you want with Mr. Serrano?"

"Um, it's a personal matter. We were hoping to talk with him."

"So you've said, gorgeous, but you haven't told me why."

"What are you, his keeper?"

She inspected the long red fingernails on her left hand. "You might say that."

"We wish to speak with him about a painting. *Sunflowers in a Vase*."

Mitzie was abruptly curious, her left eyebrow rising. "What about it?"

Angela said, "We own a gallery, and we're interested in purchasing it for a client."

"I doubt it's for sale. I know Mr. Serrano's fond of it."

"Please, it's crucial we see him," Randy said.

"Well, I'm sorry, sweetheart, but he isn't here."

"He's not?" Randy tried to peek over her shoulder into the office behind her.

She shifted the door to block his line of sight. "Sorry. He's in Ventura. He has a new apartment complex under construction."

"Will he be there long?"

Mitzie shrugged. "I haven't the foggiest."

"It's important. We're desperate to chat with him."

"How'd you find out Mr. Serrano owns *Sunflowers in a Vase*?"

Randy realized they wouldn't get to see Serrano without Mitzie's consent. "It's complicated. There may have been some irregularities in his purchase of the painting."

"Eugene bought it from a respected gallery."

"I'd like to speak with him about the transaction."

"He'll be coming here for dinner this evening."

"May we speak with him then?"

"That's up to him."

Randy's eyes locked onto hers. "I bet someone as influential as you could arrange an appointment."

"Maybe."

He gave her his best dazzling smile. "Maybe yes or maybe no?"

She winked. "Come back around seven. I'll see what I can do."

Randy smiled even wider. "Thanks, Mitzie, we'll see you tonight."

NINETEEN

RANDY AND ANGELA were back at the Sleepy Hollow Motel. Randy was lying on the bed closest to the door, and Angela was on the other one. Using the remote, she turned on the battered television, the volume low.

"So far, it's been a pretty unproductive day," Randy said.

Angela nodded.

There was a knock at the door, and they both stared at it in fear. Randy stood and glanced through the curtains. "It's Wayne."

Relief melted across Angela's face. "My heart's pounding so hard."

Randy opened the door. "Hey, stranger. Where've you been all day?"

Wayne carried a six-pack of beer into the room. "Don't get me going. I told you my crap was in storage in places all around L.A.? Well, I'm way down in Irvine when the U-Tote trailer develops a flat and the spare's flat too. I couldn't find a gas station. I wasted half the morning."

"Did you collect all your furniture?"

Wayne sat on the corner of a bed. "Yeah, but with the cost of the gas, the U-Tote, and the flat, I could've bought everything new. But it's packed, and I'm taking it all to Vegas."

Angela said, "At least one of us is getting something accomplished."

"No luck locating Mrs. Nicosia's ex?" He popped open a beer and took a swallow.

"None at all," Randy said.

"Angela," Wayne said in an excited voice, pointing with the beer can, "turn up the television. I just saw Randy's picture."

Angela picked up the remote, increasing the volume, and the television blared. The afternoon anchor for Channel Two was describing the murders of Cynthia Nicosia and casino magnate Conrad Hale. "In another bazaar twist," the anchorman said, "it seems the alleged murderer has kidnapped a woman who also works at the Desert Palm Resort. The woman, identified as Angela Grisham, is a cashier at the casino. Yesterday afternoon, the police found the front door of her townhouse smashed in. Witnesses at the scene say clothing spattered with the blood of Cynthia Nicosia was found at the home."

"Oh my god," Angela said. "Randy, they believe you've abducted me."

Randy's shoulders slumped. "This is a nightmare."

"Listen," Wayne said, mesmerized by the news report.

The anchorman said, "Desert Palm Resort owner Walter Parker has put up a million-five-hundred-thousand-dollar reward for information leading to the arrest and conviction of the person responsible for the murders that have sent a chill through Las Vegas. In an exclusive interview, Parker told our reporter he hoped the reward will assist the police in finding out what happened."

"A million and a half," Wayne said, whistling. "They've put a million-five bounty on your ass." He finished off his beer and crumpled the can in his hand. "Well, don't worry about me. I won't rat you out. I'm expecting my host gig will eventually make me more than a million and a half."

Randy closed his eyes and rubbed his hands over his face. "Oh, man. What am I going to do?"

Angela looked at him sympathetically. "I'm so sorry."

"I have to somehow find Cynthia's killer. It's the only way I can begin to clear my name."

"We'll do that."

Wayne stood up and began pacing in front of the beds. "I have to get back to Vegas. I'm due at work tonight, and I need to hit the road. If I don't show up, I'll be terminated. I'm sorry, but I can't afford to lose my goddamn job."

"Don't get yourself fired," Randy said. "You've already done far more than anyone could expect."

"Dude, all I've done is given you a ride and bitch about it." Wayne picked up the remaining beers and walked to the door. "Anyway, I have to take off. I put some minutes on my phone, so if you need something, give me a call. Hang in there."

"I'll try, thanks."

Wayne said goodbye to Angela and left the motel room.

Randy turned to her. "It's just the two of us now. There's a chicken restaurant up the street. Let's go grab a bite to eat before meeting Serrano."

"Ahh...that won't work for me."

Randy's whole face transformed into a frown. "You have other plans?"

"I promised Brett I'd join him for dinner. After that, he's giving me a tour of his art studio."

Randy slapped his clenched fists to his chest. "This is my life we're talking about. I thought we'd hash out a few ideas I have. You'd rather spend time with Brett?"

"That's unfair," Angela snapped. "Brett offered to show me his paintings. He's been helpful to us, to say the least, and I figured I owed him the courtesy. I assumed the last thing you'd want to do is look at modern art."

He gave her a contemptuous wave. "Be my guest."

"We'll be back in time to meet with Serrano." Clearly annoyed at Randy's jealousy, Angela put her hands on her hips. "It's just dinner."

Randy shook his head. "If you say so."

"I'm going to call the police in Las Vegas and tell them that I haven't been kidnapped."

"No," Randy said, immediately panicked. "They might be able to trace the call."

"But they think you've abducted me. At least we can straighten that out. I have to do something. My family, Dixie, my boss—they're frantic, I'm sure."

"Go ahead and call your parents, but don't tell them where we are." He lifted one of the curtains.

Angela glared at him, her cheeks tinted pink. "Believe it or not, I'm on your side. I know how difficult this is for you, but I have little incentive to help if you speak to me like this."

Randy's mouth fell open. He jerked his head back and spun around. "You're right, I'm sorry. I'm so sorry. I'm tired and not thinking straight. I need you." His expression was again beseeching. "If I fly off the handle, stop me."

Angela closed her eyes for a moment, her emotions plainly mixed. "Let's calm down and keep focused on what we're planning to do."

HIS PHONE RANG, and Gus Hadley scooted through the studio and picked it up. Seeing it was Kevin Delfino, he trembled as he tapped on the screen and put it to his ear. "Hello?"

"I received your text," Delfino said. "Are they legitimate?"

Hadley cleared his throat. "I suppose so. They say they have a client who's interested in Van Goghs."

"How are you doing on the replica of the *Sunflower*?"

"It's coming along. It should be ready in a month or so."

"Not fast enough, my friend. If I work this right, I can make twice as much money."

"I still think you're crazy, selling another fake of *Sunflowers*. That worked once, but you're pushing your luck trying it again. If Serrano finds out, we could both get ourselves killed." He heard a pop and hiss as Delfino opened a can.

"That's your opinion. I disagree. Now get your ass in gear. If you'd like a piece of the action, I suggest you step up the timetable."

"I'll do what I can, but if you want a credible copy, it can't be rushed." Hadley's voice was so shaky, he didn't sound like himself.

"Get it done. Don't give me any of your pansy-ass excuses."

"I'll do my best."

"I expect better than that. The black market for Van Goghs has dried up, and if I miss this opportunity because you couldn't finish the painting, there'll be hell to pay. I now have an alcohol fueled murder under my belt, and it's not that bad; I feel no guilt at all."

"What are you saying?"

"I killed Dee for that painting; now get the copy done before you suffer the same fate."

Hadley eyes widened, his lips quivering. "I'll get back to painting right now."

The line went dead. Hadley's hands were trembling as he poked the screen of the phone. He looked across the room at the unfinished reproduction of *Sunflowers in a Vase*. He couldn't stop shaking.

ANGELA PICKED UP the receiver in the filthy phone booth and dialed Las Vegas. On the second ring, Dixie answered. "Hello?"

"Dixie, it's Angela."

"Oh my god, are you all right?"

"I'm fine."

"Where are you? What happened?"

"Don't worry."

"You have to be kidding me. I've been sick with concern."

"I promise I'm okay."

"What's going on? Are you with Randy Kennedy?"

Angela said quietly, "He didn't kill anyone."

"What kind of nonsense has that man put into your head?"

"I don't want to argue. I called to let you know I'm safe. Please do me a favor and get hold of my parents. I haven't been able to contact them. Tell them not to worry. I know the police think I've been kidnapped, but that's not true. I'm trying to help Randy find the real murderer."

"Oh honey, why?"

"He's innocent. I have to go, but know I'm all right. With any luck, I'll be back soon."

"Where are you?"

"I'd rather keep that a secret. It's safer if our whereabouts aren't known."

"Don't you trust me?"

"Of course I do; don't be ridiculous."

"Please come home, Angela."

"Soon, Dixie. Soon."

ANGELA AND BRETT were at the kitchen table of his West Hollywood house.

Brett took a bite of pasta and dabbed his lips with a napkin. "So tell me, Angela, why are you with the suspect in my sister's murder?"

She looked down quickly to hide her shock. "I don't know what you mean."

Brett smiled and sank his teeth in another mouthful of pasta, chewing it and sipping from a wineglass. "Randy Kennedy—

that's his name, isn't it? Not Randy King. What the hell are you two doing?"

Her cheeks turned a guilty red. "How'd you know?"

"His picture—when he had dark hair—and yours have been plastered on the front page of every newspaper in town. You're all over the TV news. There's a million-and-a-half-dollar reward for Randy's capture."

"He's innocent, Brett. He didn't kill your sister."

Brett picked up his wineglass. "I wondered why you guys were always wearing sunglasses. They say you've been kidnapped. You don't seem like you've been abducted to me."

"See? Just like my supposed kidnapping, it's all a huge misunderstanding."

He tasted his wine. "Why should I believe you?"

"We wouldn't be here if Randy were a murderer. Do you think we'd risk exposure—a danger you've made clear is real—by trying to find the painting? We wouldn't do this if he weren't innocent."

"It's obvious he's got you convinced."

"I am. I want you to accept it too. I need you to trust us."

Brett was quiet, thinking about that as he stirred his pasta. "It's apparent you have feelings for him."

Angela blinked a few times. "I don't know what I feel."

He laughed. "Yes, you do. You're kidding yourself if you don't recognize that."

She shut her eyes and tipped her head back. "I guess I'm afraid."

Brett chuckled. "Afraid to commit yourself to him but not frightened about running across two states with a fugitive?"

"Crazy, huh?"

"In my experience, love's always unpredictable."

Angela said in a wistful voice, "So I'm finding out."

BRETT HELD THE door of Tapas Grille open, and Angela stepped into the restaurant. He gazed at Randy and said with exaggerated sarcasm, "After you, Mr. Kennedy."

Randy's spine stiffened. "I didn't kill your sister, Brett."

"I wouldn't be here if I thought you did. If I believed you murdered Cyndi, I'd be calling the cops and collecting a million-and-a-half-dollar reward."

Randy released a discouraged sigh. "A million five. I'd almost turn myself in for that much money."

They walked up to the lectern, and a pretty, auburn-haired hostess led them to a table in the corner of the dining room, then went to get Mitzie. The place was busy.

Angela asked, "Are we using the same story we did with Gus? That we're gallery owners interested in the Van Gogh?"

"It's the most reasonable cover," Brett said.

"Who tells Serrano we think he has a fake?"

"I'll do it," Randy said. "It's my ass we're trying to save."

"I wonder if Mitzie will still be wearing that super tight sweater."

Randy's eyes twinkled at her. "Me too."

Angela sniggered.

Randy gestured with his chin. "Here she comes now."

Mitzie was no longer sporting the gray sweater she'd had on that afternoon. Instead, she was wearing a red leather mini-skirt and a white top that exposed her bare midriff.

"Holy moly," Brett said.

"Hi, guys," Mitzie said. As she had earlier in the afternoon, she stared at Randy, seeming quite enchanted. "You have beautiful eyes. Did anyone ever tell you that?"

"Oh, I suppose a few times," Randy said. "Thanks for noticing."

"May we meet with Mr. Serrano?" Angela asked.

"He's not here yet," Mitzi said. "I'm sure he'll show up soon. Let's enjoy a few cocktails while we wait."

Randy stood and pulled out a chair.

Mitzie gave him a lustful smile and sat down. She gestured for a waitress, and the woman came up to the table and took their drink orders. A few minutes later, after the drinks had been delivered, Mitzie sipped her cocktail and asked, "So, tell me, what's the name of your art gallery?"

Angela winked at Brett and said, "Art Works. It's in West Hollywood, just off Sunset."

Mitzie pointed across the restaurant. "There's Eugene now."

Angela, Brett, and Randy turned their heads and peered at the man. Serrano was an imposing gentleman in his mid-sixties, with a strong build and a full head of thick black hair that was groomed to perfection. He was wearing a dark suit and a red silk tie that looked expensive.

Serrano strode to their table, bent down, and pecked Mitzie on the cheek. "Hey, babe." The look he offered Randy, Angela, and Brett was guarded.

"This is Eugene Serrano, my husband," Mitzie said.

"Your husband?" Brett said. "I thought you were his secretary."

Mitzie grinned. "Used to be."

Serrano shook hands all around, then sat next to his wife. "Mitzie tells me you have questions about my Van Gogh."

"Yes, sir," Randy said. "To tell you the truth, we're a little confused. We heard the painting might be on the market and wanted to see if we could act as the broker. After some digging, we found out you were the registered owner of that piece. But we've been told by a reliable source that yours is a forgery and the real work is now up for sale."

Serrano's face flushed a dark red, a deep scowl flaring.

"That's impossible. I have the genuine *Sunflowers in a Vase*. I had it appraised when I made the purchase."

"Who did the appraisal?" Brett asked.

"The gallery arranged for it. It was done by a man named Kevin Delfino, as I recall. The dealer gave him a great recommendation. He signed the certificate of authentication. My insurance company also said it was an original Van Gogh."

"Mr. Serrano, I urge you have that painting reappraised. And not by Mr. Delfino. He's an imposter and may be in possession of the original."

Serrano's black intimidating eyes bored into him. "I don't believe any of this." He waved his hand in the air. "I have the original work of art."

Brett's tone was matter-of-fact. "A new appraisal will bear out whether we're correct or not. Make sure they examine the composition of the paint. That's key to a proper authentication."

"How would Delfino get my painting?" Serrano growled with increasing hostility.

Randy said, "The saleswoman at the gallery, Cynthia Miller, was working with Delfino to make the switch. She's been murdered, and we're confident he has the bona fide *Sunflowers in a Vase*."

Serrano stared at him, a vein in his temple throbbing. The possibility that he'd been duped didn't seem to be sinking in. "No. I don't accept any of this."

"You can argue all you like, but you have a forgery. I guarantee it."

Brett said, "We have reason to believe that Delfino is now trying to unload the original."

Serrano shook a finger at him. "If what you're saying is true, I must call the police."

"Do you know how to contact Delfino by any chance?"

"I have a business card in my office." He glanced at Mitzie. "Babe, would you go get it? It's in my card file on the corner of the desk."

Mitzie rubbed one of his arms. "Okay, honey. I'll be back in a second." She rose from her chair and headed toward the office.

Serrano watched his wife stroll through the restaurant. "I still can't comprehend that I might have been swindled. There must be a misunderstanding."

"Many others have been conned as well," Brett said.

Serrano glowered at him. "Is that supposed to make me feel better?"

"I just wanted you to know you aren't alone. Delfino had quite a scam going. Did you purchase any more paintings from this gallery?"

"No. I almost can't believe this. It's a respected gallery with a client list full of wealthy and famous people."

"Have you contracted with Delfino to appraise other works?"

"No. Thank god. I remember not liking the man and didn't seek him out again. There's a woman I trust for appraisals; she's employed at the Museum of Art."

Coming back to the table, Mitzie handed a card to her husband, shaking her head as she said, "He's sure got himself some business cards that make him look legit."

Serrano eyed it with a frown. "If I do have a reproduction, I'll need to give this to the authorities."

"Can I see it?" Randy asked.

Serrano shrugged and passed him the card.

Randy studied it. "Could I have a copy of this?"

Serrano nodded. "I don't see why not. Mitzie can xerox it for you."

"I'd appreciate that."

"Now, if you'll excuse me, I have some phone calls to

make." Serrano stood and adjusted his jacket. "I need to track down my museum appraiser and insurance agent." He marched away from the table, grumbling to himself.

Brett, Randy, and Angela followed Mitzie to the office, where she made a copy of Delfino's business card. "Boy, I wouldn't want to be this guy," Mitzie said.

"Why's that?" Randy asked.

Mitzie gave him the photocopy. "Eugene did a good job of holding his temper. At least in front of you. But if you're right and he has a forged painting, this Delfino's in grave danger. Eugene has some pretty tough associates, if you know what I mean."

Randy folded the paper and put it in his back pocket. "If he hears anything about the painting, will you let us know?"

Mitzie winked lasciviously. "Sure, sweetheart."

"We'll get back to you."

"Fine by me. Maybe the two of us could go out for cocktails."

RANDY YANKED THE curtains of the motel window shut and sank down on the bed next to Angela. She patted his hand, and he smiled at her.

"It's frustrating," she said.

Randy traced a design on the bedspread with his finger. "How'd I get into this?"

Angela slowly shrugged.

Randy stretched out on the bed, staring at the ceiling. "We've made some progress. At least we have a copy of Delfino's business card." He sat up, dug in his jeans pocket, and took out the white sheet of paper Mitzie had given him, unfolding it.

Angela nodded. "I wonder if the number's any good."

"I'll run down to the phone booth by the office and see." Randy leapt up off the bed and moved to the door. He hurried to the phone booth, dropped a few coins in the slot, and dialed the number from the business card. A second later, he heard a recorded voice: "We're sorry, the number you have dialed is no longer in service." Randy hung up, and the phone swallowed his quarters. He gritted his teeth in disappointment.

Randy folded the copy of the card and shoved it back in his pants pocket. He walked to the motel room, opened the door, and shot Angela a disillusioned look. "Number's disconnected."

"What's the address on the business card?"

Randy again retrieved the paper from his pocket, reading it. "It's in Marina Del Rey. It looks like it's an apartment or condo."

"Tomorrow, we should ask Brett if he'll take us out there. It may be a long shot, but it's worth a try."

Randy stared at her with narrowed eyes. "You haven't told me about your dinner."

She inhaled deeply. "Brett quizzed me about your real identity. He seemed to believe me when I insisted you're innocent."

"Can we trust him?"

"I think so. Right now we have no alternative."

TWENTY

A SEAGULL CRIED out, and Randy watched the bird swoop into the water. He was walking down Venice Beach with Angela and Brett. They were a few strides in front of him, talking as if they'd known each other for years.

Doesn't she realize how much she means to me? Randy wondered. He eyed the two of them and felt a growing jealousy. He said under his breath, "Does she like Brett in more than a friendship kind of way? Sure, he's attractive, but..." He shook his head.

Randy slowed, and Brett and Angela pulled away from him, so deep in conversation they didn't notice. *She's here,* Randy thought. *She wouldn't be with me if she didn't have strong feelings.* He picked up his pace and joined them. "Do you know where we're going?" he asked Brett.

Brett pointed. "Those white-and-gray apartments over there."

"How are we approaching this?"

"The same as we did with Hadley and Serrano. Art gallery owners. It's a good ploy. If Delfino has the painting, you want to broker the sale. Act confident you have a buyer. I can't be there, you understand. He knows me."

Randy was anxious, his expression troubled. "I guess we have no choice."

They followed a winding cobbled pathway until they reached the first row of buildings in the apartment complex. The units were stacked three high, with steel-blue balconies and sliding glass doors.

"The apartment's in building B," Randy said.

Angela and Brett scanned the complex, seeking some sort of marker. "There," Angela said, gesturing. "Two buildings over."

Brett led the way to the structure with the large letter B on the side.

Randy drew the photocopy of Delfino's business card from his pocket and glanced at it. "Number three-oh-seven."

"I'll wait here," Brett said. "I need a smoke."

They set out for the stairs, hiked up the three stories and down a passage to number 307. Randy pressed the doorbell. There was no answer. He rang the bell a couple more times. Again, nothing. "I wonder if he still lives here."

Angela held up a hand. "It's the middle of the afternoon. He could be working."

Randy flipped open the black metal mailbox that hung next to the door. It was empty.

Angela blew out a frustrated breath. "What should we do now?"

"Let's locate the management office. Maybe they'll know where we can find him. If Delfino doesn't live here anymore, perhaps we can get a forwarding address."

Returning to the ground floor, they told Brett no one was home, then searched through the apartments until finding a unit marked *Manager*. They opened the door and entered a small reception room. No one was behind the counter, and Randy rang the bell that sat on it.

A minute later, a heavy-set older woman with brown permed

hair came through a doorway and up to the counter. She smiled. "Good afternoon."

"Are you the manager?" Randy asked.

She shook her head. "No, I'm not. He's at a home improvement store, pricing carpet."

"Would you be his wife?" Angela asked.

The woman smiled with obvious satisfaction, a sparkle in her eyes. "Forty-one years next month."

"Congratulations," Randy said. "We were wondering if you could help us. We're looking for the tenant in unit three-oh-seven. Kevin Delfino."

She rubbed the side of her nose. "Three-oh-seven, three-oh-seven, ah yes, young man with the muscular build. I haven't seen him in a while. He may not live here anymore."

"Can you find out?"

"I don't keep track of the occupants of the apartments. I leave that to my husband. I don't even know how to log on-to the computer. I'm only the cook around here."

"Do you expect him back soon?" Angela asked.

"Can't say. He's at Home Depot. The man loves that place. I've known him to spend hours pacing up and down the aisles, drooling over this gadget and that."

"Well, thanks for your time," Randy said, knowing that, for now, they were at another dead end.

"Sure. I'm sorry I can't be more help."

"We'll get back with your husband."

"You do that. Now, if you don't mind, I'd like to return to my shows. My husband relishes hardware; I love the *Family Cuisine Channel. Peggy Sue's Country Kitchen*'s my favorite."

Angela smirked, saying, "You don't want to miss her latest recipe, which includes five pounds of butter."

"Right you are, honey." The woman shuffled through the doorway behind the counter.

Brett turned to Randy and Angela. "Maybe Kevin's moved out," he said.

"To Vegas?" Randy asked.

"Could be," Angela said, "and committing murder."

STRAUB WAS SEATED in a leather chair in the parlor of Nicosia's Beverly Hills mansion. Nicosia handed him a cigar, lit his own, and within minutes, the room was gray with smoke. "Kennedy's here, in the Los Angeles area," Straub said.

Nicosia tapped his cigar in an ashtray. "How do you know?"

"One of my men spotted him at your wife's funeral. He's a towhead now."

"He was at Cynthia's service?"

"He stayed clear of the interment procession."

Nicosia puffed on his cigar. "How'd you know to have surveillance at the cemetery?"

"I cover all my bases, Mr. Nicosia. You hired me to do a job, and I'll do it well."

"Where is he now?"

Straub looked down, admiring his Brietling timepiece. "An old motel off Sunset. My people are keeping tabs on him."

Nicosia again tapped his cigar on the ashtray. "That's what I like to hear. It's critical you take care of this soon."

"That's what you're paying me for. He's still with Angela Grisham."

Nicosia scratched his head. "Her so-called disappearance has become quite a sensation in Las Vegas."

"So I hear."

"I met her after Cynthia's death. She came to my suite at the Desert Palm and pretended to be concerned about my welfare. I'm sure Kennedy sent her."

Straub stared at the glowing ash of his cigar. "Why would he do that?"

"It was some kind of taunt."

"That doesn't make sense."

"It's not your place to question my conclusions. Your job's to eliminate the man who killed my wife. Nothing more."

Straub blew a thick smoke ring into the air. "I just returned from Mexico an hour ago. I plan on taking him out later this evening."

SITTING ON THE living room sofa of her apartment with a football game on the television, Jennifer Crichton massaged Wayne's shoulders "Why are you so preoccupied?" she asked, kneading deep into his muscles.

"What?" he asked and took a swallow of his beer. "I'm sorry, what did you say?"

Jennifer laughed. "Wayne, your mind's a million miles away. Are you sure you want to be here?"

He smiled. "Yes, Jennifer. Believe me, I rushed back to Las Vegas so I could see you."

"What were you doing in Los Angeles?"

Wayne glanced at her over his shoulder, wondering what he should say. "When my new boss called and said he was giving me the host job at the Desert Palm, I drove up here with almost nothing. I went to L.A. to pick up everything that was in storage." He sipped his beer.

She continued to rub his shoulders. "Did you get it all?"

"I did. Why don't you have dinner at my apartment tomorrow? You can see how I have it decorated."

"It's a date. I want to see your taste in décor."

"It's better than you might expect from a jock like me."

"I want to be surprised." Jennifer wrapped both arms around his neck and hugged him.

"That'll happen no matter what." He kissed her on the cheek.

"Is that so?" She caressed his chest. "What do you have in mind?"

He gave her a lecherous grin. "What do you think?" He put his beer on an end table.

"That I shouldn't have to wait until tomorrow."

Wayne chuckled, desire in his eyes. "Take off your clothes, baby."

DIXIE WAS COUNTING hundred-dollar bills at her workstation in the Desert Palm's casino cashier, somewhat annoyed, as every time she started, a patron would interrupt her and she'd have to begin again.

Her supervisor tapped her on the shoulder. "May I have a word with you?"

Dixie frowned, put the stack of hundreds in a drawer, and turned to face the woman. "Sure, Simone."

"There's a police lieutenant in my office. He'd like to speak with you about Angela."

Dixie swallowed hard. "Why?"

"He told me he wants to talk with you about her—he didn't tell me the reason. It must be related to her disappearance."

She covered her mouth with her hand. "You say he's in your office?"

Simone nodded. "Yes."

"I wonder what he wants from me."

"There's only one way to find out."

"You'll watch my window?"

"Certainly. You better go in there; he's waiting."

Dixie left the main casino cashier's cage and walked down the stark linoleum hallway to Simone's office. She paused outside the door, trying to compose herself, then entered the room.

The lieutenant looked up as Dixie came into the office. "Mrs. Holiday?"

She was nervous, her hands trembling. "Yes, sir."

"I'm Lieutenant Schultz with Metro." He gestured to a chair. "Please have a seat."

Dixie sat down, her discomfort palpable, and crossed her legs.

"Please relax. I only have a couple questions. There's nothing to be afraid of."

"Sure." Dixie's mouth was dry, and she licked her lips.

Schultz leaned forward. "I'll get to the point. It's my opinion Angela Grisham wasn't kidnapped by Randy Kennedy."

"Is that so? Why do you believe that?"

"An educated guess."

"I see. Then how do you explain her disappearance?"

"You tell me."

She fingered her wedding ring nervously. "I don't understand."

"What's the relationship between Angela Grisham and Randy Kennedy?"

"I, I, I don't know."

The lieutenant's gaze was probing. "Why don't you tell me what's going on?"

Dixie hung her head, her eyes fixed on her shoes, fighting to hold back tears.

Schultz leaned closer. "Is Angela with Kennedy of her own volition?"

She sat there, fumbling with the pleats in her dress.

"Mrs. Holiday," he said with more emphasis, "please tell me what you know."

Her lower lip quivered. "Angela's fine. She insists Randy didn't kill anyone."

"You've spoken with her?"

Dixie closed her eyes.

"Everyone will be safer if you tell me the truth. Have you talked with Angela?"

She nodded slowly. "Yes, earlier today. She called me."

"She wasn't abducted by Kennedy?"

"No, I told you—she's okay. Randy didn't kidnap her. She says she's with him because he's an innocent man."

"Did she tell you why she thinks that?"

Dixie shook her head. "We only spoke for a minute. Angela phoned to tell me she wasn't in any danger. She's seen the newspaper and television reports and knew I'd be worried. She asked me to call her parents."

"Where is she?"

"I don't know."

"Please," Schultz said, his voice louder. "She must've told you where she was."

"She didn't."

"Two people have been murdered. Your colleague Angela's with a man we suspect is responsible."

Tears streamed down Dixie's cheeks. "I told her he was no good, but she wouldn't listen."

"We can't protect her if we don't know where she is."

Dixie blinked through the tears. "Angela wouldn't tell me. She's with Randy because she wants to be, but that's all I know."

BRETT DROPPED ANGELA and Randy off at the Sleepy Hollow Motel, and they sat in the cramped room, pondering the day's events. "I feel sorry for Brett," Angela said. "Cynthia died with their relationship strained, and he isn't going to be able to forget that." She walked over to the window and watched cars speed past the grungy motel. It was another moonless evening, and the streetlights were struggling against the dark, leaving the area in a hazy gloom.

Randy adjusted the pillow he was leaning on. "He won't

recover from it soon. My parents were killed in a car crash, and I can tell you, it's something you don't blow past in a hurry."

"I'm sorry."

"I was young, in grade school when it happened."

"Who raised you?"

"My grandmother. Toughest woman I've ever known. She's the one who christened me the Lucky One."

"She knows your reputation with women?"

He waved his hand. "That's not what it means. I'm Irish, and things come to me pretty easily. At least, they did."

"You should call and tell her you're all right."

"Can't do that, Angela. She passed away last summer. I'm all alone on this earth."

Angela didn't know what to say at first, but her expression reflected sympathy. "No, you're not."

He smiled at her. "Thanks."

Angela stared back out the smudged window, her eyes narrowing. "Randy, come over here."

His eyebrows drew together. "Why?"

"Get over here now."

He jumped off the bed and hurried to the window. "What is it?"

"See that police car there?" Angela gestured.

"Yeah." His voice was tight.

"It's been circling the block. Each time it drives by the motel, it slows, and the officer's peering in this direction."

Randy watched the police cruiser creep past the motel.

"You don't suppose..." Angela's face was pale.

"We can't take that chance. Let's get out of this dump."

"How would they know we're here?"

"Brett Miller."

"I don't believe that."

"That doesn't matter right now."

Randy took Angela by the hand and opened the door. Seeing that all was momentarily clear, they dashed out of the room and across the parking lot. Sirens blaring and lights flashing, a police car barreled down the street toward them. They froze for a second; then Randy said, "This way." He turned, and they bolted in the opposite direction.

At first, Angela's hand dragged hard against his, but then she was sprinting along next to him. They scurried around the side of the motel and scrambled past several old vehicles. Running toward some apartments, they heard a deep voice yell, "Freeze. Stop where you are."

Randy and Angela ignored the man and leaped behind a dumpster. Panicking in the darkness, they sped into an alley strewn with trash. Randy heard the cops shouting but didn't look back. His lone concern was keeping Angela with him as they fled. He'd seen her conflicted expression.

A police car, red lights flashing, moved into the alley in front of them, and Randy veered between two dilapidated apartment buildings. They stumbled in the dark, feeling their way past beat-up metal garbage containers and discarded beer cans. They slid between a building and a large thicket of bushes and stopped. Randy put his hands on his knees, trying to catch his breath without making a sound doing so. Angela recovered her wind a tad faster and said in a whisper, "We have to find a better place to hide. They're sure to discover us here, and we can't keep running. I don't have the stamina."

They heard footsteps in the alley and saw a beam of light blaze in their direction. Angela put her hand over her mouth, clearly afraid she might release an inadvertent gasp.

A brawny policeman walked between the apartment buildings, his flashlight in one hand and a forty-five in the other. He shined the light over the bushes that camouflaged

Angela and Randy, who stayed as still as possible until the man continued down the ally and out of view.

Randy exhaled. He'd been holding his breath the entire time the officer had been standing there. He took in a deep gulp of air.

"My heart is pounding in my ears," Angela said. "What are we going to do?"

"I don't know. We can't stay here. Any minute now this entire block will be crawling with cops." He inched out from behind the bushes, Angela his shadow. The sound of a barking dog stopped them both. After a moment of hesitation, they continued to creep between the buildings.

Angela said in raspy whisper, "I believe we should keep away from the alley. It's best if we stay in the maze of apartments."

Randy followed her around the corner of a building. They heard the ever-increasing sound of sirens and the cops surrounding the area.

"If there was a moon, we could see," Randy said.

Angela looked at him. "So could the cops."

They skulked between the buildings, close to the grimy clapboard walls. Randy plodded forward and frightened a cat, which yowled and darted through the dark. He put his hand over his heart. It felt to him like it was pounding a thousand beats per second.

"It's just a cat," Angela said and marched forward.

Randy shook his head. They heard the sound of footsteps and froze.

Randy motioned to the walkway above. "Up there." He ducked back and crawled up a wooden staircase. Angela did the same. At the landing, they hunkered down against the walkway's four-foot-high half-wall.

Below, two policemen were coming down the sidewalk. They stopped in front of the stairs. A Hispanic officer shined his flashlight at the second-floor walkway. The light shone only feet above where Randy and Angela were crouched.

"There's a dumpster up ahead," the red-haired cop said.

The Hispanic policeman turned his flashlight, and they disappeared down the alley.

Angela and Randy sat there paralyzed, unsure what to do, their hearts beating frantically.

Angela glanced at the window next to the front door of a nearby apartment, where a light was on. "Randy, that window's open."

He shrugged. "So?"

"Maybe we can get into that unit."

He stared at her like she was a space alien. "What if someone's home?"

"Let's ring the bell and find out."

"No," he said in a sharp whisper. "We can't risk it."

"What's the alternative? The entire area's surrounded by cops. If somebody answers, say you're at the wrong apartment."

Randy gaped at her. "Okay." He edged his way over to the door. The sound of barking dogs and the growing wail of police sirens was everywhere. He slunk up and peered through a dirty window, surveying the small apartment. The living room and kitchen were lit and empty, as was the hallway to the back. The apartment appeared to be vacant, but he couldn't be sure. Randy rang the bell and waited. He hit the doorbell again. "I don't think anyone's home."

He pried off the screen and leaned it against the wall, then slid the window open wider and told Angela to climb in. With one swift movement, she lifted a leg over the windowsill and slipped into the apartment. "Open the door," Randy said. "I'll replace the screen."

Angela did as instructed while Randy put the screen back in the window. Hearing voices between the units below, he zipped into the apartment and shut the door. For now, they were safe.

ROBERT STRAUB PULLED his black Cadillac off the street and drove into an alley, stopping behind a police cruiser. He sat there, the flashing lights on the cop car illuminating his face in crimson every few seconds. He was angry, his teeth clenched. His plan to take Kennedy out had been interrupted by the arrival of the authorities.

A police officer crossed the alley and walked up to the driver's side of the Cadillac. He knocked on the glass with the butt of his flashlight.

Straub lowered the window, holding up his hand to shield his eyes from the beam of light. "Yes, officer?"

"You can't park here."

"What's going on?"

"A fugitive's on the loose. It's not safe for you to be in this area."

"What did he do?"

"Murder. He's wanted on a couple homicide charges out of Las Vegas."

"And he's here?"

The cop nodded. "Yeah. That's why you have to leave. I need you out of here now, before something happens."

"Yes, sir. I'll be on my way." Straub put the car in gear and backed out of the alley.

CARTER CAMP POUNDED his fist on a counter in the Las Vegas Metro police station. "For the amount of money I've put up, I demand to know what's going on."

The police officer on the other side of the counter said, her expression unyielding, "This is a police matter. I'm not at liberty to discuss the details of our investigation."

Camp's pasty skin turned a bright pink. "I demand to speak to someone in charge."

The woman rolled her eyes. "All right, let me see if I can find the lieutenant. In the meantime, calm down, or I'll have your ass thrown in jail for disorderly conduct."

"Fine." Camp turned away from the woman and paced in front of the counter. Two policemen escorted a stocky Asian man wearing handcuffs down the hallway.

"I didn't hurt her," the prisoner said.

"Tell that to the judge," one of the officers said.

"She's a lying bitch."

The cop pushed him forward. "Aren't they all?"

Camp watched them guide the man away and disappear around a corner.

"Mr. Camp," a voice said from behind him. "I hear you're asking for me."

Camp swiveled around and looked at the lieutenant. "Yes, sir."

"I'm Lieutenant Schultz. We spoke at Angela Grisham's townhouse."

"Can you tell me the status of the Randy Kennedy case?"

Schultz stared at him with a thoughtful eye. "Let's go back to my office."

"Is there any news on his whereabouts? Do you know if Angela's with him?"

"My office." Schultz turned and headed down the hallway.

Camp rushed after him and trailed the lieutenant through a maze of cubicles until they reached a glass office door. The lieutenant opened it and moved behind his desk, pointing Camp to a chair.

Camp sat down. "Lieutenant, you have to tell me what's going on. I've put up a million-and-a-half-dollar reward, and for that kind of cash, I deserve some answers."

Schultz cocked his head to one side. "It's my understanding Walter Parker put up the money."

"At my request. You know he's my uncle. He wouldn't have offered the cash if I hadn't persuaded him to do so."

"The reward has certainly resulted in the phone ringing."

In an excited voice, Camp asked, "You have some leads?"

"Every crackpot in Las Vegas has called with a Kennedy sighting."

"Then you have nothing solid?"

"I didn't say that."

"Stop being so evasive. Has the reward produced a useful tip?"

Schultz put on his reading glasses. "We received numerous calls through *Secret Witness*. Two hours ago, there was one we believe may be legitimate."

"Where is he?"

"Nothing's been confirmed."

"I understand that." Camp rubbed his hands together. "What did the caller tell you?"

The lieutenant shuffled some papers on his desk, obviously stalling as he tried to decide what he was going to say.

"A million and a half bucks, Lieutenant. That's what my uncle put up at my request. You have me to thank for your *Secret Witness* call."

Schultz studied Camp over the top of his glasses. "Our tipster said Kennedy and Grisham are staying in a motel in the Hollywood area."

Camp's mouth dropped open. "They're in Southern California?"

"Yes."

"Then why do you think the tip's credible?"

"He knew information that made me feel he's telling the truth, including that Angela Grisham was with Kennedy by choice."

"That's not true."

"I'm sorry, sir, but it is."

Camp's eyes were now the thinnest of slits. "No. It can't be."

"It is."

"Why?"

"You know the most likely answer to that."

"I won't accept it."

"Suit yourself. The *Secret Witness* caller confirmed what I'd found out already. Ms. Grisham phoned a cashier at the Desert Palm and told her she went with Kennedy voluntarily."

Camp's face twitched. "You say they're in Hollywood?"

"Some run-down motel. We've contacted the Los Angeles Police Department, and they're on their way there this very minute."

"When will you know if they have Kennedy?"

"Soon, I expect."

"They wouldn't harm Angela?"

"I'm sure they have no intention of hurting either Ms. Grisham or Mr. Kennedy. Their only goal is to capture them and extradite him to Las Vegas. If he gives up without incident, they're in no danger."

"They'll send Kennedy back, but what about Angela?"

Schultz took off his reading glasses. "We'll need to find out why she's with him. She could be charged with aiding and abetting a fugitive."

"That can't be true. She wouldn't assist a murderer."

"It appears as though she is."

Camp bit his lip, his face stony. "No way."

"We'll know soon enough."

"You'll find out Angela's one more victim of Randy Kennedy."

RANDY AND ANGELA stood in the apartment, listening to the thunder of their hearts. They surveyed the interior of the small room in the dim light. A beat-up sofa with a garish green-and-white pattern sat against the far wall, the cushions stained. Next to it was an end table. Across from the sofa was a vintage television set on a yellow plastic milk crate. The smell of stale beer and tobacco smoke permeated the space.

To the left of the living area was a kitchenette with a compact refrigerator, stove, and a sink filled to the top with dirty dishes. A Formica table sat in the corner of the room, mounds of newspapers stacked on it, along with a large red ashtray that was the grave of a few dozen cigarette butts.

"Let's make damn sure we're alone," Randy said, making his way down the short hallway. Angela followed close behind. They passed a tiny bathroom, which reeked of urine, and inched their way into the bedroom. The floor of the room was piled high with soiled clothing, more newspapers, and empty Budweiser cans. A double mattress lay on the floor in the middle of the room.

Angela asked, "Can you imagine living in a place like this?"

Randy shrugged. "For now, it's our home. Let's attempt to relax, if that's possible." They walked back into the living area.

Angela wrinkled her nose. "How long do you suppose the police will hang around?"

"I have no idea. Not all night, I hope. The occupants of this fine villa are bound to come home at some point."

Angela cringed at the thought and eyed the door apprehensively.

Suddenly, a helicopter roared overhead, its flood light blazing down between the buildings and brilliantly lighting the area where they were standing. "Close the blinds," Randy said, tearing over and shutting the ones next to the table in the kitchenette. Angela dashed to the living room window and did the same.

The chopper flew past but returned for a second look. It seemed to be just feet above the building. They heard the obscenity-laced yelling of the tenants in the adjoining apartments. The helicopter, sirens, barking dogs, and people's shouts created a symphony of confusion that assaulted Angela and Randy.

"We're trapped for now," Randy said. "Let's try to make the best of it."

Angela nodded, and he led her to the sofa. They sat down, and he put an arm around her in a futile attempt to give her comfort. Hours passed, and they both dozed, jolted awake every few minutes by a siren or a howling dog. Once, there was a knock at the door. "Police!" a man said. Randy and Angela sat there with their muscles frozen until the authorities continued to the next apartment.

"What do you guys think you're doing?" the high-pitched voice of the woman next door asked the cops. "You've kept me awake all night. I have to be at work in a few hours, and I need my rest."

The muffled sounds of the officers' deep voices could be heard but not understood.

The shrill woman said, "Everyone in this goddamned neighborhood's a fugitive. Now leave me alone." The slamming of the door shook the apartment.

Randy listened, his mind numb. *How can this be happening?* A week ago, he was a happy-go-lucky casino host, and today, he was wanted for kidnapping and the murder of two people and was hiding in a tenement almost three hundred miles from home.

Angela had fallen asleep, and he watched her breathe. *She's what keeps me going*, he thought. She'd done so much for him, both for his morale and to help him. He had to clear his name, if for no other reason than to validate Angela's belief in him. He pressed his head against her shoulder and shut his eyes.

The jingling of keys and the metal-on-metal sound of one

being unsuccessfully inserted into a lock awakened Randy. He nudged Angela. She woke instantly, cold fear crossing her face. The rattle of keys was like an alarm, and he could feel the terror rip through his body and knew Angela felt the same. They sprang off the sofa and into the kitchenette, dropping down behind the counter and holding their breath.

The jingling of keys and scraping of the lock continued. "What's going on?" Angela asked in a curt whisper.

"I'm guessing whoever it is can't find the right key."

They heard slurred swearing on the other side of the door, then the successful insertion of a key and the clicking noise of the lock being turned. An old man in a disheveled brown suit staggered into the apartment. He pushed the door shut and stumbled to the hallway, slamming into a wall as he attempted to enter the bathroom. More obscenities. He flicked on the light and moments later, they heard the steady stream of a man who desperately needed to urinate.

After what seemed forever, the man lurched out of the bathroom, zigzagged into the bedroom, and flopped on the mattress. Almost instantly, the reverberation of drunken snores echoed throughout the apartment.

"He's asleep," Angela said. "Let's get out of here."

Randy shook his head. "No. That guy will be passed out for a while. We're better off in here with him then out there with them."

TWENTY-ONE

As EARLY MORNING arrived, the sounds of sirens, helicopters, and even barking dogs subsided. Randy and Angela sat on the sofa, wide-eyed, bracing for the police to burst in or their drunken roommate to awaken. As best they could tell, the foot patrols by the cops had stopped. And the snoring man in the other room was oblivious to everything.

When the sun crept over the horizon, there was a stirring in the apartment buildings as the tenants got ready for work. "It's time for us to leave," Randy said in a gravelly voice.

Angela rubbed her eyes. "Fine by me. The anxiety's too much."

"I wonder if our friend in the other room has some clothing we can wear."

She tugged on a shirtsleeve. "I doubt we wear the same size."

Randy yawned. "Let's take a look anyway."

They slunk down the short hallway, careful not to make a sound. At the door to the bedroom, they peeked in. The man had his rumpled suit jacket pulled up over his head. His chest was rising and falling with the accompanying sound of adenoidal breathing. He snorted, and they both held their breath, waiting

286

for the snoring to continue. The man turned over on his side, and the reassuring buzzing resumed.

Angela and Randy tiptoed to the closet and stared at the contents. There wasn't much to see. More clothing was piled on the floor than hung up. Randy grabbed a baseball cap—the L.A. Dodgers—and placed it on his head. He took a brown fedora off a shelf. Angela inspected it and grimaced. Randy smiled and put it on her head.

Angela mouthed, *I'm going to look like a clown*. She glanced down and saw a blue sweatshirt on the floor. Lifting it, she pressed it to Randy's chest and nodded.

He grinned and laughed silently. He picked up a gray sports jacket and threw it to her. Angela slipped it on. It was a bit large and scruffy, but a quick peek at the closet told her there was little choice. She snickered quietly, mouthing, *It'll have to do*. The old man continued to snore in what sounded like total contentment. Randy pointed to the hall, and they exited the bedroom and shut the door.

Back in the living room, they looked at each other in the morning light. He was dressed like a refugee from a homeless shelter, and Angela resembled someone on their way to a speakeasy. "Won't we be a tad conspicuous?" she asked.

Randy raised his shoulders. "We can't be seen in the clothes we were wearing last night. We just need to get out of this neighborhood."

"Easier said..."

Randy pulled down the bill on his hat and reached for the doorknob. "Wait," he said, "before we go." He pulled out his wallet, removed three-twenty-dollar bills, and set them on the kitchen table. "For our friend in the other room. He can either buy new clothes or booze; I don't care which."

Angela chuckled. "That's noble of you. Want my guess which it'll be?"

Randy smiled, turned to the door, and slowly opened it. He looked down the walkway in both directions, then gestured to the stairs. "Let's find a bus or taxi. I believe there's a pretty busy street nearby."

After they made it to the ground floor, they pivoted to the south and followed the pathway through the apartment buildings. A young boy on a bicycle rode between them, and when he glided by, he knocked the fedora off Angela's head. "Hey, you moron," she said. The boy laughed and peddled away. She frowned, picked up the hat, and put it back on.

Randy swerved toward the sounds of traffic. Approaching the end of the apartment complex, they walked into a crowded parking lot. "Follow me." He hooked a hard right toward the street.

Angela put a hand on his shoulder. "I have a better idea. Come on."

Randy was curious but trailed after her without hesitation.

Angela meandered between parked cars and up to an old green Toyota with its engine running. She strolled to the driver's side and looked through the open window at the young black man sitting behind the wheel. The pulsating sound of rap music blasted through the air.

"Would you like to earn an easy twenty bucks?" she asked.

The man was rocking to the rhythm. "What?"

"Twenty dollars. I'll give you twenty bucks."

He kept on jiving back and forth.

Angela raised her voice. "Turn down the stereo."

The man drummed on the steering wheel. "What?"

"The stereo, turn the damn thing down." Angela put her hands over her ears.

Randy watched, bewildered, thinking, *I thought we weren't going to bring attention to ourselves.*

The man extended his hand to the dashboard and lowered the volume. "I love that Kid-Z."

"Me too," Angela said. "How'd you like to make twenty dollars?"

"What do you have in mind?" The guy was interested but eyeing her outfit with a raised eyebrow.

"We need a ride. It's really important. Our car broke down, and we can't find a taxi."

"I don't know...I have to be at work in thirty minutes."

"We don't want to go far—a mall about three miles from here."

"The Beverly Center?"

"That's the place."

"Okay. There, but no farther."

Angela smiled. "Great."

The man beamed back at her. "As they say in the movies, show me the money."

Randy retrieved his wallet, took out a twenty-dollar bill and handed it to Angela, who gave it to the man.

"Hop in," he said with another large grin.

Randy ran around to the passenger side of the car, while Angela jumped in the backseat. The man ratcheted up the stereo and, swaying his head to the beat, cruised out of the parking lot. Driving down the street, he settled into the traffic, still playing his imaginary drums on the steering wheel.

The man rocked along until stopped by a red light, the thunderous beat of the stereo vibrating across the intersection. A police cruiser drove up next to them, and Randy sank down in the seat and lowered his head. Angela did the same. When the light changed, the cop car raced away, and they sped off for the Beverly Center Mall.

LIEUTENANT SCHULTZ PACED around Walter Parker's office at

the Desert Palm Resort, a deep frown on his face. "Mr. Parker, I'm sorry to inform you of this, but Randy Kennedy somehow dodged the police in Hollywood. Considering the amount of money you've put up as a reward, I thought you should know."

Parker leaned back in his chair. "I appreciate that, Lieutenant. Have you told my nephew?"

"Mr. Camp hasn't left the police station in two days. He's quite distraught, to say the least."

"I'm sorry if he's being a pest. He's smitten by Miss Grisham and has been consumed with her kidnapping."

"I assumed you knew…She wasn't abducted."

"Ah." Parker patted his desk. "I thought that might be the case. I know Randy quite well and knew he wouldn't do something that stupid."

"I wish your nephew was as clear-headed."

"All his life, Carter's been one-upped by people like Randy Kennedy. I can understand him not believing the truth."

Schultz grunted. "The truth. If only it were that easy."

"Why do I get the impression you're not satisfied with how this investigation is shaking out?"

"Certain aspects are bothering me."

"Such as?"

"Randy's lawyer says his prints were on the murder weapon because he picked it up to defend himself from Joseph Nicosia and his bodyguard. Nicosia's a well-known mob boss."

"The mob, huh?"

"Yes, Mr. Parker. One way or the other, Nicosia's behind a great deal of the criminal activity on the West Coast."

"If he's so bad, why isn't he in prison?"

"You know how these crime bosses work. They have their minions carry out the dirty work. They direct the illegal activities but stay out of jail by not doing it themselves."

"I guess it should trouble me that the funds he wagers at my gaming tables are the fruits of illegal activities."

Schultz put his hands in his pockets. "Perhaps."

"I'm not in the habit of inquiring where my guests obtain their bankroll."

"With all due respect, maybe you should."

"It was my understanding he was involved in financial institutions—making payday loans. I didn't know he had a sideline. I understand, though, why you'd have an issue with Nicosia's claim about what happened."

"It's given me pause."

"Lieutenant, let me give you my opinion on this whole sordid ordeal. Number one, I don't believe Randy killed Cynthia Nicosia. I never have. Two, to think Randy took out Conrad Hale is preposterous. He had no motive whatsoever. Three, if Nicosia's the kind of man you say he is, then both Randy and Angela may end up in the same condition as poor Mr. Hale."

"I may be inclined to agree, but there's nothing to prove that."

"In time, the facts will unfold. I ask you to investigate every possibility before you unjustly crucify Randy."

Schultz cleared his throat. "Why do you care? He's just an employee gone bad."

"I don't have employees. The people who work for me are my family. In a way, I consider Randy a son."

"For a man with no living relatives, Kennedy sure has a lot of people worried about his fate."

Parker clasped his hands. "That must tell you something."

"It might."

"Keep digging. You'll find your murderer if you're persistent."

TUCKED BEHIND A directory kiosk between the Beverly Center and a beauty supply store, Randy and Angela debated their next move. "We should call Brett," Angela said.

Randy's voice rose. "He turned us in for the reward money. We can't go to him."

Angela also raised her voice. "He didn't call the cops; I know it."

"How can you think that?"

"The same reason I know you didn't murder Mrs. Nicosia or Conrad Hale. I'm a good judge of character, and just as I know you didn't kill anyone, I'm sure Brett didn't call the police."

He stared at her. "I can't argue with that logic."

"Trust me."

"I am, with my life."

"We'll be fine."

Randy adjusted his baseball cap. It was too big for his head and kept sliding forward. He fished in his pants pocket and pulled out a couple of quarters. "Okay, we'll call Brett."

Angela reached in her pocket. "I have his number." She handed Randy a slip of paper.

He pointed to a booth next to a sandwich shop. "There's a payphone."

They walked to the phone, and Randy inserted the coins and dialed. On the third ring, Brett answered. "Are you guys okay?" he asked after Randy identified himself.

"We've had better days."

"The TV news has shown nothing but footage of the area you fled to."

"I can imagine. I wouldn't call us out of danger yet. We're just about four miles from the Sleepy Hollow Motel, and we need a place to hide."

"I'll come get you. Where are you?"

Randy hesitated. "I know I have to take your word for this, but reassure me you weren't the one who called the police." A long silence filled the air. "Brett, did you hear what I said?"

"I want my sister's killer. Nothing more."

"The cops think I murdered her. Are you sure you don't agree?"

"I trust Angela, and she believes you're innocent. For now, that's good enough for me. I didn't call the police, and I won't until or unless you give me reason to."

"Fair enough. We're near the Beverly Center on the La Cienega side. There's an Old Navy across the street."

"I know the place. I'll be there in twenty minutes." Brett clicked off.

Randy hung up the phone and stared at Angela, his eyes filled with concern. "He's on his way."

LIEUTENANT SCHULTZ POURED Anthony Chapman a cup of coffee. "Cream or sugar?"

Chapman shook his head. "No, black's fine. There's no sign of them?" He took the coffee from Schultz.

"No. Somehow, they slipped right out from under the Los Angeles police."

Chapman savored the aroma of his coffee and sipped. It didn't taste as good as it smelled, and he scowled. "Where were they?"

"In an old motel in Hollywood. We received a *Secret Witness* call giving their whereabouts."

"How the hell did the police let them get away?"

"They're sure not happy. They had the motel staked out, but Kennedy must've seen them. He and Grisham ran down an alley and disappeared in a jungle of run-down apartments."

"I assume they searched the area?"

"Of course they did. Helicopters, foot patrols—everything they had—but they escaped."

Chapman drank another swallow of his coffee. "That's unbelievable."

"You say you've heard from your, um, ex-client?"

Chapman nodded. "Randy called me yesterday afternoon."

"He seems to be keeping in touch with you. Why would he stay in contact with his...ah, ex-lawyer?"

"His attorney or not, Randy and I are friends, and I'm one of the few people he has to call."

"Hopefully, you've attempted to set him straight—convince him he should turn himself in."

Chapman placed his coffee on Schultz's desk. "I've about given up on that."

"What did he want?"

"He has a theory about Mrs. Nicosia's murder."

"Oh, I bet he does."

"He thinks it has to do with a painting—*Sunflowers in a Vase* by Vincent van Gogh."

Schultz's expression became peevish. "I'm listening."

"It's complicated, but as Randy explained it, Mrs. Nicosia had a Van Gogh."

"Yeah, so? As I understand it, her husband's a wealthy individual. I'm sure they own many expensive works of art."

"Randy says Joseph Nicosia wasn't aware she had this particular painting."

"How'd she obtain it?"

"Before Mrs. Nicosia married Joseph, she was involved in some kind of forgery scam. She worked at an art gallery and would sell fake paintings to people, then sell the originals on the black market."

"Forgive me, but what does this have to do with her murder?"

"Listen, Lieutenant, please. Mrs. Nicosia had a partner named Kevin Delfino. Randy told me that he was her boyfriend before she married Nicosia and did the actual fencing of the genuine canvases."

"I still don't see what this has to do with her death."

"Mrs. Nicosia screwed over her ex-boyfriend and kept

Sunflowers in a Vase for herself. Just days before her murder, she hung it in a suite at the Conquistador Resort, the one she was slain in. It's missing, and Randy's certain the killer has the painting."

Schultz flexed his right hand. "There was an empty picture frame in the suite. We assumed the painting that was in it was stolen. You say it was a Van Gogh?"

"Yes. Randy believes the murderer has the work in his possession."

"Who does he suspect?"

"It's his opinion that Delfino has the most compelling motive. The Van Gogh's worth a million and a half, maybe more. Cynthia Nicosia screwed him by taking it and left him for Joe Nicosia to boot. As I understand it, they didn't part on good terms. Randy believes those are damn strong reasons for Delfino to kill the woman."

Schultz rubbed his chin. "The painting could just as easily be Kennedy's motive."

Chapman said firmly, "Randy's adamant it's Delfino. He told me I was wrong when I said I thought the killer was Joe Nicosia."

"I've questioned Nicosia, who has an alibi."

"From a reliable source? She cheated on him—motivation for murder if I ever heard one."

"A Desert Palm blackjack dealer gave a statement that she was with Nicosia during his wife's murder."

"It's a motive for killing Conrad Hale as well. What does he say about that?"

Schultz looked at the papers on his desk. "I haven't questioned him about Hale."

"Why the hell not?"

"Kennedy is Hale's assailant."

"You're fricking kidding me. You haven't even interrogated Nicosia?"

"He's gone back to Beverly Hills. We'll get to him eventually."

Chapman glared at the lieutenant in disbelief. "Will you at least consider Randy's theory that Delfino should be a suspect in Mrs. Nicosia's murder? And mine that Joe Nicosia took out Hale?"

"I have more than enough evidence to place Kennedy at the scene of the Nicosia homicide. Her blood's all over his clothing. His fingerprints were on the murder weapon."

"Please, Lieutenant, do me this one favor; keep an open mind."

"I've been trying, but the case against him is airtight."

"He doesn't have the Van Gogh. The killer does. Don't you owe it to all of us to check every possibility?"

"I wish I didn't like you, Chapman. I'd throw your ass out of my office and never give it a second thought."

"But you do." Chapman fought to hold back a grin.

"I guess I better book a flight to Los Angeles and speak with our friend, Joseph Nicosia. I'll need to arrange for a search warrant too, if I want to rattle him and search his home for the Van Gogh."

Chapman unleashed that smile. "If you let me tag along, we can use my firm's private jet."

RANDY MOTIONED TO the blue Honda pulling to the side of the road. "There's Brett's car."

Angela smiled. "At last. It took him log enough."

Brett idled at the curb as Randy and Angela crossed the sidewalk and walked up to the car. Angela beamed at Brett and waved, seeing his puzzled face as he scrutinized their outfits.

Brett reached across the passenger side and unlocked the doors. Angela opened the front one and lowered herself into the seat, saying, "I'm glad to see you. I wasn't sure you'd ever get here."

"Sorry, the traffic's brutal."

Randy heaved open the rear door. He was slipping into the Honda when a gust of wind caught the bill of his baseball cap and flipped it off his head. He lunged for the hat, which was spiraling under the car. At that moment, the door window shattered into pieces, shards of glass spraying through the air. Angela screamed, and Randy threw himself on the backseat as a second blast blew out the rear window. "Go, Brett, go," Randy shouted.

Brett hit the accelerator, and the car rocketed away from the curb, tires smoking. He glanced in the rearview mirror, his face rigid and ghost-white. "What the hell was that?"

"Why would the police be shooting at us?" Angela asked. Her skin was also pale, eyes wide as she crouched in the seat.

Randy peered over the top of the backseat and out the shattered rear window. "It's not the cops."

"Who, then?" Brett asked.

"Nicosia. It's him, I know it."

Brett drove down La Cienega Boulevard at an unnerving speed, hitting potholes, the remaining pieces of broken glass bouncing across the trunk of the car. "Nicosia? Why?"

"He wants me dead," Randy said hoarsely.

"I didn't know that hanging around you would make me the target of the mob."

"Now you know. If you're not willing to continue, let me off at the nearest corner."

"Brett," Angela said, eyeing Randy over the top of the seat, "he didn't mean that. Keep driving."

Brett weaved through traffic. "Are we being followed?"

Randy took a labored breath. "I don't believe so. Slow down a little. At this speed, you're certain to attract attention."

Brett eased up on the gas, and the Honda slowed to a more reasonable speed. "You're sure we're not being followed?" He licked his lips and checked the side mirror.

Randy was watching the cars behind them. "No." He pointed. "Take a left here."

"Where are we headed?" Angela asked.

"Nowhere now. We need to get lost in traffic and zigzag around until we're confident we're not being followed."

Brett was paying more attention to the rearview mirror than the road in front of them. "Okay," he said. He looked forward again and braked fast, the car lurching as he almost ran into the truck ahead of them. "Sorry, guys."

After a few miles, they all calmed a little. Randy noticed that Angela was being extra quiet and said in a soft voice, "Are you feeling all right?"

The dark circles under her eyes were getting deeper. "Randy, with all that's happened, I'm more scared than ever."

He put his hand to his chest. "I know. So am I."

TWENTY-TWO

NICOSIA SAT IN a lounge chair next to his swimming pool, a cigar in one hand and a foamy glass of beer in the other. He was wearing a red Speedo, and his bare, tanned torso was covered with black and gray hair. His potbelly was a convenient location to rest his drink.

Robert Straub sat across from him in obvious discomfort. Dressed in a dark suit and without the benefit of the umbrella shading Nicosia, he was perspiring profusely.

Nicosia looked at the assassin. "So, Mr. Professional Hit Man, what's taking you so goddamn long?"

Straub considered Nicosia's query with the dark eyes of a shark. "I told you I planned to take Kennedy out last night. The police arrived before I had a chance. I watched the cops chase Kennedy and Grisham through the motel parking lot and down an alley."

"The news said they disappeared near some public housing slum."

"No one can vanish, Mr. Nicosia. The police gave up, but I didn't. I waited them out. Sure enough, they sneaked out of one of the apartments about seven this morning."

"Why didn't you do your job then?"

Straub's crazy, piercing eyes drilled into Nicosia's. "They were wearing disguises, and by the time I realized it was them, they'd hitched a ride with someone." Straub was incensed; he couldn't remember the last time he botched a hit this badly.

Nicosia inhaled smoke from his cigar. "Where's Kennedy now?"

"With your wife's brother. I noted down his license plate, and bribed a clerk at the DMV to get the address. We're staking out his home."

"Miller? What's Kennedy doing with him?"

Straub whisked a hand through his hair. "Hiding out, I expect."

"That fruity little artist. Why would he be consorting with the man who murdered his sister?"

"Your guess is as good as mine."

"Get this over with. It's taken more time than I wanted."

"It won't be long, I assure you. This is personal."

Nicosia took a sip of his German Pilsner. He smacked his lips and gazed around the pool and garden. "Beautiful day, isn't it?"

Just then, Samples came toward them, his expression stressed. "Mr. Nicosia, the cops are here."

Nicosia glowered at him. "Why?"

"They have a search warrant."

"For what? Where are they?"

"At the front entrance."

Nicosia rolled out of the lounge chair.

"I'll be leaving now," Straub said.

Nicosia's mind was obviously on the police. "Fine." He waddled to the house, his bare feet slapping against the patio. He crashed through the door and into his home, calling, "Conchita, bring me a robe." He saw two men in suits and two uniformed police officers near the front door. "What's this about?"

Lieutenant Schultz stepped back as the half-naked man, coils of hair on his head shooting in all directions, charged toward him.

"Are you deaf?" Nicosia demanded, louder. "What's the meaning of this?"

Schultz held out his right hand. "Good day, sir."

Nicosia ignored Schultz's hand. "I want to know what this is about."

"Mr. Nicosia, we met in Las Vegas. I'm Lieutenant Andre Schultz with the Las Vegas Metropolitan Police Department. These are officers Hansen and Price with the Beverly Hills P.D." He didn't introduce Anthony Chapman. "We have a warrant to search the premises."

A Hispanic woman scampered up to Nicosia and handed him a black robe, which he put on. "And what, may I ask, are you looking for?"

"A painting; *Sunflowers in a Vase* by Vincent van Gogh."

Nicosia tied the belt of the robe. "It's not here."

"It's missing from the suite Mrs. Nicosia decorated in the Conquistador Resort. We're seeking it in connection with the murder of your wife."

Nicosia shook his fist at the lieutenant. "Randy Kennedy killed her."

"This is an ongoing investigation."

"I demand my lawyer be present."

"You're more than welcome to call an attorney." Schultz pulled a piece of paper out of his jacket pocket and scanned it. "Judge Leroy Rankin signed this warrant about an hour ago, and we're starting our search. Now." The lieutenant and the two policemen walked past the slack-jawed Nicosia and entered the parlor. Anthony Chapman smiled at him and followed the officers.

THE PUDGY LAWYER was short and could best be described as

pig-like, his fat frame covered with an expensive gray wool suit. He retrieved a handkerchief from his pocket to wipe off his temples and said with a squeal, "I must protest this blatant abuse of power."

"Take that up with Judge Rankin," Lieutenant Schultz said.

"I told you," Nicosia said, "I don't have any goddamn painting."

Schultz crossed his arms. "Not here."

"Lieutenant, I don't know anything about a Van Gogh. If my wife had it, I guarantee you, it was without my knowledge."

"As I told you, she'd hung the painting in the suite she redecorated. It's now missing, and we believe you've hidden it."

With insulting slowness, Nicosia said, "I was unaware Cynthia had a painting."

"You know nothing about the whereabouts of the Van Gogh?"

The lawyer said, "I must object to this badgering of Mr. Nicosia."

Schultz ignored the man. "Mr. Nicosia?"

The lawyer took a few paces closer to the lieutenant. "That's enough of this. You've searched the house; the painting isn't here."

The lieutenant motioned to Nicosia. "As I understand it, your wife announced at a public event that at one point, she'd planned to leave you for Conrad Hale." He eyed Nicosia, waiting for a cataclysmic response. He received it.

"You piece of trash," Nicosia said, his face red. He thrust himself forward, his nose within inches of the lieutenant's. "I ought to punch you silly."

The two police officers moved in around the lieutenant. Both of them had that "make my day" look.

Schultz rubbed his hands together. "Mr. Nicosia, what do you know about the death of Mr. Hale?"

Nicosia said through gritted teeth, "Nothing. Now get the hell out of my house."

The lieutenant reached inside his jacket and pulled out a notepad. "No, sir. We're visiting for a little while longer."

THE DESERT PALM Casino was busy, and there were lines at the cashier's cage. "Good luck," Dixie said to an older lady after cashing her check.

"I need it," the woman said, scooping up the currency and tucking it in her purse. "I have almost seventy-five dollars invested in that machine."

"I'm sure it's due to hit."

"From your mouth to the slot god's ears." She tottered away from the counter to a row of slot machines.

Dixie watched her sit down at a slot, feeling sorry for her. She smiled at the next guest and cashed out his chips. When the line in front of her window was gone, Dixie spotted Carter Camp crossing the casino and called out to him.

He came over to the counter and up to her workstation, his expression sullen. "Hi, Dixie," he said, sounding depressed.

"Have you seen the news today?" she asked eagerly.

"I've been at the police station. Kennedy escaped."

"Any word on Angela?"

He bowed his head. "No."

"She phoned me yesterday."

His eyes narrowed. "You're the one she talked with?"

"She wanted to tell me she was all right."

"Kennedy hasn't harmed her?"

"No, Carter. I don't like this any more than you, but she's with him by choice."

He stared at her. "The reward flushed him out once, and I'm sure it will again."

"You know, when the police find them, Angela's going to be in a lot of trouble."

"She made her own decisions, and she'll get what she deserves."

BRETT TOOK A soft drink from the McDonalds drive-in crew member. "Would you like any ketchup?" the woman asked him.

He nodded. "Please."

She took a handful of ketchup packets and passed them to him.

"Thanks." Brett steered the car out of the drive-through and turned to Angela and Randy. "There's a park about a block up the street. I'll find us a shady spot."

"I'm starving," Randy said, seizing a few french fries from the bag and stuffing them in his mouth.

Angela leaned over and grabbed a couple. "Me too."

"What's your next move?" Brett asked.

Randy said around a mouthful of fries, "Find a safe place to hide."

"You're welcome to stay at my house."

"I don't believe that'll work."

"Why not? The neighborhood's quiet, secluded. No one will know you're there."

"Whoever shot at us—and I'm certain it was one of Nicosia's men—would find us there too easily."

"You think so?" Angela asked as she plucked a single french fry from the bag.

"If the gunman snagged Brett's license plate number, he'll know where to start looking. I don't want to take that chance."

"You're right," Brett said, his eyes showing how jittery he felt. "I don't enjoy being shot at one iota."

"It's not my favorite pastime either. While holed up in that apartment last night, I had some time to deliberate. We need to be more aggressive. Let's tell Gus Hadley we have a client willing to pay two million for the painting. He'll get the word out on the street. Hopefully, that'll attract Delfino's attention and lure him out in the open."

Angela asked, "Where will we find a client willing to offer two million?"

Randy chuckled. "We need to visit Eugene Serrano again."

"How can he assist us?"

"I'm thinking Mitzie may be able to help."

ANGELA AND BRETT decided to take a walk and left Randy on a park bench. He used the time alone to make some more calls with Brett's phone. Wayne didn't answer his mobile, so he dialed Anthony Chapman's number. As the telephone rang, Randy felt his anxiety heighten. "Pick up, Anthony. Please answer."

After the fifth ring: "Chapman."

"Anthony, it's Randy."

"Jesus, this stealth calling's driving me crazy. Where are you? Are you all okay?"

"Been better, but right now, I'm hanging in there."

"How'd you evade the police?"

"Luck and Angela."

"She's all right?"

"Yes, she's fine. If it weren't for her, I couldn't keep going."

"I take it you've won her over?"

"Even after all we've been through, I still don't know if she's doing this because she believes I'm innocent or what."

"Bull crap. I know you and females. You're the Lucky One, remember? You have her mesmerized, one way or the other."

"That's just it; I'm not certain I do. I can't discern her feelings."

"I've known you a long time. Being insecure with regard to women isn't like you."

"I haven't met anyone like Angela Grisham before."

"Enough about Angela. Randy, you're in a heap of trouble. You're fortunate that Lieutenant Schultz from Metro's being half-way open-minded about this case. In my opinion, he's been more than fair."

"We know for sure that two people knew Cynthia had the Van Gogh—Conrad Hale and Kevin Delfino. I don't know if anyone else was aware she had the painting. Maybe Nicosia."

"He doesn't have it."

"How can you be so positive of that?"

"I returned to Vegas forty-five minutes ago. Lieutenant Schultz and I have been busy men. We made a quick trip to Southern California in my firm's private jet. Schultz interrogated Nicosia about Hale's death, and while there, he and the Beverly Hills police searched the premises. There was no Van Gogh."

"He could've hidden it elsewhere."

"He denies any knowledge of the painting's whereabouts. I believe him."

"Anthony, this makes it clear that I've been right all along. There's only one person who could have the Van Gogh. It has to be Kevin Delfino."

"Any idea how you're going to prove that?"

"I might. I'm not sure yet how to make it all fall into place, but if I get lucky, I will."

BRETT SHIFTED THE Honda into a lower gear and turned onto a winding, tree-lined street. The clear plastic sheets they'd taped over the blown-out windows made a loud flapping sound in the wind. Eugene Serrano's mansion was to their right, and

Brett turned off and drove up the driveway toward the estate. An expansive rolling lawn led to a circular parking area with a large fountain in the center, jets of water streaming into the air.

Randy glanced at Angela and said, "Some digs."

She nodded as Brett parked the car in front of the double doors. Randy, Angela, and Brett piled out of the vehicle and walked up to the ornate front doors, which were framed by stained glass. Randy pressed the doorbell, and they heard an elaborate chime. "I hope he'll listen to us."

Angela and Brett exchanged nervous looks.

The giant doors opened, and a pale butler stood there, assessing the three of them uncertainly. "May I help you?"

"We'd like to speak with Mr. Serrano," Randy said.

The man shook his head. "I'm sorry, but he's unavailable."

"Please," Angela said. "It's important."

The butler leered at her. "He's working from home today, reviewing the blueprints of a project that begins construction next month. I'm sure he doesn't want to be disturbed."

"We're aware he's working from home," Randy said. "I talked with Mrs. Serrano earlier. She gave us this address. I think she called and told him we'd be dropping by. We'll only take a moment of his day."

"I don't know..." The butler glanced at Angela again. "I'll ask him, but there are no guarantees. Who should I say's calling?"

"Tell him Brett, Angela, and Randy. We met him at Tapas the other night. It's about the Van Gogh."

The man bounced a finger against his lips. "Very well."

Angela smiled. "Thank you."

"Wait here in the foyer. I'll see what I can do." The three of them entered the house, and the butler marched down the hallway.

"What if he won't see us?" Brett asked.

"We can't give up," Randy said. "We'll camp here until he will."

Angela asked, "Do you expect him go along with your plan?"

"I suppose it depends on how badly he wants to get the original painting."

"He spent a lot of money for a forgery," Brett said. "You know he's pissed and wants what he paid for."

"Tell us about Van Gogh," Angela said. "His flower paintings."

Brett nodded. "He crafted a series of *Sunflowers* paintings. Some are worth more than others. I believe Serrano's canvas isn't as valuable as most."

"Most?" Randy asked. "More than a million dollars isn't a lot?"

"I know one painting that sold for more than thirty-eight million."

"Thirty-eight million," Angela said with a gasp. "I still don't understand how Mrs. Nicosia could get away with selling forgeries. Serrano didn't just rely on the fake authentication from Kevin Delfino. He said his insurance company appraised the piece as well. Why didn't they spot that it was a replica?"

"That's the problem with Van Gogh's canvases. There are no contemporary sales records to authenticate the Dutch Master's art because he sold almost nothing during his lifetime. The popularity of his paintings soared after his death."

"How could anyone make credible forgeries?" Randy asked.

"Vincent van Gogh's diaries have been published, and he described works in progress. From this information, and pictures that are out on the internet, a convincing counterfeit can be made."

Angela looked doubtful. "That seems so difficult to do."

"I told you, Gus Hadley's a talented artist. He can make

copies of Van Gogh's paintings that are difficult for even the most experienced art expert to detect. The easiest way to identify a fraud is to examine the canvas and paint itself. Today's synthetic paints have a texture that can be spotted by qualified experts, no matter how talented the forger. I'm assuming Serrano's insurance company just screwed up and didn't do the proper testing."

"I wonder if Serrano's arranged for a new appraisal."

The butler emerged from the hallway and walked into the foyer. "Mr. Serrano's very busy, but if you'll keep it brief, he'll see you."

"We'll be in and out as fast as we can," Randy said.

The man ogled Angela. "This way, please."

They followed him out of the foyer and down a tiled corridor. Angela felt like Dorothy in the *Wizard of Oz*, making her way down a vast passage to an uncertain destination. Moving into a room lined with bookshelves, they saw Eugene Serrano behind a large cherry-wood desk, wearing reading glasses and studying a thick stack of blueprints.

"We're sorry to bother you," Randy said. "We know we're interrupting, but we'll take only a little of your time."

Serrano looked up at him, a frown on his face. "That would be appreciated. I need to sign off on this construction project today if I'm going to lock in the price."

Randy gazed at a painting on the wall across the room. "Is that the copy of *Sunflowers in a Vase*? The forgery?"

Serrano's dark eyes flashed. "A damned good one. I was given the appraisal results earlier this morning. Unfortunately, you were right. It's a fake. I called the police, and they're sending out some officers. I expect them within the hour."

Brett, Randy, and Angela eyed each other, concerned the authorities could show up any minute.

"Why haven't you taken the copy down?" Angela asked.

Serrano stood and strode to the painting. He took off his

glasses. "My dear, when I bought *Sunflowers in a Vase*, Mitzie and I threw a party and bragged about being the proud owners of an expensive Van Gogh. It was a nice addition to my collection, and I wouldn't want my neighbors to know I was duped. For that reason, the reproduction will remain on the wall until I can get the genuine one home."

Randy said, "We have an idea that might help you retrieve the original work."

Serrano angled his head. "What would that be?"

"As we told you the other night, we believe Kevin Delfino has *Sunflowers in a Vase*. You want what you paid for, and we want to see Delfino behind bars. With your help, we can ensure that happens."

Serrano put his glasses back on. "Delfino in prison is a kinder option than I had in mind. Regardless, how do you propose we do this?"

Brett said, "We intend to let Delfino know we have a buyer who wants to purchase the original Van Gogh, no questions asked. Two million should be appropriate."

"What do you want from me? I can't be the buyer of a painting I'm supposed to already own."

"Does Delfino know your wife?"

"No. They never met."

"We'd like to get a letter of intent from her under her maiden name, saying that she'll buy the painting from the Art Works Gallery. The two-million-dollar offer is to draw him out from wherever he's hiding. Once we know where he is, the police can take over."

Serrano went over to his desk and sat down. He poured himself a glass of water from a pitcher and took a sip. "An interesting plan." He scratched his chin. "You can make this work?"

"I believe so."

"I'll consider it. Let me talk this over with Mitzie and my lawyer, and I'll get back to you."

"Thank you, Mr. Serrano, that's all we can ask."

TWENTY-THREE

BRETT DROVE UP Sunset Boulevard, a lit cigarette in his mouth.

"Where are we going?" Angela asked.

Brett removed the cigarette and blew smoke out the window. "I want to stop by my house and pick up a change of clothes. Then we're going up to Santa Clarita. I have a friend who lives out there. It'll be a safer place for you."

Angela looked at Randy in the backseat. "I sure hope Serrano will act on our proposal."

Randy brushed a few shards of glass from the seat. "I see no reason why he wouldn't."

"I wish he wasn't making us wait."

When they arrived at Brett's home, he ran in and grabbed a knapsack, filled it with some clothes and toiletries, and made a hasty return to the car. With the plastic-covered windows of the Honda rattling, Brett threaded the car though heavy traffic to I-5 and took the onramp north.

For the next half-hour, they drove down the freeway with little conversation. Every once in a while, Brett and Angela would engage in small talk, but Randy just stared out the window.

"You okay?" Angela asked him after a long period of silence.

He was concentrating on the passing countryside. "I've been thinking."

"About anything in particular?"

"A few things about this whole mess bother me. Ones I can't settle in my mind."

"Like what?"

"I'm not sure. I can't put my finger on it. But I know something's wrong."

"This all troubles me, Randy."

He turned away from the window. "I know. I've been pretty selfish, asking you to endure this with me."

"I'm not here against my will."

Randy gave her an appreciative smile. "I'll call Serrano first thing in the morning. With Mitzie's letter of intent and a little good fortune, this part of our nightmare can be over."

Brett said, "Tomorrow, we should pay another visit to Gus— see if he's found out if the Van Gogh's on the market."

Angela said, "Assuming the Serranos agree to our plan, we'll have a firm two million to offer for the painting. That'll get someone's attention. With any luck, Delfino's."

"I'd like to give Wayne another call," Randy said. "I couldn't contact him earlier. I want him to do me a favor and meet with Walter Parker."

"Mr. Parker? Why?"

"The reward money. Wayne's got to convince Walter to cancel the bounty. With it on offer, half the world's searching for me. If he cancels it, that might buy me some more time."

"You're dreaming. There's no way Mr. Parker will cancel the reward. I bet you anything he's doing it at Carter's prompting."

"Walter has to know I'm innocent. When he knows the truth, he'll do what's right."

"Are there exhaust fumes coming in through the plastic in the back window? There must be, because your thinking's fuzzy."

"I'm a desperate man, Angela. What else am I going to do?"

WAYNE STOOD BACK to admire his living room. Jennifer had bought him some colorful pillows, and they looked nice on the black leather sofa. He smirked, thinking about the marathon sex they'd had on it that morning. Hearing his cell phone ring, he walked into the kitchen and picked it up. "Hello?"

"Wayne," Randy said.

"What the hell. Are you okay?" He opened the refrigerator and pulled out a beer.

"About as good as I can be, considering the circumstances."

"What's happening? The news said the cops found you. How'd you get away?"

"Angela spotted them, and we took off before they could capture us. We're still in Southern California with Cynthia's brother."

"How'd the police find you?" He cracked open the beer and took a sip.

"I don't know. That's something I haven't been able to figure out."

"I can't believe you evaded the authorities, even if you did have a head start."

"We were lucky; that's all I can say. There were cops in helicopters and on the ground searching for us. Never in my wildest dreams would I have thought I'd be in a situation like that."

"How's Angela?"

"Coping better than I am. She's been a rock. The only one I can rely on. With that bounty on my ass, it's been hard to trust anyone else."

"I wish there was something I could do to help."

"Convince Walter Parker to withdraw the reward."

"You know he won't do that."

"Yeah, but I can hope. I'm calling from Brett's mobile. Call me back at it if you have any success."

"I'll see what I can do."

STRAUB LEANED BACK in the chair and cradled the phone between his neck and shoulder. "Okay, Yazzie," he said, "tell me about this painting."

He bent over and picked up the gun case lying on the floor next to the chair. He flipped up the latch and opened it, lifting out a shiny rifle, then put the case down, broke the gun open, and peered down the barrel.

"What do the police believe?" Straub closed the chamber and caressed the stock. "Is it possible Kennedy didn't kill Cynthia Nicosia?"

Straub listened, absorbed in thought, while continuing to rub the stock of the rifle. "Interesting. You think this Delfino did it?" He reached for a cloth and wiped the barrel. "Hey, I appreciate the heads up. Who told you to call me?"

Straub smiled. "Eugene Serrano, huh? I'll have to thank him. Okay. I'll talk with you later."

Straub hung up, his crazy eyes animated. He brought the rifle up to his eye and aimed, but his mind was still on the conversation with Yazzie. Who was Kevin Delfino, and what part did he have in the death of Joseph Nicosia's wife? Straub had to find out. He might be able to make a whole lot more money.

THE NIGHT WAS calm, and the chirping of the crickets was the only sound echoing up the canyon. Randy sat alone on the patio of an acquaintance of Brett's. Doris seemed a little bewildered by their presence but clearly trusted Brett and asked few questions.

The sliding door opened, and Angela stepped out onto the patio wearing a fresh cotton T-shirt. No doubt she'd borrowed it from Doris, as it was a little baggy. "Care for some company?" she asked.

"Sure." Randy motioned to the plastic chair to his right.

Angela sat down. "It's peaceful here. Just what I needed."

"Brett's friend seems like a sweet person."

Angela nodded. "Yes, I like her home." All day, their conversation had been stilted.

"Brett said her father bought her this house. She's an artist too, just struggling a little more than he is. It must be nice having a parent who takes care of problems, like a mortgage and such."

Angela's eyes drifted up to the stars. "I wish my dad were here. When I was little, he solved all my problems."

"Could he crack the mystery of who killed Cynthia and Hale?"

"If I were still five, I'm sure I'd believe it."

"But not now?"

"It looks a little bleak. We're chasing after a painting in hopes it'll lead us to Cynthia's ex-boyfriend, who we think might be her killer. That's not much to go on."

He said, wistfully, "I have no other alternative."

"I know."

Randy peered into her eyes. "Angela, where are we?"

"In a canyon north of Los Angeles."

He made a face at her. "You know what I mean. Where's our relationship going? Do we even have one? You know how I feel about you, but I'll be damned if I understand what's in your mind. You're here—that gives me comfort, but I'd like to hear you say what you feel in your heart."

Angela bowed her head. "I, I don't trust my heart, and my mind tells me to take it slow."

"Why not follow your instincts?"

She twisted a few strands of hair that were hanging over

her shoulder. "I've come with you because of my feelings, but that's as far as I'm willing to go."

"Were you ever in a bad relationship?"

Angela blinked a few times. "No, and I aim to keep it that way."

"You have to believe in me at some point."

"I'm not going to let myself get hurt."

Randy reached out and touched her arm. His gaze was intense and gripping. "I won't ever hurt you."

"Your reputation says otherwise."

He raised his voice. "That's not fair. Sure, I've dated quite a bit, but I haven't harmed anyone."

"That's not what Dixie says. She says you two-timed a girl she knows."

"Who?"

"Does it matter?" she asked, aggravated. "I don't know why I'm attracted to men like you."

"Have you ever had a man tell you he's falling in love with you?"

"That's none of your business."

"Angela, I haven't been in love with a woman, and told her so, until you."

She said mockingly, "Never said it and meant it."

A trace of red highlighted his cheeks. "I'm a cad, okay? But with you, it's different. You have to understand that."

"I've avoided being hurt by your kind before. I'm not about to go down that road now. My mind tells me I'd be stupid to make that mistake."

"Sooner or later, you're going to fall in love and have to take some risks."

"I haven't fallen for anyone yet."

"Do you make a habit of following wanted men across the country?"

"I'm a kind soul. For now, let's leave it at that."

He put his hands on top of his head. "Okay. Let's change the subject. Doris has a computer, and I need to use the Internet."

"Why's that?"

"I have to Google a man named Frank Titan. Hale mentioned him when I confronted him at his office. I wonder if it could have any relevance to my situation."

This seemed to puzzle Angela. "How so?"

"That's what I need to find out."

TWENTY-FOUR

DORIS WALTERS—A plump woman in her mid-fifties with bottle-blond hair and about two inches of dark roots showing—walked across the kitchen with a plate full of buttermilk pancakes. "Who wants more?" she asked, wiping a trace of flour from her chin.

"They're delicious, Doris," Angela said. "I'll take a couple. This syrup's wonderful."

"I buy that at a farmer's market in the valley. I can thank that decadent liquid for the extra twenty pounds I've packed on."

"Sometimes, you have to indulge."

"Indulge I do. Brett, how about another pancake?"

"No, thanks," Brett said. He wasn't paying much attention to her; he was eavesdropping on Randy's telephone conversation with Eugene Serrano. Randy was nodding a lot.

"You're sure?" Doris asked. "You're looking a little thin. Some meat on your bones would do you good."

Brett shook his head. "I'm stuffed. Thanks, though, you're a great cook."

"Suit yourself. If you folks don't mind, I'm going out to the garden. The morning light's just right, and I'd like to get working on a painting I have in progress. I'm inspired and want to take advantage of my mood and the right ambiance."

"It's your house. Do whatever you want and try to ignore us."

"I'll be out back. If you need anything, help yourselves."

"Thanks for the hospitality," Angela said. "I hope we haven't put you out."

Doris took a paintbrush from a jar on the counter. "Not at all."

Brett's eyes were back on Randy, and Doris waltzed out to the garden, humming.

"Thank you, Mr. Serrano," Randy said. "I'll see you later to pick up the letter of intent." He hung up and moved over to the kitchen table.

Angela said, "Doris has some pancakes warming for you in the oven."

"Thanks, but I'm not hungry."

"What did he say?" Brett asked.

Randy sighed with great relief, a smile on his face. "He's agreed to let us broker the purchase of *Sunflowers in a Vase*. Mitzie has signed a letter of intent that can be shown to Delfino. Her maiden name's English, by the way."

"Thank god," Angela said.

"Now," Brett said, "we just have to confirm that Delfino has the painting. Let's go visit Gus and see if he's heard anything. We can tell him about our two-million-dollar offer."

Randy said, "After that, I want to go back to Delfino's apartment in Marina Del Rey. He may have left a forwarding address."

"That's a good idea," Angela said. "Maybe we'll get lucky."

"Angela, I'm about out of hope. Luck's all I have left."

ANTHONY CHAPMAN RAPPED on the door to Lieutenant Schultz's

office. Schultz looked up and gestured for him to enter. Chapman came in and sat in front of the desk. "What's the latest?"

"The same as the last time we talked. Your client, friend, whatever, is wanted for two murders."

"Where's that open mind you were demonstrating yesterday?"

"Shrinking by the minute."

"What about the missing painting?"

"You say it's gone; I say Kennedy has it."

Chapman narrowed his eyes at the lieutenant. "What are you talking about?"

"Kennedy made several visits to Cynthia Nicosia's suite at the Conquistador Resort, both before and on the night of her murder. To visit the pool-view VIP floors, you have to go past a security guard. Kennedy sweet-talked his way past the guard each time. I just talked with her, and she remembered him. The night of the murder, he made two visits within forty-five minutes. Knowing the Van Gogh was in the suite, I'm sure he took it. I just received word from forensics, and his prints were on the frame. I surmise that Mrs. Nicosia caught him in the act of taking it, and he killed her. He stashed the painting elsewhere, then went back to the suite to hide the evidence. That's when Joseph Nicosia surprised him and he ran off."

"Lieutenant, let me remind you it was Randy who brought the existence of the painting to our attention. He wouldn't do that if he stole it."

"He's trying to confuse us."

"It's been my observation that the police have had issues with this case from the get-go."

Schultz shook his fist. "On the contrary, when looking at the evidence, this case's been settled from the beginning. We have Nicosia's account, Kennedy's fingerprints on the murder weapon and empty frame, the deceased's blood on his shirt, and a statement from the security guard that he made two visits to the suite on the night of the homicide. I agree the painting's a good motive for murder. Kennedy's. And on top of all that, an innocent man doesn't flee."

"He's afraid. He keeps in touch with me, which must mean something."

"Not that he's innocent. He wants to know how close we are to capturing him."

"He doesn't need me to determine how close you are. It's been on television twenty-four-seven."

"Not everything's been reported by the media."

"Like what?"

"Conrad Hale was killed by a blow to the head."

"That's common knowledge."

"The murder weapon was a golf putter from the set of clubs Hale kept in his office. I just obtained that report also. The putter has Kennedy's fingerprints on it."

Chapman was struggling to keep his dismay from showing on his face. "Hale and Randy went golfing together a couple days before the murder. Randy must've touched the club then."

"Oh, come on, Chapman."

Chapman's voice notched up. "It was a mob hit, and you know it. Nicosia's revenge for Hale screwing his wife."

"You always have an answer, don't you? Every tangible piece of evidence points to Kennedy's guilt. I'll admit I had my doubts, but I did a little research on the value of the missing Van Gogh. It's worth millions. Having that painting would make life for a fugitive easy. He could enjoy a pretty nice existence on the beaches of Brazil with that kind of money. It's time to resign yourself to the fact that Kennedy's a murderer."

Chapman covered his face with his hands. "There must be an explanation."

"I'm sorry. I know he's your friend, but it's gotten to the point where the evidence of his guilt is overwhelming."

STRAUB SAT IN the keno lounge of the Desert Palm Casino. He picked up a keno ticket from a rack attached to the chair and marked an eight-spot with a black crayon. He stood, wandered to the keno station, and handed the ticket to a woman writer. He took out his wallet and removed a twenty-dollar bill, pushing it across the counter.

"Twenty-dollar eight-spot," the keno writer said and processed the ticket. "One of these hit about an hour ago. It paid fifty thousand dollars. Maybe yours will do the same."

Straub smiled. "One can hope. Thanks." He took the keno ticket and walked out of the lounge and into the casino. His crazy eyes widened when he saw a guy he thought was Kevin Delfino. Straub pulled a grainy picture of Delfino out of his jacket pocket and examined it. The gap in Delfino's teeth was noticeable. Straub smiled. He propped himself against a slot machine and watched Delfino move through the casino to the elevators.

The doors of an elevator opened, and Delfino boarded the car. As the doors closed, Straub turned and put a five-dollar bill in the slot machine he'd been leaning against. He poked the max credits switch, hit the spin button, and watched the reels respond. A seven lined up. Another seven. Straub's heart raced a little. Blank. The machine stared back at him hungrily. He didn't oblige.

Straub walked out of the casino and to the far corner of a cocktail lounge. He took a seat, dug in his jacket pocket, and took out his mobile phone. He dialed a number in Beverly Hills. "Joseph Nicosia, please," he said when it was answered. "It's Robert Straub."

Straub looked through the lounge and into the crowded

casino. Despite his distance from the slot machines and gaming tables, the ringing bells and craps dealers' calls were still audible, and he cupped his hand over the mouthpiece of the smartphone.

Nicosia asked in a rude voice, "Where are you?"

"Las Vegas."

"Is Kennedy there?"

"No."

"I'm paying you to do a job on him. Why the hell's it taking so goddamn long?"

"Mr. Nicosia, what if I told you I can make a hit on your wife's killer and acquire a valuable piece of art I bet you want?"

"What are you talking about?"

"If my information's correct, and I believe it is, Kennedy didn't murder your wife."

"You're insane."

"Do you know much about your wife's past?"

"What are you insinuating?"

"Are you aware Mrs. Nicosia sold forged paintings?"

"She worked in an art gallery. That's how I met her. But I didn't know she'd been peddling fakes."

Straub switched the phone to his other ear. "She was."

"What does this have to do with her murder?"

"She had a partner in the forgery scam—a man named Kevin Delfino. Do you know him?"

"The name sounds familiar. An art appraiser, as I recall. I haven't met him, but he signed the certificate of authentication for several paintings I bought."

"Did you know a Van Gogh's missing?"

"So I deduced when the police made a visit to my home."

"Delfino has it."

"You're sure?"

"I'm positive. He killed your wife to get it and is trying to sell the work."

"There's no question?"

Straub looked at his watch. "Not in my mind. My source says Delfino approached him about unloading the Van Gogh."

"Why are you in Las Vegas?"

"Delfino's here, working at a casino."

"Take Delfino out and get that painting."

"That's why I'm in Vegas."

"Kennedy too. I want him gone. Kill him; he slept with my wife."

An insidious grin spread across Straub's face. "I was hoping you'd say that. I do expect a double fee for the killings and some kind of reasonable compensation for the acquisition of the Van Gogh."

"I'll pay what's fair."

Straub smiled wider. "Excellent."

"Where's Kennedy?"

"We reacquired him at Miller's home. As I told you, we had it staked out. Kennedy, Miller, and the Grisham woman are now in Santa Clarita, at the home of a woman named Doris Walters, a friend of Miller's."

"When will you finish off Kennedy?"

"One at a time, Mr. Nicosia."

"I suppose you know your business."

"I do. I'll keep you informed."

"Fine."

The line went dead.

HARLAN SAMPLES STOOD in Nicosia's mansion, a telephone in his hand. He placed the handset gently in its cradle and smiled. "Doris Walters in Santa Clarita," he said aloud.

Samples had been angry with Nicosia ever since Straub was called in. It wasn't his fault Kennedy somehow evaded them, yet the way Nicosia had been treating him, you'd think he'd driven the getaway car. Samples felt wronged and couldn't wipe that out of his mind.

He retrieved his iPhone from his jacket pocket and did a search for Doris Walters. There was no Doris, but five D. Walters were listed. He wrote down the addresses and hustled out to his car.

GUS HADLEY OPENED the door to his loft and stared at Randy, Angela, and Brett. "Back so soon?" he asked.

"Hi, Gus," Brett said. "Mind if we visit for a while?"

Hadley looked back over his shoulder. "Ah, sure, come on in." He pulled the iron door open wide, and they entered the loft.

Brett and Angela grabbed a seat on the sofa, and Randy sat on a wooden stool.

Hadley crossed into the kitchen alcove and looked at Brett. "Are you thirsty?" he asked, opening the refrigerator.

Brett didn't reply but bounced up from the couch and walked through the studio. He stopped in front of an easel. "What are you painting?"

Hadley slammed the refrigerator shut, rushing out of the kitchen and up to Brett. He snatched a cloth from a table and draped it over the painting. "Never you mind. That's a work in progress, and it's not ready for viewing."

"My, my, Gus." Brett lifted one corner of the fabric and studied the work. "If I'm not mistaken, and I'm not, that's Vincent van Gogh's *Sunflowers in a Vase*. Now why would you be painting a copy of that? And why did you lie to us about working with Delfino?"

Hadley's hands were shaking. "It's a beautiful painting, and I have the perfect place for it in my bedroom."

Brett shook his head. "Cute, but I want the truth."

Hadley's face turned ashen, and sweat streamed down his temples. "It's true." He wet his lips.

"You knew we were interested in the original. You weren't painting a fake for someone to sell us, now were you?"

Hadley turned away. "No."

"Why are you painting that work?"

He peered back at Brett. "I told you—"

Brett's voice crept up. "Cut the crap. Does Kevin Delfino have the original?"

Defensively, Hadley said, "He asked me to paint a copy of *Sunflowers in a Vase* almost five months ago. I don't know why."

Brett's eyes ripped into Hadley's. "You don't know why? Who are you trying to kid?"

Hadley cast his gaze down. "I suppose." He hunched his shoulders. "Okay...right. I guess I do. I'm sorry I lied, but I was scared."

"Angela and Randy have a client willing to make a strong offer for the real Van Gogh. Where's Delfino?"

Hadley rambled over to where Randy and Angela were seated and lowered himself into a chair. "I didn't know when you visited me the other day. I swear I'm not lying about that. Like I said, he contacted me five months ago and asked me to paint a replica of the Van Gogh. I hadn't heard from him for months when I spoke with you. He knows it takes me a while to make a credible reproduction."

"But you've since talked with him?"

Hadley nodded. "I have his cell number. I texted him, and Kevin called. I told him about Angela and Randy and that they were looking to buy the Van Gogh. He told me to get my ass busy and finish the fake. His tone was intimidating, and it frightened me."

"I want you to set up a powwow with Delfino so we can discuss the purchase of the real painting. Randy and Angela have a client who's willing to pay up to two million. Here's her letter of intent. It's a woman named Mitzie English."

Hadley took the letter and read it. "Impressive. I'll set up a meeting."

"Where is he, Gus?" Randy asked.

Hadley hesitated for a second and licked his lips nervously. "He's moved to Las Vegas."

Brett said, "You know that's where my sister was killed."

Hadley bowed his head and stared at the floor. "I know, and I'm really sorry. He's been terrorizing me. I'm afraid—I know he's capable of murder when he's drunk."

"How can we contact him?"

"I'll organize a meeting, but you may have to go up to Vegas."

"We can do that."

Hadley sighed deeply. "Okay, Brett. I'll try to arrange a meet-up as soon as possible."

Randy asked, "Do you have a physical address for him in Las Vegas?"

"No, just a phone number. I'll call him right away. I should be able to put together something soon."

Randy closed his eyes. He hoped soon didn't feel like an eternity.

BRETT DROVE INTO the parking lot of the Marina Del Rey apartments. He'd been quiet on the drive up from Long Beach, listening to Randy and Angela discuss ways they could trap Delfino. The three of them climbed out of the vehicle and wound their way through the apartment complex to the manager's office. They entered the reception room and stood in front of the counter. "It's time for the manager's wife's favorite cooking show," Angela said. "If he's not here, we're going to be blown off pretty damn fast."

Randy tapped on the bell. The thunder of heavy feet could be heard through the doorway behind the counter, and an overweight man with a round, pale face entered the room. He had a full head of sandy hair and was wearing tan overalls. The sound of a too-loud television came through the door behind him. "Afternoon," he said.

"Are you the manager?" Angela asked.

"Yes. Rex Thornton. Are you interested in an apartment?"

"Is unit three-oh-seven vacant?"

"It's available. It's a great place and even has a partial view of the marina. The rent ain't half bad for a prime spot like this. I'll get a key and show it to you."

"We're not in the market for an apartment," Randy said. "We're hoping to find the former tenant, Kevin Delfino."

The manager scratched his day-old stubble. "He's a popular man. The police were here this morning asking about the guy. I told them he moved away a few weeks ago. I don't know what he did that would attract the authorities. The officers wouldn't tell me."

"I'm guessing art theft," Brett said.

"Any idea where Delfino went?" Angela asked.

Thornton turned to her. "Las Vegas."

"Do you have a forwarding address?" Randy asked.

"Like I informed the police, I don't have a good one. I sent his security deposit to an address in Vegas, but the envelope was returned. It said no such person was at that location."

"Did you keep the envelope?"

"It's in the file."

"Can we see it?"

"The address is lousy."

Brett stroked his goatee and said, "We'd still like to take a peek."

The manager eyed the three of them. "Oh, all right." He went over to a filing cabinet.

They waited, subjected to the blare of the cooking show

emanating from the doorway behind the counter. A woman with a high-pitched voice was saying, *"To make the perfect macaroni and cheese, you need at least a cup and a half of shredded cheddar. And you know me, everything I make has lots and lots of creamery butter. Now mix in two cups of whole milk..."*

"Sounds delicious," Angela said.

Randy and Brett chuckled as the apartment manager came back to the counter. He slid the envelope to Randy, who picked it up and read the address. "Two-twelve Tropicana—" His voice faltered, and he didn't finish reading it aloud.

Concerned, Angela put a hand on his arm.

He handed the envelope back to the manager. "Thanks for your time."

"You're welcome," Thornton said. "I'm going to see if I can pry my wife away from the TV long enough to make me a snack. Have a nice day."

"You too," Angela said.

The manager nodded and left through the doorway behind the counter.

As they walked back to the car, Angela looked at Randy. "What's wrong?"

"I recognized Delfino's address, but it doesn't make sense."

"The post office says he doesn't live there."

"I know he doesn't. Someone else lives there."

Angela eyed him uncertainly but decided not to push it any further. "We should go back to Vegas."

"Do you think so?" Brett asked.

Angela nodded. "Yes. We're not getting anywhere here. And that's where we'll be meeting with Delfino."

Randy didn't comment, deep in thought.

"Randy, don't you agree it's time we returned to Las Vegas?"

He stopped and faced her, his expression strained. "Yeah.

Vegas." He spun around and set out for Brett's car, shaking his head.

GUS KNEW HE couldn't stall anymore. He gazed across his studio at the unfinished Van Gogh replica as he picked up his iPhone and dialed, his hands trembling. He blew out a fretful breath and held the phone to an ear.

After the third ring, he heard Delfino say, "Gussy, have a painting for me?"

Hadley wiped his brow with his shirtsleeve. "Not yet, but I'm close.

"Goddamn it. I'm going to kick your ass if you don't hurry up."

"Soon. I promise. I had another visit from the gallery people interested in the Van Gogh. They have a client willing to pay up to two million for the piece. They showed me the letter of intent from the buyer."

"Oh, Gussy, that's what I like to hear. Arrange a meeting so we can broker the deal. Tomorrow or the day after. And I need the replica at the same time. I figured out a way to get a million-and-a-half-dollar reward using it."

"How?"

"I'm going frame the asshole casino host who the cops think killed Dee. I'll put the copy in his condo and collect the reward for turning him in."

"I told you, the replica isn't ready. I need at least a week."

"You son of a bitch, I'm tired of waiting. I'll give you five days because I know the painting will be scrutinized with care. But not a day longer. I don't give a crap if you don't sleep a minute to get this done. I've been giving you a break, but my patience is running thin."

"Okay. I can finish it by Sunday. Where do you want to get together with the buyers?"

"Can they come to Las Vegas?"

"Yes. They're willing to travel, but they insist on seeing the painting before they negotiate the deal. So you'll need to bring the original to the meeting."

"Are you confident they can produce the cash?"

"The letter of intent from their client says a wire transfer will be made at the appropriate time."

"Okay. Let's meet at the lower level observation deck of the Conquistador Tower. There's a deck area with cabanas that are conducive to private conversations."

"All right, Kevin. I better get to work." Hadley ended the call and looked down at his quivering fingers. There was no way he'd be able to paint with shaking hands. He went over to an oak cabinet, grabbed a bottle of whiskey, unscrewed the cap, and took a healthy swig.

TWENTY-FIVE

DORIS WALTERS BRUSHED paint on the canvas and leaned back to admire her handiwork. In her mind, she was a budding Monet. In actuality, her work was destined for many a garage sale.

Dabbing her paintbrush on a smeared palette, she heard the sound of dried leaves crunching in the bushes to her right. She laid down her brush. "Who's there?"

Hearing nothing, she rose from her chair, charged into the yard, and rounded a tall evergreen bush. A mountain of a man stood there, frozen in place, obviously not sure whether to stay put or flee.

Doris put her hands on her hips. "Who are you? And what are you doing on my property?"

He scratched his head. "Me? I'm Har... Harry, I'm Harry. Um, I, I'm going for a hike."

She studied the giant man in front of her. He was wearing black from head to toe. Black hat, suit, shirt, socks, and shoes. "Dressed like that?"

He frowned and glanced at his clothing. "What wrong with what I'm wearing?"

"It's not hiking attire."

"So?"

Doris glared at him. "Well, you're trespassing on my land, and I demand you leave."

"I was looking for the trailhead."

Doris knew he was lying; she saw it in his eyes. He was snooping around. She thought of Randy and Angela. His presence had something to do with them. She wasn't sure why Brett had brought his friends to stay at her house, but he was a good man and someone she trusted. She owed him too. He'd encouraged her when others did nothing but criticize. Brett must have had a good reason for bringing those people into her home. "There's no trailhead near here. It's all private land."

The man stared at the ground. "You're positive?"

"I am. Now get off my property or I'm calling the cops."

He waved his hands in the air. "Hey lady, I'm going. Sorry if I scared you." He trudged toward the road.

She watched him go, her heart still pounding, angry with Brett for getting her involved in something that would attract such visitors. She returned to the garden. Whatever reason Brett had for bringing Angela and Randy into her home, they weren't safe here.

WAYNE ANXIOUSLY TAPPED his foot. *I have to make this work*, he thought. Sitting in Walter Parker's outer office, he picked up a magazine and flipped through the first couple of pages, but couldn't concentrate. He threw it back on the coffee table. Randy wanted him to convince Parker to call off the bounty. "The stupid asshole," he said under his breath. "A lot of good that will do." Every law enforcement agency in the country was searching for him. The reward might make a few more people interested in locating Randy, but in the grand scheme of things, it wasn't changing matters.

Wayne puffed out an uneasy breath and stared at the secretary at the desk in the corner of the room. She was a pretty woman, but didn't have Jennifer's voluptuous body. He grinned, remembering the previous night and the best sex of his life.

"Mr. Parker will see you now," the secretary said.

"Thank you." Wayne pushed himself up from the chair and crossed to the door of Parker's office.

When he went inside, the old man walked up to him, his hand outstretched. "Come in, Wayne, please."

"Thank you, sir." Wayne shook Parker's hand with a solid grip. He spotted a seated Carter Camp and looked at him curiously.

"You know my nephew, Carter, of course." Parker shuffled behind his desk and sat down.

Wayne nodded. "Yes. Hi, Carter."

Camp grunted in acknowledgment. The permanent scowl on his face was getting deeper by the day.

Parker gestured to the chair next to Camp. "Have a seat."

Wayne dropped into it. He crossed his legs, felt uncomfortable, and uncrossed them.

"My secretary tells me you want to speak with me. If it's a private matter, I'll ask Carter to leave."

Wayne glanced at Camp, unsure if he should be wary. He shrugged. "I guess he can stay—that's not a problem."

"Fine." Parker clasped his hands in front of him. "Wayne, I must tell you that in the short time you've been with us, I've heard some good reports on your progress. Eric Frazier speaks well of you."

Wayne smirked, pleased to hear that. He hadn't been working all that hard. The opposite, in fact. Most of the time, he only pretended to be busy. He'd just been lucky with the new guests he met. He was willing to take credit, however. "I appreciate that. I've been following some advice Randy Kennedy gave me, and I've been able to cultivate a small pool of new customers...oh, I mean guests."

"Kennedy," Camp scoffed. "Ha."

"Carter," Parker said, "despite Randy's current situation, there can be little doubt he's an excellent casino host. For Wayne to fashion his hosting style after Randy is commendable and prudent as well."

"Uncle Walter, Kennedy's a murderer."

"I'm talking about his hosting skills."

"Randy gave me a lot of good tips," Wayne said. "Using those, I've attracted some strong guests. One lady's a Charleston Resort player, and she dropped twenty thousand dollars on her first visit here."

A smile blossomed on Parker's face. "No wonder Frazier speaks so well of you, son."

Camp said, "I'd be careful how far I'd emulated Kennedy. You could end up behind bars."

Parker flicked a dismissive hand at his nephew. "Enough of that. Wayne, what is it you want to speak with me about?"

Wayne cleared his throat. "I'd like to talk with you about the million-and-a-half-dollar bounty you've put on Randy's head."

DORIS PRESSED THE button on the garage opener, and the door clattered up the tracks. She climbed in the vintage Volkswagen bus and, after two attempts, started the engine and backed it out of the garage. "This isn't going to fool him," she said. Crouched on the floor of the bus were Randy, Brett, and Angela.

"Be quiet, Doris," Brett said. "We don't want him to see you talking."

Doris grimaced and backed the bus down the long driveway to the street. After she crunched a few gears, the bus rolled forward. She drove a short distance before saying through clenched teeth, "To the right, in that old black sedan. It's the man who was lurking in the backyard."

Randy crept off the floor of the bus and peeked through a window. "Samples."

"Who?" Angela asked.

Randy ducked back down. "Harlan Samples. He's Nicosia's bodyguard and part-time gopher—one of the thugs at your townhouse."

She winced. "Oh, no." She looked up at Doris. "He was in the bushes behind your house?"

Doris shifted gears. "Yes. Man what a moose—biggest guy I've ever seen. He said he was hiking, but wasn't at all dressed for it."

Randy said, "Samples isn't one of the world's brightest bulbs."

"Doris, is he following us?" Brett asked.

She checked the rearview mirror. "I can't tell. The trees are blocking my view."

"Do you have enough gas to get to Las Vegas?" Randy asked.

Doris's eyebrows ticked up. "Vegas?"

"Can this old tank make it that far?" Brett asked.

"I suppose."

"Do you mind?" Randy asked.

Doris eyed Brett for reassurance. "Las Vegas?"

"Please," Angela said. "We need your help."

"Las Vegas it is. Okay, Bessie." She rubbed the steering wheel. "Let's show these people what you can do. If Mama gets lucky at the craps table, maybe she can buy you a new set of tires."

THE VOLKSWAGEN BUS idled in the parking lot of the apartment complex. "I'm sorry it took so long," Doris said. "Bessie doesn't like hot weather, and the trek through the desert was a little too much for her."

Brett said sarcastically, "I've always dreamed of spending three hours in a Barstow service station."

Annoyed, Doris shook her finger at him. "I didn't plan this trip."

"You don't need to apologize," Randy said and slid open the door. "The delay may've been fine. We saw no sign of Samples while we were waiting."

"Do you think Wayne's home?" Angela asked.

He massaged his stiff neck. "He works day shift this week. He should've been off a couple of hours ago. I tried calling him, but it just went to voicemail."

Angela nodded.

Randy caught Brett's eye. "We won't be long. I want to let Wayne know we're back in town and see if he spoke with Parker." He jumped out of the bus and walked to the front of the vehicle.

Angela hopped out, slid the door shut, and joined him. "Let's hurry," she said. "I feel exposed out here, and I'm still not comfortable knowing Samples may be around somewhere."

"It's this way." Randy pointed and led her along the pathway toward Wayne's apartment.

Angela looked at the lush foliage. "This is a nice place."

"Yeah. There's a pool and tennis courts right next to Wayne's unit. He told me he was lucky to find a vacancy. The location makes it pretty desirable."

Angela followed Randy up the stairs to the second floor. He walked to the blue metal door marked 2C, looked at Angela, and knocked hard three times.

A short wait later, the door opened, an obviously surprised Wayne standing there holding a beer. "My god," he said. "What are you doing here? Come in, come in. Quick."

They slipped into the apartment.

Wayne shut the door. "How the hell did you get to Vegas?"

"A friend of Brett's brought us," Randy said.

Wayne leveled a hard look at him. "Where is he?"

"Brett and Doris—she's our chauffeur—are waiting in the parking lot." Randy moved into the living room and surveyed their surroundings. "Whoa, there's furniture."

"Yep. It's the stuff I picked up when I took you to L.A."

Randy walked over to the fireplace and scrutinized the painting above the mantel. "Angela, the last time I was here, a folding chair was the single furnishing."

Wayne nodded. "It's nice not having to sleep in a sleeping bag on the goddamn floor."

"I like your taste in décor," Angela said.

"Who gives a crap about my decorating skills? What the hell's going on with you two?"

"It was time we returned to Vegas," Randy said. "Cynthia's ex-boyfriend is here."

"He is?" There was a catch in his voice. "Huh. What's your plan?"

"Hide out. For now, we don't have a choice."

"Then what? You say the ex-boyfriend's in Vegas. Where?"

"We don't know. We just know he's here."

Wayne stared at Randy for a second. "It must suck being you."

"It hasn't been fun for any of us," Angela said.

"Randy, I talked to Old Man Parker about the reward."

"And?" he asked.

Wayne hung his head. "Camp was there too."

"The answer's no," Angela guessed.

"Sorry, dude. I tried."

"Hey, I appreciate the attempt," Randy said. "We better get going. I just wanted to see if you'd spoken with Parker and let you know we're in Vegas."

Wayne escorted them to the door and told them to watch

their backs. They assured him they'd try and exited the apartment, heading down the winding sidewalk toward the parking lot. Before reaching it, Angela asked, "What now?"

Randy shook his head. "I don't know. I have a lot of thinking to do."

BRETT HANDED HIS mobile phone to Randy. "It's Gus," he said.

Randy put the phone to his ear. "Hello?"

"I spoke with Delfino," Hadley said. "Like I told you, he has the original Van Gogh and is eager to peddle it."

Randy's heart skipped a beat. "Let's negotiate a sale as soon as we can."

"When I told Kevin about your offer, I could almost hear him drooling."

"I need to meet with him right away. He has to bring the painting. I must see it. Don't try to fool me with your forgery."

"I've made arrangements for Sunday night."

Randy groaned, his shoulders slumping. "Couldn't we make it sooner? Five days is a long time to wait."

"That's the earliest he's available."

"Damn it."

"He made it clear he has to be satisfied you can produce the money."

"I'll bring the letter of intent to purchase the Van Gogh from our client. Our client's extremely wealthy. There won't be a problem. Where do we meet?"

"In Vegas. This Sunday night at seven. Kevin wants to get together in the cabana area of the lower level observation deck of the Conquistador Tower."

Randy wasn't happy about that and frowned. "Why up there?"

"I suppose he likes the view. It's as good a place to meet as anywhere."

"I guess so. I just want to finalize the purchase as soon as possible."

"So does Kevin."

"Okay. Thanks for your help, Gus." Randy tapped the phone off.

TWENTY-SIX

RANDY HADN'T SLEPT well. It didn't help that the motel they were staying at was close to a busy freeway. Running low on funds, they'd selected a cheap motel. Unfortunately, in their haste to leave Doris's house, Brett had left his wallet. Doris spent her money repairing the bus. All they had was the remaining cash Randy had won from Wayne, and a hovel was all he could afford. The noisy location was the least of the reasons Randy couldn't sleep, though. His mind ran at Mach One all night. Kevin Delfino had the painting, and he could end this nightmare if he timed everything just right. Somehow, he had to get Delfino, the Van Gogh, and the police all in the same place at the same time. It would be difficult—one miscalculation and the entire plan would blow up in his face.

He needed to talk with Anthony Chapman, his connection with the authorities. Randy glanced at his watch. It was a little before seven. Anthony would be awake; he always woke up early to go to the gym. Randy looked at the adjoining bed. Brett was asleep, a slight snore coming from somewhere under the covers. Angela and Doris were no doubt also still slumbering in the room next door. He threw his legs over the side of the bed and scanned the motel room. On the nightstand between the beds was a lamp but no telephone. What did he expect for $19.95 per night? He glanced at Brett again. He didn't want to wake him to get his mobile phone.

Randy moved to the window and peeked through the dingy plastic blinds. It took a moment for his eyes to adjust to the early morning sun rising above the mountains. He looked across the parking lot and saw a payphone near the street. He grabbed his shirt and pants from the foot of the bed and put them on. He pulled a baseball cap on his head, tilted the brim over his face, and padded to the door.

Randy strode past parked cars and into the phone booth. It was in terrible condition. The door had been ripped off, and there were just a few remnants of a phonebook. Given the popularity of mobile devices, he was grateful that a couple phone booths—and this one in particular—were still in existence. He picked up the receiver, deposited some coins, and dialed Anthony Chapman's number.

As the phone rang, Randy felt the barrel of a gun between his shoulder blades. He froze, and the hair on his neck stood up as Anthony said hello.

"Put the phone down," Samples said.

"Hello?" Anthony said again.

Randy's breathing was shallow. "Don't shoot."

"Hang up," Samples said.

"Hello?" Anthony said. "Randy, is that you? Hello?"

Randy hooked the phone in its cradle and stepped out of the booth.

"That way," Samples said, gesturing with the gun.

Randy's face felt stiff. "Whatever you say, Harlan. Just don't shoot me."

Samples waved the gun some more. "Don't give me a reason."

"Please give me a break."

"Hell, no. You're worth a million and a half dollars to me."

"I'm innocent. That money isn't going to be paid."

"I was there, Kennedy, remember? You were crouched over Mrs. Nicosia's body. I saw the blood on you, and I know you killed her." He poked the gun into Randy's side and pushed him forward. "March."

Half-way across the parking lot, Randy stopped. Samples' gun rammed into his spine. "Ouch," Randy said and arched his back. "Let's discuss this, Harlan."

"You moronic jerk. There's nothing to talk about. You're worth a million and a half bucks. With that kind of money, I won't have to take Nicosia's crap anymore. I can buy myself a little cabin on a lake and enjoy the rest of my life. Now quit yapping and start walking." Samples shoved Randy toward an old black Ford sedan.

Randy watched for an opening, counting on Samples to make a dumb mistake. He cursed himself for his own stupid blunder. He'd suspected Samples was following them, three-hour delay in Barstow or not; he should've been much more cautious.

Samples herded Randy to the passenger side of the vehicle. He groped in his pants pocket and lifted out a ring of keys. "Slide over to the driver's side."

Randy opened the car door, slid across the seat, and settled in behind the steering wheel. Samples kept the gun trained on him as he leaned down to make sure Randy was in the driver's seat. He was about to get in the car when there was a flash of movement behind him. Samples groaned and fell to his knees, dropping the gun and reaching up to touch the back of his head. Behind him, Randy saw Brett holding a tire iron, Angela next to him. She lunged for the gun, which had fallen into the foot well of the Ford, slapping it out of Sample's reach, then picking it up and tossing it under the vehicle.

"Let's take off," Brett said.

Randy shot out of the car.

Running to the front of the motel, Angela asked, "Are you all right?"

Randy looked her in the eye. "No. But I'm not going to be as long as I'm on the lam and there's a million-five reward on my ass."

Entering the parking lot, they spotted Bessie, Doris's venerable VW, inching toward them. They scrambled into it, and after a few backfires, the bus with its scared passengers chugged up the Las Vegas Strip.

ANTHONY CHAPMAN SAT alone in the steam sauna of his gym and took a moist breath. The steam was thick, and beads of sweat trickled down his temples. The door to the sauna opened, and a muscular man wrapped in a towel entered and sat on a bench in the corner.

The dense steam made it impossible to see the guy very well, but Anthony didn't care; he wasn't in the mood to socialize. He'd just finished a hard workout and wanted to take a quick steam and get to the office.

"Anthony, is that you?" Randy asked.

Chapman turned his head toward him. "Why am I not surprised?"

"I need your help."

"Was that you who called me earlier?"

"I tried to. Harlan Samples, one of Nicosia's goons, interrupted me."

"How'd you get away?"

"With a little help from my friends."

"It seems you have your share of those."

Randy wiped moisture from the corners of his eyes. "In that, at least, I *am* the Lucky One."

"Randy, I know you don't want to hear this, but you

should surrender yourself to the police. Let justice take its course. If you're innocent, and I do believe you are, the courts will set you free."

Randy massaged his temples. "I wish I thought that."

"Can it be any worse than it is now?"

"It's changing for the better. I now know for certain who killed Cynthia Nicosia. I need you to help me interface with the cops."

"You said you thought it was Kevin Delfino."

"It is. No question."

"What makes you so positive?"

"Delfino has the Van Gogh. There's no doubt."

"Okay, let's say you're right. How do you plan to shift the police spotlight off of you and onto Delfino?" By now, the steam had dissipated enough Anthony could see Randy's face.

"Like I said, it's time the cops got involved."

"You'll get no argument from me on that."

"Do the police agree that the person who has *Sunflowers in a Vase* murdered Cynthia Nicosia? It was the motive?"

"Yes, and they think you have it. They say you made several trips to the Nicosias' hotel suite. Your fingerprints were on the Van Gogh's frame."

"I went there to host the wife of my best player. I touched the frame when it was on the wall with the Van Gogh in it."

"It's your word against the evidence."

"I can prove it."

"How?"

Randy wiped his forehead. "Delfino killed Cynthia and took the Van Gogh. He has the painting, and I've made arrangements to meet with him here in Vegas. He believes I'm going to broker a sale of the work."

"What does this have to do with proving your innocence?"

Randy threw his head back in frustration. "Anthony, you're

not listening. I'm meeting with Delfino Sunday night to cut the deal. He'll be there with the Van Gogh—I've insisted on seeing it before we complete the sale. I need the cops to be there too. Delfino will have the painting, the police will have Delfino, and I'll be off the hook for the Cynthia's murder."

Anthony massaged his right arm. "You expect me to coordinate the capture of Delfino by the authorities?"

Randy nodded. "That's the idea."

"What if they won't go along? This sounds pretty bizarre."

"Do they want to solve the murder?" Randy snapped.

"There's still the issue of Conrad Hale and his death."

"I know who killed him too."

"Delfino? Why?"

"You have to convince the cops to work with me, and it'll all make sense."

"I'll see what I can do. It's not going to be easy getting Lieutenant Schultz to agree with this arrangement."

"You must persuade him. You know as well as I do that this is my only chance."

"I do see some optimism brewing your eyes. It's a long shot...Blondie."

"I know, but it's the only one I have."

Anthony swabbed droplets of water from his face. "Okay, let's give it a try."

CHAPMAN WATCHED LIEUTENANT Schultz attack a jelly donut with a vengeance. They were once more in the lieutenant's office, drinking bitter coffee and arguing about Randy's fate. "Lieutenant, just how many jelly donuts do you consume in a morning?"

Schultz looked at him and lifted his shoulders. "According to my doctor, too many. I can't please that man. First it was give up cigarettes, then red meat. Donuts are about the only pleasure I have left."

"You should slow down a little."

The lieutenant brushed crumbs from his lips. "No way. I'm even considering taking up ciggies and eating steak again. The way I figure it, if I don't enjoy life, what's the point in living a few extra years?"

"Your family might disagree."

"I'm insured in full. They can enjoy the payout."

Chapman chuckled.

Lieutenant Schultz smiled, and then his face darkened. "We've had a break in the Kennedy case."

Chapman squinted at him. "How so?"

"Walter Parker's reward money has once more attracted an informant who can lead us to your boy."

"Care to elaborate?"

"No, I don't." Schultz picked up his mug and took a sip of coffee.

"Why not?"

"I'm uncertain whose side of the fence you're on."

"I'm on the side of justice."

"I'm not yet ready to explain what's going on. When the time's right, I'll tell you what you need to know."

Chapman said in a subdued voice, "I saw Randy this morning."

Schultz's eyes narrowed. "He's here in Vegas?"

"Yes, he arrived last night."

"Where is he?"

"Right now, I don't know. Our meeting was fleeting, to say the least."

"Chapman, let's put an end to this. If you know where we can find Kennedy, save everyone a great deal of trouble."

"Lieutenant, I don't know where he is. I spoke with him just long enough for him to ask for my assistance."

"That's wise. He'll need a good lawyer."

"That's not what he has in mind. He insists Kevin Delfino killed Cynthia Nicosia and has the missing Van Gogh."

The lieutenant slapped his hand on the desk. "Of course he does. He's desperate to point the blame at someone else."

"I don't think so. Hear me out. Randy says he can prove Delfino has the painting. It just might work."

Schultz fixed a skeptical gaze on Chapman. "I don't need to listen to this. I have a credible source who can take me to Kennedy. Our informant's positive we can capture him. I'll make the arrest, and that'll be the end of it."

Chapman said in a straightforward tone, "Ever since this case began, you've had some qualms about Randy's guilt. You've even admitted it at times. Give him a chance to prove his innocence. The way Randy explained his plan, in the worst case scenario, he'll end up in your custody. In the best, you have the real murderer of Mrs. Nicosia and a valuable stolen painting as well."

Schultz reached across the desk and took the last jelly donut from the plate. He brought it to his mouth but stopped. He eyed Chapman and the donut, then threw the pastry back on the plate. "All right, Anthony. Tell me about Kennedy's idea, and I'll decide how much latitude I'm going to give him."

Chapman smiled. "Thanks, Lieutenant." He grabbed the donut and took a bite.

The lieutenant threw him a dirty look.

LIEUTENANT SCHULTZ WALKED out of his office and through the busy squad room to Captain Buckley's office. He rapped on the glass door, opened it, and peered inside. "Captain, you have a few minutes?"

The man glanced up from his papers. "Sure, Andre, what can I do for you?"

Schultz entered the room and parked himself in a metal chair. "It's the Nicosia murder."

"I hear you've had a break in the case."

"I have two, and they're both happening at the same time."

Buckley grinned, showing coffee-stained teeth. "That's fantastic. Commissioner O'Leary will be pleased. He's been driving the sheriff crazy. I know you've put in some long hours, trying to put this case to bed."

Schultz's droopy eyes seemed to sag even more. "Unfortunately, my two breaks in the case come with different outcomes."

Buckley tipped his head to the right. "I don't understand."

"The Parker reward has produced a viable informant, who can take us to Kennedy."

"So I've been told."

"At the same time, Kennedy has proposed a plan through an emissary."

"Emissary?"

"Anthony Chapman, the attorney. Do you know him? He played b-ball for UNLV."

"Yes, I do. He's a good man and an excellent lawyer."

"Chapman's a friend of Kennedy's and, I suppose, his de facto counselor."

"He's been in contact with Kennedy?"

"On and off."

"What does he have to say?"

"All along, he's professed Kennedy's innocence. He says Kennedy's just been guilty of being in the wrong places at the wrong times."

Buckley rocked in his chair. "That's a typical defense attorney position."

"Somehow, I get the feeling Chapman's viewpoint is more than lawyer-client. He really believes Kennedy's not guilty."

"It's clear you have doubts as well or you wouldn't be here."

"That's the problem. Despite the evidence, and it is

substantial, I have this nagging misgiving about Kennedy being responsible for the murders."

"Andre, you're a thirty-five-year veteran of Metro. With your experience, I trust your instincts."

Schultz appreciated the comment and bowed his head. "Thanks."

"Go with your gut. I'll stall Commissioner O'Leary if necessary."

"Okay, Bert. I'll keep you in the loop on what's going on."

"I expect no less."

TWENTY-SEVEN

RANDY AND ANGELA sat next to each other in a dark booth at a dive called Kilroy's Diner. They'd spent five nerve-racking days, waiting for the meeting with Delfino. Angela's head was on Randy's shoulder, and it'd been a long time since either had spoken. Randy felt a mixture of emotions. The woman he loved was next to him, the faint scent of the perfume she'd gotten from Doris wafting into his nostrils. As much as he wanted to forget everything and spend all his time building a relationship with Angela, he had to face the fact that his fate was soon going to be decided.

It could be perilous. If something went wrong, he'd end up in jail for the rest of his life, or worse yet, be given the death penalty. *Why take the risk?* he thought. Being a fugitive wasn't all that bad. Not as long as Angela was with him. They could slip out of the U.S., maybe go to Mexico or Canada, and start a new life.

Canada, sure. It wouldn't be difficult getting into that country, not with three thousand miles of open border. He'd secure a job, as a waiter perhaps. He'd done that before and made pretty good money, adept at coaxing tips from female customers. He and Angela could rent a little house with a white picket fence and start a perfect life.

He smiled at the idea and caressed her hair. But what if Angela didn't have any intention of going with him? She'd made it clear she wasn't sure a relationship with him was what she wanted. He'd never loved someone like this. How could she not want to spend the rest of her life with him? Why didn't she understand that the man she knew, the one she'd gone on the run with, was a good person who wouldn't do anything to hurt her?

He questioned whether he was being selfish. Would it be fair to take her out of the country? No, of course not. She had friends and family she'd never leave. No, as tempting as it was to chuck it all and escape to Canada, he couldn't do it. He was going to have to face his fears, take his chances, and pray for the best. He put his lips to her ear and whispered, "I love you, Angela."

Angela closed her eyes and felt her heart flutter once more. *Why am I so confused?* she wondered. She'd spent more than a week with Randy, and it would've been impossible for him to hide his true self under those circumstances. The man she'd been helping evade the police, was everything she'd hoped for deep down inside. *You're falling for his charms*, she remembered Dixie saying. *He's just a peacock. He's a dirty nasty bird, but you're not seeing that because he has beautiful feathers. A leopard doesn't change his spots.* Dixie's clichéd words of wisdom.

Randy had probably been with hundreds of women. Gee, in her whole life, she'd had five boyfriends. Just one was serious. She'd seen some of the girls he'd dated. They were centerfold material. Angela turned to Randy and looked him in the eye. He smiled at her. A tingle ran up her spine. *Why shouldn't I believe I'm more than another notch in his bedpost? I can't even be that, however; we haven't slept together. We haven't even kissed.*

Maybe if a man loves a woman, he treats her differently than a one-night stand and doesn't pressure her for sex. Could it be he does love me? She shook her head. How long would that last? A man with Randy's reputation would have a short attention span. At first, he'd lavish her with love and devotion, but for how long? A year, maybe two? His eyes would wander, and sooner or later, he'd stray. It was bound to happen.

What if you're wrong? she thought. *Are you giving up your chance at the proverbial golden ring?* What if her heart was right? What if he could love her and nothing would come between them? No, she was going to have to face her fears, take her chances, and pray for the best.

"A lot's at stake tonight," Randy said.

Angela swept a few wisps of hair out of her eyes. "I know, and I'm afraid."

"I'd like to tell you I'm not, but I'd be lying. I don't know why I'm so on edge. I've got to keep my cool and set the plan in motion."

"I should go with you."

"Oh no, Angela. There's no way. As I told Brett, it's best if I go alone. You need to stay with him."

"The police will be there."

"You don't know what could happen."

Angela crossed her arms. "Randy, haven't I risked my life for you?"

He nodded.

"Haven't I left my job and friends and slogged through the country-side with you?"

"Yes." It came out as a hoarse croak.

"Haven't I believed in you from the beginning?"

He nodded again. "Sure."

"Then you owe me. I'm accompanying you to your meeting with Delfino. I've earned that right."

Randy's forehead furrowed. "I just don't want anything to happen to you."

"It'll be fine. I'll be by your side."

Randy gazed deeply into her eyes and touched her face. "I meant what I said earlier. I love you." He leaned over and kissed her.

Angela grasped his hand. "Then let me go with you."

Randy took an anxious breath. "I can't say no when you put it like that."

RANDY JERKED ON the stick shift, and the VW bus lurched into the intersection. "I guess we should be honored Doris let us borrow…what does she call this thing, Bessie?"

Angela patted the scratched dashboard. "Good old girl."

"In some circles, a vehicle like this would be considered a classic."

"It is to people who reminisce about the sixties."

Randy drove the bus into the Conquistador and headed for the parking garage. "Since we're fugitives on the run, we better skip the valet."

Angela smirked. "I do believe fugitive protocol does require discretion in parking."

Randy grinned, feeling a nervous tremor in his hands, and drove the VW up the ramp of the parking garage, finding an open space on the third floor. After another discussion about fugitive protocol, they took the stairs to the main floor of the casino.

The Conquistador was busy, the slots and table games packed with gamblers. The sound rose around them—craps dealers yelling out the rolls of the dice, shrieks of laughter from the winners and the low moan of the losers. All around the casino, patrons were focusing on the top of the Aztec temple, waiting for the start of the laser light show.

"This way," Randy said and led Angela through the maze of slot machines to the escalators. As they rode up, the beat of a band reverberated across the cavernous casino, playing a familiar country song called On the Run, and it seemed appropriate, considering their situation.

At the top of the escalator, they followed a group of German tourists through the Tower Shops at the Conquistador, where Victoria's Secret, H&M, and Cartier were intermingled with T-shirt and souvenir stores. Randy motioned to a jewelry shop. "I'd like to buy you a bracelet."

"Let's clear your name first." Angela placed her hand on one of his elbows and led him past another long row of retailers. After passing the last one, they crossed into a large lobby area with lines of people queuing up to enter the tower elevators.

Randy said, "We need to buy some tickets for the elevator. They walked up to the cashier and purchased two tickets, then took their place at the end of the snaking queue of people waiting for the elevators.

Concerned, Angela said, "I wonder how fast the line is."

"Quick, I hope. We're supposed to meet Delfino in ten minutes."

Naturally, the line just crept along. One of the elevators appeared to be out of order, and the others, even filled to capacity, didn't make much headway on the lengthy procession of sightseers.

"Delfino isn't going to wait long," Randy said. "If we don't meet with him, I'm toast. Everything's set. This is our one chance to get Delfino, the painting, and the cops in the same place."

"Wait here," Angela said.

Randy gave her an intense look. "Why?"

"Just stay here."

"Angela..."

"I'll be right back." She ducked under the stanchion ropes

and walked to the front of the line. Randy watched curiously as she engaged in a conversation with the woman who was admitting people to the elevators.

Angela was quite animated and kept pointing to him. The ticket taker said something to her, and she nodded, then came back to him. "We don't have to wait in line."

He squinted. "Why not?"

"Follow me."

"What's up?"

"Limp."

Irritated, he grimaced. "What are you talking about?"

"I said limp."

"You're crazy. Why would I do that?"

She leaned over and, in a hushed voice, said, "I explained to the ticket taker that you're disabled and can't wait in line."

He said in a loud whisper, "You told her what?"

"Limp."

"I can't believe you lied to her."

She poked him in the chest and said through gritted teeth, "Do you want to wait and miss Delfino or get on the elevator now?"

"Now, of course."

"Then limp."

He said through tight lips, "This isn't right."

Again, she whispered. "Randy, you're wanted for two murders you didn't commit. I'm sure the disabled will understand this one time."

He looked at the people on each side of him and sighed.

"Make it convincing. I told her you were injured in a car crash."

"Don't worry. It's amazing I survived the horrible accident." Randy hobbled out of the line and toward the elevators, dragging his right leg behind him. "This is wrong," he said in an annoyed whisper. "Besides, I'm a fugitive, and someone might recognize me. You too."

"With your blond hair, no one's going to make out who you are. We're more likely to be recognized while standing in that endless line."

Randy dragged his leg, more obviously.

Angela tapped him on the shoulder. "Don't get over-dramatic. Remember the fugitive's protocol."

He shrugged. "I can't win."

Angela grabbed his arm and pretended to assist him to the elevators. "We appreciate this," she said to the ticket taker. "Standing for long periods is painful for him."

"We always try to accommodate," the woman said, giving Randy a sympathetic smile.

"Thank you," he said.

They stood in front of the elevators, and when the next one became available, Randy, with Angela aiding him, shuffled into the car. When the doors closed, a grin seeped onto Angela's face. "We made it."

Randy blew out a relieved breath as the elevator operator recited her speech on the features of the Conquistador Tower. As the elevator rose, his trepidation increased. The stakes were high. He had to keep Delfino from getting spooked before the police made the arrest.

"What are you thinking about?" Angela asked.

"Not screwing this up."

The elevator stopped at the lower level observation deck, and the occupants streamed out. Randy limped at first, but soon remembered the charade was no longer necessary and trailed Angela into the lobby. They examined the directory sign hanging from the ceiling. "Have you been here before?" she asked.

He nodded. "Yes. Once with Cynthia Nicosia, and I was given a tour by Conrad Hale."

Angela frowned. "That's not a good omen. Both of them are dead."

He let out a short, ironic laugh. "I know. This way." They maneuvered through the large group of sightseers to their left. Nearing the double glass doors to the observation deck, he could see out over the city of Las Vegas, millions of tiny colorful lights twinkling a hundred and ten stories below. His acrophobia heightened with each step, until his stride faltered and he stopped.

Angela turned to him. "What's the problem?"

Randy chewed his lower lip. "Ah, nothing."

Angela gave him a disbelieving look. "Are you afraid of heights?"

"No, not at all."

"Don't think about how high up you are. Concentrate on the deck."

"I'm not afraid of heights." Randy bent his head and pushed tentatively through the glass door that led onto the observation area. The deck was crowded with people.

Angela moved with confidence in front of him. "The next time you set up a rendezvous with someone, think about the location before you agree."

Randy's cheeks were pale as he glowered at her. "Goddamn, it I'm fine." She was right, of course, but when he arranged the meeting with Delfino, his fear of jail and the death penalty had overshadowed his fear of heights.

They stood near the railing, their eyes roving up to the next level, where they saw a bunch of high school kids boarding the rollercoaster. The riders' demeanor was a mixture of anxiety and excitement.

"It seems like fun," Angela said.

Randy craned his neck back. "It's crazy. Cynthia tried to persuade me to ride it. What if it sailed off its tracks?"

"I'm sure it's well-engineered." The rollercoaster took off with its load of passengers and slid toward the edge of the tower. "Any sign of him?"

Randy scanned the observation deck, which was dotted with hundreds of sightseers. An older man and woman stood next to them. The guy was looking through a tiny pair of binoculars while she tugged at his shirt, asking for a peek. "He could be stuck in the line to get up the tower."

Angela stared out over the city. "What an amazing view."

Randy planted a firm grip on the railing and looked out far across the horizon. They were silent for a minute as they watched the twinkling lights of one of the world's most vibrant cities.

Angela glanced at the doors that led to the Cabana Bar and saw Wayne Cork standing there holding a Bloody Mary. "Look who's here."

Randy turned, and his expression made it clear he was pleased.

Wayne walked over to them. "What the hell are you two doing here?"

"Where's *Sunflowers in a Vase*?" Randy asked.

Wayne head snapped back. "What?"

"You're here to meet with the gallery owners and discuss the sale of Cynthia's painting. That's us. Brett Miller said to say hi, by the way."

Wayne stared at them, dismayed. "What do you mean?"

Randy eased in front of Angela. "You can cut the subterfuge, Delfino."

Kevin Delfino gave a sudden, lopsided smile. "You should call me Wayne. Wayne Cork." He chuckled. "You know, my instincts told me you knew something wasn't quite right." He took a big swig of his drink.

Angela turned to Randy. "It's shocking he pulled off the ruse."

Randy gazed across the observation deck, looking for the police. "I know."

Delfino placed his Bloody Mary on a table. "How'd you figure it out?"

"No one thing, but eventually, the pieces began to fall into place. Or should I say out of place? Randy inched to his left, Angela his shadow. He wanted more space between them and Delfino. "There were a few clues. Your ex-girlfriend's name. Dee, shortened from Cyndi."

Delfino tapped his finger on his temple. "Very smart."

"Then I thought about how you and her brother were never together. Whenever we were planning to meet with Brett, you always had to be somewhere else. Then we drove to Kevin Delfino's apartment, yours, in Southern California—you weren't there, of course, and when the landlord showed us the address your mail was being forwarded to, I recognized your Las Vegas address instantly."

Delfino's eyes flickered. "Hmm, I bet you did."

Randy scowled. "You've been trying to screw me since the day I first ran from the police. It was you who called Nicosia and told him I was staying at Angela's townhouse."

Delfino gave them a cunning grin, the gap in his teeth prominent. "I also called the cops and informed them you were at that flophouse of a motel in L.A. Boy was I pissed when you weren't captured."

"You're a bastard, Kevin," Angela said.

"I'd rather be called Wayne. It's the name I've chosen for my new life."

Randy asked, "How were you able to get a casino work card?"

"If there's one thing I know how to do, it's arrange for something to be forged."

"Why did you kill Cynthia?"

"It was an accident," Delfino snarled. "I loved Dee."

"Who are you trying to fool? She was bludgeoned to death with a bookend."

"She owed me my half of the money for the painting."

"How'd you get past the security guard and into her suite?"

"I went to VIP Services and got a keycard. I told them I was Nicosia, and they made me one, no questions asked. Imagine that—they didn't even ask for ID."

Randy continued to slide along the railing, Angela following, still uncomfortable being so close to Delfino.

Delfino burst out, "Don't move another goddamn millimeter. I mean it. I have a gun, and I'm not afraid to use it." He pulled a small handgun from inside his jacket, let them see it, then put it in his jacket pocket, the press of his knuckles creating a bulge in the fabric.

Randy and Angela froze in place, both wondering where the cops were.

Angela said, "I still don't understand why you had to kill Mrs. Nicosia. You could've worked it out."

"She didn't want to do that," Delfino said. "Dee was a greedy slut who only cared about accumulating more cash. That's what really angered me the most. She didn't need the Van Gogh—she had Nicosia and his money. She kept *Sunflowers in a Vase* to spite me."

"So you murdered her," Randy said.

"It didn't happen that way. I was reclaiming what was mine, and she tried to hit me with the bookend. I was defending myself."

"With a half-dozen blows to the head? I saw the body, Kevin; you can't expect me to believe it was self-defensive."

"It was."

Randy glared at Delfino, his nostrils flaring.

"Now you tell me..." Delfino said in a superior tone. "Why did you kill Conrad Hale?"

"He had nothing to do with Hale's death," Angela said.

"Is that so? Well, I suppose it was Nicosia then, or one of his people. I bet you top his list of enemies, Randy."

"Where's the painting?" Randy asked. "You were supposed to bring it with you."

Delfino pointed to the Cabana Bar. "I left it with the bartender. I gave him a hefty tip to hold it for me. I wanted to check you out before producing the painting. Turns out, I was right to be cautious. Obviously, it was a waste to bring it here. I know you don't have two million. But, you know, that's okay. I'll collect the million-and-a-half-dollar reward for turning you in to the police."

"Why do that?" Angela asked. "The Van Gogh's in your possession. You have what you believe is yours. So sell it and get on with your life."

"I'm afraid he can't do that," Randy said.

She frowned. "Why not?"

"Brett told me the black market for Van Goghs is nonexistent right now. The Feds have been more diligent, and no one's willing to make a sale. That's why Delfino jumped at our offer so fast."

Angela's lips twisted. "So wait a while. The painting's worth a lot of money. At some point, he can surely unload it somewhere."

"What am I supposed to do in the meantime?" Delfino asked. "Work as a stinking casino host? No way. I have plans, big ones, and they don't include escorting gray-haired little old ladies around a casino floor. But thanks to you, I don't need to wait a day longer. Walter Parker's bounty will hold me over until I can sell the painting. I told you I met with him. Not to ask for him to rescind the reward but to tell him I knew how to get in contact with you. He put me in touch with a very grateful police lieutenant."

Randy said, "We've been in discussions with the cops as

well. They know we're meeting here. I expect them to be joining us any minute."

Delfino leaned against the railing. "Who are they going to believe? You, a fugitive two-time murderer, or me, an upstanding citizen who's turning in his coworker because it's the right thing to do?"

"They know about the Van Gogh and that Cynthia's killer has it." Randy motioned to the Cabana Bar. "And you were accommodating enough to bring it."

"And when the police look for the painting, my bartender buddy will say he's got no idea what they're talking about. And guess what, the stolen painting will be found in your condo. Gus Hadley delivered the replica this afternoon. I had to threaten the little bastard to get him to finish it in time, but it's here now and hidden in your bedroom closet."

Randy clenched his teeth. "You son of a bitch."

"I'll corroborate Randy's story," Angela said firmly.

Delfino waved his hand, saying, "As far as credibility goes, Angela, you're not much better than him. You should've stuck to your original opinion and stayed away. You were right; he's a cretin." His upper lip curled. He fished out his mobile and made a call, pausing as the phone rang. "Lieutenant Schultz," he said when it was answered, "it's Wayne Cork. I'm at the Conquistador Tower lower level observation deck. Kennedy's here, ready to be arrested." He listened for a moment. "You're on your way? Okay, I'll see you in ten minutes. When do I get the reward?" A smile danced over his face. "We'll be waiting for you." He flicked the phone off and turned to Angela and Randy, giving them a condescending sneer. "It won't be long now."

"You're a despicable human being," Angela said. "What's funny is that I knew that the first time we met."

Delfino grinned. "Oh, I am. That's been the toughest part of this whole charade—pretending to be a good ole boy casino host and not the asshole I am. Now why don't you relax? Enjoy your final minutes of freedom—taking in the view."

The whine of police sirens reached them faintly from far below. Delfino stepped to the railing. "The sound of money." He picked up the Bloody Mary and took a deep swallow.

Randy was confused. Surely the cops were all around them. They had to be. He was positive Anthony had convinced them to come to the observation deck.

Randy glared at Delfino, who laughed contemptuously.

A man behind them shouted, "Delfino."

Randy sagged with relief; his nightmare was finally ending. The police were here. He turned to his right and saw a man wearing a silver foil jacket pointing a semiautomatic at Delfino's head. The man's eyes had an insane intensity. The hair on the back of Randy's neck stood up as he realized it wasn't the cops. A gunshot rang out, and Delfino dropped, blood exploding from his head. The Bloody Mary glass shattered on the deck. Angela screamed, as did the people around them.

"Oh, my god!" Randy grabbed Angela and flung her toward the tower doors.

"You're next, Kennedy," the shooter called out and aimed the gun. But there were so many frightened tourists scrambling in every direction, he was having difficulty getting a clear shot at his target.

Panicked, shouting tourists fought for the exits. Randy thrust Angela hard to their left. They were running in a zig-zag pattern through the crowd when they heard a gunshot, and a bullet whizzed past Randy's ear.

Angela asked tremulously, "What's happening? Who's that man?"

"I don't know. It must be one of Nicosia's men." He looked back and saw the man with the foil jacket trying to spot them in the crowd. The gunman's eyes were even more crazed.

They dashed into the tower lobby and shoved their way through frantic sight-seers. A flood of tourists were clambering through the doors to the fire escape, hollering angrily at each other. Randy turned back, saw the shooter out of the corner of his eye, and pushed Angela to the stairs leading to the next level of the tower. They flew up the steps three at a time and burst through the doorway that led to the upper observation deck and the boarding area of the rollercoaster.

Randy zipped across the deck, Angela just behind him. They ran to the boarding area and crouched behind the rollercoaster cars full of passengers. The riders gave them questioning looks as a bell clanged and the cars started to roll forward. Randy and Angela crouched alongside the string of cars as they traveled along the track, the ride attendants yelling for them to get away from the moving cars.

The shooter was at the glass doors, surveying the area, looking for his target. Randy and Angela's cover would soon career off the side of the tower, revealing them to the gunman. Freaked out, but with no other option, Randy yelled to Angela, "Hop into the last car. We have no choice."

There was no alternative, and Angela hoisted herself into the empty car. The safety bar was down, so all she could do was hang on. Randy ran, hunched over, along the track, trying to judge when to make the same jump. The edge of the tower was approaching. He threw himself into the car just seconds before it swooped off the edge, and the cars climbed away from the observation deck. The ride attendants were screaming at them. Randy had a death grip on the safety bar, his nerves shrieking with fear.

"What are we going to do?" Angela shouted. "Sooner or later, this thing's going back where it started, and our friend with the gun will be waiting for us."

"I don't know," Randy mumbled, terrified and too afraid

to think. Seeing the skyline of Las Vegas open up in front of him, feeling that nothing was keeping them from plummeting to earth, he clamped his eyes shut and tightened his hold on the safety bar. The rollercoaster roared around the perimeter of the tower, plunged back over the side, and zoomed up by the massive spire in the center of the structure. Before the cars had a chance to start back down, they slowed, then jerked to an abrupt halt.

Angela peered back at the rollercoaster boarding area, where she saw the ride attendants surrounded by police officers and pointing up at them. "It's crazy down there."

Randy couldn't bring himself to turn to see. "What's going on?"

"It's the cops. They're everywhere." She looked at the lower observation deck and saw more police officers surrounding the body of Kevin Delfino. The last of the frantic tourists were pouring down the emergency exits.

"Why did they stop the rollercoaster?" Randy asked.

"They must think they have you cornered up here and can keep you contained until they've taken control of the situation on the observation decks."

"I suppose."

"We have to get off this thing."

"Yeah, right," Randy retorted. "Can you fly? I can't."

Angela glanced over the side of the rollercoaster car. About a yard and half away was the colossal Conquistador spire, and on it was a white metal ladder, which ran from the top of the spire to a ledge below. "We're just a few feet from that ladder," she said. "It leads to a landing, and I'm sure there's a way down from there. The ladder must be used to service the floodlight on top."

Randy knew he couldn't do it. It was as if his muscles were paralyzed. "I don't know."

"Someone's trying to kill us and we don't know where he is. We have to climb down the goddamn ladder."

He didn't want to admit he was terrified. "I don't...we shouldn't..." He turned toward her and, past one shoulder, saw the sparkle of the crazy-eyed man's silver foil jacket near the base of the massive spire. He was taking off the jacket and staring at them, his gun tucked in his pants. A chill ran up Randy's spine as he wondered if the presence of so many police officers would deter the man from taking another shot. He wasn't going to take that chance. "Okay...you're right. Please be careful."

Angela reached out and grabbed the ladder with the lithe grace of a ballet dancer. She kicked her legs free of the rollercoaster and swung them to the ladder. Once she was secure, she gave Randy an encouraging smile. "I'll be waiting on the ledge below."

Looking out of the rollercoaster, all Randy saw was how high up he was. It was at least a hundred feet to the upper observation deck and another a hundred and ten stories to the ground. Mortified, he bit his shaking lips. "Goddamn it, do this," he said to himself and leaned toward the ladder. He grabbed a rung and was reaching for it with his other hand when the coaster began to creep forward. Randy had one sweaty hand on the ladder, and the car was pulling away with his legs still inside.

Panic overtook him, sending a charge of adrenalin through his veins. He kicked his legs free of the car, leaving him dangling from the ladder by one trembling hand. With all the strength he could muster, he heaved himself up and grabbed on with his other hand. Soon after, both feet were planted on a rung. He clung to the ladder like a child to its mother and didn't budge.

From Angela's prospective, it didn't look like Randy had any intention of coming down. "Randy," she shouted, "get over here. What are you doing?"

Randy was still, every muscle contracted, his eyes shut tight. He felt light-headed and thought he might pass out.

"We're an easy target for the gunman against this white spire. You have to climb down here."

Randy opened his eyes and stared at her. She was twenty feet below and right about being a target. For her sake, he had to descend the ladder. After another personal pep talk, he took an unsteady step to the next rung. Each movement was agonizing, but he was determined. One of his feet would dangle, feeling for the next rung. When he found it, he would release a reluctant hand and reach down. His hands were moist and quivering. When his foot hit the ledge, his knees wobbled, but he was relieved to be on solid footing.

Not letting go of the ladder, he looked out at the black sky and the sparkling lights of the city. Dizzy, he dropped to his knees. Breathing heavily, he tightened his trembling grip on the ladder and looked over the side of the ledge. The observation deck was seventy-five feet below. He didn't see the shooter.

"Are you all right?" Angela asked.

"Never been better," Randy said in a gruff voice. "Can't imagine a more enjoyable way to spend an evening."

"Where do we go from here?"

Randy scoped out the area, gasping as his peripheral vision told him that any second they'd plunge a hundred and ten stories. Still clinging to the ladder, he stood. "Over there—a small door." Randy pointed with his chin to a hatch in the ledge. "Let's hope there's no lock." He let go of the ladder and took a short stride, then dropped to his knees and crawled along the narrow landing to the door. He looked back at Angela and saw the gunman below them. He took an uneasy gulp of air, yanked on the handle, and swung it open. He hoped no one was on the other side. There wasn't, just a red metal ladder. He seized it and climbed down into the darkness. Angela followed without wavering.

Expecting the ladder to lead to a room at the bottom of the spire, Randy was surprised, and then horrified, to see they were in a ten-foot-wide cylinder that spanned the entire height of the Conquistador Tower. Electrical conduit and heating-and-cooling pipes clung to the walls. Although the lighting was minimal, he saw what seemed to be miles of ladder. He stiffened, his spine tingling.

"What's wrong?" Angela asked, stepping on his hand. "Oh, sorry."

"This ladder goes all the way to the bottom of the tower."

"This must be our lucky day."

Randy's hands were clammy. "Angela, I'm not certain I can keep going." His grip on the steel rungs of the ladder was so tight that his knuckles were white, but the moisture on his palms made it feel like he'd slip off any second. His whole body was quaking.

"Why not?"

"I know this doesn't make sense—"

Angela interrupted. "You're afraid of heights. I'm not stupid, Randy. It's more than noticeable. Quit trying to deny it."

"It's overpowering. I can't describe the fear."

Angela said with an encouraging lilt, "Focus on the ladder and nothing more. I'm sure there's a place to get off somewhere below."

Randy tentatively lowered his right foot to the next rung. When he was confident he had a firm footing, he released his grip with one hand and grabbed the next rung. With slow and methodical determination, he climbed down the ladder. Angela was patient, but he knew she was concerned about the pace they were descending at. Randy was the first to comment about the time it was taking. He stopped. "The gunman might be coming up or down this thing any minute." His voice echoed through the tower. "I pretty sure he saw us enter the hatch."

Angela nodded. "I know. Just keep at it. I see a landing of some kind about thirty feet below us."

Randy's eyes swung down, but Angela reprimanded him. "Don't do that. Keep climbing."

Rung by rung, they made their way down the ladder until they reached a perch, where a catwalk led from the ladder to a door. Randy stepped off the ladder onto the landing. He made the mistake of peeking over the side, and every muscle in his body screeched with terror.

Angela said supportively, "You can make it."

Each inch forward was agony. Randy slumped to his knees, crept to the door, and clasped the handle. He turned it and opened the door, overwhelmingly relieved to see a room with four solid walls. He rushed inside and flopped down in the middle of the floor. Angela hurried in and shut the door behind her.

STRAUB WAS ENRAGED. His easy hit had blown up in his face. He'd missed one of his marks, and for some reason, there were cops all over the place. He hadn't been spotted by them and ditched the foil jacket before heading toward the fire escape stairwell. He's seen Kennedy enter a hatch at the ledge in the spire and figured he could find him somewhere in the tower pod below. Most of the frantic sightseers had evacuated the tower and he was alone as he descended the stairs. He was so angry and wanted Kennedy so badly that he dismissed the danger of going after him with the police in the tower.

"I FEEL LIKE such a wuss," Randy said, still trying to catch his breath and lower his heart rate. His face and hair were wet with perspiration. "All my life, I've thought of myself as a big stud who electrifies the ladies. Now, in front of the one woman I want to impress more than anyone I've ever met, I almost fall apart."

Angela smiled. "Even Superman has his weaknesses."

"I'd rather mine were Kryptonite." He boosted himself up off the floor.

She inspected the space. "You're safe now. It's my guess we're somewhere near the bottom of the tower pod. I wonder if we should lie low and wait this out."

Randy looked at the walls of the room, which were covered with electrical panels. "No. I saw the shooter just before we went through the hatch, and he almost certainly saw me. I want to get us out of this tower; there's nowhere to hide in here." He walked over to a door in the corner of the room and placed his hand on the handle.

"Go slow, Randy. The gunman could be on the other side."

"Angela, I'm far less concerned about who's out there than I am with the thought of returning to that damn ladder."

"You prefer being shot to death over acrophobia?"

"I'd rather take my chances this way."

"It's your skin."

"No, it's ours. You've gone too far in this to be an innocent bystander."

Angela stared at him, obviously disturbed. "Throughout this ordeal, I've always felt that, in the end, I was on the right moral ground. For the first time, I'm realizing it might not turn out okay. Not that I don't believe in your innocence. I do. But we're both guilty of evading the authorities, and I'm aiding and abetting a wanted man.

"When I thought there'd be a quick conclusion to this nightmare, I pushed those thoughts away. But three people are dead—Cynthia Nicosia, Conrad Hale, and now Kevin Delfino, who was shot five minutes after he called the police and told them he was with you at the top of the Conquistador Tower. Oh, god, how did I get into this mess?"

Randy looked at her compassionately. "You listened to her heart. But I didn't kill Delfino, and there must be plenty of witnesses. And his bartender friend has no reason to continue hiding the painting for him now. I can clear my name. But we can't do that with a gunman after us."

She stared at him.

He gestured. "I'm opening this door. Stay where you are. If it's all clear, I'll signal to you."

She said in an anxious whisper, "All right."

"If the shooter's out there, you get back on that latter. Don't try to help me; just get out of here."

"I'll be okay."

His eyes tore into hers. "You can't understand what you mean to me."

"I think I do, Randy. Just be careful."

Randy took a deep breath, turned the handle, and opened the door a crack. It was a service hallway, and he heard male voices coming toward them. When they drew closer, he shut the door and waited a minute before opening it half an inch. He saw two uniformed maintenance men heading away from him down the corridor.

Randy watched the men disappear around the corner and motioned for Angela to follow him, slowly walking in the opposite direction. "I assume there are three ways out of this tower," he said. "The elevators, a fire escape, and the infamous ladder from whence we came. I'm not taking the ladder. That leaves the stairs or the elevator. What's your pleasure?"

Angela shrugged. "Neither alternative sounds good. The gunman could be in either place."

"I'm sure this floor has a service elevator somewhere. Let's see what our options are." Randy led her down the hallway, moving tentatively due to the short lines of sight. Like everything in the tower, the corridor was curved around its central core.

They kept conversation to a minimum, listening for any noises indicating someone was coming their way.

They were creeping along the passageway close to the inside wall when they came upon a single elevator. They eyed it, unsure what to do.

"The stairwell's over there." Angela said, pointing to the marked door.

Randy walked to the stairwell door and pressed an ear against it, listening intently.

"Anything?" Angela asked.

"It's quiet. The sightseers are probably down near the bottom of the tower by now, but the gunman, and maybe the police, could be anywhere. This is spooky."

"It's a large tower."

Randy put his hand on the door handle, rotated it, and poked his head inside the stairwell. There were voices below him that seemed far away, but footsteps above that were getting louder. "I have an idea. There are two ways down—the stairs and the elevator. Let's let fate decide."

Angela tilted her head. "What do you mean?"

"We push the elevator call button but wait here in the stairwell. If the elevator's empty, we board it. If not, we take our chances with the stairs."

"What happens when we arrive at the first floor?"

"Hope there's enough chaos we can make it out of the building."

Angela squinted at him. "Chaos?"

Randy gestured to the elevator. "Hit the call button."

"If you say so." Angela scurried to the elevator and pressed the down button.

She ran back to the stairwell, and they waited for the elevator to arrive, leaving the door cracked. Above them, they heard heavy footsteps descending toward them. The sounds were getting closer, and they both knew discovery was eminent. They peeked at the elevator. The doors remained closed, and Randy looked with growing concern at the lit elevator button. "I wish there was a floor indicator."

"Whoever's above us," Angela whispered, terror in her voice, "and it could be the gunman, will be here any minute."

He gave a jerky double nod. "I know."

They watched the closed elevator doors, willing them to open but terrified the car would hold a passenger with a gun. Angela clung to Randy's arm as the echo of footsteps grew nearer and the elevator doors remained shut.

They gave audible sighs of relief when the elevator clanged and the doors slid open on an empty car. They exploded out of the stairwell, and Angela ran to the elevator, jumping into the car and tapping the *one* button several times.

"Hold the elevator," Randy commanded.

"Why?"

"The chaos."

"What do you mean by that?"

"Just hold the door." He bolted over to a fire alarm that hung on the wall, flipped the lever, and waited a fraction of a second for the alarm to begin screaming, then hurried to the elevator.

Angela asked in clear disbelief, "That's how you're creating chaos?"

Randy nodded. "That's part of my plan."

"What's the other part?"

"When the fire alarm's pulled, all the elevators go to the bottom floor."

"We're going to the first floor anyway. I pressed *one*."

"I'm not sure if we'd go all the way to the ground. If you remember, we entered the tower elevator on the mezzanine. I'm guessing that with the fire alarm going off, we'll go all the way to street level."

"I pray you're right, but—"

"Plus, with the alarm blaring, there'll be confusion throughout the casino. The place was pretty busy. The shootings on the observation deck already created a stir, and with a few thousand tourists trying to leave the building, there's certain to be—"

"Chaos?"

"Yep."

With a loud bang, the door to the stairwell burst open, and the gunman looked right at them as the elevator doors closed. "Hit the floor," Randy screamed and they both dove down.

Bullets ripped through the doors of the elevator as it started its descent.

"God damn," Randy shouted. "Whoa."

"That was close," Angela said in a shaky voice.

"We've got to get out of this tower before the shooter catches up to us."

As the elevator descended, Randy knew both their pulses were pounding in anticipation. After about a minute, the car stopped and the bullet-riddled doors made a grating sound as they opened. They scrambled out. They were in some kind of maintenance room. Randy saw a door he hoped would lead to the casino and sped over to it. He grabbed the handle and smiled when he opened the door and saw the casino, a frantic mass of patrons clambering for the exits. Clasping Angela's hand, he charged into the crowd.

"There's a gunman in the tower," a man cried out, his voice panic-stricken. "He's shooting at people."

A woman fell trying to reach the front doors. She screamed. People were leaping over her, more concerned about getting out of the casino than her welfare.

Angela and Randy were zigzagging through the mob. Racing toward the exit, Randy squeezed Angela's hand.

She looked at him. "Where to?"

"Follow everyone else and hope we get lost in the swarm. Just stay with me and keep moving." They ran through the front door and out to the porte-cochere. An armada of police cars and fire engines surrounded the entire area. The police stood helpless as hordes of gamblers poured out of the casino. Their radios were squawking that the shooter was still in the tower, and no one knew the whereabouts of Randy Kennedy.

Angela and Randy bounded into the stalled traffic on Las Vegas Boulevard. Horns blared as they weaved between the cars. They ran into the parking lot of the Savage Garden topless bar and darted behind a large sign that said, "Las Vegas' most popular gentlemen's club." Angela stopped to catch her breath, her lungs on fire.

"We made it," Randy panted. He hunched over, sucking in air.

"The chaos," she said, her chest heaving, "it saved us."

Randy felt a strange sense of exhilaration. "I can't believe we made it out of that place alive."

They peered around the corner of the sign and looked at the confusion surrounding the Conquistador Casino Resort and Tower. People were spewing out of the exits like water. The sirens of ambulances, fire engines, and police cars competed stridently. There was no way they could get safely into or out of the garage in that mess. Bessie would have to stay where she was for now.

Randy spotted a taxi in front of the Savage Garden entrance. "Let's hitch a ride."

Still on an adrenalin high, they skipped over to the cab and dove into the backseat. The East Indian driver turned to them but didn't utter a word.

"The Hazy Days Motel," Randy said.

"Big doings at the Conquistador," the cabbie said with a thick accent.

Randy clapped his hands together. "Yeah. Big doings."

TWENTY-EIGHT

RANDY HELD THE mobile phone to his ear, his hands shaking with apprehension. Angela sat next to him on the motel room bed, her eyes giving him encouragement. Brett was pacing in front of them.

"Lieutenant Schultz, please," Randy said when his call was answered. He closed his eyes and waited to be connected.

"Schultz," the detective said.

"Lieutenant, it's Randy Kennedy."

Silence filled the air for a moment.

"Did you hear me?" Randy asked.

"Where are you?"

"That's not why I called."

Schultz raised his voice. "What did you call for, Kennedy? Do you want to talk sports? Women?"

"I want to turn myself in."

"That's more like it."

"I didn't kill anyone."

"That's not what it looks like from where I'm sitting."

"Wayne...Kevin Delfino murdered Cynthia Nicosia."

"Dead men can't confess."

"I didn't kill him."

"I know that. Delfino's assailant was arrested at the Conquistador Tower. We sealed it off, and Robert Straub was caught trying to slip down the fire escape. My men were monitoring your meeting with Delfino from a distance. We saw Straub shoot him and go after you. Of course he didn't expect Metro police to be in the tower. It took us a while, but we were able to find him."

"I bet this Straub works for Nicosia."

"Knowing the police saw him make the hit, Straub accepted a plea bargain to avoid the death penalty. He fingered Nicosia as the man who hired him for the murders. Nicosia was arrested an hour ago. Straub had been keeping tabs on you and Kevin Delfino. He was surprised and pleased when you both showed up at the Conquistador Tower, allowing him to hit two targets at once."

"Why was he so brazen? Why would he do that in such a public place?"

"The guy's half nuts. Most insane man I've talked with in a long time. He thought he'd pop you and Delfino and be out of there in seconds."

"Good thing we were fast on our feet and he missed."

"You were fortunate. The panic of the crowd made it difficult for Straub to get a clear shot. If he had, you'd be in the morgue alongside Delfino."

"I heard a bullet whizz past my head."

"You got lucky."

"Delfino admitted that he killed Cynthia. He took the painting. He had it at the tower when he was shot."

"The bartender turned over the Van Gogh."

"That proves my innocence."

"There's still the murder of Conrad Hale."

"I know who killed him."

"And who was that? Pointing the finger at Delfino again? Dead men can't defend themselves either."

"It wasn't Wayne, Kevin, whatever the hell his name was. I know who murdered Conrad Hale, but you have to give me some latitude to prove it. I'll turn myself in, but you must give me a chance to prove I'm innocent."

"I'm listening."

"You'll work with me?"

Schultz paused. A few seconds later, he said, "Yes."

"I'll be at Metro headquarters in fifteen minutes."

RANDY PUSHED OPEN the solid oak door and went into the deserted outer office. He glanced over at the vacant secretary's desk, then gazed beyond it to the closed double doors. It was almost seven in the evening, and he knew the man he wanted to see always worked late. He stood there, his hands moist, once more taking the risk of his life. Hard to believe, considering what he'd gone through in the last few weeks.

Lieutenant Schultz and his officers were stationed outside the suite. A wire was strapped to Randy's chest, recording every sound.

Randy walked up to the double doors and opened the right one just a fraction. He saw the old man inside, staring out the window. The vibrancy of the early-evening Las Vegas Strip was shimmering through the large pane of glass, and he appeared to be mesmerized by the blinking lights.

Randy slipped into the room, cleared his throat, and asked, "Why, Walter?"

Walter Parker swiveled around and looked at him. "Aren't you full of surprises? Blond hair and all. What, pray tell, are you doing here?"

"You know the answer to that."

Parker lowered his eyes. "May I get you a drink, my boy? My throat's a little dry. How about a whiskey?"

"You've asked me not to drink at the Desert Palm."

That visibly annoyed Parker, and he snarled. "Considering the circumstances, I suppose an exception's called for." He limped to the bar, lifted two tumblers from a rack, and poured several fingers of whiskey into each one. He handed one of the glasses to Randy, then lifted his own glass up in a salute. "To survivors like us."

Randy clicked his glass against Parker's and downed the whiskey. It burned his throat, and he said hoarsely, "I didn't have to kill anyone to get this far—no matter what the cops believe."

"What's that supposed to mean?"

"I'm clearing my name."

Parker sipped his whiskey. "You're wanted by the authorities for two brutal murders."

"Cynthia Nicosia was killed by her ex-boyfriend. The police recognize that now."

"And Hale?"

"You know the answer to that. But you still haven't answered my question."

Parker stepped back to the window, his jaw clenched. He turned and stared at Randy with a furrowed brow. "Ever had a dream?"

Randy nodded. "Sure, I'd imagine everyone does at some time or other."

"True, most people have dreams, but there's a difference between ones that can become reality and ones that are out of reach."

Randy gave a short shrug. "Maybe."

"Some folks dream of hitting the lottery or marrying some glamorous movie star. It's not a dream but a wish."

"In my experience, dreams and wishes are interchangeable."

Parker wagged a finger. "Yes, but some dreams are achievable. Okay, wishes too, I suppose."

"It's the hope that dreams and wishes will come true that keeps us going in a world that sometime seems overwhelming."

"My dreams were more than far away wishes. I knew that with hard work, mine could come true."

"What were they, Walter?"

Parker waved his hands in front of him. "The Desert Palm Resort. Everything about it was a dream. Fifty years ago, I'd walk into the Flamingo and the Golden Nugget, and my imagination would go wild. I wanted to own a place like those magnificent resorts. The pools, the showrooms, the casinos. I knew what the guests desired, and if given a chance, I'd make it big. Finally, I saw my opportunity to enter the casino industry, and when I did, I never turned back. With each expansion of the Desert Palm, my dreams became a reality. I beat the odds and made my dream come true."

Randy looked contemptuously at Parker, and his upper lip curled. "If it were only that simple."

Parker ignored Randy's tone. "It was easy. I knew what the guests sought in a resort experience, and I fulfilled a need in the Las Vegas market. How do you think I've survived despite all these mega-resorts being built?"

"Walter, I know you're a hell of a good casino operator. It's one of the reasons I enjoyed working here. But as we both know, getting into the casino business wasn't easy. Sure, once you developed this place, you made it sing. But you had to obtain it first."

Parker frowned and roamed back over to the bar, pouring himself another generous glass of whiskey.

Randy watched him sip his drink. "Tell me about Frank Titan."

Parker laughed, softly and regretfully. "I hadn't heard that name in decades. Now I seem to every other day. How'd you find out?"

"Conrad Hale mentioned it when he told me you were his alibi for Cynthia Nicosia's murder. I did some digging. There wasn't a lot about Frank Titan. Just an old archived story from the *Las Vegas Review/Journal* saying he died in a fiery accident on the Red Rock highway. He was drunk.

"Then I thought I'd Google Walter Parker. Lots came up when I searched that name. Plenty of stories on the Desert Palm and your charity work. But I ran across a funny story I didn't expect. It was also an old archived story from the *Review/Journal*. It was some kind of society column that described how a man named Wally Parker won twenty-five thousand dollars at a craps table at the Golden Nugget.

"The columnist said the man who won the money was going to use his winnings to purchase the Kincaid homestead about seven miles out of town. He wrote something like, *doesn't that foolish guy know the soil at the Kincaid homestead's nothing but alkali?*"

Parker's eyes met Randy's, his expression despairing.

"There was a picture of Wally Parker," Randy said. "He was a small African-American man in his mid-thirties. Walter, you don't look like a diminutive black man to me."

Anguish covered Parker's face. "How was I to know some egomaniac casino tycoon would use that against me to steal away my dream?"

"I'm pretty sure that, like Hale, I've figured this all out, but I want you to tell me how you managed to assume another man's identity."

Parker sat down in his chair. "You won't believe how shocked I was when Hale confronted me with my past. It's been so long. I'd almost wiped any knowledge of Frank Titan out of my mind. I was young, driven. I had a dream. What I didn't have was a way to make it come true. I was a bartender in Bakersfield, pouring cocktails for the farm workers. One of my regulars was a little guy named Wally Parker. A loner. He didn't have many friends. Just me and a man named Jack Daniels. Parker and I sort of became buddies.

"He kept telling me about this plot of land he'd bought outside of Las Vegas. Said that at first, he'd intended to grow vegetables, but it turned out the dirt was bad. Then he decided he'd open a bar and snag the tourists on their way to Vegas. He hoped I'd work for him."

Randy folded his arms. "So how did Frank Titan, a bartender from Bakersfield, become Walter Parker, the sole owner of five acres in what would become one of the most valuable spots in Las Vegas?"

Parker's lips twitched, and he leaned back in the chair. "One drunken day, Wally showed me the title for the five acres. He was really proud of his purchase. He asked me to give him a ride to Las Vegas so he could show me the land. I figured what the hell and drove him up here. It was scrub brush, but I saw the potential. Large resorts had been popping up all along the road leading to Los Angles, and the location was a gold mine.

"Wally—he liked to be called Wally rather than Walter." Parker stopped speaking, his expression morose. He peered over at Randy and shook his head. "I guess that's why I've always insisted on being called Walter. Anyway, as always, he was drunk and bragging about how valuable the land was going to be. He's waving the title around like a crazy man. At that instant, it dawned on me...and, well, I saw a way I could make my dreams come true."

Randy felt sickened, a metallic taste in this mouth. "The newspaper article said Frank Titan died in a flaming wreck."

"I'm not proud of it, Randy. I hit Wally on the head with a pipe, then placed the body in my old Chevy. I drove out to the desert and rolled it off a steep embankment. I'd doused the truck with gasoline and lit it before I sent it plunging over the edge." Parker's eyes were moist, and Randy could see he was reliving the emotions he'd felt as he watched the vehicle burn.

Parker said in a shaky voice, "I walked back to town and called the sheriff. I identified myself as Walter Parker and said I was concerned about a friend. I told the cops he'd been drinking and I wasn't able to keep him from getting behind the wheel."

Randy's eyes were questioning. "Did the authorities find the truck right away?"

Parker nodded. "The next morning. They called and told me Frank was dead."

"Didn't they do any kind of investigation?"

"No. In those days, the sheriff wasn't wasting time on a dead drunk. Wally didn't have any living relatives. Neither did I. Frank Titan was just another lost soul who killed himself after a few too many drinks. That was the end of him. I built a twelve-seat bar, financed using the land as collateral. The casino followed soon after. Back then, obtaining a gaming license was easy—they didn't do background checks if you greased the right palms."

"You thought you were in the clear until Conrad Hale came along."

Parker's expression darkened. "He threatened to expose me, to tell Marian. I couldn't bear for her to find out the truth."

"She knows nothing of your past?"

"I hired her as a cocktail waitress soon after I opened the bar. I fell in love the day I met her. I took it as a good omen that she'd come into my life so soon after the death of Frank Titan. We married six months later."

"Was Hale forcing you to sell the Desert Palm?"

Parker pounded his fist on the desk. "He was planning to destroy my life's work. I was wrong for killing Wally. I know I told you that I killed the man as if the end justified the means, but I haven't erased the guilt. I've been trying to work through that remorse by being a fair and charitable businessman. No casino owner in Las Vegas has been more giving than I. My foundation's bestowed millions. I give money to any charity that asks. I send fifteen students through college each year. Full-ride scholarships. St. Vincent's built a new church with the funds I donated. I've done almost forty years of penance."

"There's no doubt you've been generous with your money."

"Hale didn't care," Parker said with distain, his lips thin. "He wanted the Desert Palm. Or should I say the land under it. He threatened to expose me if I didn't agree to sell. I had no choice. Either way, I was going to lose the Desert Palm. You have to believe me when I tell you that, as I negotiated the sale of the resort, I tried to ensure the team members would be taken care of."

"I'm sure you did."

"I knew, though, that Hale had a strategy to get around our agreement. I was positive he'd throw my beloved team members out in the street without a second thought, and Mrs. Nicosia confirmed that. I knew there were no surveillance cameras in Hale's office area. During our negotiations, we'd had a discussion on the merits of privacy versus security. Hale opted for privacy, and I took advantage of it. I had to stop him. I had to kill him."

Randy looked at the withered old man with pity. "I'd be more understanding if you hadn't let the police think I murdered Hale. You put me and the woman I love through hell."

"I had no idea you'd be accused of his murder."

"You knew I was in his office."

"Yes, I saw you enter. I was standing against the back wall in the outer room. I stood at the door and listened to your conversation. As you know, it was brief. Too quick. I expected a longer exchange of words. You zoomed toward the door so fast, I just had time to slip out of sight. I ducked behind the secretary's desk when you ran out of Hale's office."

"I know. That's how I first connected you to the death of Conrad Hale. As I ran out of Hale's office, I tripped on something. It was your cane." Randy strolled to the side of Parker's desk and picked up the mahogany walking stick with the elaborate silver tip. He twirled it in his hands. "At first, I suspected that Hale was killed by Joseph Nicosia. After all, he was the logical choice—Hale made nice with Joe's wife. But a bludgeoning isn't the mob's style. It took me a while, but eventually it clicked that I'd seen your cane just minutes before Hale was murdered. That's when I started trying to figure out why Hale had mentioned talking about Frank Titan with you."

Parker scowled. "It took more than forty years, but I finally had enough incentive to kill again." He dropped his face into his hands and wept. "I didn't want my dream to end," he sobbed, his chest shuddering. "Randy, you understand, don't you?"

Randy shrugged. "I've been sought by the authorities for two murders I didn't commit. I'm pretty sure I've cleared my name of Cynthia Nicosia's death. But I've spoken with an understanding police lieutenant, and I'm still on the hook for Hale's murder."

Parker took a handkerchief from his jacket pocket, dried his eyes, and glared at Randy. "I can't give up my dream. Even if it means you go to jail for a crime you didn't commit."

Randy was surprised at Parker's tone. "I won't be going to prison."

Parker slouched forward in the chair. "Of course, you're right. That isn't necessary. I guess we can work out a financial arrangement. Have you ever considered living in Mexico? I've heard they're going to be legalizing casinos. The resorts down there won't find a better host than you."

"You're dreaming. The cops are waiting outside." Randy lifted his jacket, revealing the wire.

Parker's lips tensed, his cheeks paling. "Then it's official, my dream's come to an abrupt halt and turned into a nightmare."

"I'm sorry, Walter. It didn't have to be like this. You should've taken Hale's money and retired."

"I couldn't see past the hatred I felt for the man obliterating my lifelong passion. I guess, in the end, I'm the one who destroyed everything."

Randy scrutinized the broken man in front of him and shook his head. He spun around and walked out of the room.

RANDY ESCORTED ANGELA out onto the balcony, where they stood and watched the twinkling lights of the Las Vegas Strip. It was a typical Southern Nevada evening, with a much-needed cool breeze blowing in from the north.

Randy said, "Lieutenant Schultz says we should get off with a stern lecture from the District Attorney and be asked to do a couple of hours of community service."

"We've been lucky," she said, greatly relieved.

"We're in the casino industry. It's a staple of the profession."

"Conrad Hale and Walter Parker were in the business too. Their luck ran out."

"Let's pray this incident didn't use up our lifetime supply."

Angela chuckled. "Mr. Parker made it eighty years before his ran dry."

Randy watched the blinking lights of an airplane in the distance. "It's sad. He did try to do some good in his life."

"Randy, he killed two people in cold blood."

"I know. I guess I'm having difficulty believing the kind old man I liked so much has a wicked side. You know…Before

I told him the police were outside his office, for a second there, I saw a look in his eyes that scared me. In that moment, I saw the cold stare of a murderer."

"You said he offered to give you money to go to Mexico."

"He did, but I've been thinking about that. Sending me there would've been a temporary solution to his problem. How long would he have let me blackmail him?"

"You believe he'd have killed you?"

"I'd hope not, but that look in his eyes makes me wonder."

Angela shrugged. "His fate lies with the courts now."

"Did you hear the Wyman Corporation's buying the Desert Palm?"

Her face was tight with worry. "Do you think we'll get our jobs back?"

"I've got my fingers crossed. I have a friend who works at the Charleston Resort, which is owned by the Wyman Corp. He says Sal Wyman's a pretty good man to work for. If not, well, some casino's going to want to hire a host with a bit of notoriety and a pretty good guest list."

"You have that, but what about me?"

"I won't let anything happen to you." He reached over and put his hands on her shoulders.

"You know you saved my life."

She wagged her finger at him. "I did not."

"Yes. When we were on the rollercoaster, I was ready to give up. Thank you." He pulled her into his arms and kissed her, deeply and passionately. "It's time you understand that I do love you."

"I have for a while." She looked into his eyes.

His heart was pounding. "Why didn't you say anything?"

"I guess I was still afraid."

Randy's smile reached his eyes. "There's nothing to fear now." He held her in his arms, not wanting to let go, and kissed her again. "I hope to spend the rest of my life with you." He was so happy, he thought his heart was going to explode.

Angela squeezed him. "Me too."

"Now I know for sure I'm the Lucky One."

The sliding glass door opened, and Anthony Chapman stepped out onto the balcony. "Hey, you two. This party's for you. No hiding. There are a couple dozen people inside celebrating your return to the real world."

Randy smirked. "Okay, Anthony, we're coming." He put his hand on the small of Angela's back and ushered her inside to join the party.

Dixie and Brett approached them. Dixie hugged Angela and pointed at Randy. "I'm keeping an eye on you, young man."

He gave her a wide grin. "I bet you will."

"He's a good man, Mrs. Holiday," Brett said. "And a friend I hope to have for the rest of my life."

Randy thrust his hand toward him. "Count on it."

"He is cute," Dixie whispered to Angela.

"Let me get you a drink," Anthony said. "A beer and a chardonnay?"

"Oh, that's okay," Angela said. "Dixie and I will get the drinks. We have girl talk to catch up on. If you gentleman will excuse us, we'll be right back."

Dixie looked at Anthony. "You're in charge of keeping track of Randy."

He saluted her, obviously trying to hold back a laugh. "Yes, ma'am."

She chuckled.

Anthony, Brett and Randy watched the two women chatting as they moved across the room. "God, she's gorgeous," Randy said.

Anthony gave him the briefest of nods. "She's some woman."

"I'm going to marry her."

Anthony looked doubtful. "It's still difficult for me to believe the biggest stud in Las Vegas is settling down."

"Like I told you a while ago, I hadn't met Angela Grisham before."

"I'll give you that. She's special."

A curvaceous redhead wearing tight jeans sauntered across the far corner of the room. Randy's eyes followed her to the kitchen.

Anthony followed Randy's gaze, and his eyebrows shot up.

Randy grinned, a faint blush tinting his cheeks.

Anthony rolled his eyes.

"I didn't say it would be easy."

About the Author

Steve Trounday has been a senior marketing executive at many of northern Nevada's most prominent casino resorts. He is writing a series of mystery/thrillers set in the fascinating world of casino gambling, each with intrigue and a little romance. For more information on Steve's books go to his website at stevetrounday.com.